THE

WIFE'S SECRET.

A ROMANCE.

BY THE AUTHOR OF "KATHLEEN," OR THE SECRET MARRIAGE," "HEBREW MAIDEN'" &c.

LONDON:

PUBLISHED BY E. LLOYD, SALISBURY SQUARE, FLEET STREET.
MDCCCL.

PREFACE.

~~~~~~~~

The Author of "The Wife's Secret," feels grateful to the indulgent public for the great support they have rendered to him in this particular emanation of his pen, and he can assure the public, and especially the readers of his productions generally, that no exertion shall be wanting on his part to induce a continuance of their favour; and he begs leave to say that assiduity to subject, clear delineation of character and an adherence to facts, shall form the main features of his future perseverance. The present Romance is taken from the Popular Play of the same name, which was performed at the Haymarket Theatre; and gives the reader an introduction to the Commonwealth era, when civil war was shaking society to its foundation from one end of the kingdom to the other, and before the Protector had had time to consolidate his power.

THE PUBLIC'S HUMBLE SERVANT,

THE AUTHOR.

London,

THE
WIFE'S SECRET;

OR, THE

DEFEAT OF THE CRAFTY STEWARD.

A ROMANCE.

CHAPTER I.

A DISCOVERY.—LADY AMYOT BECOMES CONVINCED THAT SHE HAS A DISHONEST SERVANT IN HER HOUSE.—JABEZ SNEED LEARNS A FACT THAT MAKES HIM FEEL VERY UNCOMFORTABLE —PERCEIVES HIS DANGER, AND THREATENS RETALIATION.—ARRIVAL OF AN UNEXPECTED VISITOR.

"DEPEND upon it, lady, Jabez Sneed is neither more nor less than an old rogue, who takes advantage of his master's confidence, and is robbing him every day that he lives."

Lady Eveline Amyot threw upon the table some of the steward's accounts which she had just been looking over, and glancing towards her faithful attendant, Maud, who had just given utterance to these words, inquired how long she had suspected the acts of dishonesty of which they had been speaking.

"Long enough, my lady, to be quite convinced that I am not making an unjust charge against him."

"Is he aware that you suspect him?"

"I think he is," answered Maud, "for he scarcely can venture to look me in the face, and all his actions go to prove that he is conscious of being unworthy the trust that has been placed in him."

"Well," replied Lady Amyot, "it would be in vain for me longer to conceal the fact that our steward's accounts are anything but satisfactory. He has scandalously abused the confidence reposed in him by his master; and from what I have just now seen, I am afraid his defalcations will amount to a very considerable sum."

"Ay, my lady!" exclaimed her attendant, "who would have supposed that Jabez was such an old hypocrite as he has turned out to be? But so much for your Roundhead Puritans, who all prove to be so many rogues in grain, though they profess to be so much better than their neighbours. Even Oliver Cromwell himself is no better than he should be, in spite of his affected piety amid the rigidness of manners that he outwardly exhibits."

"Hush! these are dangerous words, Maud," interrupted her mistress, "for whatever may be his faults, he is our ruler, and has the power to punish those who show themselves hostile to him. Besides, you yourself wear the garb of a Puritan, though probably not a very strict follower of the sect you apparently belong to."

"Ah! my lady," answered Maud, "my only reason for putting on this plain, homely-looking garb, is that I may remain constantly near you, which would never be allowed if your husband, Sir Walter Amyot, thought I was one of what he calls the daughters of Belial. Perhaps it was hardly right to impose upon him, but as he wanted you to be surrounded by none but people of his own over strict principles, I fancied there could be no great harm in acting the part of a Puritan hand-maiden of your ladyship's."

"But if Jabez Sneed should happen to make the discovery, he will not fail to inform his master of it."

"I am aware of that, my lady," answered Maud, "and for that reason I always contrive to look as demure as possible whenever I am in his presence. The old man likes me not, I know, but as he don't suspect anything at present, I think it will not be difficult to keep him in the dark as long as he is suffered to remain in this house."

"Which will not be long, I think, after Sir Walter returns home."

"That is to say if he will be convinced that his accounts have been falsely kept," observed Maud.

"How can he help being convinced of it when we have his own hand-writing to prove the facts against him?"

"Your ladyship will of course take care that Jabez Sneed don't get the accounts out of your possession?"

"They will remain locked up in this room till Sir Walter's return," answered Lady Amyot. "I shall then show them to him with the remarks I have made upon some of the items, and it will then be for my husband to say how much longer he will suffer that man to remain under his roof."

"May I be so bold as to ask when Sir Walter is expected to return home?" asked Maud.

"At present it is quite uncertain how long he will be required upon the service that called him away from me," answered her ladyship. "Some say that his troops have already scattered a body of royalists who had collected together under the command of my brother, Lord Arden; and if there be truth in the rumour, we may hourly expect the return of Sir Walter Amyot."

"And if my Lord Arden should have the misfortune to fall into the hands of his enemies, he will meet with the same fate that has befallen so many of the loyal friends of our exiled king."

"That is what I am afraid of," sighed Lady Eveline, "for my brother has always been amongst the most zealous in advocating the cause

of King Charles, and has consequently brought upon himself the vindictive anger of the Protector Cromwell. Rewards have long been offered for his apprehension, and now that he has made another attempt to overthrow the present government, I fear his chances of escape are but small."

"Has he no way to leave the country?"

"I know of none unless he can bribe the captain of some ship to carry him over to France, where his royal master is sojourning, till he sees an opportunity to return and get back possession of his kingdom."

"Which people say there is very little chance of his doing."

"Ay, Maud," replied her mistress, "at present it must be acknowledged the cause of royalty seems to be in a most hapless condition. Those, however, who desire to see the king return, are full of hope that things cannot remain much longer in their present state; and there are many who venture to say that at no very distant period Englishmen will gladly hail the return of the exiled Charles."

"Is it fair to ask if your ladyship be one of those who are anxious to see his return?"

"For some reason I am," answered Lady Amyot, "for my family were all royalists so long as the struggle lasted between the late King Charles the First and his people. On the other hand, however, my husband has fought and bled on the opposite side, and it is perhaps my duty to sacrifice my opinion to him who has a right to expect so much submission from me."

"Wasn't it rather a singular circumstance, my lady, that you, the daughter of a Royalist, should have united yourself to a Roundhead?"

"Sir Walter Amyot," answered Lady Eveline, "is a Puritan, but he has never proved himself to be a bigot. He was a determined foe of the late monarch, but bearing no enmity to those who still adhere to the family of the king, who a few years ago perished upon the scaffold."

"As a proof of which," observed Maud, "he wooed and won your ladyship, the sister of Lord Arden, as stout a cavalier as any who fought in support of the royal prerogative, and who, at this time, is supposed to be a fugitive, on account of the part he has taken to restore the monarch whose cause he advocates. That your husband loves you, my lady, no one can doubt; but somehow I am afraid Jabez Sneed is only looking for a chance to injure you in his good opinion."

"And yet," observed her ladyship, "the old man always appears to treat me with the greatest respect."

"That of course he would do if he expects to blind you as to his real feeling towards you."

"But I have never given him cause for complaint."

"So you may fancy, my lady," answered her attendant, "but I can see reasons though for the dislike that he entertains towards you."

"Have I not always treated him with kindness?"

"With a great deal more than ever he deserved," replied Maud. "That, however, has had little effect upon Jabez Sneed, who would hate you if it were only for your difference in the forms of religious worship."

"He may think my notions in that respect are wrong, but surely he would not try to injure me on account of a mere matter of opinion?"

"Ay, my lady," answered the girl, "you little know how bitter the feelings are that arise out of a difference in religious opinions. Jabez Sneed is one of the most vindictive Puritan that ever I had the misfortune to be acquainted with; and if there were no other reason for his wishing to injure you in the estimation of your husband, one would be found in the fact that your discovery of his knavery may lead to his dismissal from the service of Sir Walter Amyot."

"How is he to injure me in the eyes of Sir Walter?" asked her ladyship.

"'t may take some little trouble before he succeeds," she replied; "but when bad people are determined to carry out a purpose, they will try scheme after scheme till they at length succeed. Now I have no wish to injure Jabez Sneed, so after the caution I have thought it right to give, your ladyship will of course act as you may think best to guard yourself against any plots that he may invent."

"I shall certainly keep a watch upon his actions," answered Lady Eveline; "and, if it should appear to be necessary for my own safely, shall inform my husband of his steward's antipathy to me."

"So far, that will be all very well," exclaimed Maud; "but, begging your ladyship's pardon for venturing to give an opinion, I should think it nothing more than right to tell Sir Walter of the glaring errors that you have discovered in the accounts of his steward."

"Will it not be better to leave my husband to detect the wilful errors as I have done?"

"Anything that your ladyship does will no doubt be right," answered Maud; "but if I may venture to give an opinion, I should say that the conduct of Jabez Sneed ought not to be concealed for a moment. As far as pity goes, he deserves none, for he has been base enough to rob the master who has placed all his confidence in him."

"I believe you are right, Maud!" exclaimed her mistress; "and if I wished to conceal the dishonesty of this old man, it was in order to spare him the shame of a public exposure."

"And yet he deserves not your pity."

"You think then he ought to be immediately dismissed?"

"A poor dependant like me has no right to give an opinion," answered Maud; "but, since your ladyship is not offended at my freedom, I must needs say that I can see no reason why Jabez Sneed should be pitied after the scandalous robberies he has been guilty of."

"Perhaps he may be able to explain away a great deal of that which at first sight appears to be so much against him."

"Then by all means let Sir Walter Amyot be the judge of how far he has been wronged by his steward."

"That of course he will do on looking over his accounts," answered Lady Eveline, "and therefore I can see the less necessity for me to interfere in a matter that I would rather have nothing to do with. That the old man bears me no good will is certain, and, to confess the truth, I feel somewhat alarmed lest he should afterwards endeavour to injure me in retaliation for exposing his conduct to Sir Walter."

"So he would, I have no doubt," returned Maud; "but I would take care to watch him so narrowly that no opportunity should be offered him to carry out any of his vindictive projects. Besides, Sir Walter has always placed the fullest confidence in your ladyship, and it would be strange, indeed, if he were to listen to the false representations of a mischief-making old man."

"But you forget that Sir Walter has always placed the utmost reliance in the steward, who has been so long in his service."

"I know he has, my lady," replied Maud, "but he will not disbelieve the evidence of his own senses. The figures in the accounts you have been looking over, speak for themselves, and they afford a proof that even the cunning of Jabez Sneed cannot get over."

"Ay," answered Lady Eveline, "but Sir Walter has always held so high an opinion of his steward that he will accept of any explanation that may be given of the affair."

"What explanation can he give?"

"He will say that all people are liable to errors; and that is so reasonable an excuse that Sir Walter will overlook the first offence on condition that the fault is not repeated."

"In that case, your ladyship, I am afraid Jabez will try to do you all the injury in his power."

"So he may, but strong in conscious innocence I can still defy the mischief he may attempt. My husband will not believe the idle tales of a man who has committed himself as Jabez Sneed has done, and I shall triumph over all the evil reports he may raise against me. Nay, more, what can he say against his mistress which will prejudice her in the sight of an affectionate husband?'"

"Oh, my lady," exclaimed Maud, "you have indeed every reason to be certain of an impartial consideration from Sir Walter, who, though I don't like his puritanical ways, is as good a man as is to be found from one end of England to the other. Under any common circumstances he would not injure you even by listening to any of the tales Jabez may relate to him but then the old man may repeat them so often and throw such an appearance of truth into them, that I am almost afraid to think of what the consequences may be."

"Do you imagine, then," asked Lady Eveline, "that my husband would take the word of his steward in preference to mine?"

"It's impossible to say how that may be," answered Maud, "for unfortunately, this Jabez Sneed is such a crafty, insinuating villain, that—"

A slight scream of alarm from the girl as she started back, roused the attention of Lady Evelina Amyot, who, turning in the direction towards which her attendant was looking, perceived the subject of their discourse standing within a few yards of them. There was a malignant scowl upon the countenance of the old man, but this quickly changed as he perceived that his presence in the room was known, and assuming a look of calm indifference, he said—

"Your ladyship will, I hope, pardon this intrusion, but knowing that you have been examining my accounts, I ventured here to ask if you are satisfied with them."

"I suppose you have been listening long enough to know that I am by no means satisfied with them?" answered her ladyship coldly.

"Indeed I came not here to listen," exclaimed the steward, with assumed humility, "but finding that you were engaged in conversation with your attendant, I remained where I was till an opportunity presented itself to enter upon my own affairs."

"And I hope you have been gratified by all you have heard since you came into the room?" observed the girl, tartly.

"I know not that I have heard anything to fill me either with anger or alarm," replied the steward. "It may be true that her ladyship is not satisfied with my accounts; but conscious of my own rectitude, I can wait with perfect calmness for the less prejudiced opinion of my master, when he returns home, which, happily for me, may be expected in the course of a few hours."

"May I look for Sir Walter's return so soon?" demanded Lady Eveline.

"A messenger has just reached the hall for the purpose of bringing you that happy news," answered Jabez Sneed, "and I have lost no time in coming to announce that which I know would afford your ladyship the most lively satisfaction."

"Did the messenger say that he was on his way home?"

"He left him within thirty miles of home, and Sir Walter would have arrived here before now, but that the roads are in such a dreadful state af.er the late rains. Besides, he is still looking after Lord Arden, your ladyship's brother, who is supposed to be concealing himself somewhere upon this part of the sea coast."

"Surely——urely," cried her ladyship in despair, "he w.ll not hunt to death one who is so dear to me?"

"My master never neglects his duty," answered the steward, "and when a rebel is to be taken he will follow in pursuit of him even though that person may be the brother of his wife."

"It may be all very well to say so," exclaimed Maud; "but Lord A den will be aware of his danger, no doubt, and it is to be hoped he will either find some place to conceal himself in or get over to France, where he will be safe till the time comes for him to return here with a better chance of succeeding in his designs."

"Are you aware, girl," exclaimed the old man sternly, "that you are wishing for the escape of a traitor to his country?"

"Jabez Sneed," returned his mistress, "I ask if _you_ recollect that it is of my brother you are speaking?"

"It matters little to me who or what he may be," answered the steward, "for all are alike when we speak of an enemy that has appeared in arms against his country. Sir Walter Amyot, too, is not likely to be influenced even though a rebel may claim close affinity to his wife; and I believe before long we shall hear that the fugitive has been either taken or slain."

"And wouldn't you afford him assistance if it were in your power to do so?" asked Maud.

"By no means, girl," he replied. "Am I not threatened because a few items of my accounts cannot be satisfactorily explained at a moment's notice, and has her ladyship—who has threatened me with dismissal—any right to expect a favour from me?"

"If you had been listening long enough," answered the girl, "you would have heard her ladyship declare that she would not even mention the circumstance on Sir Walter's return home."

"Lady Eveline Amyot may have said so," he replied bitterly, "but she had one at hand who was ready enough to persuade her to do that which would terminate in my being dismissed from this house with the character of a dishonest steward. So much I know to a certainty, Maud, and it is now my turn to warn you that _your_ tenure of office will not last much longer if I have any power or influence with my master."

"Sir Walter," answered her ladyship, "neither engages nor dismisses those domestics who belong solely to myself. With Maud he has nothing to do; and in order to put him on his guard against any evil reports that you may whisper to him, I shall take an early opportunity of informing him of the threat you just now uttered."

"Am I then to have no protection against the insolence of the girl who shields herself under your protection?"

"Insolence!" exclaimed Maud; "of a verity I think all the insolence has come from your own side, for you have dared even to threaten our mistress for no other reason than that she has been the means of discovering the system of robbery that you have been carrying on."

"Who says I have ever wronged my master?"

"Your own accounts prove it."

"So says prejudice," he replied; "but Sir Walter will treat the accusation with the scorn it deserves, when he has carefully gone over the items that have been disputed. The charge has only been got up to ruin me, and yet I am expected to favour her ladyship's brother if he should happen to fall in my way."

"I will not ask you the same favour again," answered Lady Eveline, "for, upon further consideration, it is not likely that he will venture to come near the hall. Nay, I am in hopes that before now he has succeeded in reaching a coun ry where he need fear no more from the malice of vindictive and blood-thirsty enemies."

"You must not expect that he is going to escape quite so easily as that," exclaimed Jabez Sneed, with a grim smile of satisfaction, "for the troops have been ordered to watch the coast all round England, and not a vessel will be allowed to depart till she has been searched for any rebels that may be on board. So you see Lord Arden will have but an idifferent chance, even if he has been lucky enough to elude the pursuit of your husband."

"My husband will not hunt to death the brother whom his wife so fondly loves."

"Perhaps he might show him some favour if he were not compelled to do his duty," answered the steward. "He has, however, the watchful eyes of Oliver Cromwell upon him, and, favourite as he is of the Protector's, he must not knowingly permit the escape of Lord Arden, were he twenty times your brother."

"There is no doubt Sir Walter will do his duty well and fearlessly," answered Lady Eveline. "Indeed, the fugitive knows that he has not the slightest favour to expect from him, and therefore it will be his chief care not to cross his path. A few days concealment will be enough; and as soon as the search after him begins to relax, he may find a vessel ready to transport him to the land where so many other faithful loyalists are wa ting the opportunity when they may seat their king upon the throne from which he has been driven."

"Have a care, my lady!" exclaimed Jabez, "for words like these, if spoken in any other presence than mine, might lead to the most unpleasant consequences to yourself."

"I know what you mean, but defy you to do your worst!"

"What meaning do you put upon my words?"

"The true one, I have no doubt," resumed Lady Eveline. "You know that it is in my power to report unfavourably of you to Sir Walter on his return home, and those words have been uttered only to intimidate me from such a purpose. Now, however, I know you for an enemy, and you may leave me, Jabez Sneed, with a perfect conviction that I am not to be deterred from the performance of a duty by any threats that you may utter."

"Very well!" exclaimed the steward, "I shall expect the worst then; but I suppose your ladyship will have no objection to let me have the accounts to look over again?"

"Why do you wish to look over them?"

"To see if I can rectify any of the errors you speak of."

"No," she replied, "such as they were when you placed them in my hands, so will I give them to Sir Walter on his return home."

"Then it is your wish to injure me?"

"Indeed I have no such desire, but I would see justice done between your master and yourself. Let him be the judge of whether your accounts have been rendered fairly or not, and for my own part I will not even hint my own suspicions unless cause is given me by any misconduct of your own."

"That may all be very well," he replied. "but I see no reason why I should not be allowed to look over my accounts again."

"Be content," she exclaimed, "with the decision you have already heard, for nothing will ever induce me to alter it. Enough, too, has been said for the present upon this unpleasant subject, and you will therefore leave me, Jabez, for I am in no humour to argue with you any longer upon a matter that cannot be arranged till the return of your master, who you tell me may be hourly expected."

This was said in a tone of sufficient command to prove that either reply or remonstrance would be useless; and after glancing at the accounts, which were still lying upon the table, though he durst not touch them, he left the room, grumbling within himself at the reception that he had met with.

"That man has mischief in his mind or I am very much deceived," exclaimed Maud as soon as he was gone. "I have kept my eye upon him ever since I first discovered his presence here, and as sure as your ladyship is alive, he'll never be satisfied till he has paid off some of the scores that he fancies he owes."

"You think he meditates mischief against me, I suppose?"

"I feel almost certain about it, my lady."

"Then all I can say about it is, that I care not for anything he may plot against me," answered Lady Eveline. "He knows well that my husband is not to be easily led away by any falsehoods that he may invent, and I have therefore nothing to apprehend from the malignancy of a man whose revengeful feelings have already begun to show themselves."

"Ay, my lady," exclaimed Maud, "I am glad to find that you are not afraid of him; and yet I should like you to be more upon your guard against a person who is governed only by the worst of principles."

"What do you think he intends to do?"

"That is more than I can tell, but I can fancy that for one thing he means to lie in wait for Lord Arden; and if he should happen to come into this neighbourhood, I am afraid he would have but a very poor chance of making his escape."

"But my brother, I hope, will not be so imprudent as to trust himself where he is almost sure to be seen."

"Oh! my lady," cried Maud, "but when a man is driven about from one place to another, what is he to do at last but seek the best refuge he can, even though there may be some danger in it? Here we are near the sea side, where there are always plenty of vessels; and if he could only find some one to give him shelter for a few days it would not be very difficult to get out of the country."

"You speak, Maud, as if there were no risk to be run."

"I know what you mean, my lady," answered the girl, "but where there is great danger all sorts of risks are run to get out of it."

"Will any one be found to give shelter to a fugitive when the punishment would be so severe in the event of a discovery?"

"Some one, no doubt, might be found to run the hazard, if money enough were offered to pay for it," replied Maud.

"Lord Arden, I am afraid, has it not in his power to give any money in advance, unless he was to venture here,—which would be most imprudent under present circumstances,—to obtain from me the sum that may be required to meet his exigencies."

"If he were to come here, my lady, how should we ever be able to conceal the fact from Jabez Sneed?"

"That," answered Lady Eveline, "is the danger of which I was apprehensive. The steward is only desirous for an opportunity to revenge himself for the discovery I have made of his evil practices, and nothing would so fully gratify his vindictive feelings as to destroy the man who, next to my husband, is most dear to me."

"There's no denying that he is capable of any act of villany," answered Maud, "but I rather think Sir Walter would not be best pleased with him for getting your brother into trouble."

"Yet my husband is now in pursuit of him."

"That's because he can see no way of getting out of it," returned the girl. "As an officer in the service of the Protector he is compelled to perform this duty, however much it may be against his inclination; but I dare say if the opportunity were given to him he would rather assist in the escape than the capture of Lord Arden."

"I am sure he would," answered her mistress; "but unfortunately, he has no alternative when so many jealous eyes are directed towards him every moment. My brother is well aware of the difficulty, and for that reason I am in hopes he will direct his flight towards any part of the country rather than to this."

"And yet what part of England is he so likely to go to as to the place where his sister might be able to assist him?"

"Alas!" cried Eveline, "glad as I should be to afford him my assistance, how can I do so when his presence here must be immediately discovered? My husband, too, is expected to return, and should he learn that an enemy of the commonwealth was lurking about the neighbourhood, he would consider it an act of duty to surrender him into the hands of his enemies, even though it might be his wish to afford him shelter and protection. The steward, too, will be more than usually vigilant when he thinks there is mischief to be done, and especially so if he knows that the blow would fall heavily upon me."

"Well, then," exclaimed Maud, "under all the circumstances, it is to be hoped his lordship will not think of venturing here. Not that I think it impossible to harbour him for a short time without a discovery taking place, but that I would not give a chance to old Jabez, to gratify the malignancy of his heart. However, there can be no doubt that Lord Arden will weigh in his mind the perils he would have to encounter in the neighbourhood of Amyot Hall; and in order to avoid the risk of being taken by his pursuers, he will take some other route when the search is not going on with as much activity."

"But from what I have heard they are looking for those who were concerned in the late outbreak in all parts of the country."

"I believe they are, my lady," replied the girl, "and that is one very good reason why my Lord Arden should seek refuge where he is at once likely to find it. Not that I should be glad to see him here, because his pursuers would be sure to lead you as well as himself into trouble. In truth, I see nothing but difficulty and danger, if Sir Walter Amyot should, by any unfortunate chance, hear of his being within his reach."

"And yet, one would scarcely think it possible that he would do aught to endanger the life of his wife's brother."

"Very true, my lady; but you needn't be reminded how strict he is in the discharge of his duty. Besides, there must be no favour nor affection when the safety of the country demands every sacrifice to be made; and I'm afraid your brother would not be spared any more than any body else if the place of his retreat should happen to be discovered."

"Nay," exclaimed Lady Eveline, "this is looking on the worst side of the question, when we ought rather to hope for the best."

"But where there's uncertainty there can be no real ground for hope," answered the handmaiden. "To be sure, Lord Arden may by this time have got out of the country, which, of course, he would attempt to do if the slightest chance were given him. Time, however, will show what is to be the upshot of this affair; and all we can do is to wait with patience till we receive intelligence that may be depended on as to what has really become of him; at all events, let us pray that he may keep out of the reach of Sir Walter Amyot, who, I am afraid, would not shield him, even though he be your brother."

At this moment, a sound as of some one climbing up to the window was heard, and both Lady Eveline and her attendant moved from the place where they had been standing, as if already forewarned that some great danger was to be apprehended. But apparently some still stronger motive prevailed upon them to remain where they were, for suddenly pausing, they directed their gaze towards the spot from whence the sound had proceeded, and remained as if rooted to the floor, till the window flew open and discovered to them no other person than the persecuted fugitive, Lord Arden.

CHAPTER II.

THE BROTHER AND SISTER.—A FUGITIVE'S LAST RESOURCE.—THE PROMISE OF SECRECY.—THE CONCEALMENT. — JABEZ SNEED STILL REMAINS UPON THE WATCH, AND AT LENGTH THINKS HE HAS DISCOVERED A MARE'S NEST. —THE ROYALIST NARROWLY ESCAPES A DISCOVERY BY HIS MOST ACTIVE PURSUER.

FORGETFUL of the danger with which her brother was threatened, and giving way only to the feelings with which she had ever regarded him, Lady Eveline rushed into the arms of Lord Arden, and was for some few minutes unable to give utterance to the words with which she would have greeted his unexpected appearance. At length, however, on being supported to a chair, she began to recover herself, and gently chiding her brother for his temerity, she implored him most earnestly to leave a place where it would be dangerous for him to remain. But he, more sanguine than herself, persisted in remaining where he was till she had heard the explanation he had to give, and the motives that had induced him to seek refuge where nothing but danger was to be apprehended.

"Indeed, my dearest sister," he added, "imminent as the peril may appear to yourself, I, who have the greatest cause to shun it, am by no means alarmed at the efforts that are being made to bring me within the snares that have been laid for me by my enemies."

"Has no one traced you hither?" she asked with alarm.

"As far as I am able to judge, I have succeeded in reaching this house without having been seen," he replied. "As you may imagine, I was most cautious in proceeding hither, and it was only under cover of the darkness of night that I have ventured to pass from place to place, till good fortune, and my own perseverance brought me so far in safety on my dangerous journey. By the by," he added, glancing towards Maud, "there is a third party here who it may be dangerous to speak before."

"If you mean my faithful attendant," answered Lady Eveline, "I could pledge my life that you have nothing to fear from anything that she may say or do. She is, indeed, so entirely devoted to me, that I believe not even a threat of torture would ever induce her to say aught that might lead to your apprehension."

"Ay, my lord," exclaimed the girl, "my mistress does me no more than justice when she says, that I am to be trusted in all cases where her happiness, or that of any one dear to her, is concerned. I would not, however, say so much for all the servants in this establishment, for there is at least one under the roof who, I am certain, would exult if he could be the means of leading to your being taken by those who are looking for you."

"And who pray," he asked, "am I indebted to for the ill-feeling of which you are speaking?"

"She alludes to a steward, who has been long in the service of my husband," replied Lady Eveline; "and, I believe, to revenge himself upon me, he would be guilty of any act, however excusable it might be."

"Have you ever given him any cause of offence?"

"I believe," answered her ladyship, "that my being of a different religion to that which he follows was the original cause of the dislike he has manifested towards me. There is, however, another cause which has served to excite his hatred, and it is one that he is never likely either to forget or forgive."

"He is aware that you like him not, I suppose?" suggested her brother.

"He is quite certain of that," replied Lady Eveline: "but there is still another reason why I have to anticipate evil from the machinations of the man we are speaking of. In short, I have discovered that he has been in the habit of giving false accounts to his master, and I have thought it my duty to reprimand him severely for his dishonesty, and to acquaint Sir Walter with it immediately on his return home."

"And what harm can the man do you?" asked Lord Arden, "even though he should seek for revenge?"

"Perhaps not much to myself," answered her ladyship, "but should any chance bring it to his knowledge that you are here, he would not fail to give immediate information to my husband."

"And do you think Sir Walter Amyot would take advantage of information thus obtained?"

"I know not how he would act," answered Lady Eveline, "for the oath he has taken to serve the Commonwealth faithfully, would, I am afraid, urge him to do that which he would shrink from under any other circumstances."

"But surely not when he knows the fatal consequences that must follow, if he gave me up to my enemies?"

"He would remember only his duty, without reflecting upon the consequences of such an act."

"Then you would have me fly from here even though I know my pursuers are hunting for me in every direction?"

"Nay, my dear brother," cried Lady Eveline, "you know how much I would sacrifice to preserve you from the great danger with which you are threatened. My own life should be freely given, were it possible to save yours; but I know the rancour of those who are opposed to the royalists, and am but too certain that they would exult in sending you to the scaffold, were it your misfortune to fall into their hands."

"Which I assuredly shall do, if compelled to leave this house."

"Do you not think your danger is greater here than it would be elsewhere?"

"That will depend upon whether there is any part of this house in which I might remain concealed for a few days."

"As far as I am myself concerned," replied Lady Eveline, "I need not say how gladly my assistance should be given, were there any chance that it would rescue you from this imminent peril. I, however, too plainly perceive the probability of Jabez Sneed discovering the fact of your being here; and, were such a thing only suspected, no prayers or entreaties of mine would prevail upon him to forego his evil purpose."

"Surely he might be kept in ignorance of the fact for the short period of my sojourn here?"

"You know not the man you speak of, my lord," interposed the attendant, "or no kindness or pity would be expected from Jabez Sneed. At all times he loves mischief, and when an opportunity offers itself for revenging himself upon my mistress for having made the discovery of his dishonesty, he will not fail to take advantage of it. In short, my lord, though it is not for me to say so, this is the last place where you ought to have sought an asylum from your enemies."

"And pray, good Mistress Maud, what would you have had me do in such an extremity?"

"As for that, my lord," she replied, "as I said before, it is not for me to say what you ought to have done; but I should have been rejoiced to have heard that, like many other cavaliers, you had escaped over to the French coast after the skirmish that proved so disastrous to the cause of the banished king."

"And so I should, my pretty Maud," exclaimed his lordship, "but that, being compelled to pursue my journey only at night, I missed the vessel which was lying off the coast to convey away those who had escaped after our defeat. Since then, the search after me has been so hot, that I was compelled to direct my steps hither, as the nearest place where I could hope for a temporary refuge."

"And yet," observed Lady Eveline, "you know the danger that is to be apprehended from my husband."

"I expected that you would be surprised at my request, my dear sister," he exclaimed; "for, of course, I knew the enmity of Sir Walter Amyot towards me, and the difficulty that was likely to follow. There was, however, no alternative, and I must therefore ask shelter beneath his roof, but with the understanding that he must not, on any consideration, be informed of my presence here."

"How is it possible to conceal it from him?"

"I think less of the difficulty than you do," he replied, "for the time I require to be here is very short, and any chamber which is not in constant use will serve my purpose during the period that I am waiting for the arrival of a vessel to convey me over to France. That Sir Walter hates me, I know; yet it seems scarcely credible that he would betray the brother of his wife, when he knows the fearful consequences of such an act."

"There I believe you do him no more than justice," answered Lady Eveline; "for, much as he is opposed to the cause you have embraced, he would not, I venture to hope, injure one who is so nearly and dearly connected with the wife whom he fondly loves."

"In that consists my chief reliance," exclaimed the fugitive lord; "but at the same time he knows that I was always opposed to your marriage with him, and surely he cannot have forgotten the many insults I have heaped upon him."

"I believe he never recollects the past."

"He may not speak of them to you," answered Lord Arden, "yet I know it is quite impossible that he can either have forgotten or forgiven certain events in our former life. I have even challenged him to mortal combat, and when he refused to meet under the plea of my near relationship to his wife, I accused him of cowardice, and endeavoured by every other means in my power to draw upon him the contempt of his fellow men."

"True," answered his sister; "yet, do I believe from my heart that he has forgiven the injury you did him."

"Impossible!" exclaimed his lordship; "for I have repeated my insults over and over again; and, judging of his feelings by my own, I should think nothing would gratify him more than to revenge himself at the first opportunity that may offer."

"Why then did you venture to come here?"

"Because we must run into any port in a storm," answered Lord Arden, "and being compelled to seek shelter somewhere, I ventured to enter the house of the man I look upon as my greatest enemy, though I knew the danger to be apprehended from him, were he to learn the secret of my being beneath his roof."

"Believe me, brother," exclaimed Lady Eveline, "whatever enmity Sir Walter Amyot may bear towards you, he has too much honour to betray even the man that he looks upon as an enemy."

"So, your love for him would make you believe," returned the young nobleman; "but I, who know mankind better, will not pin my faith on the honour of any one who has his own revenge to serve. Besides, as an officer in the army of the Commonwealth, he would, indeed, be forgetful of his duty if he were knowingly to afford protection to one who has lately been in arms to restore our banished sovereign to his throne. Do not, however, understand that I am saying anything that is prejudicial to your husband, who, I dare say, would act only as every other man would, under similar circumstances."

"In that you have done him no more than justice," returned Lady Eveline; "but I believe, for my sake, he would go even farther than what he might otherwise conceive to be his duty."

"Do you think he would permit me to remain here till I am able to get on board a vessel that is hourly expected to make its appearance off this coast?"

"I am afraid he would not go so far as to do that," replied Lady Eveline; "but, at all events, I have good reason for believing, that he might permit your departure on condition that you leave England with as little delay as possible."

"And having been forced to leave his house, what chance should I have of avoiding those who are searching for me?"

"That is, indeed, a thing to be dreaded," answered his sister, "yet it is to be hoped, matters will not be driven to such an extremity, since it is possible you may remain here without the fact coming to the knowledge of my husband, whose return home is momentarily expected."

"You have heard from him, then?"

"Yes, Jabez Sneed, a short time since, informed me, that news to that effect has reached the Hall."

"In that case, it is to be hoped the pursuit is at an end?"

"I know not how that may be," answered Lady Eveline, "but from the anxiety that has been shown to take you, I fear there is little chance of the search being ended, till you have either been captured or certain intelligence has been received that you are safe in a foreign country."

"Has any one been here to look for me?"

"At present, we have been spared so unpleasant a visit," replied his sister, "but, of course, if any person has chanced to trace your footsteps towards this neighbourhood, there is no saying how soon the soldiers of the Commonwealth may arrive, for the purpose of searching our mansion, and the buildings connected with it."

"And yet," observed Lord Arden, "I should have thought, that his well-known zeal would have spared him and yourself the unpleasantness of such a proceeding. He has always been a stern and uncompromising republican, and should be one of the last persons suspected of harbouring a friend of the royal cause."

"But if you have been seen near our house, there will at least be a plea for such an intrusion."

"So it would," answered his lordship; "yet surely there are places in so large a mansion as this, in which I might be concealed for the short time I shall require to be here?"

"There are," she replied, "were it not for the vigilance of Jabez Sneed, who would gladly avail himself of an opportunity to gratify his revenge, for the discovery I have made of his dishonesty. He, in short, is the only person I fear, and there are but too good reasons for believing that he is even now keeping a vigilant watch in the event of your coming here to seek for shelter."

"Let him beware, then, how he braves my fury," exclaimed Lord Arden, "for I am well armed, and those who attempt to betray me must take the consequences of their own rashness."

"Would you, then, shed blood in the house

where you have been received as a fugitive and wanderer?"

"Only under the most pressing circumstances," he replied, "and not even then if there should be any means of avoiding it. Life and liberty are, however, too precious to be lost without an effort being made to preserve them; and, being once driven to extremities, I might surely be pardoned for an act that I was driven to."

The loud, joyous shouts of the tenants and peasantry outside the mansion, at this moment, announced the near approach of Sir Walter Amyot. The danger being thus more imminent than had been anticipated, Lord Arden expressed his determination to leave the house, though, to all appearance, escape was rendered impossible by the close proximity of those who had been charged with his capture. In Sir Walter, too, he could place little reliance, when duty urged him to secure one who was regarded as an enemy of the state; and therefore, disregarding all entreaties, he still persisted in leaving the place; and, if necessary, fighting against the most fearful odds rather than fall into the hands of his enemies. In this emergency, and urged by her terror, Lady Eveline entreated her brother to conceal himself behind the tapestry till other means could be thought of to secure his safe retreat to some other place of concealment. Lord Arden paused for a moment to consider, and then taking the hand of his sister, he said—

"On one condition only will I consent to remain a moment longer beneath the roof of your husband."

"What is the condition?"

"You must swear to keep my presence here a secret from Sir Walter Amyot," he replied.

"And what if I hesitate to take the oath you have mentioned?"

"In that case I will leave the hall this instant."

"Nay, that you cannot do, for those whom you would avoid are now within sight of the house."

"Then, I will remain here till your husband comes, and dare him to the worst!"

Driven to extremity by the situation in which she found herself, Lady Eveline could no longer hesitate. At the same moment, too, footsteps were heard coming along the corridor, so that not an instant was to be lost, and reflecting only on the fearful peril that threatened her brother, she took the oath that had been insisted on. Maud also was prevailed upon to promise silence, with regard to his having sought refuge in the house; and then as the young nobleman glided behind the tapestry, the door of the chamber was thrown open, and Jabez Sneed made his appearance.

"I have come, my lady, to announce the near approach of your husband," exclaimed the steward, "and to learn if you are still determined to charge me with dishonesty before I have had time to look once more over the accounts that have been disputed?"

"Of Sir Walter's approach I was aware," answered Lady Eveline, "for the shouts of his tenantry announced that fact to me some few minutes since."

"And what say you to the question I asked?"

"At present I have no reply to make to it," she replied.

"Then, I am to understand that you are determined to charge me with having cheated him?"

"Were I to hesitate I should be forgetful of my duty."

"Very well, my lady," he replied in a half menacing tone; "it is, of course, not for me to say how you ought to act, but I may, perhaps, be pardoned for suggesting that it may be one day or other my turn to be deaf to the voice of entreaty. I only ask you to suspend your judgment for a time, lest in the suddenness of his wrath, Sir Walter should dismiss an old, and—I will still say—a faithful domestic, from his service."

"Sir Walter Amyot will do nothing without giving the matter a full and fair consideration," answered Lady Eveline. "If your accounts are such as they ought to be, there can be no reason for apprehension on your part, and should my suspicions prove to be ill founded, I shall be ready to acknowledge that I have been guilty of an act of injustice towards you."

"That may be all very well, my lady," he replied, "but a man like myself, who has lived so long in the service of one family, cannot endure the thought of being suspected even for an instant."

"Perhaps so," answered the lady, "but Sir Walter Amyot never condemns till after a full and impartial inquiry, so that, however serious the charge may be, he will take no steps against you till he has gone carefully through your accounts. If innocent, the result of the ordeal will be so much the more gratifying to you—but if guilty, you must expect instant dismissal from his service."

"And how," demanded the steward, "am I to be satisfied that you will not use your influence against me?"

"I shall merely inform my husband of what I myself suspect, and then leave him to form his own conclusions."

"Then your ladyship will not give up the papers to me that I may have an opportunity of looking over my accounts once more before they are submitted to Sir Walter?"

"The accounts," she replied, "have been rendered, and should therefore be correct, even to the smallest item."

"And so I believe they are."

"If so, my false impression will soon be removed."

"But Sir Walter will never place so much confidence in me as he has previously done."

"On the contrary, I believe he will place more confidence in you," answered Eveline, "for it will afford him an opportunity of judging for himself how far you have conducted yourself ever since the commencement of your stewardship. If your management of his affairs has been uniformly honest, he will gladly acknowledge it and reward you for the zeal you may have manifested in his service.

"It may be all very easy to say so, my lady," exclaimed Jabez Sneed, "but when once a slur is thrown upon a man's character, it is not a trifling matter to convince the world of his honesty. Now, character being everything to me, I ask once more if you are determined to seek the ruin of a faithful servant."

"I would not do so upon mere suspicion," answered his mistress, "but the accounts you have delivered speak for themselves, and they pass not from my possession till with my own hands do I place them in the hands of Sir Walter Amyot."

"Then my ruin is determined on!"

"Not by me," she replied, "for I only do my duty in giving them to my husband exactly in the same state as I received them from you. If he be satisfied with them, the blame of the whole transaction will fall, not on you, but on myself."

"Ah!" exclaimed Jabez Sneed, "it may be all very well to say so, but is it likely that he would blame his wife for doing what she supposes is her duty?"

"He would blame me," answered Lady Eveline, "were it to appear upon an examination of the accounts that I have suffered my zeal to outreach my discretion. Remember, Sir Walter is a strict lover of justice, and nothing would offend him more than to discover that an old domestic had been wrongfully charged with dishonesty."

"Then it seems you are still positive of my guilt?"

"I shall pass no opinion till my husband has

carefully gone through the accounts, that I have objected to," she replied. "At present it must be admitted my mind is strongly biassed in favour of the notion that I have entertained from the beginning, but a prejudice has nothing whatever to do with it. I should rejoice as much as yourself to find that I have been mistaken."

"And that you are mistaken," exclaimed the steward, "you will be convinced as soon as Sir Walter Amyot has gone carefully through the papers which are the subject of this unpleasant suspicion."

"Which I suppose will be as soon as he returns home."

"I rather think we shall have some time to wait," answered Jabez Sneed, "for there seems to me a notion that Lord Arden is somehow in this neighbourhood, so that of course my master will deem it his duty to go out in quest of him as soon as he hears that the fugitive is supposed to be within his reach."

"Do you remember," asked Lady Eveline sternly, "that the fugitive you speak of is my brother?"

"I do" answered the steward, "and pity him no more than you do me when I am in trouble."

"If I understand rightly, you would betray him were his place of concealment known?"

"That will depend upon circumstances," returned Jabez Sneed, "for I can either be grateful or vindictive, according as I receive favour or injury from your ladyship.'

"You threaten me," she replied "but I am not to be intimidated from what I know to be my duty. The papers, therefore, will remain in my possession till they are given into the hands of my husband, who shall not fail to know the means you have taken to prevent my performing an act of duty."

"Very well, my lady," he exclaimed, "you will, of course, do as you please about it, but revenge is sweet, and it may, by-and-by, be my turn to torture your feelings as you have mine. That Lord Arden is not far off I am certain, and it shall be no fault of mine if he be not in custody before many hours are over."

"Do you know where he is?" asked Lady Eveline, with a feeling of anxiety that it was impossible to conceal.

"It is not my intention, at present, to say whether I do or not," replied the steward; "but if it be any satisfaction to your ladyship, I will confess that a very little exertion and watchfulness on my part will serve to put me on the right track. Nay, more, I will undertake to say that Lord Arden shall not be at liberty twelve hours hence, if the information I have received is to be relied on."

"Then you do know where he is?"

"Perhaps I do."

"And for the mere gratification of your own revenge, you would send to the public scaffold a man who has never offended you by word or deed?"

"He may not have offended me," replied Jabez Sneed, "but his sister has, and that is nearly the same thing."

"So then you would revenge yourself upon him because I have threatened to expose your evil doings to the master whose confidence you have so cruelly abused?"

"I repeat that the error is on your side and not on mine."

"In that case you have nothing to fear from your accounts undergoing a strict examination."

"So your ladyship may imagine," answered the steward with a frown, "but I know that when a man is once suspected, he never again thoroughly recovers his former good character. You, however, have resolved to take a decided part against me, and it is likely I may be the sufferer through

it, but at any rate, I shall have the satisfaction of carrying out my revenge. So, beware, my lady, for so surely as you deliver those papers into the hands of my master, Lord Arden shall be surrendered to those who are searching throughout the country for him."

Upon uttering this threat, Jabez Sneed strode insolently from the presence of his mistress, and scarcely was the door closed behind him than the fugitive nobleman of whom he had been speaking, emerged from behind the arras which had concealed him.

"So," he exclaimed taking his sister's hand, "the steward is no less revengeful than you imagined, and I had need act with caution or he may have it in his power to carry into effect the threat with which he parted from you."

"You overheard him, then?" asked Lady Eveline.

"Not a word that he uttered escaped me," he replied, "and it was with no little difficulty that I could restrain myself from rushing out and punishing him upon the spot for his insolence."

"'Tis well you had sufficient command over yourself to forbear," exclaimed his sister, "for had he seen you, an alarm would have been instantly raised, and your capture would have been certain."

"But not without so desperate a defence on my part that some of my assailants would have perished through their fool-hardiness."

"And where, my dear brother, would have been your satisfaction, when a death of shame must have been the consequence?"

"There would have been little satisfaction I must admit," he replied, "except that my first victim should have been the villain who betrayed me. However, a truce to that now, for your husband has by this time arrived at home, and it is necessary that I should decide quickly whether to remain here or venture once more to make my way towards the sea-coast."

"Let me conjure you not to leave this house whilst so many of your enemies are about the place!" exclaimed Lady Eveline, in an agony of alarm. "Nothing can prevent your being seen by some of those who have followed Sir Wa'' hither, and should a pursuit be commenced, would not be the slightest chance of your e

"What would you have me do, then?"

"Remain where you are," answ Eveline, "and I will do all I can to p covery, that must prove fatal to you.'

"In what part of the house can I main undiscovered?" asked the fu man.

"I know of no place where you safe than in this room," answered h is the one which I usually occupy in of my husband, and at all other time except on very rare occasions. He you may hope to remain undisturbed turn y fortunately presents itself for to France."

"Well, then, since it is your wish, seems to be some little probability of re. discovered for a few days, I will conse. kept here a prisoner, you, of course, bei. jailor."

"And a harsh one I shall not be, you may depend upon it," answered Lady Eveline. "As a matter of prudence, however, I shall not visit you very often, but Maud—who may safely be relied on—will convey all messages between us, since her coming to the room frequently will not be likely to awaken suspicion."

"And I suppose I may rely upon you for some of the crumbs that fall from your table?"

"Depend upon it, my dear brother," she replied, "I will take care that the hospitality for which our house is celebrated, shall not be forgotten on this occasion. My attendant will watch her opportunities to bring all that may be required, and you may rest assured that she will prove no niggard in providing for your comforts."

"How," exclaimed Lord Arden, " am I ever to repay the kindness you lavish on me in my misfortunes?"

"By taking care that no one shall know of your being here," she replied. "Caution will be necessary, or all that I am endeavouring to do for your preservation, will be thrown away."

"You may rely upon my prudence for that," answered his lordship, "for the vigilance of my enemies has warned me that I have nothing to expect from their mercy if it should be my evil destiny to fall into their hands. Besides, the apartment you have assigned me, seems to be comfortable enough, and though it may not be pleasant to part with one's liberty, even for a few days I will endeavour to remain within the limits of my chamber, till the happy hour arrives when I may leave it to seek a home in another country.'

"I do not know that you need keep yourself quite so close a prisoner as all that," replied his sister, "for at night, when all have retired to the house, there will be little danger in your descending from yonder window to the terrace, where you may exercise yourself without much fear of being discovered. When an opportunity offers, too, I will venture out to bear you company, and you will then be able to learn how the search is proceeding, and what chance there is of your leaving the country."

"Take care, Eveline," exclaimed her brother, "or Sir Walter may grow suspicious and watch where you are going to.""

"Leave that to me," she replied, "and I will so arrange the meetings I speak of, that no one shall wonder at my absence. Besides, Sir Walter is one of the last persons in the world to be suspicious, and he would rather——"

"My lord! my lord! you have not a minute to lose," exclaimed Maud, who had been watching at the door—"Sir Walter is coming up the stairs, and will be here almost before you have time to conceal yourself."

e warning thus conveyed was instantly followed, and almost at the same moment that Sir Amyot entered the room, Lord Arden concealed himself behind the arras.

CHAPTER III.

EETING.—SIR WALTER RECOUNTS
TS OF HIS FRUITLESS SEARCH.—A
WKWARD PROPOSITION, AND THE
TIES ATTENDING IT.—THE COAST
ONCE MORE CLEAR.—MAUD AND
LIER.

d affectionate was the greeting that between the husband and wife; but the of the former soon observed the pale agitation of Lady Eveline. This, however attributed to the suddenness of his arrival, half in joke, half in earnest, inquired why she had thus given way to her feelings when the wife of a soldier should always be prepared for surprises of every description. But perceiving that she wished to change the subject, he spoke of other matters relating to the affairs which had compelled him to leave home, and held out hopes that his absence from her would be no more required, since the result of the last skirmish had so completely discomfitted the cavaliers, that there was no probability of their ever making another attempt to disturb the peace of the country. This, though in some respects it was welcome intelligence, was far from allaying the fears of Lady Eveline, and at length taking advantage of a pause in the con-

versation, she ventured to ask if anything had been heard of her unfortunate fugitive brother.

"At present," answered Sir Walter Amyot, "all is doubt respecting the place of his concealment—but it is generally supposed that he is still in England, though in what part no one has yet been able to ascertain."

"And would you," she asked, "assist in hunting out one who is so dear to me?"

"What am I to do when duty calls upon me to fulfil the oath I have taken to serve my country faithfully?" he asked. "As your brother, I would gladly have shielded him from the consequences of the rashness he has been guilty of, in drawing his sword against those who are in authority; but the commands issued are most imperative, and those who disobey them will do so at the risk of meeting with a disgraceful punishment."

"And yet," sighed Lady Eveline, "he has only attempted to serve the cause of the prince who he believes to have been unjustly deprived of the crown of his royal ancestors."

"That may be," answered her husband, "but the voice of the whole nation has declared against the restoration of monarchy, and it is therefore nothing short of madness to resist in the behalf of one who has been forced to seek for safety in exile. Your brother has unfortunately linked himself to the weaker cause, and it being well known that he was engaged in the late attempt to overthrow the Commonwealth, it is little to be wondered at that he has been denounced as a traitor to our country."

"My brother is no traitor," said Lady Eveline, proudly; "but has acted upon the impulse of a generous mind that is devoted to the cause of a family that he was taught always to regard as the rightful rulers of the land."

"And like some few others," observed Sir Walter Amyot. "he has brought ruin upon himself through following a mistake. We will not, however, speak further upon this subject, for it has ever been my wish to avoid even an allusion to the only affair upon which it has been our misfortune to differ."

"But though we differ, my dear husband, we never disagree upon it," she replied, "because you are always considerate enough to excuse the warmth with which I advocate views that are entirely opposite to your own. Besides though I know you are in duty bound to hunt out all those who our present laws call traitors to their country, I believe you would rather assist at the escape than the capture of my unfortunate brother."

"As far as inclination goes," answered Sir Walter, "I should be sorry were chance to throw us in each other's way, because I know how heavily the blow would fall upon you, were Lord Arden to fall into the hands of those who are in pursuit of him. On the other hand, however, I cannot conceal from you the fact, that were I to receive intelligence of the place of his concealment, I should feel myself bound to use all my exertions towards making him my prisoner."

"And suppose," asked Lady Eveline, trembling with emotion, "he should ever be so hard pressed as to seek a shelter beneath your roof, would you, under such circumstances, break the law of hospitality, by giving him up to his enemies?"

"That," returned Sir Walter, "is a question so difficult to answer, that I know not what to say. The probability of his ever doing so is, however, so remote a one that it is to be hoped my feelings and hospitality will never be tried by so severe an ordeal. Still, I may again receive orders to search for him, and should that be the case, I must obey them, even though the task would be the most painful one that could be imposed upon me."

"But, perhaps you would take care not to be excessively strict in your search?"

"I certainly would afford every opportunity I could for his escape," replied her husband; "but were chance to throw him in my way I should have no alternative but to apprehend him as an enemy of the state I am bound to serve with my best energies."

"Yet there are some who would say that he is a friend rather than an enemy of the state."

"So they might, my dear Eveline," he replied. "but those only would say so who, like himself, have devoted themselves to a bad cause. As your brother, I feel the deepest regret at the unfortunate side he has taken in this affair, but since he has so far involved himself, all I can now hope is that he may have succeeded before this in getting clear out of this country."

"Do you think it possible he may have done so?" asked her ladyship.

"At all events," answered Sir Walter Amyot, "there is good ground for presuming that he may have done so, because it is well known that a vessel lately left our English shores with a large number of persons who were engaged in the recent insurrection. Your brother may have been among them, and I need hardly say how glad I should be to hear my supposition confirmed."

"Then during your search you have heard nothing to lead to the belief that he is still in this country?"

"I have not."

These few words served to allay a good deal of the alarm which had been experienced by Lady Eveline, and recovering some of her usual composure, she inquired whether the search was supposed to be nearly at an end.

"Not by any means," answered Sir Walter Amyot, "for a report has just been received that he has been seen travelling at night, as if making towards the coast under cover of darkness. In consequence of this, orders have been given to keep a strict look-out for his lordship, so that he may not be suffered to escape."

"And do you believe so improbable a report that he is still in a country where there is so much danger?"

"I can scarcely give it credit," he replied, "but, of course, I am equally bound to exert my vigilance in case he should be rash enough to venture upon making another attempt to overthrow the government as is at present established by law. He, however, so well knows the consequences of being taken, that it is only reasonable to infer that he will take warning by the past and give up a cause that can only end in his own discomfiture and ruin."

"Would that I knew he was safely out of the country," exclaimed Lady Eveline, "for never till then can I rest satisfied that he is beyond the reach of danger."

"A few days will serve to confirm or contradict the fact," answered her husband, "for Cromwell has his agents in most of the foreign countries, so that he may receive the earliest information respecting those whom he has occasion to regard as his enemies. These people are constantly communicating with him, and it will, therefore, be soon publicly known whether Lord Arden be among those who have lately succeeded in escaping from England."

"And in the meantime," exclaimed her ladyship, "may I ask for your promise not to take active part in the search that you say is still making for him?"

"I can make no promise of that kind," he replied, "because it is a point of honour to obey all orders that proceed from our superiors, even though the duty we are called upon to perform may be against those who are nearest and dearest to us. With respect to Lord Arden, though we have never been upon terms of friendship with him, yet, as the brother of my wife, I would not join myself with those who are in pursuit of him, unless commanded to do so by those who I am bound to obey."

"May I ask again if you would betray him were circumstances at any time to compel him to ask, beneath your roof, a shelter from those who are in pursuit of him?"

"The question is so difficult a one to answer, that I would rather not be questioned any further upon it, just now," replied Sir Walter Amyot. "Indeed, considering the coldness that has always existed between us, I should think my house is the last place he would think of choosing as an asylum."

"So I have thought myself," answered her ladyship, "but we know not what necessity may drive us to, and I have sometimes thought with terror that, as a last resource, he might some time or other find himself compelled to throw himself upon your mercy and generosity. And, when a thought of that kind has struck me, Sir Walter, I have almost ventured to hope that his confidence in you would not be thrown away."

"Perhaps not," he replied; "but I would make no promise, because the duty we owe to our rulers is the chief consideration that ought to govern our actions."

"Then why not grant the same privilege to him?" asked Lady Eveline. "He regards the son of the late King Charles as the sovereign he is bound to serve, and surely he would be a traitor to his cause were he to desert him now that he so much needs the services of those few friends whom misfortune has left him."

No answer was given to this, and Lady Eveline's anxiety was raised to the highest pitch, for, from the beginning to the end of this conversation she had been a prey to the greatest uneasiness, lest her brother should be discovered. At length, breaking the silence which had followed her last observation, she proposed adjourning to another apartment where refreshments had been prepared in anticipation of his expected return. Against this suggestion Sir Walter good-humouredly remonstrated, as he knew the chamber in which they were was her favourite one; but again her request was urged with so much earnestness, that, all unsuspecting as he was, he determined to offer no more serious opposition. Seeing, however, how anxious she was upon the point, he said, gaily—

"How is it, my dear Eveline, that you are so resolute not to take your refreshment with me in this room, which I always understood was your favourite one?"

"It is still my favourite one when you are absent," she replied, "because it is more retired, and has been fitted up according to my own taste. But when you are at home there are many other parts of the house that I prefer, as being more convenient for the reception of friends who may happen to call upon us."

"But I have brought no friends with me now," answered her husband, "and there is, therefore, the less reason why I should not have been indulged in this whim of mine."

"Had I been aware of your wishes earlier," exclaimed Lady Eveline, "I would have made my arrangements differently; but having no idea of your immediate return home, till a short time ago, I may be pardoned for anything that may appear like an omission of duty."

"Yet we have often used this apartment, and I never till now have heard you make any objection to it."

"Nay, Sir Walter, I hope you do not think I have any improper motive for wishing you to go elsewhere?"

"How can I think so," he asked, "when I have never known you to be guilty of either secrecy or deception? However, why should I speak further upon this subject, since it has already been agreed that we shall occupy our usual sitting apartment, and I know well that any motive you may have is a good one? Besides, it is likely I shall be called away again very soon, so that it can matter very little what part of the house we inhabit."

"Must we then part so soon?" sighed Lady Eveline.

"There is every reason to believe so," he replied, "for orders have been given for securing all the insurgents who yet remain in England, and part of the duty of searching for them through the country will, as a matter of course, fall upon me."

"In which case it will be your evil fortune to be sent in quest of my unfortunate brother."

"That may indeed be," he replied, "but you may be sure that the task will be the most disagreeable one that could be entrusted to me. ... differing from him both in politics and ...ligion, I feel for him as your brother, and would do anything that would not compromise my duty to save him from the consequences of his rashness."

"But you do not consider that his rashness, as you term it, was exercised in a cause that he considers as just as you do yours."

"Perhaps so," answered Sir Walter Amyot, "nor will I blame him for doing that which he considers right, and which he has probably entered into as a matter of conscience. On the other hand, however, it must be recollected that he has been fighting under the banner of those who are in rebellion against the state; and having failed in changing the form of government, he will be made to bear the consequences of his act unless he has succeeded in leaving the country."

"And supposing he was to be taken?"

"I fear nothing would save his life, which has been declared forfeited."

"Would not even your influence be sufficient to save him from so terrible a fate?"

"The hope," replied Sir Walter, "would be so remote a one that it would be madness to indulge in it. It is true I am in high favour with Cromwell, but he is sternly resolved to carry the extreme penalty of the law against all those who have been concerned in the late outbreak; and I am afraid there is no one who possesses influence enough to obtain pardon for any of those who may be taken."

"But this is the first time my brother has appeared in arms."

"I know it is," answered her husband, "but that, it is to be feared, will make very little difference. In fact, though Lord Arden has not taken an active part till lately, it is well known that he has been long engaged in several intrigues, and he is marked as being one amongst the most dangerous enemies of the Commonwealth. Thus you see, my dear Eveline, how poor a chance he would stand in the event of his falling into the hands of his pursuers."

"Yet it seems that you may be the very person to capture him."

"I earnestly pray, however, that it may not be my misfortune to be so circumstanced," he replied; "but if destiny has so willed it, my duty must be fearlessly performed; even though it be at the sacrifice of your love, which I esteem beyond all earthly blessings. You however may, if he be still in England, receive some communication from him, and if that should be the case, you must earnestly exhort him to quit the country with as little delay as possible."

"Do you think he would venture to let even me know where he has found concealment?" asked Lady Eveline in the hope of ascertaining whether any suspicion was entertained of where he was.

"Why should he fear to trust you with the secret?" asked her husband.

"Because he would not trust any one with a message for fear of being betrayed."

"True," exclaimed Sir Walter Amyot, "but there are people who say he has been seen in this neighbourhood; and if there should be any truth in the rumour, I am afraid he would apply here for an asylum till he is able to get away."

"Why are you afraid of it?" asked Lady Eveline anxiously.

"For no other reason," he replied, "than that I should be compelled to take measures for his immediate arrest."

"And would you then refuse your hospitality even to the man that you regard as an enemy?"

"How could I do otherwise?" he asked. "Am I not a soldier of the Commonwealth? and would it not be an act of treachery on my part were I to harbour one who has appeared in open insurrection against the authorities to which I am bound to yield obedience?"

"I know not how that may be," answered Lady Eveline, "but I cannot believe that you would refuse your protection against one who has no friends nor place of refuge to fly to. Besides, though my brother and you have never been upon good terms, your promise has often been given to me never to seek reparation for the insults he has sometimes heaped upon you."

"Nor would I for any private quarrel," answered Sir Walter; "but upon public grounds I am compelled to treat him exactly as I would any of the other persons who were engaged in the recent outbreak. For your sake I would gladly have given him any assistance in my power, but upon public grounds I must seek for him whenever called upon to do so."

"But suppose you were to see him before any orders were given to you upon the subject?"

"Ay," returned her husband, "that is a question that I own somewhat puzzles me, for I know not how I might act upon the impulse of the moment. As far as my own feelings go, I should rejoice to have it in my power to return good for the evil opinion he has ever entertained against me; but, knowing as I do, that he is a proclaimed traitor, it would be a breach of confidence on my part were I in any way to connive at his escape."

"Yet what harm could result from it," exclaimed Lady Eveline, "seeing that, should he succeed in getting abroad, he would never again venture to return to England where it seems he is so much dreaded."

"It is by no means certain that he would not return," observed Sir Walter Amyot, "for it is pretty generally feared that those who have succeeded in effecting their escape, will concoct fresh schemes for another attempt at an insurrection the first time that an opportunity offers. That, indeed, is the principal reason why so much severity is manifested towards those who have been already taken, for it is hoped that a terrible example may prevent any further outbreak which might otherwise be expected."

"A mere excuse," sighed Lady Eveline, "for the horrors that have been perpetrated from one end of the country to the other."

"Nay, my love," exclaimed her husband, "you know not the difficulties which our country has to contend against. Abroad, the fugitive royalists are perpetually endeavouring to prevail upon foreign courts to send their armies into England, and, failing in this, have every now and then ventured here in disguise to ferment dissatisfaction amongst those of our countrymen who would otherwise be well disposed towards their present rulers. Upon such enemies mercy would be thrown away, and it has at length been resolved, as the only way to secure the peace of the nation, to visit with the severest punishment all those who happen to be captured."

"Would not mercy and kindness be more likley to answer the same purpose?"

"I has been tried, but I am sorry to say without any favourable result," answered Sir Walter. "At those times when men fancy the peace of the country most secure, evil-minded persons take advantage of the general confidence, and a sudden insurrection rouses us to a sense of the danger which had not been foreseen. This has happened on several occasions, till at length it has been found necessary to show the enemy that we are still strong enough to punish those who presume to disturb us with their treasons."

"Ay," exclaimed Lady Eveline, "I know that laws must be respected; but who broke them so much as those who imprisoned and afterwards beheaded the late king?"

"The late king was a tyrant," answered Sir Walter, with more sternness than he had yet manifested, "and deserved the fate he met."

"Then you defend the act that sent a crowned monarch to end his life upon the scaffold like a common felon?" exclaimed Lady Eveline.

"Let us speak no more, my love, upon a subject upon which we can never agree," returned her husband. "Come with me to the apartment where the refreshments have been prepared, and we will speak further of your brother, whose misfortunes grieve me almost as much as they do you."

They then left the room, Maud remaining behind for the purpose of speaking to Lord Arden, who once more emerged from behind the tapestry on finding that he could do so without fear of discovery.

"Ah! my lord," she exclaimed, "there is danger here, as I suppose you just now heard; for my master is not at all inclined to favour you any more than he would a perfect stranger, and poor Lady Amyot is in terrible trouble through you, though she has not yet said anything about it."

"How do you know then that she is in trouble about me, my pretty maiden?" asked his lordship.

"I could tell that by her looks," answered Maud, "for I have lived with her quite long enough to tell when she is pleased or angry, without a word being spoken upon the subject."

"But why," he asked, "need she feel any alarm on my account, when Sir Walter seems to have no notion of my being here?"

"That may be all very true at present," she replied, "but then, my lord, you have no idea what a prying, inquisitive old fellow we have to deal with in Jabez Sneed, who is as revengeful as he is cunning; and if, as is only too likely, he should discover that you are in the house, he would betray you as sure as fate."

"Very likely," exclaimed Lord Arden, "but knowing the sort of customer we have to deal with, we must be the more careful not to let him know that I am within reach of his malice."

"I'm afraid that will not be quite so easy as your lordship imagines."

"Nay, but I hope I shall be able to leave this house in the course of a few days at the very farthest."

"And if you do, it will be at the risk of falling into the hands of some of the people that are looking out for you."

"But so far, I believe, my presence here is unsuspected and the secret may still be kept if I remain closely confined to this apartment till the time comes when I can embark on board some vessel for a foreign coast."

"Ay, my lord," answered the girl, "it seems to be all easy and smooth enough to look at, but my master has a terrible feeling of revenge against all you cavaliers, and I'm afraid he would have no more pity upon you than upon any one else,

if he should happen to learn that you have found shelter beneath his roof. And my lady thinks so too, I am certain, for I saw what looks of terror she every now and then cast towards the place where you were concealed, whenever Sir Walter turned his head in any other direction. And, oh! if he had only guessed who was there, he would have dragged you forth, and delivered you up to the constables with as little remorse as if you had been quite a stranger."

"How do you know his feelings are so bitter towards me?"

"Because I have heard him say that he would not shelter even his own brother if he took up arms against the Commonwealth."

"But his wife has great influence over him."

"So she has, my lord, in almost anything else but this. He, however, is such a red-hot republican, that he considers it to be his duty to give up any royalist that may happen to come within his reach. My mistress would, of course, try to shield you as much as possible, but her persuasions would be nothing in comparison with the pleasure of surrendering up to the laws any one that he considers to be an enemy to the state."

"In that case," exclaimed Lord Arden, "I can only see the greater reason for avoiding every chance of my presence here being known to any more than are already aware of my being in the house. And I should suppose there can be no great difficulty in that, as I believe this room is seldom entered by any other persons than yourself and your mistress."

"Not very often, my lord," answered the girl, "but we have that terrible mischief-making Jabez Sneed to guard against, and that will not be a very easy matter if he only sees the slightest cause to suspect that there is any mystery that he is not acquainted with."

"How can he know that any one is here when I am certain no one saw me come into the house?"

"But the merest trifle will make him suspect, and the moment the notion enters his head, he will go and tell Sir Walter, who would soon have the place searched from one end of it to the other. And then, my lord, if a discovery should happen to take place, he would give you up to the laws, though he knows it would be certain to send you to the scaffold."

"You seem to think, my good girl, that I am unable to defend myself, even if your worst fears should be realised."

"Ah, my lord," she exclaimed, "but you know not the mischief that such an affair would cause. Sir Walter would be the more incensed against you if the lives of any of his people were sacrificed, and no prayers or entreaties of Lady Amyot would save you from the vengeance of those that look upon all royalists as the greatest enemies to the country."

"That may be, my good girl," answered Lord Arden, "but it cannot be expected that I would tamely surrender myself up so long as I had arms in my hands with which to protect myself. I am no lover of violence, yet if need be, I will fight to the very last, rather than give myself up to my deadly enemies."

"Well then, my lord," exclaimed Maud, "the best thing you can do will be to remain quietly where you are, and not suffer yourself to be seen by any one except my mistress and myself. I will take care to bring your meals whenever I can do so without much danger of being seen, and at the same time Lady Amyot can send any messages that she pleases through me. In that way I think the old steward may be deceived for a time; but if my advice may be offered without giving offence, I should say that the sooner you get over to France the better it will be for all parties."

"I suppose then I am looked upon as an intruder here?"

"Nay, my lord, if my mistress wishes you to leave this place, it is only that she is afraid of the danger that will surround you as long as you remain in the house."

"Sir Walter Amyot, I believe, very seldom comes to this room?"

"Very seldom," answered Maud, "for it is looked upon as my lady's own private apartment, where no one is to intrude upon her without express permission. So I believe you may consider yourself as being tolerably safe here, if you are only careful not to let any person see you standing at the window."

"How then am I to amuse myself in my solitude?"

"If your lordship is fond of books, you will find plenty on yonder shelves; they are such as my lady finds amusement in, and may serve to pass away the time that would otherwise hang heavily on your hands. Besides, Lady Amyot will be able to pay you a visit now and then, for I can keep watch on the outside of the door, and give timely warning in case anybody should be likely to break too suddenly into the room during your interview."

"But will not Sir Walter wonder at her absence?"

"The meetings," replied Maud, "must only take place when he is either absent from the house, or so engaged that he will not be likely to discover the absence of my lady. In short, you may trust to me for making those arrangements; for I know the danger that would follow a discovery; and we'll take good care that neither Jabez Sneed nor anybody else shall have the gratification of learning the fact of your being here."

"Does the fellow ever come to this room?"

"Only when sent for my lady, as was the case a little time ago," answered the girl. "Once, to be sure, he used to try very much to make his way into the chamber; but on my mistress complaining of his intrusion, Sir Walter rebuked him for it sharply, and since then he never comes unless his presence is particularly desired."

"Is there any reason to believe that the old man acts the part of a spy upon my sister?"

"He would do so if he dared," answered Maud, "but my master is above the paltry meanness of employing a spy, and Jabez would find no sort of encouragement from those that he might wish to seek favour with."

"Then, if I can understand, this steward is no favourite of Sir Walter's?"

"Why, as for that, my lord," answered the girl, "he has always been rather favoured because he has been a great many years in the family. But I fancy he'll find things a little different when my lady tells Sir Walter of the false accounts that have been made out."

"Perhaps Jabez may have made a mistake without being aware of it."

"So he would like to make it appear," replied Maud; "but my lady says, she is pretty certain the system of fraud has been going on for a long while; and if that can only be proved against him, the old man will soon be dismissed from his stewardship,"

"Which will only make him the more determined to seek occasion to injure Lady Eveline."

"I shouldn't at all wonder if he tries to do my lady a mischief," replied the girl; "but then, Sir Walter is a man that always judges for himself, and Master Sneed may say whatever he will without making the least impression, unless his master was convinced upon better evidence than an accuser could bring forward. In truth, the only danger I can see is lest he should happen to suspect that you are in the house; for, in that case, a search over the place would be sure to follow."

"But you could give such early information that I should be able to leave the house before they come to this part of it."

"I should most likely know of it in good time," answered Maud; "but if it should be suspected that you are anywhere about the place, the old hall would be surrounded by Sir Walter's people, to prevent all chance of your getting away. However, I don't want to make things appear worse than they really are; so if your lordship will favour me with your confidence, I'll do my best not only to conceal all knowledge of your being in the house, but think of some plan to insure your escape if matters should come to the worst."

Having received his assurance that he would leave the management of the affair entirely in her hands, Maud left the room to attend upon her mistress. The situation in which Lord Arden found himself was an extremely critical one, but he had no other choice but to remain where he was; and taking up a book, he endeavoured to forget for awhile the perilous condition into which he had fallen.

———

CHAPTER IV.

THE STEWARD REMARKS SOME SUSPICIOUS CIRCUMSTANCES, AND TAKES HIS MEASURES ACCORDINGLY. — MEETS WITH MAUD, AND IS RATHER TOO FREE IN HIS INQUIRIES.—TOM DINGLE COMES TO THE RESCUE.—SIR WALTER AMYOT APPEARS ON THE SCENE, HEARS THE CAUSE OF THE DISPUTE, AND SUMMARILY DISPOSES OF IT.

Two or three days passed over after the events related in the last chapter, and still none but the two persons who were in the secret suspected that the mansion contained more than its usual number of inhabitants. At length, however, Jabez Sneed, who was continually upon the watch, began to discover that frequent visits were made to the bower chamber by Lady Eveline and the attendant. This excited his curiosity still farther, and induced him to be more prying than ever; and when he made the notable discovery that sundry articles of the nicest description were continually disappearing from the pantry and the wine-cellar, he suspected they must have been conveyed to some person who was secreted in the apartment, to which even Sir Walter Amyot himself was denied admittance. Any one less cunning than the old man would have immediately informed his master of his suspicions; but it was not so with Jacob Sneed, who preferred abiding his time and opportunity; and feeling satisfied that some important discovery was about to be made, he preferred waiting till his whole scheme of action was ripe for execution. The exultation he felt as he thought of the mischief he was preparing was excessive, but he was determined not to lose the chance by being too precipitate; and resolving to continue his watch upon the parties he suspected, he waited with intense anxiety for the moment when his plans were to be carried into effect. In fact, from the time when the idea struck him, he resolved, at a fitting opportunity, to communicate his suspicions to his master; and thus, by exciting his jealousy, to effect a quarrel that should lead to the speedy downfall of the unsuspecting Lady Eveline. Gloating with fiendish delight over the scheme he was forming, Jabez Sneed was slowly proceeding towards his own room, when he heard light footsteps behind, and looking quickly around, perceived Maud with a basket on her arm, walking sharply in the same direction that he was. It appeared evident that she had not yet perceived him; but no sooner did she observe who was before her than, suddenly coming to a full pause, she appeared as if about to retrace her steps, when the steward suddenly pounced forward; and seizing her by the arm, inquired what errand of mischief she was going on.

"Good gracious, Mr. Sneed, what do you mean by mischief?" exclaimed the maiden, recovering herself with surprising quickness. "I suppose I have my business in this house to attend to as well as you, and yet I have not presumed to ask what mischief you are going on."

"You are equivocating with me, girl!" returned the old man, in a tone of voice that was intended to terrify her. "There's something going on in this place that ought not to be, and I am determined to know what it is, or I shall acquaint Sir Walter with your doings, and he will soon force you to tell the truth."

"Well, I'm sure, Mr. Sneed!" exclaimed Maud, indignantly. "You have been well set to work, I think, to invent a parcel of falsehoods, for the sake of setting my master against me."

"Ay, ay," he replied, "you can put on a very innocent look when a discovery of your goings-on has been made; but I have Sir Walter's interest to look to, and I shall not let you go till you have told me where you have been with that basket."

"The basket has nothing in it as you may see, if you choose to take the trouble of looking at it."

"Ah!" exclaimed Jabez Sneed, "I see it is empty now, but what did it just now contain?"

"Nothing."

"Are you in the habit of carrying a basket about with nothing in it?"

"I'm not going to be questioned and cross questioned by you nor anybody else," answered Maud tartly.

"Very well, then I shall acquaint Sir Walter with the artful doings that are going on in his house."

"Artful doings!" said the girl indignantly; "and pray what right has a prying inquisitive old fool like you to do with me? Sir Walter wouldn't accuse me of acting wrong, and I dont see why I'm to be accused by an under-trapper like you."

"The truth is you are vexed at being found out. But never mind, I have a duty to perform and I'll do it too, however much you may be offended at my question."

"It would be a good thing, Mr. Sneed, if you were to attend a little more to your duty, as you call it, for I rather think by this time Sir Walter must have seen good reason to believe that he has not been served by a very honest steward!"

"Humph! I find you have been taking a lesson out of your mistress's book," exclaimed the old man, upon whose brows had gathered a dark and ominous frown. "She has dared to accuse me of dishonest practices, but I am conscious of my own innocence; and Sir Walter, when he comes to examine my accounts, will acknowledge that I have been made the victim of a foul conspiracy."

"And who, pray, do you accuse of conspiring to injure you?"

"Those," he replied, "who will soon enough feel that they have been practicing against one who has both the power and the inclination to retaliate any evil that may be inflicted on him. I know Lady Eveline has accused me of having made up my accounts falsely, but my own conscience acquits me of any blame; and I shall by and by be able to prove to my master that I have never wronged him of a single penny."

"Single pennies I know nothing at all about," answered Maud, "but my lady has gone over the accounts carefully, and she declares that there is a large sum of money kept which ought before now to have gone into the pocket of Sir Walter Amyot. So before you find fault again with other people, Master Sneed, look to your own evil deeds, and try if you can't amend them."

"I see what all this is done for," exclaimed the old man. "You see that I have discovered some

of your goings on, and this is the way you think to intimidate me from doing my duty. But I know strange things have been going on in the house for this last two or three days, and I'll know the truth of it before I have done with you."

"What do you mean by strange things, Jabez Sneed?"

"Why, I should like to know in the first place what has become of that roasted capon that I saw in the larder no longer ago than this morning? It has found legs and walked, it seems."

"Or rather, if it be not there, it has found wings and flown," returned Maud, nothing abashed by this rather puzzling question.

"You equivocate, girl, but I am not so easily turned away from my purpose," exclaimed the angry steward. "The capon was safe enough this morning, and I shall insist upon knowing where it is."

"Indeed!" she retorted; "and suppose, the thing being no great novelty in this house, I ate it myself?"

"In that case, Mistress Maud, I should say you have a most extraordinary appetite, for half a neat's tongue disappeared at the same time."

"Really, sir, you seem to keep a very keen watch upon Sir Walter's larder!"

"And with good reason," he replied, "for if I am accused of dishonesty in my transactions, it is high time that I should discover those who are continually practicing these petty thefts. And yet they are not so petty either, for in the last three days, as many bottles of wine have been missed from Sir Walter's favourite bin."

"And pray, sir, what have I to do with that?"

"A great deal, or I am very much mistaken."

"You mean to say then, I suppose, that I have drank it?"

"No—I don't mean to say anything of the kind, Mistress Pert," exclaimed Jabez Sneed; "but I have a notion some one is secreted in this house that ought not to be here, and I shall not rest satisfied till I have routed out the whole of the secret."

"Pray, who do you suppose is concealed here?" asked Maud, nearly taken off her guard by this latter observation.

"At present that is a mystery that I have not been able to clear up," answered the old man; "but I can bide my time patiently; and sooner perhaps than you expect, the truth will be discovered. So you may tell your mistress that, as she has tried to do me a bad turn, I shall not rest quiet till I have had my revenge."

"Indeed!" exclaimed Maud ironically. "So you can boast of intending to injure a female, for no better reason than that she has discovered some of your pilfering propensities?"

"She has accused me unjustly."

"If so, it will be easy to prove your innocence, and Sir Walter will recompense you for any trouble or annoyance you may have been put to."

"How can I expect that," demanded the old man, "when the accusation comes from the lips of his own wife?"

"It matters not who it comes from," exclaimed Maud, "for Sir Walter is too fond of justice to condemn you without a fair hearing; and if your accounts are as fair as you say they are, he will not punish you for what has never been done. As for my lady, she would never have accused you of dishonesty, had there not been good ground for believing that the practice she complains of has been successfully carried on for some time past."

"Ay, I see how it is," answered Jabez Sneed; "a dead set has been made against me, and I must be crushed if I have not resolution enough to bear me through these unfounded charges. But Sir Walter Amyot is too just—too considerate to believe everything just as he hears it, and a very little explanation will serve to show him that I have never been guilty of a breach of trust. Your mistress, however, has thought proper to be the first person to throw scandal upon my name, and you will therefore do well to warn her, that she has made an enemy where she might have found a friend."

"And do you really think her ladyship will care about your enmity or your friendship either?"

"She may, perhaps, before long see reason for doing so."

"Suppose I tell Sir Walter of the threats you have uttered against his wife?"

"Do so if you please, and I shall retaliate by telling him that I believe her ladyship has secreted a man in some part of his house."

"Monster! dare you insinuate such a vile slander?"

"Slander or no slander," answered Jabez Sneed, "I am well satisfied that there is sufficient ground for what I have said; and if Lady Eveline is innocent of having done as I have said, she can have no objection to a regular search being made through the house."

"I am sure she would offer no objection," replied Maud, scarcely knowing what she said; "she is aware of the innocence of her actions, and can defy you or any other incarnate fiend to prove that she was ever guilty of an immoral action in her life."

"Well, girl," exclaimed the steward, "I have no wish to argue upon that subject any further, for it seems pretty clear that you and I shall not agree upon the matter. You deny that any stranger is concealed in the house, but I still contend that your frequent visits to one part of the place, have a very suspicious look."

"What part of the place do you mean?"

"The Bower Chamber, in particular."

"Why that is my mistress's favourite room, and surely there need be no wonder at her sending me there frequently on errands."

"But how is it," asked Jabez Sneed, "that you always have a basket on your arm, which appears to be very heavy as you go to the room, but very light when you return from it?"

"Am I obliged to answer every impertinent question that you choose to put to me?"

"You can do as you please about answering them," he replied; "but I shall still make it my business to discover what motive you can have for going to one part of the house so often. You may call me impertinent for my pains, but never mind —I have an object in view, and Lady Eveline will find out what it is if she chooses to urge me on after the warning I now send through you."

"Suppose I don't think proper to be the bearer of our message?"

"Then you may take upon yourself the blame of anything that may happen afterwards," replied Jabez. "Had she never interfered with the business that is between myself and my master, she would have avoided the troubles that I can see are threatening her. And you, too, my girl, had better mind what you are about, for my eye will be constantly upon you, and before long I shall discover the reason of your frequent visits to the Bower Chamber."

"Oh, if that is all you want to know," exclaimed Maud, "I go there merely for the purpose of feeding my lady's favourite dogs, many of which she keeps in that room."

"Indeed!" exclaimed the steward, in a tone of the most provoking unbelief; "and does her ladyship feed her dogs upon well-fatted capons and other luxuries of that sort?"

"Sometimes she does," answered Maud, sorely puzzled to know how she should reply to him.

"Well," continued the old man, "I will grant that there may be something possible in that but does her ladyship also indulge her favourite dogs

in sundry bottles of the choicest wines that are contained in her husband's cellars?"

"Really, Master Sneed, you say such strange things that I have not the least idea what you mean."

"Perhaps you may understand them better by-and-by, when Sir Walter insists upon knowing who is concealed in his house."

"Sir Walter!" exclaimed Maud with alarm; and then suddenly checking herself, she added—"Oh, you must not suppose that I am going to be alarmed by your threats, for I know well enough that if the house were to be searched from top to bottom, no one would be found in it but those who have a right to be here."

"Well, we shall see."

"But mind," exclaimed Maud, "you will stand a good chance of being turned out of the place for your pains; for Sir Walter will not thank you for doing that which would draw the eyes of the whole world upon his wife. Besides, it will not prevent his looking strictly over the accounts you gave her ladyship during his absence; and if he finds any attempt has been made to cheat him, you may expect to be sent away from this house with all the contempt you deserve."

The steward was about to make an angry reply to this, but at that moment he was interrupted by the arrival of Tom Dingle, one of Sir Walter's grooms, and the accepted love of Maud. He had been attracted to the spot by hearing rather high words, and addressing himself to Jabez Sneed, he demanded what he had to say to the girl, and whether he had not better quarrel at once with a man.

"I had neither thought nor intention of quarrelling," answered the old steward, "but was merely questioning Maud about some stranger that I suspect is lurking about the house without Sir Walter's knowledge."

"Male or female?" demanded Tom.

"That's more than I can tell you at present," replied the steward—"but judging by the appetite, I should say it's a man that is concealed here."

"What do you mean about appetite, Master Sneed?"

"Maud knows well enough what I mean," returned the other, glancing with mischievous delight towards her. "She can tell you who it is that she visits three or four times every day with the choicest viands that the larder of her master affords. Then, too, the wine that goes to that same quarter must needs be of the very best—the supply being taken from the same bin which Sir Walter calls his own."

"Is this true, Maud?" asked Tom Dingle, whose jealousy now became somewhat excited.

"You hear what this mischief-making old fellow has said" she replied, "and it only remains for you to say whether it is to be believed, before you have an opportunity of judging for yourself."

"But you can contradict him if there be no truth in what he has been saying about you."

"Indeed, Tom, I shall do no such thing," answered the girl, resolutely, as the only way of getting out of the dilemma. "If you choose to be fool enough to believe all he says against me, let it be so—but you must never dare to speak to me again, for I can never venture to marry a man that would always be jealous and suspicious."

"Don't be foolish, Maud," exclaimed her lover, "for when a charge like this is made, it's enough to make one look about to discover whether there be any truth in it or not."

"Then you would rather believe an old scandalmonger like that, than me!" cried Maud angrily.

"I would rather not believe him," answered Tom Dingle, "but what am I to do, when a charge is made by one party and the other don't think proper to contradict it?"

"But I do most flatly contradict it."

"Ask her to take us both to the Bower Chamber," exclaimed Jabez Sneed, "that we may be convinced nobody is concealed there."

"He may ask what he pleases," answered Maud, "but I shall not take any person to a room, which even Sir Walter himself never enters except on express invitation from her ladyship."

"Excuses will not pass with me, whatever they may do with your lover," muttered the old steward.

"And who do you suppose wishes to make an excuse to you?" asked Maud. "I have but one master and one mistress, and if either of them had said to me half as much as you have I should have left the house before now."

"I'll tell you what it is, old gentleman," exclaimed Tom Dingle; "you are a great deal too free with your tongue; and if you don't take care, you and I shall fall out presently."

"I shall not give you the opportunity," answered Jabez Sneed, "for I am now going to leave you, to seek my master, who ought to be made acquainted with what is going on in the house."

"Humph! you want to curry favour with him by turning tale-bearer, do you?" asked the groom.

"I want no man's favour," replied Jabez, with hypocritical smoothness; "but we have all of us a duty to perform, young man, and I should be forgetful of mine were I to suffer Sir Walter to remain in ignorance of the facts which have come to my knowledge."

"What facts do you mean, sir?" demanded Maud.

"Your frequent visits to the Bower Chamber, and the marvellous increase in the consumption of our supplies."

"'Tis well for you certainly, to pretend great concern for the interests of your master, when we have pretty good proof that you have been robbing him for years past!"

"Maiden!" exclaimed the steward, "you forget that nothing has yet been proved against me. The charge of rendering false accounts has been invented by your mistress, and she had best take care of herself, for I believe she is now in my power more than I am in hers, and I shall not fail to make use of my advantage."

"Ay," answered the girl, "but happily Sir Walter will not believe a word you say against his wife."

"Then I will endeavour to prevail upon him to visit the chamber in which I believe a man is secreted."

"Why you prying, inquisitive knave," exclaimed Maud, "how dare you say my mistress has concealed any one in her room?"

"I have dared to say it," he replied, "and shall not fail to repeat it, unless proof to the contrary is given by showing me over the room where I suspect some one is lurking."

"Indeed!" exclaimed Maud, "then you had better tell Sir Walter as soon as you like, for neither you nor anybody else shall ever enter that room unless they have first received the permission from my mistress. The chamber is the only one in the house that can properly be said to be devoted to her own private use, and I have not the right, even if I had the inclination, to suffer anybody to enter it."

"There must be some other reason for your refusal than it would be convenient for you to let us know."

"You are very cunning, Master Jabez Sneed," she replied; "but neither your sneers nor your threats will compel me to act otherwise than I have said. If Sir Walter wishes to search the room, he had better speak to his wife first, and I dare say he will find her so willing to yield to his request, that he will at once be ashamed of having suspected, even for a moment, a wife who has never done any thing to deserve such abominable treatment."

"Are you aware there is no one in the room, as Master Sneed says?" asked Tom Dingle, who, to confess the truth, felt sorely perplexed the more he heard the accusation and denial repeated.

"Am I sure that you are a great fool, Tom!" exclaimed the girl, tartly. "Do you suppose, then, that if any one was concealed there I should not have known it?"

"Of course you would," he replied, with all due humility; "there can be no doubt about it, my love; but———"

"Don't love me, sir, I beg," interrupted Maud, angrily. "You have thought proper to heed the mischievous words of this old man, and you may now join with him if you please in concocting all the villany you can think of against my poor mistress. But remember, sir, if you don't at once acknowledge your error, you need not trouble yourself any more to speak to me about our marriage."

"Nay, I merely wanted to know if there be any truth in what Master Jabez Sneed has been saying."

"Believe whichever you please," she replied; "for it's a matter of indifference to me, even if you choose to indulge in the foolish notions he has been putting into your head."

"You know I would rather believe you, Maud, than anybody else," replied her lover; "but I can't help noticing, that you have never once given a flat denial to what Master Sneed has said."

"Of course I have not," she replied, indignantly, "and what is more, I never should think it worth my while to contradict anything that an old mischief-maker like that may choose to say. My mistress, I know, would be very angry with me, if I were to humble myself through anything that Jabez Sneed may say; and as for Sir Walter being told of these wicked surmises, and inventions, he may hear of those for aught I care; for he has too much sense to give credit to every idle tale that spite and rancour can invent."

"But," retorted the steward, "perhaps he may insist upon going into the room that you would exclude him from."

"He will not do so without my mistress's permission."

"If he takes my advice he will ask no permission, nor, indeed, suffer any one to know where he was going."

"And, pray, why should you give him such advice?"

"Because," replied Jabez Sneed, "when he has women to deal with, he may expect to be outwitted if he gives them notice beforehand of what he intends to do. That there is some one in the Bower Chamber I am quite sure; and equally certain am I, that he or she, or whatever it may be, would soon be sent elsewhere till the search was at an end"

"Really, Master Sneed, you appear to have a remarkable faculty for worming out a plot!"

"So I should have," he replied, "when such cunning persons as you are to be dealt with."

"I'll tell you what, old fellow," exclaimed Tom Dingle, "you had better mind what you say to Maud, or you and I shall presently fall out. She is not to be insulted in my presence, so let's have no more of this if you don't want to have every bone in your skin broken."

"Psha! I am only doing my duty to my master"

"Sir Walter Amyot is above placing you as a spy over his wife," exclaimed Maud.

"That may be," replied the steward; "but he would not be foolish enough to turn a deaf ear to me, when I have any information to give that may touch his honour."

"Do you dare say, then," exclaimed the girl,

"that my mistress would say or do anything that her husband would not approve of? If that's your opinion of her, you had better inform Sir Walter of it, and at once you will then see what sort of a reception will be given to the mischievous falsehoods you would spread against the name and fame of a lady who is so dear to him. Nay, if he were not to dismiss you from the house immediately, the whole world would cry shame upon him for any longer suffering the presence of a villain who is trying to cause his separation from his wife."

"You may call me villain now, girl," returned the old man fiercely, "but the time may not be far distant when you will repent having given cause for my vengeance. I can bite as well as bark, so you had better beware of me, or I may show the marks of my teeth sooner than you expect."

"Come, come," exclaimed Tom Dingle, "let's have none of these threats, because I am not going to suffer you or anybody else to bully and bluster Maud for merely speaking her mind. If you don't like what she has said, the best way is not to speak to her any more, which I know will be a consolation to her, for it seems, by this quarrel, that there's no love lost between you."

"As far as I am concerned," answered Maud, "I have always held him in contempt, as a paltry, mischief-making, ear-wigging old fellow, that ought to be kicked out of all respectable society. So now he knows exactly what I think of him, and he is quite welcome to do his worst, for the only person I care about he will never be able to injure me with."

"You mean your mistress?"

"Yes, Jabez, I do; so now seek out Sir Walter as soon as you please, and tell him some one is concealed in the Bower Chamber. He may be rather startled at first, but not being one of those who condemn after hearing one side only, he will seek an explanation from my mistress, and then you'll see how soon all your fine projects of mischief will be overthrown by a few words of truth.—Ah! Jabez Sneed, then will come the time for our triumph; and if my mistress does as I would, she will tell her husband of the cheating and robbery that you have been carrying on for such a along time past."

"Who can prove that I have ever wronged Sir Walter?"

"Your own accounts will prove it."

"Where are they?"

"Safe in my lady's custody, where they will remain till given into the hands of her husband?"

"If there be any error, why am I not allowed to look over them and correct what may be wrong?"

"You had better ask Lady Eveline, for she alone can answer your question," replied Maud.

"I see how it is," exclaimed the old man. "I am to be sacrificed to gratify some feeling of revenge."

"You are a good-for-nothing, worthless fellow for saying so," retorted the girl, indignantly. "Revenge, indeed! is it likely that my lady can feel anything else but contempt for a man that has proved himself unworthy of either confidence or respect?"

"Beware how you enrage me, girl, for I cannot endure these taunts much longer."

"I care not whether you can or not," she replied; "for you have brought it all upon yourself, and it is only fair that you should suffer some of the annoyance that you intend for others. Nor is this the worst you will have to put up with, for I am much mistaken if you do not find yourself in a much worse situation when standing in the presence of Sir Walter Amyot, to answer for the misdeeds you have been guilty of to your best friend and benefactor."

"These are lies, invented only to injure me," exclaimed the steward. "I know the motives that have led to all this ill-feeling, but Sir Walter will fairly judge between the accuser and the accused, and we shall then see in which direction justice will guide him."

"You really imagine, then, that he would turn a deaf ear to my mistress when she tells him that you have for a long time past been plundering him to a considerable extent?"

"Let her prove that I have done so, and I will submit to anything that may follow."

"Your accounts will be proof enough."

"There may be errors in my accounts, but they will not be sufficient to prove that I have wilfully robbed my employer."

"Ay, Master Jabez Sneed," she replied; "it is very easy to call them errors; but how is it that all those mistakes happen to be on one side?"

"I know not yet that they are so."

"Then, the best way will be to remove the doubt at once by referring the matter to Sir Walter Amyot."

"Her ladyship can do as she pleases about it," answered Jabez Sneed, between his closely compressed teeth; "she may seek to ruin and destroy me, but the triumph shall not be all on one side."

"Ay, you are still harping I find, upon your old notion that some one is secreted in this house, and that you will be able to dismay my mistress by mentioning your suspicions to Sir Walter."

"That is what I intend to do," answered the old man: "for I have had my misgivings that it may be one of the fugitive royalists who has sought shelter here, and if so, it is my duty, as well as my inclination, to give him up to justice."

"Upon my word!" exclaimed Maud, with well-dissembled surprise, "you have made a notable discovery certainly in supposing it, really, that a royalist would venture to seek shelter beneath the roof of as stern a republican as is to be found in England."

"But her ladyship is well known to belong to the family that has fought and bled in the cause of monarchy."

"And has not the family suffered for it?" asked Maud.

"Some of them may have done so," answered the steward; "but her ladyship has so far escaped very easily through having married a man who stands high in the estimation of the Protector. But a turn may yet come in her fortune; and if she tries to do me an injury, she may rely on it I will not rest satisfied till I have discovered whether she has not been affording shelter and protection to an enemy of the State."

"What is the meaning of all this?" exclaimed Sir Walter Amyot, who, on approaching, had overheard the latter words. "You, Maud, and Dingle, will do well to go about your business instead of wrangling and quarrelling in this unseemly manner beneath my roof. Leave me, for I would speak with Jabez Sneed in private."

Maud and her lover, somewhat mortified at the peremptory tone in which they had been addressed, went as they had been desired: the one to look after his duty in the stables—the other to seek her mistress, and acquaint her with what had taken place. For a moment or two Jabez Sneed exulted in what seemed to be a complete triumph over the parties he had been contending with; but when he saw that an angry frown was still upon the countenance of his master, though the others had taken their departure, he began to feel that his own turn was now come for hearing that which would be anything but agreeable. At length the silence was broken by Sir Walter Amyot, who, in a tone of stern command, desired him to follow immediately to the library, where he wished to speak to him upon matters of importance.

CHAPTER V.

SIR WALTER AMYOT QUESTIONS HIS STEWARD
UPON CERTAIN EXPRESSIONS THAT HE HAS
RECENTLY HEARD.—JACOB SNEED DISCOVERS
THAT HIS ROGUERY IS NOT YET KNOWN, AND
RESOLVES TO WATCH THE TURN OF AFFAIRS.
—SIR WALTER AGAIN PROPOSES TO LADY
EVELINE THAT THEY SHALL OCCUPY THE
BOWER CHAMBER.—HER PERPLEXITY THERE-
UPON.

As soon as they had reached the library, Sir
Walter threw himself into a seat, and addressing
his steward somewhat abruptly, demanded of him
the meaning of some expressions that he had
heard at the moment when he so unexpectedly
made his appearance on the scene of controversy.
The old man knew not what answer to make, for
it was no part of his design to mention his suspicions till the arrival of a certain period that he
had fixed upon, and he felt certain that if he entered into an explanation now, Lady Eveline
would retaliate by exposing the villany he had
been practising before he had an opportunity of
warding off the evil consequences he so much
dreaded. He therefore stammered out a reply
that he had merely made an angry retort to something which Maud had said to offend him.

"You mean to say, then," observed Sir Walter,
looking hard at him, "that you had no ground
for suspecting that a stranger has been concealed
in this house during my absence?"

"The truth is, Sir Walter, I don't know whether
there is sufficient ground for it or not," answered
Jabez Sneed. "I spoke under the influence of
passion, and may have been mistaken."

"And is your mistress to be maligned because
you quarrel and fall out with your fellow
domestics?"

"Pardon me if I have unwittingly given
offence," exclaimed the old man, "but the truth
is, my suspicions have been somewhat roused
lately, and I may have given utterance to expressions that would have been much better kept
to myself."

"I will have no equivocation," returned Sir
Walter, "but insist upon knowing at once
whether you have any good ground for supposing
that a stranger is in my house?"

"There may not be sufficient reason for making
a direct charge," answered the steward, "but
Lady Amyot has herself given occasion for suspicion, and I may therefore be pardoned for having
thought it proper to see whether my notions were
correct."

"How mean you, sirrah?"

"Is it not strange that her ladyship so resolutely
objected to your remaining in the Bower Chamber
on the day of your return home?"

"I thought so at the time," answered Sir Walter, "but upon further reflection I remembered
that the apartment of which you speak has always
been set apart for her own private use."

"Exactly so," answered Jacob Sneed, "so of
course there is an end of the foolish thoughts that
entered my head."

"But there is not an end to the inquiries that I
have determined to make into this affair," said
Sir Walter Amyot. "There is something more
in all this than I have at present been able to
ascertain; but the secret shall be kept from me no
longer, for I will insist upon hearing the truth,
whatever it may be."

Jabez Sneed had already said more than he
wished to have done, and it was now his anxious
wish to allay any suspicions that his words had
given rise to. He paused for a few moments, and
then he said—

"I am sorry, Sir Walter, if any thoughtless
words of mine have made you uneasy, for whatever may have occurred to create suspicions in
my mind, I feel assured that my lady is too good
and faithful a wife to deceive you even in the
slightest instance."

"Yet, from what I overheard just now, you
have dared to believe that she has suffered a stranger to rest beneath this roof in my chamber."

"I certainly was presumptuous enough to think
so once," answered the steward, scarcely knowing
what reply to make: "but I am now inclined to
believe that I was wrong."

"Have you ever seen any one about the place?"

"No one but those you know of."

"Then what fiend of mischief put it into your
head that she was doing anything without my
knowledge?"

"I can make no excuse for it," exclaimed Jabez
Sneed, "unless it is, indeed, that Maud has been
more frequent of late in her visits to the chamber,
where I fancied some one was concealed."

"Is there anything remarkable in her going to
a room that belongs exclusively to her mistress?"

"Nothing, Sir Walter, if she had gone there in
an ordinary way."

"Tell me under what suspicious circumstances
you have seen her."

"I would rather not have said anything about
it," replied Jabez Sneed; "but since you insist
upon it, I must needs say, that I have seen her go
three or four times a day to the Bower Chamber
with a basket that appeared full, and she has
always returned a little while afterwards with the
same basket apparently empty."

"And pray what do you infer from that?"

"Nothing now," answered the steward, "but
at the time, I must confess, it gave rise to some
suspicions."

"Have I ever employed you to play the part of
a spy upon your mistress?" asked Sir Walter,
angrily.

"Never," he replied; "but had there been any
concealment, it would have been my duty to discover the cause of it."

"Indeed? and why so?"

"Because the person concealed might have been
one of the royalists who escaped after the last
skirmish; and I am too much attached to the
present institutions of our country to suffer them
to be overturned by those we look upon as our
enemies."

"Think you, then, that Lady Amyot would so
far forget herself as to give shelter to those who
are looked upon as foes by her husband?"

"Far be it from me to say anything that would
cast the slightest shadow of reproach upon her
ladyship," exclaimed Jabez Sneed; "but there
may be some among the cavaliers whom she
would favour for the sake of the cause they advocate, and it must be confessed I did at one time
fancy that some such person might have found a
temporary concealment beneath your roof."

"Did you ever hint such a thing to your mistress?"

"Never."

"Yet you have done so to her attendant, and
no doubt with the intention that it should be reported to her?"

"I confess as much," answered the steward;
"but I considered I was justified in taking such
a course."

"What was your justification?"

"I fancied her ladyship bore me no good will,
and that, in short, she intended to poison your
mind against me."

"There must have been a sufficient reason, or
Lady Amyot would not have formed such a prejudice as you speak of."

"I am not aware of ever having given her cause
of complaint."

"Be that as it may," replied Sir Walter, "she

has not yet said anything that could give me the slightest reason for supposing that she entertained a feeling of anger against you."

"I am glad to hear it," exclaimed the steward; "but perhaps her ladyship is only waiting till she can find a favourable opportunity."

"Why should she wait for that?"

"Because she may want to know whether it is my intention to inform you about the stranger that I suspected had found a lurking place in this house."

"If such were your suspicion," exclaimed Sir Walter, "you have been strangely neglectful of your duty in not having informed me earlier of that which I ought to have known immediately."

"That is easily explained when I state that I was anxious not to injure my lady, till I was quite convinced that she had deceived you."

"Deceived me!" exclaimed Sir Walter Amyot, "could you, who have known her so long, imagine that she would do anything to forfeit the high esteem in which I hold her?"

"Considering the unfortunate views in which she was brought up," answered the old man, "I am free to confess that my lady has always conducted herself with great prudence and circumspection."

"And you must also acknowledge that she has as little prejudice as most people against those who differ in religion or politics."

"Most people would say the same," answered Jabez Sneed; "but towards me she has certainly taken a very marked prejudice."

"That must be merely your own imagination."

"Nay, Sir Walter, she has herself told me that she believes I am not trustworthy."

"Perhaps others have told her so."

"No. the notion is entirely her own," answered the old man; "but why she should have formed such an opinion of me I am quite unable to discover. True, I may have enemies watching to do me an injury; but, even granting that to be the case, I know not how her ladyship can reconcile it to herself to believe that I, who have been so many years in the service of this family, am unworthy the confidence that has been reposed in me."

"Doubtless there is some mistake in this," exclaimed Sir Walter; "for Lady Amyot would never suffer any paltry prejudice to operate against you, unless there was sufficient proof that you had acted in some manner unworthily."

"Then, I must have a concealed foe somewhere."

"Many persons besides yourself have, but it is not usually a difficult task to discover who they are."

"Such is the case with myself, Sir Walter," he replied; "for I feel pretty certain that Maud is the person to whom I owe all the ill-feeling of which I have complained."

"And that, I suppose, is the reason why I heard you rating her so soundly a short time since?"

"My anger," he replied, "was provoked by her refusal to tell me what she had been doing with the basket she was carrying."

"Upon my word," exclaimed Sir Walter, "I am not surprised at her refusal to answer such paltry questions as that. No doubt the girl was attending to the affairs of her mistress, and she was perfectly right not to answer the impertinent questions you asked."

"And yet," returned Jabez Sneed, "I should not have interfered in the matter but that I thought it might bring out some information that you would consider of importance. However, the girl has thought proper to insult me, and I shall now watch more closely than ever to discover what takes her so often to the Bower Chamber."

"You had much better give it up as a bad job," exclaimed Sir Walter Amyot; "for you may take my word for it, that in the end you will only get laughed at for your pains."

"Let them beware that I give them not more cause for weeping," returned Jabez Sneed, savagely.

"Why should you desire to do that, when you have not yet shown me that you have received injury from any one?"

"The truth is, Sir Walter," he replied, "I have seen more to complain of than I have yet seen proper to repeat. However, I shall not long suffer things to remain as they are, so those who have reason to fear me had better be upon their guard."

"I think you said just now, Jabez, that you were pretty certain one of the late insurgents is at this time concealed in some part of my premises?"

"I am."

"How is it then that you have not yet taken measures for apprehending a man who is considered as an enemy of the country?"

"There are many reasons why I have abstained from doing so," replied Jabez Sneed; "not the least of which was that I thought I might be the means of giving up to justice some one who is regarded as a favourite by Lady Amyot."

"Scoundrel!" exclaimed Sir Walter, passionately, "what do you mean by such an insinuation as that?"

"Nothing offensive, I assure you." replied the steward, rather staggered by the anger which his words had conjured up. "I merely meant that her ladyship once had many friends amongst the royalist party, and of course it would occasion her very great grief if any of them were to be sent to die a death of shame upon the scaffold."

"Lady Amyot," answered her husband, "has long since severed herself from the party you speak of."

"But she has a brother among the cavaliers."

"True, but I am not sorry to hear that he has contrived to escape while the search was going on after him."

"Not sorry, Sir Walter! I always thought you had pledged yourself to pursue all the enemies of the country to death?"

"So I did," answered Sir Walter Amyot, "but I have since learnt to pity those who are perhaps only misguided. My Lord Arden, for instance, though entirely opposed to my own views, has many noble qualities to boast of, and I should be glad for his own sake, as well as my wife's, that he should have found means to escape from the dangers that threaten him in this country."

"May I ask, Sir Walter, if you would refuse to go in pursuit of him, were you ordered to do so?"

"Most assuredly I would not refuse to do my duty," answered his master; "but I must confess it would occasion me no little sorrow, were I to be forced to make him my prisoner."

"And yet," exclaimed Jabez Sneed, "I have heard many people say of late, that Lord Arden was last seen making his way by night towards this neighbourhood."

"Indeed! then how was it that no attempt was made to take him by the people you speak of?"

"I don't know exactly how it was," replied the steward, "but I believe he was too well armed to have rendered it safe for any one to attempt to make him a prisoner."

"In that case they were cowards," replied Sir Walter Amyot. "for when we have a duty to perform we have no right to look to the consequences, however threatening they may appear to be."

"I don't know how that may be, Sir Walter," exclaimed the steward, "but it seems likely enough Lord Arden may be lurking about the neighbourhood, and I have more than once had a notion, that it may be he who is concealed in the Bower Chamber."

"Ha!" returned his master, "what has put such an idea as that into your head?"

"Why, sir," he replied, "the truth is, when there is so much secrecy, people are apt to think all sorts of strange things."

"Are you sure the suggestion has not been offered, in order to carry out some feeling of revenge?"

"Indeed, Sir Walter, I have only your interest to care for."

"Then think not of my interest," exclaimed the knight, "and in future trouble not yourself with matters that concern you. Lady Eveline's prudence must not be doubted, nor will I hear another word in which her name is mentioned with disrespect."

"Is it to be understood then," asked the steward, "that even if I were certain that a royalist is concealed in your house, I am forbidden to take any steps that would cause his apprehension?"

"Do not make yourself busy with affairs that concern you not," exclaimed Sir Walter Amyot, "for it is sufficient that I keep watch in case any one should seek shelter beneath my roof."

"May I be allowed to suggest that her ladyship should be questioned upon the subject?"

"So far," replied his master, "I see no reason why the feelings of Lady Amyot should be insulted by suspicions, which at present I see not the slightest foundation for. There is, in fact, more in this than I can just now see through, but I shall not fail to keep a strict watch upon all your actions; and should it hereafter appear that you have been endeavouring to injure Lady Eveline, merely for the purpose of carrying out your own scheme of revenge, you may rely upon it you shall quit my services for ever."

"Do you then believe, sir, that I would be guilty of so unworthy an act as that you speak of?"

"It is impossible for me to say just now what may be your motive," answered Sir Walter Amyot, "but certain it is that a marked dislike is entertained by you against your mistress, and I am determined to know how far you are actuated by it, in the course you have thought proper to adopt. You would have me believe that she has concealed some one in the house, but nothing short of the most positive proof will ever convince me that she would be guilty of so great an imprudence."

"I may have committed myself through too much zeal in the service of my master," exclaimed Jabez Sneed, "but you will not find that I have given utterance to my suspicions for any such reason as you imagine."

"Have you ever mentioned anything of the kind to Lady Amyot?"

"Never."

"Why have you not done so?"

"Because I thought it would be sufficient for the present to hint my suspicions to Maud, who is so much in the confidence of her mistress, that she is sure to have mentioned what she has heard."

"And supposing she has done so, what good can possibly result from it?" asked Sir Walter.

"That remains to be seen," exclaimed the steward; "but if nothing else should come of it, the warning would not be thrown away upon her ladyship, who, as a matter of course, would no longer conceal anybody in your house. So you will do me the justice, Sir Walter, to confess that in spite of what you may suspect, I have a wish to save Lady Amyot instead of entertaining any design to injure her."

"You would have proved that much more to my satisfaction by not hinting at the probability of a traitor being concealed in my house."

"Would it then have been right for me to have kept the secret to myself?"

"At all events you might have done so till quite certain that your suspicions were well founded," answered Sir Walter. "As it is, you have only given utterance to your own thoughts, which I must still think have been uttered to me only to carry out your own scheme of revenge."

"There you wrong me," exclaimed Jabez Sneed, "for I have no other motive than that of saving you from the consequences that would follow if the Protector should happen to learn that you have given shelter to a traitor. I may have been mistaken certainly, but the error—if there be any—has been committed on the right side."

"How can that be," asked Sir Walter, "when you have endeavoured to injure Lady Eveline, without affording her an opportunity of defending herself?"

"But I am ready to repeat all that I have said in her presence."

"Perhaps," replied his master, "I may afford you an opportunity of doing so sooner than you expect. I shall not, however, mention what has passed till I have convinced myself that there is some probability in your story, and, even then, shall give Lady Amyot a fair opportunity to explain that which you would make of so much consequence."

"In the meantime, Sir Walter, I suppose you will not object to my trying to discover who has been secreted in the Bower Chamber?"

"I shall hold out no encouragement for you to do so," answered his master, "nor shall I commend your conduct if it should appear that you are acting as a spy upon the actions of my wife. Hitherto I have never seen anything to warrant such a proceeding, and it would be most cruel and unjust to wound the feelings of one who is all tenderness and affection."

"I have always had the highest opinion of her ladyship," exclaimed the crafty steward; "but for all that she may so far have forgotten herself as to have given protection to one of the people who hold the same opinion that she does. I am not asserting positively that she has done so; but having seen something to excite my suspicion, I thought it was only just to my master to give him an opportunity of judging for himself."

"Which I shall do," answered Sir Walter; "but not with the precipitation that you would advise. A few hours will serve to convince me whether there is such a secret as you have imagined; and if anything should occur to confirm it, I will lose no time in discovering how far your suspicions are correct."

"At all events, I am satisfied that you will find out quite enough to prove that I have not wilfully misrepresented anything to serve my own purposes. In short, I have only performed a duty which you would have blamed me for if it had been omitted."

"Still I am as far from being convinced of the truth of your story as ever I was," replied Sir Walter. "My wife has never since our marriage deceived me even in the most trifling instance, and in spite of the somewhat suspicious circumstances you speak of, my opinion of her prudence remains firm and unshaken."

"I am glad to hear it," exclaimed the steward, who saw that more was to be gained by deceit than by persisting too stoutly in the truth of his story. "Her ladyship, I can assure you, has no enemy in me, though my motives may have been mistaken; nor would I have spoken so freely upon this subject but from my anxiety to save you from the consequences that would follow in the event of its being discovered that an enemy of the State has been secretly concealed in your house."

"Which is so improbable," returned Sir Walter, "that I can never believe it except upon the clearest proof."

"I am much mistaken if the proof is not brought forward sooner than you expect," returned the old man.

"Remember," answered Sir Walter Amyot, sternly, "that I most positively forbid you to interfere in this affair. I shall myself ascertain if there be any reason for excluding me from the Bower Chamber; and should it prove that any one is concealed there, I shall perform my duty, however much it may be against my own inclination."

The knight turned away as he said this, and on being left to himself, Jabez Sneed thought over the conversation and the effects that might probably result from it. At all events, he had pretty clearly ascertained that Sir Walter at present had not been informed of the defalcations in his accounts; though it seemed equally certain that Lady Amyot would not fail to keep the promise she had made to inform him of it as soon as an opportunity presented itself. To prevent this was a matter of such paramount importance that no considerations could be allowed to stand in the way, and he therefore determined to watch for a moment when he might follow Maud without being perceived, and thus learn the secret upon which he believed so much depended. Were he to become acquainted with the fact of a royalist being concealed in the house, it would afford him the advantage he desired, and Lady Eveline would be restrained from exposing the dishonesty of which he had so long been guilty. So far, then, he began to see things were working favourably in his behalf; and he made his way to his own room exulting in the thought that his mistress would have it no longer in her power to injure him by exposing the villany he had practised against his master.

On leaving his steward, Sir Walter Amyot proceeded to the apartment in which he had left Lady Eveline, who he found busily engaged at her embroidery. She rose with evident pleasure as she perceived him approach, and proposed a walk upon the terrace to enjoy the refreshing breezes of a summer's evening. The knight, however, anxious to see the effect of such a proposition upon her, suggested that they should adjourn to the Bower Chamber, which was the pleasantest in the mansion, commanding as it did an extensive view over the whole of the surrounding country. The effect of his words was immediately apparent in the countenance of Lady Eveline, who became alternately red and pale; and at length in faltering accents demanded why he was so desirous of occupying that apartment, when, at all other times, he had regarded it as being entirely devoted to her own use.

"I can give no particular reason for it, my dear Eveline," he replied with assumed carelessness, "for the whim was merely one of the moment, and I thought you could have no reason for refusing me so trivial a favour."

"And do you *now* think I have any reason for doing so?" she asked.

"Not one that I have any wish to inquire into," answered her husband, "for I am well convinced that you would keep no secret from me that I ought to be acquainted with. It, however, strikes me as being rather singular that every time I have proposed occupying that room, you have always successfully opposed my wish."

"But not because it was your wish," replied Lady Eveline.

"In a word, then, have you any objection to passing an hour or two there this evening?"

"I can have no objection, as you may do me the justice to imagine," she replied; "but I like not the idea of being suspected, and that is the only

reason which I can at present give for refusing to gratify so trifling a favour."

"Are you aware, Eveline, that people in my house begin to suspect that some one is concealed in that room?"

"Good Heavens!" cried her ladyship, turning deadly pale at these words, "and do you also believe that I wanted to deceive you?"

"So far from it," he replied, "I have done all I can to contradict such a notion."

"May I ask if Jacob Sneed is the author of this rumour?"

"He is."

"I thought so," exclaimed Lady Eveline, "for I believe him to be the only enemy I have among your domestics."

"Are you aware, my love, of any reason that he has for manifesting this ill-feeling towards you?"

"I know his motive," she replied, "and was in some respects prepared for the cowardly act he has committed. The truth is I have lately made the discovery that he has been in the habit of robbing you for some time past, and my servant Maud has warned me that he intended to disarm me by inventing some falsehood that should make you believe I have some secret concealed from you."

"Then he will himself be deceived," exclaimed Sir Walter, "for I will listen to no tales from my domestics when they would abuse my ears with stories against their mistress. Jabez Sneed is already aware of my feelings upon the subject, and it is scarcely likely that he will risk giving me offence by repeating the improbable supposition."

"Did he tell you why he suspected that some person was concealed in my favourite room?"

"He would if I had not checked him," answered her husband, "but from a conversation that I chanced to hear between him and your servant Maud, I discovered that he has been watching her for some two or three days, under an idea that she conveys things in a basket to some person who is hiding in the Bower Chamber."

"If he really had any reason for believing anything of the kind," returned Lady Eveline, "one would have imagined that I ought to have been acquainted with it before now."

"Granted," exclaimed her husband; "but I have observed before now that Jabez Sneed is wily and cunning in spite of his efforts to appear more rigid than other people; and had it not been he has served our family so many years, I should have dismissed him from my house, as unworthy of my further confidence."

"I can see how it is," answered Lady Eveline. "The old man knows he would be immediately dismissed from your service if you find that he has been in the habit of plundering you, and as I have been the means of detecting him in his evil practices he has resolved to make this effort to ruin me in your estimation. But I trust your confidence in me is unshaken, and that you will not suffer your suspicion to be excited by the artful representations of an hypocrite."

"He has been forbidden to speak again upon the subject."

"But that will not prevent my being constantly annoyed by his impertinent curiosity."

"Let him dare to watch you," exclaimed Sir Walter Amyot, "and he shall instantly quit my house."

"Nay," replied the lady, "it is far from my wish to injure one who has been so long in your service. I only desire that he may understand how directly he is acting against your wish in thus acting the spy upon me, and if he will in future abstain from his endeavours to injure me, I shall not press for his removal till one more trial has been given to his honesty."

"He will find, though, that I expect him to give me a just and fair account of his stewardship," answered Sir Walter; "for now that my eyes have been opened to the villany of his conduct, I shall not be satisfied until thoroughly convinced that his dishonesty will never again be practised against me. However, I shall not act with too much precipitation, and in order to avoid all chance of being influenced by sudden anger, I shall allow three or four days to pass over before I insist upon his going with me through his accounts."

"Perhaps it may be as well to let the matter pass over quietly so long as he remains quiet."

"I scarcely know what to say about that," exclaimed her husband; "for if he finds that such things can be done with impunity, what security can I feel that he will be honest in his future transactions? For a few days, however, I shall content myself with keeping a watchful eye upon him, and if he conducts himself to my satisfaction, I may then think it sufficient to reprimand him severely for his past misconduct, and warn him as to the danger he will incur if he should ever again be guilty of imposing upon me."

"And at the same time," observed Lady Eveline, "I hope you will desire him not to annoy my servant by watching her about from place to place as he has done of late."

"I will tell him what you say," replied Sir Walter, with a smile; "but between ourselves, I rather think Maud has spirit enough to protect herself, if Jabez Sneed should prove too troublesome in following her about. Indeed, from what I heard to day, I am quite certain that he will get very little information from her."

"But that will not prevent him from imagining all sorts of mischief, if he has made up his mind to injure me."

"Had I treated him otherwise than I did," replied Sir Walter Amyot, "he might have imagined that his tale-bearing was not offensive to me. But I so entirely disapprove of the conduct he has pursued in this affair, that he knows how dangerous it would be to venture upon a course that I have strictly forbidden. And now, having shown how entirely my confidence is reposed in you, I will once more ask if you still object to our occupying the Bower Chamber."

"Under other circumstances I might not have objected to it," replied Lady Eveline, with some little hesitation, "but as I think there is still a lurking suspicion that some one is concealed there, I will not consent to your request until quite satisfied that you place no reliance in the reports raised by your steward."

"In that case I will not ask you again, for nothing shall make me believe that you would deceive me by concealing beneath my roof any one who is regarded as an enemy to his country."

"At all events," answered Lady Eveline, "I should not do so, except in a very extreme case."

"What case could be so extreme," asked her husband, "as to excuse our giving refuge to a foe?"

"Ah!" she exclaimed, "your heart and mine have a different feeling towards those unfortunate men who are hunted into concealment as if they had been guilty of some very great offence."

"And what greater offence can man be guilty of than that of disturbing the peace of the country?" asked Sir Walter.

"We differ so much upon that point," replied Lady Eveline, "that I despair of ever being able to convince you that the cause of our exiled monarch is worthy of being supported. He has, however, staunch and good friends, and among them are those who are now being persecuted for no other reason than that they cannot advocate the principles of those who sent the late king to the block."

"Do not let us talk upon that subject," exclaimed her husband, "for unfortunately it is one of those upon which we cannot perfectly agree. Indeed, I sometimes wish our opinions were not so diametrically opposed, for I should have been glad had it been possible for me to have offered an asylum to your brother, now that he so much needs a temporary concealment from his pursuers."

"Would you then refuse him, were he to ask you to give him shelter?" asked Lady Eveline.

"What else could I do?"

"The situation would be a most unpleasant one, I admit," replied her ladyship, "and yet a few hours concealment might be enough to save him from those who are bent upon his destruction."

"Let us hope that he has, before now, contrived to make his escape from the country," answered Sir Walter Amyot. "In many quarters it is indeed positively asserted that he has done so, and I am half inclined to give credit to the rumour, because it is most likely he would have been taken before now, if he had still been in England."

"Have many of the fugitives been taken?" asked Lady Eveline.

"About a hundred and fifty."

"And what has been done with them?"

"Several have been executed as dangerous enemies to the Commonwealth," answered Sir Walter, "and the example will no doubt be repeated upon all the rest of the prisoners, as soon as Cromwell returns from Scotland, where he has gone to put down an insurrection that was upon the point of breaking out."

"Has he then no compassion upon men, who, if they have erred at all, have done so in the excess of their zeal for the cause of the royal wanderer whom they still regard as their king?"

"How can they expect pity," asked Sir Walter Amyot, "when they have attempted to bring confusion and bloodshed into our country! The last rising was, it is true, soon suppressed by the bravery and energy of our republican troops, but the intention is well known, and the Protector sees no other way to put an end to these continual outbreaks, than by showing the disaffected that they have no mercy to expect in the event of a failure."

"Yet there is not one among the cavaliers," exclaimed Lady Eveline, "who does not firmly believe, that before many months have passed away, England will have recalled her king."

"Those who think so," replied her husband, "cannot know much of the character and determination of Oliver Cromwell. He holds the reins of government with a firm hand, and will not easily be made to surrender them, though it would be difficult to say as much for his successor, who seems to be weak and altogether unfit for the situation he will one day occupy."

"But suppose my brother should unfortunately be taken," asked Lady Eveline; "would you not have interest enough with the Protector to save him from the scaffold?"

"I am afraid not," exclaimed her husband; "for Lord Arden has so often proved that he is an enemy not to be thought lightly of, that Cromwell has determined to make an example of him in order to strike terror into the hearts of his adherents. I would, however, use my utmost exertions in his behalf, if by ill-fortune he should not succeed in escaping from the pursuit of his enemies."

"And Cromwell will scarcely dare refuse your application."

"Not dare?"

"They are bold words, I know," answered Lady Eveline, "but my brother has powerful and firm friends who would not fail to revenge his death at any and every sacrifice. Therefore, I say again Sir Walter, with all due deference, that Cromwell will not dare send Lord Arden to the scaffold."

"I should be glad were it possible to think as you do, my love," answered Sir Walter, 'but unhappily my opinion leans quite the other way. I am forced to say that nothing will ever prevail upon the Protector to shrink from what he conceives to be an act of duty."

"And yet," sighed Lady Eveline, "you would refuse shelter to my brother, though well knowing that he must perish if fate should happen to throw him in the way of his enemies."

"How can I act otherwise, when my duty is so divided?" asked Sir Walter, scarcely knowing what reply to make to this question. "Am I not trusted by the ruler of this nation with the command of a troop, and would it not be treason to the government if I were to give shelter and protection to one who has been in open rebellion?"

"But your house is large," exclaimed Lady Eveline, "and it would not be absolutely necessary that you should know of his being under your roof."

"Heaven grant that it may never come to that," answered Sir Walter Amyot, "for even though your own brother should seek shelter in my house, I should feel myself bound in honour to give him up to the authorities. Therefore, if you know where he is to be found, give him early intimation, for it may save him from a fate that would imbitter the remainder of your days."

"Have you no pity for one who never injured you?"

"Believe me, nothing would cause me greater affliction than to commit an act that would wound your gentle heart," exclaimed her husband tenderly, "but we soldiers are bound by such notions of honour that if we break through any one of them we immediately lose the esteem of the world. However, Lord Arden is well aware of the situation I should be placed in, in the event of his seeking shelter here, and it is therefore to be hoped that he will prudently seek a hiding-place anywhere than rather than in my house."

"But," cried Lady Eveline, "supposing he was compelled to come here through being closely pursued, would you have me repulse him, when by so doing I should force him into the hands of his foes?"

"That I must confess would be a situation of great difficulty and perplexity," answered Sir Walter, "and I most earnestly hope you will not be driven to so terrible an alternative. You, however, know your duty, and I fear not but you will fearlessly perform it to your own satisfaction as well as mine."

"Still you have not counselled me how to act."

"That is because I would prefer seeing you do that which your own heart prompts you to."

"Then I hesitate not to say that I would receive my brother into your house, rather than drive him forth into the world to become the victim of those butchers who would glory in his downfall!"

"As I said before," exclaimed Sir Walter, "I shall not attempt to influence your actions, because I have confidence enough in your prudence to leave all to your own judgment. But again I entreat you not to let me knew the fact if at any time he should come here, for I know my duty and should not dare to neglect it."

"But Jabez Sneed has already tried to make you believe that my brother is now in the house."

"He has, indeed, insinuated as much," answered her husband, "but, as you perceive, I am not inclined to give credit to every idle rumour that may be reported to me by my domestics. He has thus seen that it is not in his power to do mischief, and I am not without hopes that the attempt will not be repeated."

"I am not quite so sure of that," exclaimed Lady Eveline, "for he is revengeful, and the discovery I made of his dishonesty has filled him

with rage and fury that will not be easily appeased. I shall, therefore, keep a watchful eye upon his actions lest he should take advantage of some moment when I am not prepared for his schemes."

"And yet you scarcely need feel any apprehension of that kind," replied Sir Walter Amyot, "for I have myself spoken sharply to the old man, and I believe it is not likely he will again say or do anything that would give me offence."

"Will he not still believe that I have concealed some one in the Bower Chamber?"

"I know not what he may think of it in his own mind," answered Sir Walter, "but there is very little fear of his talking about it to other people, because he knows it must soon reach my ears, and that I should immediately dismiss him from my service if a report should get abroad likely to compromise either my character or that of my wife. So, for his own sake I think we may place more confidence in Jabez Sneed than you seem to think for."

"But he hesitated not to mention his suspicions to you."

"He did so," answered Sir Walter, "and the caution I gave him after telling me ought to be quite sufficient to restrain his tongue if he is not already convinced that there was not any foundation for the notion that has so unaccountably got into his head. However, if there is any chance of his saying anything upon the subject, I will speak to him about it again to-morrow, and add even a stronger caution than the one he has already received.

"It would be well to do so," replied Lady Eveline, "and yet I have a notion that his feelings of revenge against me are so great, that he would risk even your anger rather than omit an opportunity of doing me mischief."

"Let him beware how he does anything of the kind," exclaimed Sir Walter Amyot impetuously, "for as surely as he whispers a word leading to the supposition that a royalist is concealed in my house, I will take such measures against him that he will never be likely to forget. However, I cannot think he will act with so much rashness when he knows the consequences that would result from his conduct."

"And you I hope will not believe any story that he may tell about the Bower Chamber?"

"I will believe nothing upon mere hearsay," answered Sir Walter; "but in return, I trust, my dear Eveline, that you will keep nothing secret that I ought to know."

"You shall have no reason to complain of," answered her ladyship; "but I will make no promise if my brother should happen to seek shelter here. That, however, I hope is not very likely to be the case, for he knows your dislike towards him, and he would of course avoid a place where he could not expect to remain concealed for many hours. Besides, Jabez Sneed would be sure to tell you if anything of the kind was to occur."

"My steward," replied Sir Walter, "shall not be employed as a spy, nor would I listen to any report that he might make to the prejudice of my wife. Nay, I have sharply rebuked him for the conduct he has been guilty of; and, having threatened to dismiss him on a repetition of the offence, I think it hardly likely that we shall hear anything more of his busying himself with affairs that he has nothing to do with."

"Not openly, perhaps," answered Lady Eveline, "but more is to be feared from him if he sets himself secretly to work."

"Which would be a dangerous experiment for him to make," exclaimed her husband, "for I shall keep a rigid watch upon his actions, and should there be reason to believe that he is still following the old game, he will be made to suffer for it severely."

"But may he not mention his suspicions to

those who would take immediate steps to search your house?"

"What need I care even if that should be done?" asked Sir Walter Amyot. "Is it not known that I am devoted, heart and soul, to the cause of my country? And even should they come to search my house, I shall feel perfectly satisfied that no enemy will be found beneath my roof."

"Would you permit such an insult without remonstrance?"

"Certainly," replied her husband, "for it would look like guilt were I to resist those who were entrusted with the duty. Besides, there could be no insult intended when information had been given that some one had been secreted here."

"How can the government believe that you would ever be guilty of such an act?" inquired Lady Eveline.

"In times of danger," he replied, "it is the duty of those who hold the reins of power to take every care to prevent mischief. I stand high in favour, it is true, but for all that I must not feel myself aggrieved, if the same caution is observed with respect to myself as to all other persons within these dominions. Besides, it would be some satisfaction to know that those who had been trying to injure me had failed in their project."

"That is indeed true," observed Lady Eveline, "but those who had failed in one scheme would not be long in forming another. In short, my dear husband, the more I think the matter over, the more danger I apprehend from this designing man, Jabez Sneed."

"Yet, what to do with him I know not," returned Sir Walter, "for even if I were to dismiss him from my service immediately, it would only serve to add fuel to his revenge."

"Then the only way to get rid of the danger will be to punish him for the dishonesty he has been guilty of."

"With any other person I should have done so," he replied, "but Jabez has been so many years in the service of my family, that I own myself reluctant to take strict measures against him. I shall, however, watch him with a careful eye, and much will depend upon the sort of conduct he thinks proper to pursue in future. Perhaps I may caution him upon the subject, for the warning may not be thrown away when he finds that the course he has pursued is not pleasing to me."

With this he changed the conversation to another channel, though it was evident that his mind was still restless and uneasy. Not another hint was thrown out respecting the Bower Chamber and his mysterious exclusion from it, and Lady Eveline of course remained silent upon a subject that had filled her mind with inquietude. She felt alarmed at the danger which threatened her brother, and the more particularly as Jabez Sneed was not likely to relax in his endeavours to discover whether there was any truth in his suspicions of any one being concealed in the house. She, however, determined to keep her own counsel, and to hasten the departure of Lord Arden as much as possible.

CHAPTER VI.

TOM DINGLE BECOMES JEALOUS AND SUSPICIOUS—BUT MAUD REMAINS FAITHFUL TO HER TRUST.—THE STEWARD AGAIN ENDEAVOURS TO WORM OUT THE SECRET, AND AGAIN FAILS.—HE RESOLVES UPON ANOTHER STRATAGEM.—MAUD PAYS ANOTHER VISIT TO THE FUGITIVE—AND THE DISCOVERY THAT TAKES PLACE.

ANOTHER day passed away, and though Jabez Sneed was almost continually upon the watch, all the ingenuity he practised was of no avail, for

matters had been so well arranged that nothing could be learned to confirm his suspicions of any person, except the family, being in the house. His opinion upon the subject, however, remained unchanged, and believing in his own mind that his trouble would be at length rewarded in the way he expected, he determined not to relax his attempts until he was perfectly satisfied whether or not his suspicions were well-founded. Maud saw clearly enough what was passing in his mind, and resolving not to be outdone in an affair in which her zeal for the cause of her mistress was to be exhibited, she determined, at all hazards, to guard a secret upon which such serious consequences might be anticipated. Tom Dingle, too, had certain misgivings upon the subject of her frequent visits to the Bower Chamber, for the steward had taken care to instil into his mind a notion that there was some mystery with which he ought to have been made acquainted. He had, on three or four occasions, ventured to question her upon the subject, but Maud, at the hazard of a serious quarrel with him, positively refused to enter into any explanation, but promising that before long he should know all that it was at present necessary to keep from him.

"And why not at once," he asked, "when you know that if there is anything of consequence in the secret, I am quite as likely to keep it as yourself?"

"Because I am not inclined to indulge your idle curiosity, Tom," she replied. "Besides, when you know what the secret is, you will be thoroughly ashamed of yourself for having suspected that I would keep anything from you that you ought to be acquainted with."

"But Jabez Sneed has hinted as much as that some man is concealed in the room."

"Jabez Sneed is a worthless old fellow for his pains," she replied, "and he ought to be ashamed of himself for trying to fill your head with a parcel of things there's no foundation for."

"Then why has he said them?"

"I know nothing about that," answered Maud, "but I suppose its done to revenge himself for my having been the first to tell my suspicions to Lady Eveline. But he had better mind what he is about, for, woman as I am, I may perhaps be more than a match for him, if he tries to do any more mischief."

"But don't you think he'll be able to convince Sir Walter that some one is concealed in the Bower Chamber?"

"That he'll try to do so, I have no doubt," answered Maud, "but I rather think he'll find the task a more difficult one than he expects. In short, I should be quite ashamed of him if he were to take the word of a servant instead of believing his wife, who has always proved herself to be true and faithful to him."

"So we all fancy," exclaimed Tom Dingle; "yet if any credit is to be given to what the steward says, she has concealed some one in the house who ought not to be here."

"Do you believe his wicked falsehoods then?" she asked.

"If I do it's your own fault, Maud," replied her lover, "for it's easy enough to explain why one room in the house is to be closed against everybody except yourself and her ladyship."

"The secret is none of my own, and therefore I have no right to let it go any further without permission."

"But Jabez Sneed says a man is concealed there."

"And, pray what is it to you if there is one?"

"A great deal, for there would be reason enough to be jealous of your frequent visits to the room."

"Then get rid of your jealousy as soon as you can," exclaimed Maud, "for I can assure you there is not the slightest occasion for it."

"Do you mean to tell me that no one is there?"

"Once for all, Tom," she replied, "I don't mean to satisfy your curiosity if you bore me upon this subject for the next week to come. You have no right to question me, for even Sir Walter is content to remain in the dark till my mistress thinks proper to give an explanation."

"Which perhaps may never be."

"I know nothing about that," she replied; "but at all events I think you might follow the example of your master. His confidence in the prudence of his wife is a credit to him, and you ought to be ashamed of yourself for supposing that anything wrong is going on merely because I refuse to gratify your impertinent curiosity."

"Nay, you are not going to be cross with me, are you?"

"If I am, it's not to be wondered at, when I have told you over and over again that I have a reason for keeping the secret. However, I will forgive you this time, sir, on condition that you never again question me upon this forbidden subject."

"As far as I am concerned," he replied, "I'll be as mute as a mouse; but Jabez Sneed is not to be so easily pacified, and you may take my word for it that he will find some means or another to discover the mystery. The old man is constantly upon the look out, so I would have you be on your guard against him, or it will not be long before he knowe as much as he wants."

"He had better by half mind his own business," exclaimed Maud, "for I can tell him Sir Walter will not be best pleased if he finds that he is interfering with matters that he has nothing to do with."

"Jabez thinks he has something to do with it though," answered her lover; "for he suspects a royalist is sheltered under his master's roof, and that it is consequently his duty to find out the truth in order that he may give information of it to the authorities."

"Has he told you as much?"

"Yes."

"Then you may just give him a hint from me that Sir Walter will not thank him for being too busy with affairs that he is not required to attend to."

"Very likely, but the old man seems to have taken offence at something, and I rather think he'll not care what mischief he does for the sake of having his revenge."

"He had better mind what he's about," answered Maud, "for he may go a little too far, and then Sir Walter will not fail to punish him for certain acts of dishonesty that he has been guilty of. And who is there that will pity him I should like to know, when he has turned round to sting his best friend, merely to gratify a love of mischief?"

"There's a good deal in what you say," exclaimed Tom Dingle, "but the punishment of the old man would be but a poor satisfaction if he should contrive to worm out this secret, whatever it may be."

"And that he never shall do if I have the power to prevent it," exclaimed the attendant. "That he is cunning as well as mischievous I happen to know, but when he has me to deal with he will not find it quite so easy to pry into matters that don't concern him."

"How are you to help it," asked Tom, "when he is continually upon the watch to discover who is in the room that you go to so often?"

"Why, you can assist me if you think proper."

"In what way?"

"By telling him that I never go there except when sent for something by my mistress."

"Which, of course, he would not believe."

"Very much would depend upon how you manage the business," answered Maud. "Surely you can pretend to be upon friendly terms with him, and then he will believe any story you choose to tell him."

"That may appear all very easy to you, Maud," exclaimed her lover, "but it so happens that the old man and I have always been at daggers drawn, and therefore it would be impossible to convince him that I can entertain any friendly feelings towards him."

"Then you can keep your eye upon him, and let me know when any danger is to be expected."

"Ay, I'm willing enough to do that," he replied, "but you must not expect too much though, for Jabez is as cunning as the very devil himself, and he'll not move a step till he has first of all ascertained that he is not being watched. Besides, I know he suspects that I should tell you all that I may chance to discover, and he hardly ventures to say a word to me now for fear it should be turned against him."

"Well," observed Maud, "at any rate he has plenty of people looking after him, so he must take care or he may fall into the same toils that he has been laying for others. Sir Walter, too, has it in his power to send him to prison at any time he likes, and for my own part I wonder he has not done so before, for I am sure he has reason enough to get the worthless old mischief-maker out of his way."

"If Jabez Sneed has robbed his master, how is it that he has not been punished for it before now?" asked Tom Dingle.

"Why he has my mistress to thank for it," answered the girl, "for she has persuaded Sir Walter to take no notice of what has taken place, till he has thoroughly convinced himself that the charge she has made against him can be proved by an examination of his accounts. That will take some few days to do, and till then, Jabez Sneed will be suffered to remain at large."

"And, of course, as long as he is so he will be constantly endeavouring to discover the secret, answered Tom Dingle."

"He may try as much as he likes," answered Maud.

"And I," said her lover, "am very much deceived if he is to be easily defeated on a matter that he has so fully made up his mind upon. For my own part, though still rather jealous at the mystery you keep up, I am content to remain in ignorance of the truth for a short time longer; but the old steward, I'm thinking, is not to be quite so easily pacified, and especially when he has his own revenge to gratify."

"Let him take care of himself," returned the girl, "for the greater stir he makes in this affair the more will he incense those that have it in their power to punish him as he deserves. Besides, in a very few hours, all necessity for keeping this secret any longer may be at an end, and then Jabez will lose the only hold he has upon us."

"Do you think I may know what this mystery is in the course of a few hours?" asked Tom Dingle.

"I think there's very little doubt of it," she replied; "so make your mind easy and leave me for a little while, for I am now going to the Bower Chamber, and must not be watched unless you would forfeit my good opinion for ever."

Somewhat pacified by what little he had been told, Tom immediately left her, and the girl, having first ascertained that no one was observing her, proceeded along the passage which led to the room in which the fugitive was concealed. On approaching, however, she observed Jabez Sneed upon his knees, looking through the key hole, and so completely was he occupied with the object which engaged his attention, that he was not aware of her presence till she stood close to him. Then, springing upon his feet, he stammered out an excuse for the situation in which he had been found, and was about to effect a hasty retreat, when Maud, in a voice of command, desired him to remain where he was.

"Pray, Mr. Sneed," she exclaimed, "can you

offer any sort of excuse for thus meanly endeavouring to pry into matters that you have nothing at all to do with?"

"I don't know that any excuse is necessary," he replied; "for where there is so much concealment and mystery I have a right to satisfy myself whether things are going on in this house properly or not."

"Indeed!" exclaimed Maud; "then, I suppose, you will tell me next that you have the authority of Sir Walter for attempting to pry through the keyhole into my lady's room?"

"Sir Walter," answered the steward, "is too blind to his own interest to take any measures for acquainting himslf with what is going on beneath his roof. I, however, am convinced that some one is hid here who ought not to be, and it shall be no fault of mine if the whole truth is not speedily brought out."

"Did anybody ever hear such a piece of impertinence!" exclaimed Maud, indignantly. "So you can excuse yourself for peeping and peering through the key hole; and, I suppose, if the truth were known, you would have had the insolence to enter the Bower Chamber if I had not taken the precaution to keep the door locked and the key in my own pocket?"

"I think it quite likely that I should," answered the steward; "for whenever I have a purpose in view, I am not very particular as to the means I take to carry it out. However, there is no reason why I should quarrel with you upon the subject, for you may believe me when I say that I would rather there was a good understanding between us."

"I dare say you would, Mr. Sneed," she replied; "but you must be as well aware as I am myself, that you and I can never agree long together."

"Why not?"

"Because you are too fond of making mischief."

"Nay, that which you call mischief is nothing more than the performance of my duty."

"Is it your duty," she asked, "to endeavour to get Lady Amyot into trouble, and, perhaps, danger?"

"If her ladyship has done no wrong," exclaimed the steward, "she can have no danger to be afraid of. There is, however, something going on in this house that ought to be brought to light, and it shall be done by my means, too, or I am very much mistaken."

"Not if I can help it."

"It seems, then, that you don't deny there is some secret that ought to be known to Sir Walter?"

"When I make an admission it will be time enough for you to take advantage of it," exclaimed Maud sharply. "There is no secret that you can by any possibility have anything to do with, and it would be well for you to give up your inquisitive ways before your master finds it necessary to kick you out of his house."

"Girl!" returned the old man wrathfully, "your words excite my anger when it would be much more to your own advantage to assist me in discovering who is concealed here."

"I assist you!"

"Yes;—why not do so when I can promise you a reward for the utterance of merely a few words?"

"What sort of reward do you speak of?" she asked.

"This purse of gold," he replied, taking one from his pocket, and offering it to her.

"Do you think that would tempt me, Jabez Sneed?"

"If the sum is not large enough," he replied, misunderstanding her, "you shall have three times as much as soon as you have informed me of all you know."

"Indeed!" she exclaimed with bitterness. "So you would bribe me with the gold you have robbed Sir Walter of?"

"Dare to accuse me again of robbery," he exclaimed, "and you shall have cause to repent it as long as you live."

"Oh, I care not for your threats," answered Maud, "for you are in my power a great deal more than I am in yours. I have never yet been guilty of a dishonest action against those whose bread I eat, nor will I betray them even if you were to offer me ten times the amount that your purse contains."

"What proof have you," he asked, "that I have ever wronged Sir Walter of even as much as the simplest coin?"

"Your own accounts will prove all that is necessary."

"Where are they?"

"Locked up in my lady's room, where they are likely to remain till my master has time to examine them."

"Can you get possession of them?" he asked eagerly.

"Ay; at any moment."

"Then give them into my hands and I will give you any sum of money you may require from me."

"No, no, Jabez Sneed," she replied, "you and I are not such friends that you can expect any favour from me for any bribe that you may choose to offer. Besides, my mistress desires to keep them safely in her own custody, and it is not for me to do that which I know wou'd be sure to occasion her serious displeasure."

"But if a charge is to be made against me, it is only fair that I should be permitted to look over them once more in order that I may have an opportunity of correcting any errors."

"You may call them errors if you please, Jabez Sneed, but it seems rather singular that heavy overcharges should have occurred in every account that you have given in for so many years past. That, however, is no business of mine, for Sir Walter himself will be the best judge of your guilt or innocence."

"Remember," exclaimed the old man, "if matters are pushed to extremities against me, I shall not fail to retaliate in a manner that will be least expected. I have my enemies here, it seems, but none of them can deprive me of the power of carrying out my revenge. So report what I have said to your mistress, and tell her I will learn who she has secreted in her house at all risks to myself."

"You had better deliver that message yourself," answered Maud, "for I will have nothing to do with your threats against one who deserves not the enmity of any person. I may, however, relate what has just passed to Sir Walter, whose anger you must be prepared to bear."

"Are you then determined on my ruin?"

"I am only determined to punish you for trying to do mischief to those who have never injured you."

"Not injured me?" exclaimed the steward. "Is it nothing, then, to make an accusation that may end in driving me from a house in which I have passed nearly the whole of my life?"

"But her ladyship would not do so, but that she knows well you have been guilty of dishonesty."

"'Tis false!" exclaimed Jabez Sneed; "I have never done anything to deserve the charge made against me."

"Let that be made clear," she replied, "and you can have nothing to fear from Sir Walter."

"How can that be said, when he has always suffered himself to be blindly led by what her ladyship says?"

"Sir Walter Amyot is not so unjust as to be led away by anything he hears," answered Maud. "He must be convinced before he judges, and you are therefore perfectly safe if, as you say, you can prove that your conduct has been straightforward. However, this is no business of mine, nor should I have spoken at all upon the subject, if you had not been so inquisitive about a secret that you imagine is connected with the Bower Chamber."

"If there is no secret, why am I not allowed to enter in order to convince myself that I have been mistaken?"

"Be patient for a day or two longer," exclaimed Maud, "and you shall be allowed to go into the room as often as you like."

"Ay, that will not be till the bird has flown."

"And pray how do you know that any person is there?" she asked.

"Every circumstance serves to confirm the suspicion," he replied, "and your own refusal to give an explanation is quite enough to prove that some one is in this house that ought not to be here."

"That's paying no great compliment to my lady, supposing some one should be here."

"This is no time for compliments," exclaimed Jabez Sneed; "for I am threatened with ruin and disgrace, for no other reason than that I have determined to convince my master that he has been deceived."

"Deceived! do you dare say my lady would deceive her husband?"

"I dare say anything that I believe to be the truth," he replied, "and you cannot deny, with truth, that some one is secreted in the room that you exclude me from."

"You are not going to draw anything from me, I can assure you," she exclaimed; "so, as your labour would be useless, you may as well go away about your business, for I shall not enter the room whilst there is a chance of your prying about here."

It was in vain that he again urged her to accept the bribe he had offered. Maud was too faithful to her charge to admit a single fact that could do mischief, and at length he withdrew unwillingly, after the unsuccessful effort he had made to arrive at the truth. Though mortified at the result of his interview, the old man was determined not to be defeated. He had tried every scheme he could think of to get possession of the papers which were to appear as evidence of his delinqeuncy; he had endeavoured to prevail upon Maud to get them for him, and now that she had s outly refused to accede to his demand, he bethought himself of how he could obtain the key of the room where they were deposited; and in which he felt more convinced than ever, a stranger was concealed. At length, finding that every expedient was likely to fail, the thought struck him that, by climbing up a vine which grew beneath the window of the Bower Chamber, he could easily convince himself whether the apartment was occupied, and if so, by whom.

Leaving him for the present, we will now return to Maud, who, suspecting that he might return, stood outside the door to ascertain whether there was any chance of his coming back to listen. In this place she remained nearly a quarter of an hour, and then, as everything seemed to be safe, she ventured to enter the chamber, having first taken the key out, and fastened the door on the inside to prevent intrusion. The fugitive was reading near the window when she entered; and starting up as she approached, he inquired whether news had yet been received of any ship appearing off the coast in which he might hope to effect his escape over to the continent.

"At present, my lord, I have no such good news for you," she replied; "but my lady is constantly watching from the windows that overlooks the sea, so you may expect an early intimation of any vessel that may come in sight."

"And what says her husband to his continued exclusion from this room?" asked Lord Arden.

"He has his suspicions, I believe," she replied: "but my lady has been able to satisfy him that there is no ground for the rumours that have been spread abroad by Jabez Sneed."

"Does the old man still persist in what he has stated?"

"He is more obstinate than ever about it," answered Maud; "and but for my determination just now, he would have insisted upon following me here. In truth, he is a very dangerous man to deal with; for when I came to the door he was kneeling down and trying to see into the room through the keyhole."

"Do you think he saw anything to confirm his suspicions?"

"It was quite impossible for him to do that," she replied; "for having a notion that he would be prying about, I drew the screen opposite the door, as that no one can see what is passing through the keyhole. The thought was a very fortunate one, for if it had not struck me you must have been seen."

"Then, the old man is determined to ascertain the truth?"

"So much so," she replied, "that he offered me a large bribe on condition that I would allow him to come into the room. In that, however, he was disappointed, for I refused his offer, and gave him to understand that it would be in vain for him to make any such proposition to me again."

"But, I suppose, we may expect that he will continue to persuade Sir Walter to make a search here himself?"

"He may try to do so perhaps," she replied; "but luckily my master places so much confidence in his wife, that he will not believe any idle stories that may be uttered agaiust her. Indeed, if he had been at all inclined that way, his mind would have been poisoned against her before now, for Jabez has tried every means he could think of to make him believe that my lady has given an asylum to one of the fugitives that were lately defeated."

"And yet," exclaimed Lord Arden, "the old man has, by accident, given utterance to that which is strictly true."

"Ay, my lord," replied Maud, "and I am afraid Jabez Sneed will never rest satisfied till he has convinced himself of the truth or falsehood of his suspicions."

"Which he will find rather difficult to do, while I remain under lock and key," answered his lordship.

"There's no knowing what scheme he may try next," exclaimed Maud, "and, therefore, I will take the liberty of saying, that the sooner you find an opportunity of getting away, the better it will be for all parties."

"Your advice would no doubt be very good if it were practicable," returned his lordship with a smile. "Unfortunately, however, no vessel has yet arrived off the coast, and as there are hundreds of people looking out for me, I should be taken to a certainty, and the consequences of such a misfortune are very easily to be foreseen."

"Surely, my lord," exclaimed the girl, "they would not be hard-hearted enough to take away your life for taking part with the exiled prince, who you and thousands of others still look upon as the lawful King of England?"

"Indeed, but they would though, my good girl," he replied, "or I should not have been hiding from them in different parts of the country like a man who had committed some heinous offence. I, in particular, have been marked out as an object of vengeance, as being one of those who have always been foremost in endeavouring to bring about the restoration of the sovereign to whom I owe my allegiance."

"Then I'm afraid, my lord, they will soon discover that you have sought the shelter of this house."

"There I hope you are mistaken," he replied, "for the well-tried zeal of Sir Walter Amyot will convince all persons that he is the last man who ought to be suspected of harbouring an enemy of the present government."

"Ay; but I am afraid they may suspect her ladyship of concealing you though."

"Even if they do," he replied, "there would be sufficient intimation of such a suspicion to afford me time to seek some other hiding-place."

"But there's no other place to hide you in, unless it's one of the dungeons that I hear are under the house."

"Well," exclaimed Lord Arden, "any place will be to me a welcome refuge if matters should happen to be driven to extremities, and I would even submit to a few days confinement in the vaults you speak of, than run the risk of meeting an ignominious fate upon the scaffold."

"Ah!" returned the girl, "but your lordship seems to forget that it would not be very easy to get you away from this room without being seen by some of the people belonging to the house. And I'm sure none of them are to be depended on, for they are all of them Roundheads, and would be pleased enough if they could only assist in bringing a warm-hearted cavalier, like yourself, to punishment."

"It appears, then, that I was wrong in venturing to come here?"

"As far as my mistress is concerned, I am sure she is heartily glad at having it in her power to assist you. And, for that matter, I believe even Sir Walter would cheerfully afford you an asylum against your pursuers, if it was not for fear of the trouble he would get into if the fact should happen to reach the ears of Oliver Cromwell."

"Which I should think might be easily enough managed?"

"So it might, but for Jabez Sneed," she replied; "but that old man is a continual stumbling block, and I suppose nothing will prevail upon him to keep the secret now that my lady has discovered his scandalous doings that have been going on so long."

"It would, no doubt, be unwise to trust to him," answered Lord Arden, "and, in fact, I see no necessity to do so, since it is more likely than not that I shall not remain here many hours longer."

"Is there a likelihood then of a vessel arriving so soon?"

"There is."

"May I ask how your lordship knows that?"

"Because there is a smuggler in this neighbourhood who has undertaken to look out for the first vessel that passes this way, and in the event of none appearing he will endeavour to take me over to the Dutch coast in his own lugger."

"Do you think the man is to be trusted with such a secret when so large a reward has been offered for your apprehension?"

"There was no alternative," answered his lordship, "and, therefore, I was induced to promise him a still larger sum to be paid immediately upon my rejoining the friends whom I left abroad. That, I expect, will keep him honest; but whether it does so or not, I must e'en take my chance when no other hope remains to me."

"What is the man's name, my lord?" asked the girl.

"Mark Bentley."

"I have heard him spoken of before, and people say he is one of the most dangerous smugglers that live on this coast."

"That will matter very little," exclaimed Lord Arden, "for it will be his own interest to perform his task faithfully, since he would not receive more than half the amount if he was to betray me into the hands of my enemies. Therefore, his own interest being concerned, I may fairly presume that he will, at least, do his best towards conveying me safe to the place I want to go to."

"But Jabez Sneed may happen to discover what's going on."

"Jabez Sneed seems to be the great bugbear on every occasion," answered Lord Arden. "The man besets me every way I turn, and yet I have a notion that we may deceive him in this affair much more easily than we have imagined."

At this moment a cry of alarm escaped from Maud, who, looking up, had distinctly seen the form of some man, who was peering in at the window. The countenance, however, of the person, whoever it was, she had not been able to recognise, for no sooner had the intruder ascertained that he had been discovered, than he found himself compelled to make a hasty retreat, and, leaping down, he concealed himself amongst some shrubs, lest he should be seen whilst moving away to a more distant part of the terrace. The next moment the window was hastily thrown open by Maud, and from the few words that she spoke to the person that was in the room, the eavesdropper —who we need scarcely say was Jabez Sneed— had the satisfaction of learning that she had not recognised who it was that had just been intruding upon them.

Lord Arden endeavoured to persuade Maud that she had been led away by her own groundless fears; but his efforts were in vain, for she was thoroughly convinced that she had not been deceived, and her suspicions naturally turned towards the steward, who was the only person that she thought was likely to have watched them. That there was danger, she felt quite certain; and leaving Lord Arden, she once more locked him in the Bower Chamber, and then proceeded with all speed to acquaint her mistress with what had taken place.

CHAPTER VII.

NEW TROUBLES BEGIN TO FALL UPON LADY EVELINE.—HER DETERMINATION TO REMAIN FAITHFUL TO THE CHARGE SHE HAS UNDERTAKEN.—JABEZ SNEED INFORMS HIS MASTER OF WHAT HE HAS SEEN, AND OFFERS TO PROVE THAT HIS INFORMATION MAY BE RELIED ON. —SIR WALTER BECOMES JEALOUS.

ELATED with the gratifying idea that he had proofs now in support of the charge which he had hitherto made in vain against Lady Eveline, the old steward proceeded round to another part of the mansion, and having passed through the grand hall of entrance, made his way to Sir Walter's study, where he found his master, and having first ascertained that his presence just then was not an intrusion, he inquired of Sir Walter whether he had yet ascertained the truth or falsehood of a rumour respecting some person being concealed in the Bower Chamber.

"I have not thought it of sufficient consequence to trouble my head about it," answered his master in a tone of indifference.

"Then of course, Sir Walter, you imagine that I have been endeavouring to propagate a false report."

"Nay, he replied, "I will not go quite so far as to say that, but I believe you suffer yourself to be too easily imposed upon by the ridiculous notions of other persons."

"So you might have thought till now," answered Jabez Sneed exultingly, "but within the last quarter of an hour I have been convinced of the truth of all I have said by ocular demonstration."

"Ocular demonstration!—What mean you?"

"In a word I have just seen a man in the Bower Chamber."

"Impossible !"

"So you might have said a short time ago," answered Jabez Sneed; "but my eyes,—though none of the youngest,—have not deceived me this time, and you may easily convince yourself of the truth of my assertion by going to the room I speak of."

"If you saw a man there, you can of course tell me who he is."

"That is quite impossible, Sir Walter," answered the old man, "for when I looked into the room he was talking to her ladyship's female attendant Maud, who saw me the moment my head appeared at the window, and I was obliged to make a hasty retreat, though not before I had plainly seen there was some one in the room who had no business to be there."

"If there is any truth in this assertion of yours it ought to be inquired into," exclaimed Sir Walter Amyot, "but as I still think you must have been deceived, I will not insult my wife by demanding admission to the Bower Chamber unless upon the most positive proof that she has been deceiving me."

"Then my word is not to be believed?"

"If it is to be taken in this instance," exclaimed Sir Walter, "it must necessarily follow that I give up the confidence that I have always placed in my wife."

"And do women never deceive?"

"Sometimes they may," answered the knight, "but Lady Eveline's conduct has been so uniformly correct that I have no excuse for believing that she would play me false, even in the slightest particular. Indeed it would be almost criminal for me to believe that she could dare to conceal any person beneath this roof without the knowledge and consent of her husband."

"You may, perhaps, imagine that I am actuated by unworthy motives," exclaimed Jabez Sneed, "and yet I can assure you, Sir Walter, that I have brought you this news with the greatest reluctance."

"Then why came you here so immediately after making the discovery you speak of?"

"Do you give me no credit for feeling an interest in your welfare?" demanded the old man.

"I would fain believe that you have done this with a good purpose," answered his master, "but this subject has already been mentioned on three or four occasions, and it therefore begins to appear that you have some purpose of your own to serve."

"Indeed, Sir Walter, you wrong me," exclaimed Jabez Sneed, in a tone of whining hypocrisy; "for I only feared lest the person who is concealed here should be one of the fugitive royalists who escaped after the last skirmish. The thought of that has, I own, troubled me sorely, and I have therefore ventured to mention what I have discovered, even at the hazard of exciting your displeasure."

"Have I ever encouraged you to watch my wife, and report to me her actions?"

"Assuredly not," he replied, "but I thought it was nothing more than my duty to see that no mischief happens to you through the mistaken kindness of Lady Amyot to others."

"Lady Eveline," exclaimed her husband, "would not commit an act that could in any way bring me into jeopardy. She has ever acted towards me the part of a fond and faithful wife, and ill indeed should I repay all her tenderness were I to believe the first rumours that a feeling of revenge or malevolence might spread abroad for her ruin."

"Is it possible," exclaimed Jabez Sneed with affected sorrow, "that my motives can have been so mistaken?"

"You still persists then in declaring the truth of what you have just been telling me?"

"How can I possibly do otherwise when I state only things that have passed before my own eyes?"

"Again I repeat you must have been mistaken; for I dare be sworn the person you saw in the Bower Chamber was no other than one of my own domestics."

"Then it must be one that I have never seen before," exclaimed Jabez Sneed, with an inconcealed sneer. "Besides, your domestics are all Puritans, whilst the persons I saw was one of those sons of Belial that are called Cavaliers."

"Even if it were as you say,—how came he there?"

"That is more than I can propound," answered the wily steward, "but I should imagine that it is extremely probable he has been received into the house by her ladyship."

"Her ladyship would not venture upon an act that would be so certain to incur my anger."

"Far be it from me to contradict you, Sir Walter," answered the steward; "but Lady Amyot has a strong leaning towards those who favour the cause of royalty in this country, and I ventured to imagine that it was possible she had allowed one of those fugitives to obtain shelter here till he finds an opportunity to escape."

"And pray, sir," demanded Sir Walter, "how dare you imagine that your mistress would be guilty of deception?"

"If I have offended you, sir, I am deeply grieved," exclaimed Jabez Sneed. "I have, however, the consolation of knowing that I have done nothing more than my duty, and all I hope is that you may not afterwards see bitter reason to regret having disregarded the words of one who has always been faithful to your family."

"How am I to know that there may not be more of revenge than of fidelity to me in the course you have adopted?"

"My long services might argue something in my favour."

"Under other circumstances it might be so," exclaimed Sir Walter, "but not when I find that you are endeavouring to ruin the affection that I have always felt towards my wife. For her sake I will discredit all stories that are raised to her prejudice, and will never believe that she would deceive me till I have such positive proof, that further doubt upon the subject would be impossible."

"Perhaps I ought not to make so free as to say so," exclaimed Jabez Sneed, "but I cannot refrain from saying, that nothing would be more easy than for you to convince yourself in this instance."

"Ay,—by becoming a spy upon my wife?"

"Sometimes it is necessary to do that, which at any other time one would shrink from," answered Jabez, plausibly. "Where there is any reasonable ground for suspicion, a man may act unwisely in placing too much confidence, when it is within his own power to arrive at the truth. I have hinted it before, and now report it, that a visit to the Bower Chamber would at once remove all doubts upon this painful subject."

"But that cannot be done without affording Lady Eveline a knowledge of the suspicions you would fill me with."

"Would it not be easy to urge once more your wish to pass some of your time in the apartments, which she regards as being devoted entirely to her own use?"

"I have already done so."

"True, and she made some excuse I believe?"

"Excuse!—needs she any excuse when she fancies I am unreasonable in my demands?"

"Of course she has a right to do as she pleases about it," answered Jabez Sneed, "but as the request would not be a very unreasonable one, I rather wonder she was so positive in her refusal. However, I have no wish to say anything that would prejudice her ladyship in your opinion, and I will therefore say nothing more, even though I should see still further evidence than I have."

"It would be well if you keep your word," exclaimed Sir Walter, "and the more particularly if you abstain from keeping a watch upon the actions of your mistress. I myself would not be guilty of the act, and surely *you* can have nothing to do with that which never can do you any mischief."

"How can I be certain of that," demanded the steward, "when all who are in any way concerned in the concealment of these royalists are subjected to high pains and penalties?"

"'Tis to save yourself then that you would involve Lady Amyot in ruin?" exclaimed his master.

"Judge me not so, I pray you, Sir Walter," returned the old hypocrite, "for it is you only that I would preserve from the danger that I can but too plainly foresee. Ruin must surely fall upon this house should it ever be known that an enemy of the state has been concealed beneath your roof."

"Lady Amyot would not endanger me by such an act of imprudence."

"'Tis well to have confidence in one another," returned Jabez Sneed, "but sometimes we may close our eyes against the approach of danger when we ought to be most careful and vigilant. But at all events, let what may happen, I shall have the satisfaction of knowing that I have done my duty in warning you that there is reason for believing that your house contains some one who ought not to be here."

"Which information—even should there be any truth in it,—you have obtained by means such as I ought not to encourage."

"It may be so," answered the old man, "but I see no reason to reproach myself for doing that which was intended for your good."

"Or rather to gratify some private pique of your own."

"Nay, there you wrong me, Sir Walter," exclaimed Jabez Sneed, "for I can have no revenge to gratify, seeing that I have always been upon good terms with her ladyship."

"Time will best prove what your motives may have been," answered his master, "and I have a notion it will not be long before I learn the truth that is at present concealed from me. In the meantime I again warn you, not again to watch Lady Amyot, who should at least be spared the indignity of being under the espionage of one of her own domestics."

"I will endeavour to obey you," replied the old man, "but it may so happen that things come to my knowledge without my taking the trouble to inquire about them. In that case had I better inform my master of what had taken place, or proceed at once before a justice to announce the fact that one of the fugitive cavaliers has sought refuge in your house?"

"Is that question asked to intimidate me?" asked Sir Walter Amyot in a tone of anger.

"By no means," replied the steward in a tone of more humility than he had hitherto assumed. "The question was merely asked for my own guidance, in case—as I believe is very likely—I should make such a discovery as can leave no doubt that rebels have found a shelter where they should not have sought for it."

"Do you then still persist in asserting that Lady Amyot has so far forgotten her duty both to myself and to her country, as to have admitted a fugitive within my walls?"

"I have said already that I saw a man just now in one of the apartments that belong exclusively to her ladyship."

"And I believe it must either be an error or a mischievous invention of your own."

"These are harsh words towards an old, and I will still say, a faithful servant," exclaimed Jabez Sneed, "for I cannot possibly have any motive for uttering a falsehood against my mistress."

"Has she never offended you?"

"Not so much that I could entertain any feeling of revenge against her," he replied; "and even if I had received the greatest injury, I should have overlooked it if it were only through respect for the wife of my master."

"Let, then, your respect be henceforth shown by abstaining from the pursuit of such conduct as has now displeased me," exclaimed Sir Walter Amyot. "Her ladyship has never yet deserved that a word of suspicion should be uttered against her, and it would be an act unworthy of myself to listen to slanderers, for which I know there is not the slightest ground for suspicion. You may now leave me, Jabez, and forget not the injunction I have given as you would merit my future favours."

The old man withdrew at this bidding, and it would have been easy to perceive that he exulted at the mischief which he had been endeavouring to make. Notwithstanding his apparent disregard of all he had heard, the tale which Jabez had related fell like a thunderbolt upon the knight, though he still suspected that the charge originated in a pure love of mischief. The evidence, to be sure, was too conclusive to be doubted, and upon further reflection, he determined not to suffer another hour to pass away in uncertainty; and leaving the room in which the conversation had taken place, he repaired towards that in which he knew he should find her of whom he was in search.

In the meanwhile, Maud hastened to her mistress with the news of the alarm which had been occasioned her by the unexpected apparition of a man at the window of the Bower Chamber. Lady Eveline could at first scarcely credit the truth of the assertion, but reflecting on the danger to which her brother would be exposed in the event of a discovery having taken place, she became more particular in her inquiries as to all the circumstances connected with the affair.

"Are you quite certain, Maud," she asked, "that you were not deceived by your own weak feares?"

"O yes, my lady, I am quite certain of it," she replied, "for the form was that of a man, sure enough, and he slipped down from the place where he had been watching us, the moment he heard the exclamation of alarm I uttered on perceiving him."

"Did you see enough of the man to guess who he was?"

"No, my lady," she replied, "it was impossible for me to do that, for he was off so quick that, though I ran to the window directly and looked out upon the terrace, the person I was in search of was nowhere to be seen."

"Have you any reason for believing that it was Jabez Sneed?"

"Why the figure was not unlike his," answered Maud, "but the sight I caught of him was so instantaneous, that it would be impossible for me to say with any certainty who it was. It is likely enough, however, that he may have climbed up to the window, for he seems determined to find out the secret, and nothing will prevent his peeping and prying about, whilst there is the slightest chance of doing mischief."

"If I were but certain that it was he who was watching through the window, I would immediately order Sir Walter, in order that he might rid himself of so dangerous a person."

"Ah! my lady," exclaimed Maud, "I'm afraid that would be of very little use, for even if Jabez Sneed were sent away from the house, he would still find means for carrying on his mischief. There would be nothing to prevent his watching about the house, and if he were to do that, Lord Arden would be compelled to remain here for some time longer, and the chances are, that he would be discovered by some of the people in the house."

"Do you think he was seen by the person, whoever he was, that you say was watching through the window?"

"I don't see how it could have been otherwise," answered Maud, "for a lamp was burning close by the side of him, and any person could have easily seen him from the window."

"Then perhaps before this time," sighed Lady Eveline, "an alarm has been spread abroad that some one is concealed in this house."

"Oh, Jabez Sneed has, no doubt, taken care to do that before now," answered the girl, "for he is in a terrible rage about your having discovered his numerous acts of dishonesty; and in order to save himself, he will, I am afraid, inform Sir Walter of the discovery he has made."

"Are you sure he has not done so already?"

"I don't know what to say about that," answered the attendant, "but I am rather in hopes he has not, because Sir Walter has not given any hint of his suspecting that anybody is here."

"But he may when he sees a favourable opportunity."

"The worst of it is," exclaimed Maud, "there's no understanding the artful ways of Jabez Sneed, who can always appear most smiling and good-tempered [when he has mischief in view. He has, however, appeared more than usually dull and thoughtful of late, and for that reason I fancy he is only scheming within himself how he shall best carry out the views he has in contemplation."

"Can you think of no plan by which you may draw from him the schemes he is thinking of?" asked her ladyship.

"It would be of no use if I were to try," replied her attendant; "for he is not a man to be deceived by kindness, and especially when he knows that I hate him from the very bottom of my heart. Besides, it would only put him upon his guard, which is a thing to be avoided when we have such an arch old villain to deal with."

"At any rate we must watch him with a jealous eye," exclaimed Lady Eveline, "and therefore it will be better that he should remain here some short time longer in order that we may not lose sight of him whilst there is any danger to be apprehended."

"As far as I am concerned, I'll not lose sight of him," answered Maud, "and it shall go hard but I'll discover his plans, whatever they may be, before he has time to put them into effect. He has thought proper to act the part of a spy upon me, and now it is my turn to show him that I am not to be outdone in watchfulness. I have an old grudge against him, and it shall be paid off with good interest, or I am very much mistaken."

"Take care, Maud," returned her mistress, "or he may discover the designs you have against him."

"If he does it would be rather surprising," she replied, "for I will keep this secret so close that not a soul shall suspect me of having any unusual notion in my head. Besides, I am in hopes it will not be necessary for Lord Arden to remain in this house many hours longer; and when once he has made his escape on board a ship, you can acquaint Sir Walter with the dishonest acts of his steward, and it will then be for Jabez Sneed to tremble for the consequences of his own evil deeds."

"Perhaps, after all," observed her ladyship, "it may be better not to say anything to his master upon the subject."

"In that case he would commit further robberies."

"On the contrary," replied Lady Eveline, "I believe nothing would prevent his dishonesty so effectually as to keep him in continual dread of an exposure of what has already taken place. Whilst

that fear is hanging over him, I think there will not be much reason to expect that he will be the first to fish in troubled waters."

"Unless he should happen to take it into his head that he would gain the favour of Sir Walter by conveying to him all the idle whims and fancies that enter his brain," observed Maud.

"He knows not the disposition of Sir Walter Amyot if that is the notion he has formed of him," answered her mistress, "for nothing would so greatly incense him as for one of his own domestics to presume to watch the conduct of his wife. Let him only venture upon such a step as that, and I am certain he would not be suffered to remain in the house after the disclosure was made."

"Then you don't think, my lady, that Jabez Sneed has it in his power to injure you?"

"I do not, indeed," she replied, "or I should have taken steps before now to have him removed from this house."

"And yet, I cannot for the life of me help thinking that there is more mischief brewing than you reckon on."

"If you would caution me against the evil practices of the steward," answered Lady Eveline, "it is all in vain, for the more I reflect upon what is past the more certain do I feel that my enemy has no means by which he can do me an injury."

"You are not afraid, then, of his telling master that he suspects one of the cavaliers is concealed in the house?"

"Doubtless he has done that already," answered her ladyship, "and we have seen how little regard Sir Walter pays to his tattling. No attempt has yet been made to search the house, nor has my husband even pressed me since to occupy the apartments which have always been considered as devoted to my own use. That, I think, proves he is satisfied with the explanation I gave him, and it is, therefore, hardly to be expected that he will now pay any attention to the mischief-making rumours that Jabez Sneed would circulate against me."

"Ay, my lady," exclaimed the girl, "it might be all very well to think so, if it was not that the affair would come to other ears as well as my masters. All the servants in the house will be told that one of the fugitives is hiding here, and for the sake of the reward that has been offered, they would try their best to get at the truth."

"Nay, they surely will not dare to indulge their impertinent curiosity if Sir Walter forbids it."

"So one would think," exclaimed Maud, "but the temptation is so great a one, that I'm afraid none of the people here are to be depended on. Besides, they may take it into their heads that it is an act of duty to assist in taking up those that are called enemies of their country, and in that case they would care very little for any orders that Sir Walter may give to remain quiet till they have received his orders."

"Have you cautioned Lord Arden not on any account to show himself at the windows?"

"I have, my lady," she replied, "but what is the use of that, if Jabez Sneed is determined to find out the secret of the Bower Chamber? Who would have thought, for instance, of his peeping through the keyhole, if I had not caught him in the very fact?"

"Perhaps it is as well that he did attempt to gratify his curiosity," returned Lady Eveline; "for as it is probable that he knows nothing to confirm his suspicions, we may venture to hope that he will no longer believe we have sheltered one of the king's friends in our house. In that case the search will soon be given up; and as soon as all is once more quiet, we may find a fitting time and opportunity to assist my brother in escaping from a country where he is surrounded by such danger."

"You think, then, my lady," exclaimed the girl, "that Sir Walter will not again ask to enter the room where his lordship is concealed?"

"It is impossible to say how he will act,' replied Lady Eveline; "and we must, therefore, be upon our guard against any emergency that may arise. At present, he is satisfied with my denial, which is more than I can say of myself, for I often feel abashed at the resolution with which I have denied that any one is concealed in this house."

LADY AYMOT AND LORD ARDEN.

"As, my lady," answered the girl, "but how very excusable that is when you reflect upon the danger his lordship would be exposed to if it should happen to be known where he is. Indeed I don't see what else you could have done when everything depended upon his re— maining snug where he is till we are able to get him away."

"And that," sighed her ladyship, "may not be for some time."

"Never mind how long a time it is," exclaimed Maud, "if we only succeed in the end.

Luckily his lordship is in very good quarters, and I dare say he will not regret his visit to this house if we can only by and by manage to get him on board some ship."

"You say a smuggler has promised to aid in his escape?"

"Yes, my lady, and Mark Bentley, though he bears the character of being a rough fellow, is too much interested in what is to be made by it to throw away such a capital opportunity of putting money into his pocket."

"Do you think he would not betray him for the sake of the larger sum that he would gain by delivering him into the hands of the government?"

"There's no fear of his doing that, my lady," answered Maud, "for he has taken a great many of the fugitive royalists over to France, and has not once been guilty of betraying the trust reposed in him. Indeed people hereabouts look upon him as being friendly to the cause of the exiled king, though for reasons of his own, he has never yet given an opinion either upon one side or the other."

"Has he been long known upon this part of the coast?" asked Lady Eveline.

"All his lifetime," replied Maud, "and his father before him was dreaded as one of the boldest smugglers in the whole neighbourhood. Nobody, however, says that Mark Bentley is either cowardly or treacherous, and I therefore believe Lord Arden could not trust himself to a better man than the one that has undertaken to convey him over to the opposite coast."

"Should you be afraid to meet this man?"

"Not if any good can be done by it," she replied.

"You would not mind seeing him then to make arrangements for the speedy departure of my brother from a place where dangers and difficulties are increasing around him every hour?"

"I'll see him within an hour if your ladyship wishes it?"

"Do so, my good girl," exclaimed Lady Eveline, "for I see no time is to be lost if my brother is to be saved from the perils with which he is threatened. My purse shall be at your disposal in making a bargain with this man, but he must be prepared to sail at a moment's notice, and in the meanwhile I will see my brother and urge him to flee from danger whilst there is yet an hope of saving him."

There was no opportunity for making any reply to this, for the well-known footsteps of Sir Walter Amyot were heard advancing along the corridor. Maud immediately hurried away through a door which led towards a different part of the mansion, and as she did so the knight entered the presence of his wife with a countenance that showed his mind was restless and ill at ease.

CHAPTER VIII.

SIR WALTER AMYOT SEEKS AN EXPLANATION FROM HIS WIFE.—THE STEWARD'S VILLANY IS PARTIALLY REVEALED.—JABEZ SNEED AGAIN FINDS MEANS TO EXCITE THE JEALOUSY OF HIS MASTER, WHO DETERMINES TO SATISFY HIMSELF OF THE TRUTH OR FALSEHOOD OF THE CHARGE.

THE frown which appeared on the countenance of Sir Walter Amyot soon vanished when his wife addressed him in terms of affection and endearment. Then perceiving that there was no one present but themselves, he assumed as much composure as possible, and addressed her in a tone of kindness and affection.

"My dearest Eveline," he said, his voice still slightly trembling with emotion, "I have cause to speak to you upon a subject as painful as it is embarrassing. Do not, however, suppose that I am so weak as to believe every idle tale that meets my ear, for the only aim I have in view is to tell you what I have heard, in order that you may have an opportunity of contradicting the bold assertions of those who seek your injury."

"Your words fill me with surprise," exclaimed Lady Eveline, "for I know not that I have ever done anything to make an enemy."

"Yet you have one at least."

"Who is he?"

"Jabez Sneed, my steward."

"Of what does he dare accuse me?" she asked.

"Of harbouring beneath my roof some man whose presence I would not countenance."

"And you believe him?"

"Nay, I say not that," he exclaimed, "for, though the accusation is a very grave one, I would fain believe it originates in a feeling of revenge. You have, probably, in some way or other, given offence to the man who now endeavours to injure you."

"I have never done so till very lately," she replied, "and even now I have forborne speaking upon the subject, because I hoped that a little lenity would not be thrown away upon him."

"Has the old man been deceiving me?" asked Sir Walter.

"I fear he has."

"Upon what grounds do you suspect him of being unworthy of my confidence?"

"I believe that you will admit that I have not suffered myself to be too easily led away either by my own prejudice or that of any other person," answered Lady Eveline. "In fact, suspecting during your recent absence that Jabez Sneed was not acting the part of an honest servant towards his master, I demanded the immediate production of his accounts, which I perceived he was anxious to withhold."

"Did he exhibit any confusion or hesitation when you mentioned the subject to him?"

"He seemed to be much enraged, though, of course, he could not refuse compliance with my demands."

"He was reluctant, I suppose, to obey the orders of one who has never till now interfered with him."

"I observed that he was almost bursting with rage, though he endeavoured to appear more than usually submissive."

"Have you yet looked over the accounts he rendered?" inquired Sir Walter Amyot.

"I did so, immediately."

"What was the result?"

"Anything but favourable to the character of Jabez Sneed."

"You found your suspicions verified?"

"Ay, to the fullest extent."

"What have become of the papers?" asked her husband.

"Safely locked up in my own room, where they wait your leisure to overlook them."

"You mean, I suppose, that they are in the Bower Chamber, from which I have been so mysteriously excluded?"

"Yes, Walter," she replied, "I put them there because I knew they would be less likely to fall into the hands of Jabez Sneed. The old man has been tampering with my servant, for the purpose of endeavouring to get possession of them, and that fact alone is, I think, sufficient to confirm my suspicion of his guilt."

"And you think," exclaimed Sir Walter, "that the charges made by my steward have originated in a feeling of revenge for your having detected him in these acts of peculation?"

"There can be no doubt of it," answered Lady Eveline; "for he has acknowledged as much to my attendant, who has proved to be worthy of the trust I have reposed in her. Nay, he has even offered to say no more about his suspicions of some person being concealed in your house, on condition that I restore the papers he is so anxious to get possession of. But I have refused to make any terms with him, well knowing that I could rely upon your confidence in me till I find it convenient to divulge that which at present seems to wear an air of mystery."

"You know, I suppose, that he still persists in asserting that some one is secreted in the room?"

"I know he does," answered Lady Eveline; "but I still rely upon your confidence in one who till now has always been above suspicion. A few days,—perhaps a very few hours, will enable me to reveal all that which at present appears to be suspicious, and I venture to hope that you will be perfectly satisfied with my explanation."

"There is no doubt of it, my love," exclaimed her husband, "and my only fear has been lest you should have afforded shelter to any of those misguided men who are denounced as enemies of their country."

"At all events," answered Lady Eveline, "I suppose Jabez Sneed has tried to make you believe so?"

"He has declared his perfect conviction that if a search were to be made through the house I should find that he has not made the charge against you without sufficient foundation."

"And you are half inclined to believe him?"

"At first I was," answered Sir Walter Amyot; "but upon more mature reflection I have determined to wait for an explanation till you find yourself in a position to give one. I cannot, however, undertake to control those who are in my service, for they know a large reward has been offered for the apprehension of any of the royalists; and I know all my people are watching round the house in order to ascertain if there be any truth in the report circulated by Jabez Sneed."

"Can you not desire them to desist from such prying impertinence?"

"Why should I do that," asked Sir Walter Amyot, "if there be no reason to fear a discovery?"

"It may not do any mischief to be sure," she replied; "but I feel my situation to be rather a degrading one, when I find that our servants are watching round the house to discover some one who is supposed to have been concealed here with my knowledge."

"In that case," exclaimed Sir Walter, "I will give immediate orders to my people to go elsewhere in quest of those who are endeavouring to conceal themselves from their pursuers."

"Pardon my intrusion," said Jabez Sneed, who had entered the apartment unperceived, "but if your servants are sent away from the house, it will afford an opportunity for the fugitive I have spoken of to escape the punishment he deserves."

"And how know you," asked Sir Walter, "that these suspicions of yours are not founded in error?"

"If I am wrong," answered the steward, "I shall have no hesitation in making sufficient apologies for what has passed as soon as I am convinced of my error. It would, however, be easy for my lady to set the matter at rest if she would only give permission to search the chamber in which I suspect some one is concealed."

"And how dare you repeat this idle tale when I have told you that I am convinced of its utter falsehood?"

"I have offended you I see," exclaimed the steward, "but I am only doing my duty in trying to hunt down those who have lately been in arms against their country."

"Do you suppose I would afford a shelter to such rebels as you are speaking of?" demanded Sir Walter.

"Not if you knew it," replied the old man, "but it is quite possible for some of the friends of the late king to be in your house without your being aware of the fact."

"You would dare to insinuate, though, that Lady Amyot has assisted in giving shelter to the enemy."

"If it has offended you, I am deeply grieved," answered Jabez Sneed, "but I have a duty to perform to my country, and any punishment would be well deserved were I to aid the escape of any of the men who have lately been in arms against the government."

"You would take credit to yourself for the course you have adopted," returned Sir Walter, "but you will not find it easy to deceive me, for I have proof that you are only seeking to gratify your own revenge."

"Against whom, Sir Walter?"

"My wife."

"Nay, Lady Amyot knows best whether I have any reason to gratify a feeling of revenge."

"She does," answered the knight; "and it is from her lips that I have heard the cause of your having charged her with concealing some one beneath my roof. In a word, Jabez Sneed, she asserts that you have not acted the part of an honest steward; and your whole conduct proves that you are endeavouring to revenge yourself by making charges for which I believe there is not the slightest foundation."

"What proof can her ladyship bring forward in support of so serious an accusation?" asked Jabez Sneed, who could with difficulty conceal the rage that these few words had stirred up within him.

"The proofs are, I believe, contained in the accounts which you have given in during my absence from home."

"Have you examined the papers?" asked the old man.

"At present I have not had an opportunity of doing so," answered Sir Walter Amyot, "but I shall lose no time in trying to ascertain how far the accusation can be substantiated.

"May I request you to proceed with the task immediately?" asked Jabez Sneed, perceiving that he might thus find means to enter the apartment which had been closed against all but Lady Eveline and her attendant. "The papers you speak of," he continued, "are locked up in the Bower Chamber, for which I am ready to go with you this instant, in order that my character for honesty may at once be proved to your own satisfaction, and that of my lady."

"Hypocrite!" exclaimed the knight, "you would still impose upon me; but know that all your infamous designs have been laid bare, and ere long you shall receive the punishment that your black ingratitude so justly merits."

"Her ladyship has succeeded in effecting my ruin," muttered Jabez Sneed.

"Lady Amyot has but performed her duty," returned the knight, "and the lie which you have dared to invent against her reputation has been uttered only for the foul purposes of revenge!"

"At least, hear me, before I am so harshly condemned," exclaimed the old man, with more composure than might have been expected. "Your lady wife, to conceal her own shame, has accused me of acting dishonestly. If the charge is true, she can easily prove it on the instant. The papers she tells you are all in her room, which even you, for some reason or another, have not been permitted to enter since your return home. Let her take us there now, before she has time to make any preparations, and you will be convinced that I am neither the liar nor the hypocrite you have called me."

"The proposition is not an unfair one," observed Sir Walter Amyot, turning towards his wife, "and by acceding to it you will at once prove the groundlessness of the charge which has been preferred."

"What is it you would propose?" asked her ladyship.

"You have heard what Jacob Sneed says," he replied; "and I am inclined to humour him in a case which will speedily put an end to all further suspicion. Let us go and examine the papers, which are the groundwork of this charge, that I may know to what extent I have been plundered by this man."

This was a situation which had not been anticipated by the Lady Eveline, and she stood silent and evidently perplexed to frame an excuse for postponing the visit to the Bower Chamber to a future opportunity. She perceived the exultation that shone in the eyes of Jabez Sneed as he watched the effect of his proposition, and as she was anxious to maintain an appearance of composure, she could not altogether conceal the uneasiness she suffered. At length, however, seeing an answer was waited for, she faltered out—

"Another time, Sir Walter, will do as well as now, for I feel reluctant to yield, when it is easily to be seen that Jabez has only made the proposition in order to annoy me."

"Nay," answered her husband; "why should there be any delay when the matter can be so easily set at rest?"

"Again I say, not now," answered Lady Eveline, earnestly; "grant me your patience until to-morrow, and I will then go with you to the room which is the subject of all this suspicion."

"Let it be this moment, Sir Walter,"

whispered Jabez Sneed in the ear of his master.

"True," exclaimed the knight, "why should there be any delay when a falsehood like this is to be laid bare? You have the key of the Bower Chamber, Eveline, and so grave an accusation cannot be too promptly contradicted for your own sake."

"You say truly, Walter," she replied after some little hesitation, "I will not deny that the key is at this moment in my possession; but again I ask you, as a favour to myself, to defer the investigation of this affair till to-morrow."

"Why should there be this delay?" exclaimed Jabez Sneed, alarmed at the probability of a failure in his project.

"You have heard your mistress," returned the knight, sternly, "and I shall not oppose a wish that will occasion so very trifling a delay."

"But all that time my character will be suffering under the imputations that have been cast upon it."

"Nay, I shall not deem you guilty till the proofs have been placed before me."

"May there not be another delay?" he asked.

"Lady Amyot has pledged her word for to-morrow," answered the knight, "and she will not fail to keep it."

The steward, unwilling to be foiled in his schemes, was about to repeat his demand, but Lady Eveline, having already received the assent of her husband, left the room. A silence of three or four minutes' duration then ensued, which was at length broken by Jabez Sneed, who, in a tone of whining hypocrisy, asked his master if he would not grant him permission to visit the Bower Chamber, in order that he might obtain possession of the papers which had been made the groundwork of the suspicions which had been raised against his honesty.

"I will have no further steps taken in the matter," answered Sir Walter Amyot, "till the time arrives when we are to visit the room accompanied by your mistress. In this instance, at least, I have promised to let her have her own way, and it would look like a paltry feeling of distrust were I suddenly to change the determination I just now expressed."

"Far be it from me to suggest what you ought to do," exclaimed the steward, "but I am afraid lest too much confidence may lead you into more difficulties than are anticipated."

"What mean you, sirrah?"

"That if a royalist should indeed be concealed in this house, it would be sure to reach the ears of Cromwell, whose favour you might then lose for ever."

"In other words—you, I suppose, would not hesitate to give him the information if an opportunity offered?"

"Nay, I have never done anything to give rise to such a suspicion," exclaimed Jabez Sneed. "On the contrary, I have always done my best to serve you with zeal and fidelity, and till this time, no one has even ventured to assert that my conduct towards my employer has been otherwise than strictly honourable. That I am not the villain Lady Amyot would make me appear, will soon be made manifest, and at the same time I may be able to prove that I had good reasons for suspecting that one of the fugitives has been concealed in this house without either your knowledge or consent."

"I will not believe it," returned Sir Walter, "and you would, therefore, have done well to refrain from repeating this accusation till a full inquiry has been made into the whole circumstance. To-morrow will, at any rate, clear up the mystery, and till then I shall withhold any further opinion upon the subject."

"May I hope that you will also believe me innocent of the charge brought against me?"

"You may," answered the knight; "for I will confess that I have still a hope Lady Amyot may be mistaken with respect to your alleged acts of dishonesty. You have enemies, perhaps, who speak evil behind your back; but, be that as it may, I will sift the matter to the very bottom, and if you have been falsely accused, I shall not fail to give proof of my displeasure, that will not soon be forgotten. On the other hand, I shall make most particular inquiries to ascertain the truth or falsehood of the report you have raised, in order that no friend of the exiled king shall be suffered to find a refuge beneath my roof."

"Only cause an immediate search to be made," exclaimed Jabez Sneed, "and I would wager my very existence that you will find my information is perfectly correct."

"Have you seen anybody, that you are so positive in the assertion you have made?"

"At present I have not," replied the steward; "but it has been no fault of mine that I have failed, for the chamber has been carefully watched, and every precaution taken to prevent any one leaving the house without my knowledge. Maud seems to be the only person in the secret; but the girl is not to be prevailed upon either by threats or promises, and everything, therefore, will depend upon my own vigilance."

"Remember, though," exclaimed his master, "that Lady Amyot must not be subjected to the annoyance of having a spy constantly watching to discover a secret with which we may have nothing to do. As my wife, you must continue to treat her with all becoming respect, for even if she has assisted in concealing a fugitive, I am well convinced it has been done for purposes which she will not be ashamed to confess."

"But you forget, Sir Walter," exclaimed

the old man, "that no excuse can be made for harbouring persons who are known to be dangerous to the existing government."

"And those in power know well that I would not favour those who have been mad enough to attempt to excite the people of England against their leaders. I have ever proved myself a steady adherent of those who were opposed to monarchy; and if anybody has indeed found a refuge within my house, it has been without my privity or consent."

"That I know," answered Jabez Sneed; "yet the danger will be equally great if you fail to search the place, now that I have told you there is a probability of a cavalier being concealed here."

"Have I not sufficient reason to believe that you are actuated by motives of private revenge?"

"I have no private revenge to gratify," exclaimed the old man; "for though Lady Amyot has treated me with undeserved harshness and severity, I would not injure her whom I know you so tenderly love."

"Then, why are you so anxious for me to make a search that may end in the discovery that I have been deceived?"

"Merely to save you from the consequences that I fear would follow, were it known that you have favoured the foes of our glorious Commonwealth."

"I have not done so," exclaimed Sir Walter Amyot; "nor is there any one that would do me so much injustice as to believe that I would break the oath I have taken to support our present institution."

"Yet you may have enemies who would gladly take the opportunity to spread rumours to your prejudice. I do not say that to influence you in your determination, but rather as a hint to warn you against the consequences that might follow an unfortunate discovery."

"I require not your warning when I know that I am not guilty of any breach of duty," exclaimed Sir Walter, "nor will I permit any further watching upon the conduct of Lady Amyot, whose every act is far beyond the reach of suspicion."

"At all events it cannot be denied that she is very positive in her determination not to allow any one to enter the Bower Chamber."

"For which there may be a less unworthy motive than the one you have imagined," exclaimed the knight severely. "But I am not to be deceived by these evil reports of yours, and shall continue to rely upon the prudence of Lady Amyot, who, I am assured, would not so far commit herself as to involve me in danger."

Unwilling to be foiled in the scheme he had formed, Jabez Sneed was about to press the matter still further, when a servant, who was in his confidence, entered the room and whispered something in his ear. The smile which immediately followed showed that the news he had received was of a gratifying nature, and having dismissed the man, he approached his master with a look of extreme gratification.

"I have just been informed, Sir Walter," he exclaimed, "that a strange man is lurking beneath the window of the Bower Chamber, and with your permission I will go and question him as to the motive that has brought him here at this hour in the evening."

"You will remain where you are," returned the knight angrily, "for I will encourage no unworthy acts that are intended as traps to bring mischief upon Lady Amyot."

"As you please, sir," answered the steward, "but I should have thought it nothing more than a matter of prudence to ascertain who the stranger is, and why he is lurking about your premises like a man who intends to commit some evil deed."

"Perhaps it is only one of my own servants, whose motives have been thus strangely misconstrued."

"In that case, he would not have endeavoured to disguise himself by putting on a large cloak."

"That may be true," answered Sir Walter, "but on the other hand it is not very likely that a man who was endeavouring to conceal himself would venture out upon the terrace at a time of the evening when he is almost certain to be seen."

"He may just have left the chamber for the purpose of endeavouring to escape from hence."

"Who do you suspect it to be, then?" demanded Sir Walter.

"It would be difficult to say with any certainty," answered the steward, "but in my own mind I have no doubt it is the same person that I saw through the window when I looked into the Bower Chamber."

"Psha! this is mere suspicion."

"I grant you it is," answered Jabez Sneed, "but nothing can be more easy than to satisfy yourself of the truth or falsehood of the information I have deemed it my duty to give."

"How so?"

"By accompanying me to the garden, where this stranger, taking advantage of the darkness of the night, is prowling through your grounds to see if there is a chance for him to escape."

"Well," exclaimed Sir Walter; "and supposing it were so, would it not be better to suffer him to leave my place, than seek to detain a man here who it is my interest to get rid of?"

"Ay, if he really intends to go away," answered the steward; "but it is not at all unlikely that he may be merely taking the air and exercise he needs after having been closely confined in the Bower Chamber of my lady; at any rate, it would be advisable to question him upon his motives for lurking about here."

"Did your informant tell you whether Lady Amyot was seen in his company?" asked the knight.

"I understood he was alone."

"And the person who saw him, knew him not?"

"He says, that judging from his height and figure he believed him to be a stranger. Indeed, there can be very little doubt as to that fact, for had it been any of your own domestics he would not have thought it necessary to disguise himself."

"Was he endeavouring to avoid being seen?"

"I don't know how that may have been," answered Jabez Sneed; "but whether it was so or not, I think the better course would be to see who he is what motive he has for coming here. If he should prove to be one of the fugitive royalists, you will be able to show your zeal in the service of your country by handing him over to the proper authorities; but if, on the other hand, he can give a good account of himself, no great harm will have been done by your having put a few questions to him."

"But the man, whoever he is, may have taken the alarm and left the place," observed Sir Walter.

"If he has done so, there will be an end of the matter," answered Jabez Sneed; "but at any rate we may be able to ascertain whether any such person has been seen to enter or leave your premises. We shall thus get something of a clue, and it will be hard but I find out whether any of the king's friends are lurking about in a place where they have no business to be."

"Still I can perceive that you are bent only on carrying out your own scheme of revenge."

"Against whom, sir?"

"Against Lady Amyot, who has stirred up your ill feeling by an act in which she was fully justified."

"Indeed, Sir Walter, you wrong me and deceive yourself," exclaimed the hypocrite. "I bear no ill will against her ladyship for the course she has thought proper to adopt against me; but I have a duty to perform, and will not shrink from giving up a royalist whenever one of them may happen to cross my path. Once more, then, I ask, sir, if you will accompany me to see who this stranger is, and why he lurks about as if ashamed to show himself?"

"I will go with you," replied Sir Walter, "not, however, from any suspicion that I feel respecting the stranger you speak of, but in order to convince myself as well as you, that there is no truth whatever in the rumours that have been spread throughout my house."

Seeing that his master was in earnest, Jabez Sneed now left the room and led the way towards the hall-door, from whence they emerged upon the terrace, near to the place where it was supposed the stranger was to be seen. Here, however, they paused for a few minutes to listen; and then, with stealthy steps, made their way through a shrubbery which bounded a portion of the esplanade.

CHAPTER IX.

LADY EVELINE VISITS HER FUGITIVE BROTHER IN THE BOWER CHAMBER.— AN IMMEDIATE DEPARTURE RESOLVED UPON.—THE KNIGHT AND HIS STEWARD REMAIN UPON THE WATCH.—THE CAPTURE OF A SMUGGLER.

ON leaving the presence of her husband Lady Eveline was making her way towards the room in which her brother was secreted, when she was met by Maud who was going in search of her.

"Ah! my lady," exclaimed the girl. "I am glad to have met you, for I have just seen Mark Bentley the smuggler, who came to say that he will be ready to accompany his lordship this evening on board his lugger, and that in a few hours he will be able to reach, in safety, the coast of Holland."

"Does my brother know of this?" asked her ladyship.

"He does not," replied Maud, "for I thought he would rather hear the news from you in order that the necessary preparations may be made to secure his easy passage to the place he is going to."

"Where is the man you speak of?" asked Lady Eveline.

"On the terrace, just beneath the window of the Bower Chamber," answered the girl.

"Then some one will be sure to see him!"

"I hardly think that's very likely at this time in the evening," replied Maud, "for few of our people leave the house after dark, and even if he should happen to be seen no one could know him, for he is disguised in a large sea cloak that completely covers him. Besides, he is well armed, and if any person were to attempt to interfere with him it would be at the risk of losing his life."

"Will my brother be safe with a man of such desperate habits?" asked Lady Eveline, with alarm.

"Depend on it there's nothing at all to fear," answered Maud, "for though the man would fight desperately enough in defence of himself or any other person that might be under his protection, he is quiet enough when people don't interfere with him. Indeed, except that he is a smuggler, he bears an excellent character from all that have ever had anything to do with him."

" Does he say that everything is ready for my brother's immediate departure from England ?"

"Yes, my lady," she replied, " if Lord Arden can only manage to get out of the house without being seen, he may be on his passage towards a foreign country within one hour from the time of leaving the place."

"But the question is whether we shall be able to assist his departure without being discovered by Jabez Sneed or any of the other persons who have made themselves so officious in watching about to prevent the escape of those who are imagined to be concealed here.''

" As for that, my lady," exclaimed Maud, " I believe everything may be managed easily enough if we only act with a little caution. I will myself undertake to see that no one is watching us ; and when the coast seems to be quite clear, I will lead Lord Arden to the man he is going to trust himself to, and if no delay takes place, I think we may reckon upon all ending to your satisfaction."

" But how can my brother leave his room without being seen by some of the servants'?"

" The servants are now enjoying themselves as usual when the evening comes on," answered Maud, " and I don't suppose any of them will leave this hall merely for the purpose of running about in a wild goose chase. Jabez Sneed, to be sure, might feel some satisfaction if he thought there was any mischief to be done, but he has no reason to suspect what is going on this evening, and by to-morrow his lordship will, I hope, be far enough away from here."

" But I left him just now with Sir Walter, and he was endeavouring to convince him that some one was concealed in the Bower Chamber."

" That may be, my lady," answered Maud, " but his trouble will be all thrown away, for Sir Walter seems to suspect that his steward is endeavouring to gratify his own revenge against you for the discovery you made of his roguery. At all events, he has tried as hard as possible to do you an injury, and as he has not succeeded so far, it is to be hoped he will fail altogether."

" With almost any other person it might have been so," exclaimed Lady Eveline, " but the steward is as artful as he is vindictive, and it is not a single repulse that will deter him from repeating his attempt to prevail upon his master to search the room before my brother has time to leave it. However, no time is to be lost, and I will therefore hasten to the Bower Chamber, and urge Lord Arden to take his departure before it is too late to save himself from the fate I so much dread to think of."

" Do you believe, then, they would send him to the scaffold ?"

" What other destiny is to be looked for, when so many of his brave comrades in arms have already met their sad doom ?" demanded Lady Eveline. " Had it not been for the certainty I felt in that respect, I would not so far have periled my husband, as to bring beneath his roof one who has been denounced an enemy to his country."

" And yet," exclaimed Maud, "no place could have been so secure for a fugitive as the house of one who is so well known for his strong attachment to the Commonwealth. As a proof of it, he might have remained here, no one knows how long, unsuspected, if it had not been for the prying curiosity of Jabez Sneed, who had his own bad purposes to serve."

" Alas !" sighed Lady Eveline, " I fear that man will never cease his attempts till he has succeeded in proving that Sir Walter's house was the retreat of a fugitive."

" But Sir Walter could not help that, when he was not made acquainted with the facts."

" That would not weigh much in his favour if he has any enemies in the government who are determined upon his destruction," answered Lady Eveline.

" Has he any enemies, do you think ?" asked the girl.

" There are few persons who are fortunate enough to be without them," returned her mistress, " and doubtless Sir Walter has made some in the course of his life. At all events, we know that Jabez Sneed is not to be depended on if my brother's concealment here should happen to come to his knowledge, so that I am the more anxious to hasten the departure of the fugitive, in the event of some unexpected turn taking place."

" Then will you see his lordship directly ?"

" I will."

" And hasten his departure whilst Mark Bentley is in the humour to lend him his assistance?"

" I will urge him by all means to leave the house immediately," answered her ladyship, "for I see plainly that even half an hour wasted would probably lead to the most serious results. This very night, unless it should be imprudent to make the attempt, he must leave this house, and dwell once more amongst strangers in a foreign land."

" Ay, my lady," returned the girl, "but it is to be hoped that he will not be obliged to remain long abroad, for they say people here are beginning to grow tired of living under a republic ; and many go so far as to say, that if Prince Charles would only come over himself and lay claim to the throne of his ancestors, there are plenty of people in England to make him our king."

" Would that such an event were to come to pass," exclaimed Lady Eveline, " for in that case my brother would not only be safe, but his property would be rescued from the hands of those who now unjustly possess it. However, that is a question for after consideration, and I will now visit Lord Arden in order to hasten his departure while there is a chance of his getting away without being detected."

Lady Eveline then left her attendant and proceeded without loss of time to the Bower Chamber, where she found Lord Arden pacing restlessly up and down, as if in anticipation that some great change in his destiny was about to take place.

SIR WALTER AYMOT QUESTIONING JABEZ SNEED.

"Well, my dear sister," he exclaimed, as soon as their first salutation was over; "so you have come to see the poor fugitive in his cage, and to tell him I suppose that his enemies have managed to discover the place of his retreat?"

"On the contrary," she replied, "I believe, with the exception of Jabez Sneed, I believe there is not another person in the house who suspects my reason for keeping this room so carefully closed against everybody."

"Then what other news have you to tell me?"

"That a smuggler, named Mark Bentley, is now waiting on the terrace to convey you on board his lugger, which is now ready to sail for the Dutch coast."

"Have you seen him?"

"I have not yet," she replied, "but my servant has both seen and spoken to him, and he has sent a message to say that you have not a moment to lose."

"Is he quite sure that we can leave the place without being seen?" asked Lord Arden.

"I should suppose he is quite satisfied about that," answered Lady Eveline, "or he would hardly have wished you to leave this room if any danger was to be apprehended. Be that as it may, however, my servant Maud is to be relied on under all circumstances, and she has undertaken to keep a very careful look out till you and the smuggler have managed to place yourselves beyond the reach of danger."

"You say this Mark Bentley is now waiting for me? exclaimed Lord Arden.

"He is now on the terrace beneath the window of this room," answered his sister, and is willing to undertake the task of assisting in your flight whenever you may require his services."

"Which would be this very night if I could only be certain that no one is upon the look-out for me."

"And that I shall soon know," exclaimed Lady Eveline, "for my faithful Maud, upon whom we may place the fullest reliance, will take care to acquaint herself with everything that is passing either in or out of the house. Jabez Sneed is no doubt still upon the watch, but the shrewdness of the girl will be more than a match for him, let him conduct his mischievous intentions with what secrecy he may."

"But your husband may take it into his head to search this room in order to put an end to his doubts."

"Had his steward been able to persuade him he would have done so before now," answered Lady Eveline, "but Sir Walter's confidence in me is not to be easily shaken, and I feel satisfied there is no fear of his visiting here so long as I request him to postpone his purpose. I must, however, entreat of you to leave as soon as possible, for every moment serves to increase your danger, and my heart sinks with apprehension lest you should fall into the hands of your foes after all the narrow escapes you have had."

"Do you think, then, I would submit without making a desperate effort to preserve my liberty?"

"I know your bravery," she replied, "but what would that avail against the numbers by whom you would be assailed? Those whom you have most to fear are actuated by motives of gain, and they would rather slay you than suffer your escape were they once to obtain the sight of the man they are in pursuit of. Do not, therefore, delay your departure or I fear you will become the victim of malice and persecution."

"Can I see the man who is waiting to assist my flight?"

"That is a question that I shall be better able to answer when I have seen Maud," she replied, "who is now on the terrace watching for an opportunity to speak to this Mark Bentley. She will presently return, and if all goes on well you may embark this night, and avoid the danger with which you are now threatened."

"Are you sure she is not to be bribed by those who suspect she is in the secret of my hiding-place?"

"I could answer for her with my life."

"Probably your good opinion of her is deserved," answered his lordship, "and yet I have sometimes felt uneasy at the consciousness I feel of being thrown entirely upon her discretion. However, she has hitherto conducted herself with great prudence, and I will trust to her honour, in the fullest confidence that she will not disappoint your expectations."

"Be assured she will not disappoint them," exclaimed Lady Eveline, "for experience tells me that she is faithful to me, and nothing but the most positive proof would ever convince me that my confidence in the girl has been misplaced. Indeed, had she been inclined to betray her trust, it would have been when the slightest word or hint must have given you into the hands of those who seek your destruction. Nay, if proof of her fidelity were wanting it is to be found in this fact, that at no little hazard to herself, she has now gone to seek an interview with Mark Bentley, of whom she has always expressed the greatest dread."

"And to confess the truth," answered her brother, "I have myself but little faith in a man who would sell his services to the highest bidder."

"But I have sent him word that no demand will be refused if he does but succeed in landing you safely on the coast of Holland."

"Others may make him a yet more tempting offer," replied Lord Arden, "for it is hardly likely he would resist the propositions of my foes if they were to point out to him the danger he must run if it were to be known that he had assisted in the escape of one whom they insolently denounce as an enemy to his country. However, the dilemma I am in affords me no alternative, and I must e'en trust myself to this Mark Bentley, in the faint hope that he may prove himself to be one of the few friends that adversity has left me."

"And if you should escape," cried Lady Eveline, "the chances are that we should never meet again."

"Why do you think so?" he asked.

"Because your doom would be certain were you ever again to set foot on the soil of England."

"Believe me," replied his lordship, "it will not be long before I venture again to visit my native country.

"Are you then weary of your life?"

"On the contrary," he replied, "I am full of hope that a brighter period of my existence is yet to come, and that too before very long. The king's friends have not been inactive abroad, and it is confidently expected that sufficient foreign aid will be given to place our sovereign upon the throne from which he has been driven by his enemies. This indeed may be reckoned upon almost as a certainty, so that those who are now fugitives from their native soil are full of the most sanguine anticipations that the period of their sufferings is nearly at an end."

"Alas!" sighed Lady Eveline, "you seem to have forgotten the impossibility of an invading army landing upon our coasts."

"At the present moment it might be impossible," he replied, "but in a short time we shall see nearly all the difficulties removed. A strong re-action is rapidly taking place in the minds of thousands of those who were once most favourable to a republic, and in a few months we may perhaps congratulate ourselves upon the certainty that England will once more return to order and happiness by the restoration of our monarch to the crown he has been despoiled of."

"And in that case," cried Lady Eveline, "what will be the fate of those, who, like Sir Walter and thousands of others, took an active part in the civil wars against the late King Charles?"

"The king," answered Lord Arden, "will be merciful even to the worst of his enemies if he sees signs of repentance for the heinous offences of which they have been guilty. I may perhaps boast of possessing some influence over the mind of our banished prince, and you may rely upon it, my dear Eveline, that it shall be exerted in favour of my brother-in-law, who I can yet regard with feelings of kindness in spite of the difference of our opinions."

"But Sir Walter may be too proud to accept a favour from one against whom he has fought."

"Nay," answered Lord Arden, "his opinion may greatly alter when he sees that the cause he once supported is lost for ever. Besides, you possess his fondest affections, and for your sake, my dear sister, I would fain hope to see him yield when further opposition must be useless."

"In all other things he might yield to my entreaties," answered Lady Eveline, "but he is too mindful of his honour to turn against the Lord Protector, from whom he has received so many favours. But hush! Maud returns, and

we shall now hear whether she has been able to obtain any information from the man who has undertaken to convey you from this coast to Holland."

The girl of whom she spoke now entered the room, and having first secured the door to prevent intrusion, announced to her mistress in a whisper that she had failed to obtain an interview with the smuggler, as both Sir Walter and the steward were concealed in the shrubbery, evidently watching for somebody whom they suspected to be concealed about the premises. Startled by this intelligence, Lady Eveline communicated the fact to her brother, who was hastening to the window, when she earnestly implored him to reflect upon the peril he would bring upon himself if he should be seen by any of the persons who were employed in watching about the place.

"Remember, my dear brother," she added, "that everything will now depend upon your own prudence; for were you to be seen, nothing that I could say would prevent the immediate intrusion into this room of those who are bent upon your destruction."

"But the chances are that the man who was to have assisted me has been discovered, and if so, he will, to save himself, betray the fact of my being concealed in this house."

"I don't think there's much fear of Mark Bentley," exclaimed the girl, "for he owes a grudge to Sir Walter, and would not do anything to oblige him even if he were to be ever so well paid for it. In short, he has not yet forgotten the imprisonment that master gave him, and I've been told there are people who have heard him say he would rather lose his right arm than put it forth to serve a man who has proved himself to be an enemy."

"Are you sure Mark is near the house?" asked Lord Arden.

"I know he was a very little while ago."

"But he may have found that he was likely to be seen, in which case it is only natural to suppose he would leave the place before mischief came of it."

"I know not how that may be, my lord," answered the girl, "but I should think it more likely that he has concealed himself somewhere near till he sees the coast clear again. By-and-by, I shall be able to venture out again; and if I should see him, I suppose I may say that your lordship will embark to-night, if there is any probability of making sure of your retreat?"

"You may," exclaimed Lord Arden, "and tell him at the same time that I will double his reward if he prove faithful to the duty he has taken upon himself. Not that I expect much honour from the man, for he belongs to a class of persons who seldom keep a promise, unless they are certain of receiving a great benefit from it."

"Do you think then," asked Lady Eveline,

"that he will be villain enough to betray his trust, after having undertaken to convey you beyond the reach of the danger you are threatened with?"

"If I thought there was a certainty in it, I would not, of course, place any reliance in him," answered his lordship. "I shall not, however, be unharmed; and should any treachery be intended, he will discover to his cost that I am determined to sell my liberty dearly."

"You seem to have your doubts of the man?"

"Which is scarcely to be wondered at," he replied, "seeing that he belongs to a class of persons who are bound by no feelings of honour."

"Then why trust him?" asked Lady Eveline.

"Because I am so situated that I have no other prospect of escape."

"Nay, you can remain here till the search after you begins to relax, and then means may be thought of to secure your retreat to a place of greater safety. You shake your head doubtfully, my dear brother; but for all Sir Walter's prejudices against the enemies of the Commonwealth, I believe he would rather run almost any risk than hazard the life of one who he knows is so dear to me."

"Do you think I should act prudently in trusting to him?"

"Assuredly you would."

"Well, my dear Eveline," he replied "I will not doubt your word upon the subject though I am still of opinion that he would rather be influenced by what he conceives to be his duty, than by his own inclination to save the life of your brother. Besides, it might incur his severest displeasure were he to discover that you have concealed me in his house; and I would rather run the risk of being taken than do aught that might give rise to his anger against yourself."

"But," she replied, "Sir Walter Amyot is of too just a nature to blame me for sheltering a beloved relative, when he would do precisely the same thing, were he unfortunately placed in the same situation that I am."

"Have you so soon forgotten that he has formed a rooted dislike to me?"

"I am aware of the prejudice you speak of," she replied, "but nothing will ever convince me that he would give you up to the government when he knows the fearful consequences that would follow. Sir Walter is, I am aware, stern in his republican opinions; but never would he refuse his hospitality, even though it might be to one against whom he has been opposed in the field of battle."

"Then why," asked Lord Arden, "has it been considered necessary to keep me out of his sight?"

"Because I was anxious to save him from the blame of having, of his own accord, given shelter to one who is charged with being opposed to those who are now in power," answered Lady Eveline. "At present, no blame can be attached to him, even if your sojourn here should ever be discovered, for if the fact were by any chance to become known, I would confess that all the blame of your concealment was my own, and endure any punishment they might think proper to award for performing an act of duty and humanity."

"Let us hope you will avoid the suspicion," exclaimed Lord Arden, "for however vigilant your husband and his steward may be, I am determined to make an attempt to escape before this night comes to an end. There must surely be some way to evade those who Maud says are watching on the terrace; and it shall be tried, even though I lose my life in the attempt."

"And that you certainly would, my lord," cried the attendant, "unless means can be found to draw them away from the place where they were concealed. Something may perhaps be thought of to do that; and if we can only succeed, you may reach the sea-side and embark on board the vessel before any alarm is given."

"Then go, my good girl, and see what can be done," exclaimed Lady Eveline. "Observe whether they leave the place where you saw them lying in ambush; and should they leave the place, hasten here immediately, that we may take our steps accordingly."

Quickly obeying the instructions of her mistress, the girl left the room, and Lord Arden and his sister remained in a state of anxious suspense to await the result of her present mission.

We will now return to Sir Walter and his steward, the former of whom it will be recollected had been induced by Jabez Sneed to proceed to the terrace, where he was informed a stranger had been seen lurking about as if for some improper motive. They remained crouching behind some shrubs for rather more than a quarter of an hour, and as no one was to be seen, Sir Walter began to grow impatient, and expressed his determination to abandon a project which seemed likely to end in disappointment.

"Take my advice, sir, and stay where you are a little longer," whispered Jabez Sneed, "for I have no doubt some one is prowling about the place, and as it cannot be for any good purpose, it will be better that we seize the person and make him account for himself."

"But the man—if one has been here," answered the knight, "has taken alarm and fled."

"Never fear but he'll return presently," exclaimed Jabez Sneed, "for no doubt it is the person that I suspect has been concealed here these three or four days past."

THE WIFE'S SECRET.

"Psha! the suspicion is a groundless one."

"Indeed, Sir Walter, there can be no mistake in what I have told you," answered the steward, "for if no one had been concealed in the Bower Chamber, why should my lady have been so anxious to exclude you and everybody else, except Maud, from that particular room? You still seem to doubt me, but the fact could be easily proved if you would only insist upon your right of entering that apartment."

"I see how it is," exclaimed Sir Walter, "you are only anxious to be revenged upon Lady Eveline for the discovery she has made; and in order to carry out your purposes, you would fill my mind with suspicions for which there is no foundation."

"Ah," returned Jabez Sneed, with a hypocritical whine; "when too late, you will discover that I have only been anxious to preserve you from approaching danger."

"What danger do you mean?"

"That of being discovered in the act of suffering an enemy of the Commonwealt to conceal himself in your house."

"Do *you* dare assert such to be the fact?"

"Far be it from me Sir Walter, to believe that you would admit a traitor to enter your doors," answered the steward; "but there may be others who have deceived you; and if it should hereafter be discovered that there was good ground for my warning, you would be severely censured for having neglected to cause a search to be made."

"Which search you are only anxious for in order to annoy Lady Amyot for the course she has adopted against you."

"Nay," answered Jabez Sneed,, "there is no need for me to seek revenge, for it will be sufficient satisfaction for me by-and-by to hear you acknowledge that my accounts are fair and honest to the very letter. At present the case is only one of suspicion, but soon my character will be as irreproachable as it was formerly."

"Hush!" whispered Sir Walter, "I think I hear footsteps at the farther end of the terrace."

"So do I," answered the old man, "and a few moments longer will serve to prove that I have not brought you here for nothing. But we must remain quiet where we are a little while, for I have stationed three or four of your servants behind yonder buttress, and they have my orders to seize the first stranger they may chance to see prowling about the terrace."

A perfect silence then succeeded, during which Sir Walter Amyot listened with the most intense anxiety for any sound that might serve to convince him that he had been deceived by Lady Eveline. Presently afterwards the footsteps were again heard approaching; and as the persons came nearer, the steward, dark as it was, could see that they were dragging with them some person whom they had just found lurking in the neighbourhood of the terrace. These men were the servants whom the old man had stationed there, and the heart of the old man leaped with joy at the thought of having succeeded to the utmost of his wishes; but great was his disappointment, when he perceived that the person they had in custody was only Mark Bentley, the smuggler, whose vessel had been lying for the last three or four days off that part of the coast. Sir Walter Amyot also recognised the man who had made himself so notorious throughout that part of the country; but feeling somewhat relieved at the discovery that he was not the person whom he had almost expected to meet, he inquired what motive he had for intruding himself within his private grounds.

"If you would know my reason for being here," answered Mark Bentley, without losing any of his usual coolness, "I must confess that I am not able to give a very satisfactory one. However, it may be sufficient to say that I came here for no worse a purpose than to enjoy a walk upon your noble terrace."

"To enjoy which luxury, knave, you must have climbed over my wall," exclaimed Sir Walter.

"That's very true," returned the fellow; "but in these times of equality I thought I could do so without giving any offence."

"This insolence shall not pass without due punishment," exclaimed the knight, and then addressing himself to his servants, he added, "I hold you all answerable for this man's safe custody. Bear him to the dungeon beneath the hall, and to-morrow I will question him further as to the motive that brought him here."

"What right have you to deprive me of my liberty?" demanded Mark Bentley, struggling in vain to release himself from those who had laid hands upon him."

"The same right," answered Sir Walter Amyot, "that you had to intrude upon my private demain. Besides, your character is well known throughout the country, and I may fairly presume that you came here to commit some act of depredation."

"I am no robber."

"That must be inquired into."

"Well, you'll do as you please about it, exclaimed Mark Bentley, "but as there is no proof of my dishonest purpose, I shall soon be restored to liberty, and it will then be for me to consider how I ought to revenge myself for this injustice."

"You are insolent, fellow."

"And you, Sir Walter Amyot, are unjust What! is a man to be shut up in a dungeon for no worse a crime than that of being found walking on your terrace?"

"How de I know that it was not your intention to rob me?"

"Had such been my purpose," he replied, "I should not have been here at this early hour in the morning. Besides, you know well enough the sort of life I lead, and we smugglers are not the people to commit a paltry theft, even though it might be to keep them from starving."

"Ask him if he had not an appointment here," interposed Jabez Sneed, whose suspicions now began to take another turn.

"What right have you to suppose that I had any other purpose than the one I have mentioned?" exclaimed Mark Bentley, who had suspected the old man's words. "I have told the mas'er why I came, and surely that ought to satisfy the servant."

"But Sir Walter may too easily give credit to the excuses of a crafty knave," answered the steward.

"Don't talk to me about craft and all that sort of thing," returned Mark Bentley with a sneer, "for, unless the reports that are abroad are false, you have not much to beast about on the score of honesty. Now I—though knave you are pleased to call me—am open and straightforward in my doings; but you cheat those that employ you, and tremble, like a coward as you are, when people have wit enough to discover your evil deeds."

"A truce to this," interrupted Sir Walter, impatiently, "for I would yet spare you, Mark Bentley, from the consequences of your intrusion upon my premises at an hour when your motives may well be challenged. Remember, sirrah, I am in the commission of the peace, and it is my duty—as it may be my inclination—to question those whose actions are open to suspicion."

"And what is there to suspect me of?" demanded the smuggler.

"Much that you may find it difficult to answer," returned Sir Walter; "and, amongst other things, my steward believes that you are here to assist in the escape of one or more of the royalist fugitives who have been at hide-and-seek since the last skirmish in which they were so signally defeated."

"Your steward, Sir Walter," retorted the smuggler, "would do well to mind his own business instead of attributing motives to me that may never have entered my head. In short, I have told you why I am here, and, to suit your own purpose, I am to be shut up in a dungeon for thinking I had a right to enjoy an evening walk upon your honour's terrace."

"Considering what has passed between us," returned Sir Walter Amyot, "I should have thought you would rather have shunned me than thus throw yourself in my way."

"Believe me, Sir Walter, this meeting with you was one of the very last things I could have wished for."

"And depend upon it you shall have yet further reason to be sorry for it," answered the knight, "for now that I have you in my power, I shall not part with you till I know the real purpose that brought you here. If your motive is an honest one, confess it at once, and if the explanation proves to be a satisfactory one, I will immediately order you to be set at liberty."

"Whether you do so or not will not matter much," retorted the smuggler, "for I have been guilty of no crime that will authorize you to deprive me of my liberty, and a few days more or less, will compel you to let me go, however much it may be against your wish. And when once I am free, Master Jabez Sneed had better look to himself, for I shall have a reckoning to settle with him that I believe he will not be exactly prepared for."

"What means this threat?"

"Time will show you what it means, Sir Walter," answered the smuggler, "for I seldom fail in my promise whenever it is made, and your steward shall acknowledge that I have said nothing but what I mean from the bottom of my heart. It is through him that you are here watching me to-night, and as I have been deprived of my liberty he may make sure that I shall not rest till I have had satisfaction."

"Beware what you say," exclaimed Sir Walter, "or I may deem it my duty to keep you closely confined to your dungeon till I am assured that these bad feelings have been forgotten."

"Forgotten! is a man ever likely to forget such an injury as this? But Master Sneed ought to know by this time what he has to expect, for I am a desperate man, and one of those who love revenge as dearly as I do my existence."

"You hear him, Sir Walter," exclaimed the old man with alarm, "and I earnestly implore that you will take means to secure me against his evil designs."

"What evil designs do you suspect me of?" demanded Mark.

"There can be but one construction put upon your words," said the steward. "You will seek my life if my master does not take measures to prevent your villanous purposes."

"You may make yourself quite easy upon that point," returned Mark Bentley, "for I desire not to hazard my life by taking yours. There are, however, other ways to have my revenge, whilst I can at the same time steer clear of any very serious consequences."

"What is the use of these threats," demanded the knight, "when it is so easily in your power to obtain immediate liberty?"

"What would you have me do?"

"Confess your motive for coming here to-night."

"That I have done already," he replied, "and you choose to doubt my word, though I can give no other answer."

"You have not given me a true one."

"How know you that?"

"Why, it is not likely you came here merely, as you say, to enjoy a walk upon the terrace. In short, you are endeavouring to deceive me, and it is now time that you should yourself be undeceived. There is some plot going on in which you are concerned; and in order to put a stop to it, I have ordered you to be taken into custody by my people, and you are not likely to be set free again till the whole truth has been fully and fairly confessed."

"How will you be able to make me do that unless you have the power to put me to the torture?"

"Time will best show how you can endure the trials of a long and painful confinement," answered Sir Walter Aymot.

"Then I must appeal to some one that is superior to yourself."

"Which will do you little service," replied the knight, "for you are suspected of being one of those who are employed in assisting the royalist refugees to escape from England. That alone is sufficient to justify me in the course I am about to adopt; and if any change were to be made, it would only be to remove you from my custody to that of others who would perhaps be less lenient than I am."

"I am not guilty of what you accuse me."

"Prove your innocence, and you shall be immediately set at liberty."

"It is rather for you, Sir Walter Amyot," exclaimed the smuggler, "to prove that I am engaged in assisting the escape of the fugitives."

"Which may be easily done, I believe," answered the knight, "for my steward suspects that one of them is now secreted about these premises, and, if such should be the fact, there is good reason for suspecting that you are here to aid him in embarking on board your vessel, which I have observed for some days past hovering about our coast."

"Is there, then, anything remarkable in my lugger being in the neighbourhood of my home?" asked Mark Bentley.

"I have good reason for believing there is," answered the knight; "and if my suspicions should prove to be correct, you must expect to receive the full punishment that is usually awarded to those who are detected in affording aid to those who have appeared in arms against their country. At present you will remain here in my custody, but in a few days I shall receive orders from the government relative to your future disposal."

"Don't make too sure of keeping me in confinement," exclaimed Mark Bentley, "for when my comrades hear that I am a prisoner here, they'll make a desperate attack upon your house to release me from the trouble I have fallen into.

"Let them do so," answered Sir Walter, "and I can promise them a warmer reception than they expect. One way, however, remains for you to get out of this dilemma; so tell me what you know about the person supposed to be concealed in some part of my premises."

"I know nothing about any one being here," he replied; "and, even if I did, I am not scoundrel enough to betray a poor devil, whose only crime consists in having fought on the side that he believes to be the right one."

"Then, you will be guilty of treason and must be dealt with according to your deserts."

"These threats will not serve your purpose," he replied; "for I have lived in danger so long, that I can now look it in the face without fear. As for your dungeon, I can put up with it for a few hours, because I know my friends will not suffer me to be a prisoner longer than need be, and, perhaps, you will have reason to repent having deprived me of my liberty without just cause."

"Your threats will not deter me from doing my duty," exclaimed Sir Walter Amyot; "for those who are suspected of lending their aid to the enemies of this country shall receive little quarter from me whenever proof of their guilt can be brought forward. You will, therefore, be conveyed to the dungeon; and, with as little loss of time as possible, I will communicate with those in authority as to what place shall serve as your future prison."

On a sign being given by the knight, Mark Bentley was dragged by main force from the terrace and conveyed to the place where he was to remain for the present. So far Jabez Sneed had succeeded to the utmost of his wishes, for he knew that Sir Walter would continue his inquiries, and there now seemed to be every certainty that Lady Eveline would be found to have assisted in the concealment of one of the fugitives. In short, he saw that revenge was in his grasp, and that the moment of his anticipated triumph had nearly arrived.

CHAPTER X.

CIRCUMSTANCES APPEAR TO CONFIRM THE ASSERTIONS OF THE STEWARD.—DISCOVERY OF A STRANGER IN THE BOWER CHAMBER.— INTERVIEW BETWEEN HUSBAND AND WIFE.—LADY EVELINE ASSERTS HER INNOCENCE, BUT REFUSES TO AFFORD AN EXPLANATION.—ARRIVAL OF A PARTY OF SOLDIERS, AND THE ALARM CONSEQUENT UPON IT.

ALMOST convinced that some one was concealed within his house, Sir Walter Amyot turned away and was about to leave the terrace, when at that moment an exclamation of triumph was heard from the steward. Turning to ascertain the occasion which had given rise to this, Sir Walter looked in the direction towards which the old man pointed, and beheld a sight that filled him with horror, and at the same time served to confirm the evil reports which had been so often whispered in his ear. Through the spacious window of the Bower Chamber, he could distinctly see Lady Eveline enter the room with a young man upon whose arm she leant, and whose gay habiliments denoted that he belonged to the royalist party. As they advanced across the room he threw his arm fondly round her waist, and as she released herself to depart, she suffered him, without seeming to resent the act, to imprint a kiss upon her lips! Who this stranger was, Sir Walter could not see, for his face was constantly turned away from him; but all the worst reports of the steward appeared to be confirmed beyond the possibility of a doubt, and with a groan of anguish the unhappy husband sunk senseless upon the ground. In this condition he was conveyed into the mansion, and the servants having been dismissed, Jabez Sneed applied such restoratives, as soon brought the now wretched Sir Walter to a recollection of the harrowing scene which had snatched from him the last hope to which he had clung.

Having seen his master in some degree recovered, the steward lost no time in referring to the fact which they had both witnessed; and in a tone of exultation that he could not conceal, asked if anything more was required to prove that his former assertions were correct. Sir Walter was now indeed an altered man; he could no longer believe in the fidelity of his wife, whom he had loved with the tenderest affection; and groaning aloud in the fulness of his despair, he acknowledged that she was no longer worthy the love he had once bestowed upon her. Now then the steward felt that his triumph was complete; but concealing his exultation as well as he could, he asked Sir Walter, with an appearance of affectionate concern, whether he would not at once take the necessary steps to bring punishment upon the man who had brought shame and dishonour upon a once happy family.

"Ay," answered the knight, in hollow accents of despair, "the veil has at length been removed, and it is now due to myself that I should lose no time in bringing retribution upon those who have so wantonly trifled with my feelings. The villain, whoever he may be, has thrown himself into my power, and never again shall he leave my house until they drag him away to suffer the doom which has been passed upon all those who are known to have taken part in the insurrection that has lately been suppressed."

"At all events," exclaimed Jabez Sneed,

"you have the satisfaction of knowing that he cannot leave the place, for a watch is kept all round the house; and as Mark Bentley has been secured, there is no likelihood of any attempt being made to assist his flight."

"Have any of my people seen him so as to know who he is?" asked Sir Walter Aymot.

"I believe not," answered the old man, "for he has purposely avoided us, and our only chance of discovering who he is will be to search the Bower Chamber without delay. You shake your head at my suggeston, sir, but if any time is lost, the stranger, whoever he is, will find means to make his escape from the house."

"How can he do that when there are so many people constantly watching round the place?"

"Ah, Sir Walter," replied the steward, "but the girl, Maud, is cunning enough to deceive us if we are not very careful, and there may be means to secure the escape of this cavalier even when we think he is most completely in our power. It shall be no fault of mine, however, if he get away, for I have sworn deadly hatred against all who take part with the royalists, and this one, who has destroyed your happiness, shall receive the punishment he so justly deserves."

"Do nothing without my orders," answered Sir Walter, "for I believe you are actuated chiefly by a feeling of revenge against Lady Eveline, for the charge she laid against you."

"Indeed, sir, you are mistaken," exclaimed the steward, "for I am sure you will acquit me of all blame when my accounts have been carefully examined; and it will be seen that her ladyship has accused me without having any foundation for doing so. And with respect to the person she has concealed here without your knowledge, I can have no ill-feeling against him save that which every man ought to entertain towards those who are plotting to overthrow our government."

"Leave him then to me," answered Sir Walter Aymot, "for it is I who have most cause to look upon his presence here with suspicion, and with me must be the responsibility of giving him up to those against whose authority he has raised himself."

"May I not venture to observe that not a moment is to be lost if you would prevent his escape."

"I will take care that no one leaves the place unless he is known to those who are on the watch," answered Sir Walter; "and the stranger, whoever he may be, shall not elude the justice from which he is endeavouring to fly. There must, however, be no imprudent haste, for if it should chance to be known that his presence here has been discovered, means will be devised to secure his retreat, and we shall find ourselves defeated at the time when we believe ourselves to be most certain of capturing him."

"Will you then suffer her ladyship to remain in ignorance of the discovery you have made this evening?"

"No," answered Sir Walter. "I will presently tax her with the baseness she has been guilty of, and the probability is that we shall part never to meet again."

"That is to say," exclaimed Jabez Sneed, "if she does not find means to convince you that you are labouring under some delusion."

"What possibility is there of her doing that," asked the knight, "when my own eyes have witnessed the profligacy of her conduct?"

"Oh, sir, women are never at a loss for an

[MAUD PERCEIVES JABEZ SNEED AT THE BOWER CHAMBER WINDOW.]

expedient, when they want to deceive a too confiding husband."

"Think you not I may have formed a too hasty conclusion?" asked Sir Walter.

"I know not how there can have been any mistake," he replied, "for you yourself saw her with a stranger, and it appeared that they are upon terms of the greatest familiarity."

"True," sighed Sir Walter, "and yet I cannot quite give up all hope that she may be able to explain the affair with some degree of satisfaction."

"All I hope is, that you may not have deceived yourself," replied the steward. "For my own part, I see only one conclusion that we can possibly arrive at, and no explanation that can be given will ever convince me that you have not been cruelly deceived. Nay, if you have nothing worse to complain of, her ladyship has acted with the greatest imprudence in giving shelter to a man who has sided with the enemies of the Commonwealth."

"There, she has, indeed, given me just cause for displeasure," replied the knight. "That she has concealed a known foe of the state cannot be doubted; and yet, perhaps, it is scarcely to be wondered at, when I remember that she and all her family were staunch royalists, even at a time when the cause of monarchy in this country was in a most hopeless state."

"That," exclaimed Jabez Sneed, "would argue little in your favour, if it should ever come to the ears of our rulers, that a foe has found refuge in your house."

"How is it to be known unless you are about to turn traitor against your master?"

"Which I need hardly say is not very likely after the many years I have passed in your family. But my lady has very probably endeavoured to prejudice you against me; and if so, I must be content to remain under your suspicion until I am able to clear myself triumphantly."

"A few hours will serve to go over your accounts," answered Sir Walter Amyot, "and if your own assertions of innocence are borne out by facts, you cannot possibly suffer from the imputations that have been made against your character."

"In the meantime, sir, I suppose you will question Lady Amyot upon the subject of the discovery you have made this evening? There can be no doubt of a man having been in the Bower Chamber; and by taking prompt measures alone can you hope to arrive at the truth which has been purposely withheld from you."

"That there are grounds for suspicion," answered Sir Walter, "it is unfortunately impossible to deny. Upon further reflection, however, I am inclined to hope her ladyship will be able to explain that which at present seems to be so full of suspicion. At all events, black as circumstances appear to be, I will not judge her with the harshness that you do."

"Then, beware, or she will yet find means to procure the escape of her gallant."

"How!" exclaimed the knight, "do you dare, without further proof, to accuse your mistress of infidelity?"

"I know not how any one can believe otherwise, after the scene we witnessed this evening," replied Jabez Sneed. "You have yourself seen that a stranger is secreted in the apartment which has been devoted to her own use;

and that fact is sufficient to convince me that her seeming affection for you was only assumed in order that the secret might not be revealed. You, however, seem to believe that the matter can be easily explained, and it therefore only remains for me to pursue my inquiries till I have ascertained what it is that has made so free with your hospitality."

"At least you will abstain from further interference till you have received my orders?"

"In all other matters you shall not find me disobedient to your commands," answered the steward; "but in this case I am bound by the duty I owe to my country to deliver up any one that I have reason to believe is a foe to the Commonwealth. This I shall certainly do, Sir Walter; and therefore the stranger, whoever he is, will have but little chance of getting out of the house without discovery."

"In that case," exclaimed the knight, "I will lose no time in seeing Lady Eveline, and questioning her upon the subject that has filled my mind with such deep affliction."

"And do you not expect that she will deceive you as she has done before?" asked Jabez Sneed.

"Of that I shall be best able to judge when I have had my interview with her upon this painful subject," answered Sir Walter. "At present, it must be confessed, that there is too much reason to believe that she has abused the confidence I placed in her; yet it is still possible that she may be able to explain away much that just now affords you an opportunity of speaking injuriously of her."

"Can she deny that she has been seen in company with a stranger?"

"That she cannot do," answered the knight; "but still I would put the most favourable construction upon the circumstance till she has had an opportunity of stating who the person was, and why he has been admitted to my house."

"Humph!" ejaculated Jabez Sneed, "and she will have small powers of invention, indeed, if she be not able to find an excuse for one who will not believe that she is capable of doing a wrong action. However, I have discovered quite enough to convince me that something is going on here which ought not to be; and as it is my duty to do so, I shall, with all deference to yourself, employ my next few hours in endeavouring to discover who the fugitive is, and to give him up to those whose duty it is to secure all those who have been in arms against our government."

With this menace the old man turned away, and Sir Walter Amyot, after considering within himself for a little while, proceeded to another part of the house, where he found Lady Eveline, who, only a few minutes previously, had left her brother with a promise of returning to him as soon as she could do so without the risk of her being seen. The alarm of the wife may be better imagined than described when she saw the fearful alteration that sorrow and jealousy had wrought in the countenance of Sir Walter since the last time they had met. She eagerly demanded of him what had happened in the interval; and without alluding at present to what he had that night witnessed he informed her of the rumours he had heard of her infidelity, and of the credit which, from the fact of her keeping the Bower Chamber closed against him, he began to attach to those reports. Unable to divulge a secret upon which the life of her brother depended, and which she had solemnly sworn to keep from every one, Lady Eveline could only asseverate her innocence and implore Sir Walter to judge less harshly of her conduct till circumstances should permit her to reveal that which at present must remain locked up within her own bosom. This appeal was, however, made in vain, for everything seemed to confirm more and more the fact of his having been dishonoured; and with an emotion that he could not control, he informed her that he now had evidence of her having concealed a man in the apartment from which, for the last few days, he had been excluded. As Lady Eveline heard these words, she became deadly pale, and sinking into a chair, remained for some moments with her face covered with her hands. Sir Walter Amyot watched her with an angry countenance, and after a brief silence, demanded whether she could refute the accusation which had been made against her.

"I could answer all to your satisfaction," she replied, "but there are circumstances which for the present restrain me from doing that which would remove the foul stain that has been thrown upon my character."

"There is some secret, then, which is kept from me?" he exclaimed.

"There is," she replied, "and you have only to bear with me a few hours longer, when I shall be able to refute the fearful calumnies which have been raised to my prejudice."

"Why are they not refuted now?" demanded, sternly, "when by doing so you might restore to yourself that love which for the present has been forfeited by your own imprudence."

"Ask me not for an explanation at present," she exclaimed, "for even to regain your regard I dare not break the solemn oath that binds me to secrecy."

"Do you deny that a man is concealed in the Bower Chamber?"

"I do not deny it," she tremblingly replied.

"Tell me, then, who he is."

"Ask me a few hours hence, and I promise to remove this fearful suspicion."

"Nay, I demand instant admittance to the chamber."

"Do not urge me further upon this painful subject," she exclaimed, "for indeed there is a reason for my silence, which, not even your threat can overcome. The demand I make upon your patience will be but of brief duration; and when the time comes that I may reveal the secret, you will acknowledge that I have been cruelly wronged by the suspicions you have given utterance to."

"If you have suffered wrong," he replied, "you have only yourself to blame for it. I have asked but for an explanation, and even from your own words I should hear that which would exonerate you from all blame. Confess, candidly, then, Eveline; for the state of suspense in which your silence has thrown me, is so terrible, that I shall become mad under the reflection."

"Nay, you ask me that which is impossible."

"Will you accompany me to the chamber, that my doubts may be at once removed?"

"I cannot break the oath I have given," she replied; "but when once the person who has been concealed there has effected his escape, I will reveal to you everything that you desire to know."

"From what I saw of him through the window, I judged him to be one of the fugitive royalists."

"I confess it; for my promise extended not further than to conceal the name of the person who has been compelled by circumstances to seek shelter in our house."

"Know you not the danger in which I should be involved, if it happened to be known that one of the cavaliers has been sheltered in my house from his pursuers?"

"I am but too well aware of the consequences."

"Yet you hesitated not to run the risk!"

"There was no alternative," she replied; "nor did I know that a refuge would be demanded till it was too late for me to refuse the application. Had I acted otherwise than I did, the unfortunate fugitive would, ere now, have been exposed to certain death from those who spare none that entertain views which are different to their own."

"Yet it was your duty," he replied, "as the wife of a republican, to assist in the capture of those who have been endeavouring to overthrow our present government, in order to restore monarchy as it existed a few years since. All those who favour the son of the late king, are declared to be traitors to their country; yet have you afforded an asylum to one whose escape may lead to the most disastrous consequences."

"Nay, he would rather perish than betray the name of those who afforded him shelter in his need."

"That may be, Eveline," exclaimed her husband, "but how can I reconcile it to my conscience, when I know that I am failing in my duty by harbouring one of the fugitives whom I lately assisted in defeating? Lead me, therefore, to the Bower Chamber, or at once proceed thither by yourself, and desire him to quit my house immediately."

" Would you have him leave the place, she asked, " when he would be certain to fall into the hands of those who are watching for him?'

" Whether he leaves now or at any other time, the same fate awaits him," answered Sir Walter, "for the man who was to have assisted in conveying him over the water is now a prisoner in my hands, and every chance of escape is, therefore, at an end. Jabez Sneed, too, is resolved to secure him; and within an hour or two from this time your secret will have been discovered, in spite of all the efforts you may make to prevent it."

" To Jabez Sneed I owe all my present difficulties," exclaimed Lady Eveline, " for I have incurred his displeasure, and it is the malice of that man which now pursues me."

" It may be so," replied her husband, " yet I cannot blame my steward, since he is doing nothing more than his duty in trying to cause the arrest of one of the men denounced as traitors and enemies of their country."

" Can you then be deceived by the villany of one whom I have so lately unmasked?"

" That he has betrayed his trust I have good reason for believing," answered the knight; " but I cannot blame him for doing that which I conceive to be his duty."

" Then you have given him permission to keep a watch upon the house, in order that my share in concealing a fugitive may be made known to the world?"

" How could I act otherwise," demanded Sir Walter, " when I have myself seen that one of the fugitive cavaliers has been permitted to conceal himself from those who are in pursuit of him? But be he who he may, even if he were my own brother, I would give him up rather than break the solemn oath which binds me to support our present government."

" At least, you will do me the justice to believe that I am not the guilty, faithless wife you just now thought me?"

" I would fain do so," he replied, " but I must have proof of your entire innocence before I can remove the impression which the stranger's presence here has occasioned. Till now I have never entertained a suspicion to your prejudice; and believe me, nothing can ever restore me to happiness till it has been proved that my evil surmises were without foundation."

" Am I indebted to Jabez Sneed for this charge?"

" Partly so," answered the knight, " but I myself saw you with a stranger; and the secrecy which has been observed, seemed to confirm that which it was torture to me to believe. The truth, however, shall not be long withheld from me, even though in the pursuit of it I should bring to the scaffold the man whom you have endeavoured to shield from the consequences of his own evil deeds."

" Alas!" sighed Lady Eveline, " was it an evil deed to draw his sword in the defence of a monarchy, which he has always regarded with the strongest affection?"

" But he advocates the weakest side," answered Sir Walter, " and, therefore, his conduct is less worthy of estimation, though it may appear to be romantic and worthy of admiration. But he has chosen to enter, unbidden, the house of one he must have know was an enemy, and he must take the consequences, whatever they may be."

" Would you refuse him your hospitality?"

" Under present circumstances I would," answered Sir Walter; " for the duty I owe to my country is far superior to any false notions of the laws of hospitality. In short, if he has not already left my house, I shall give orders for an immediate search to be made, in order that it may not be said hereafter that I have given aid and protection to one whom it was my bounden duty to deliver up to justice."

" You would not hesitate then to yield up an unoffending man to the sanguinary laws of the country?"

" Why should I hesitate when it is the only course that I have to pursue?" demanded Sir Walter Amyot. " As a soldier of the republic, I should be acting the part of a traitor were I to connive at the escape of a foe, when I have good reason for believing that one is endeavouring to shield himself beneath my roof, from the consequences of his own want of fidelity to those who are now in power."

" And would you not afterwards repent having been the cause of sending a fellow-creature to the scaffold?"

" Why should I repent," he asked, " when the thing was forced upon me by the indiscretion of the person who throws himself in my way? Had he been wise he would have avoided this house, instead of courting danger, when it might have been so easily avoided."

" How could it have been avoided," asked Lady Eveline, " when the pursuers are scattered about all over the country, and no chance of escape remained, except that of throwing himself upon the generosity of a known enemy? He has, however, committed a fatal mistake, which no one regrets more than myself, since I have myself to blame for not having taken more care to prevent this discovery."

" But since the discovery has been made," exclaimed Sir Walter Amyot, " would it not be as well for you to tell me the name of the man you have received beneath my roof?"

"Can you ask me to break the solemn vow of secrecy that I made?" asked Lady Eveline.

"The vow was improperly given," he replied, "and therefore may be broken without doing much violence to your conscience. You will, however, act as you please in the matter; only remember, I am resolved to capture the intruder, and yield him up to those who are looking out for all those who have hitherto escaped the search that has been made for them."

"Nay," exclaimed the unhappy Lady Eveline, "let me implore of you to spare one who has never injured you, and would have given his assistance had your positions ever been reversed."

This appeal, however, earnest as it was, made no impression upon the heart of Sir Walter Amyot, for everything seemed to confirm more and more the suspicion of his having been dishonoured; and he was about to leave her, when Dingle entered the room to announce that a party of horse-soldiers had just arrived in search of a royalist officer, who was suspected to be concealed somewhere about the house.

"What is the name of the commanding officer?" asked Sir Walter Amyot, after a moment's pause.

"Colonel Latimer."

"I know him only as a brave soldier," answered the knight, "and one who will perform his duty faithfuly, even if it had been his own brother that he had been sent against. What number of men has he under his command?"

"About a score, I believe."

"And Colonel Latimer—where is he?"

"In the court-yard giving directions to the men, some of whom have already began to search over the premises."

"Tell the officer I will see him as soon as it is convenient to himself," exclaimed Sir Walter; and then, as the domestic left the room, he turned towards the terrified Lady Eveline, and continued in a tone still tremulous with emotion: "You have heard what the man says, and must by this time be convinced that all further secrecy would be in vain. A discovery must now take place, and it is for you to reflect whether it would not be better to make a confession to me at once, than to risk a public exposure by the discovery of this stranger by those who have been sent hither in search of him."

"Have I sunk so low in your estimation hat you will not assist in preventing such an exposure?"

"How can I do so," asked her husband, "when these troopers have been sent here for the purpose of searching my house? Is it not enough to be suspected of assisting the escape of a royalist, but I must also bring upon myself the anger of the Protector, by opposing myself against those who have a duty to perform?"

"But surely Colonel Latimer will not doubt your word if you assure him that you have not concealed any person in your house?"

"And how can I utter such a falsehood when it is scarcely an hour since I saw in your Bower Chamber, one who, by his garb, I know belongs to the party of cavaliers whom we have lately routed?"

"Will you not bear with me, then, till I am released from the pledge that seals my lips?"

"You know, Eveline," he replied, "that it has ever been the chief pleasure of my life to indulge your wishes on almost every occasion on which they have been urged. Now, however, I have a duty to perform to my country, and I will not fail in it, let the consequences be what they may to the fugitive whose escape you would favour."

"Then you will not remonstrate against the search that they are about to make over your premises?"

"Why should I do so," he asked, "when I know the place is polluted by the presence of a man who has brought dishonour upon my name? I have been treated with a want of confidence that I never could have suspected you of; and it is, therefore, hardly to be supposed that I will grant a favour which ought not to have been asked."

"At least, then," replied Lady Eveline in a low faint tone, "you will except the Bower Chamber from the visit of these troopers?"

"I can make no exception," answered her husband, "and even if I did so, Colonel Latimer would be the more likely to suspect that in that apartment is to be found the man he has been sent in quest of. Besides, I have nothing to fear from what is about to take place; for though a stranger may be discovered secreted in your private apartments, the disgrace will fall more heavily upon yourself than it will upon me. Reflect, therefore, before it is too late, whether it will not be better to confess to me at once who it is that you have so assisted, and your motive for committing an imprudence that might have ended in my ruin."

"Impossible."

"Is that your final answer?"

"What other can I give, when my word has been pledged to say nothing which may endanger one who has thrown himself upon our protection? I ask your patience but for a few hours, yet you have refused me the most important boon I may ever have to request."

"That is because it is one that never ought to have been made."

"Yet a few words of explanation will convince you that I am not so guilty as you imagine."

"Then why defer the explanation for a moment?"

"I have already told you that I have no alternative."

"The excuse is one that I cannot listen to," exclaimed Sir Walter Amyot, 'for a wife should make no promise of secrecy when her husband has a right to expect perfect sincerity and submission from her.'

"Have I ever been disobedient before?"

"There was never so much reason for your candour as upon the present occasion," answered the knight, "and whatever sufferings you may have to endure have been caused by your own want of proper caution. I have asked nothing unreasonable, yet you refuse compliance at the hazard of your future happiness."

"Defer your questions till to-morrow," she replied, "and there is little doubt that I shall reply to them, if not to your satisfaction, at least with sufficient fulness to exonerate me from any act of great culpability. I have done nothing more than a sacred duty called upon me to perform; and though the world may condemn me for having afforded aid to one who is called an enemy, it will at the same time do me the justice that my honour, which is dearer to me than life itself, has not been in the slightest degree compromised."

"If it must needs be so, I will wait the time you have asked for," exclaimed Sir Walter Amyot; "but, remember, I will ask no favour from Colonel Latimer, nor will I even solicit him to except the Bower Chamber from the search he is about to make."

The conversation was here interrupted by the sound of approaching footsteps; and presently afterwards the officer who had been last named entered the room.

CHAPTER XI.

THE PARLIAMENTARIAN OFFICER AND HIS MISSION—LADY EVELINE'S ALARM IS STILL FURTHER INCREASED—THE SEARCH IS POSTPONED TILL THE FOLLOWING MORNING.—MAUD SUGGESTS A PLAN FOR THE ESCAPE OF MARK BENTLEY.

"I am sorry, Sir Walter Amyot, to have come here on so unpleasant a visit," said Colonel Latimer, after having introduced himself, "but you know the duty we soldiers owe to our superiors, and it is therefore needless to say that, however disagreeable the task may be, I am bound to execute it to the very letter."

"Colonel Latimer has no need to offer any apology for performing his duty," answered the knight, "though I could have wished there had been no reason for supposing that a traitor had found refuge beneath my roof. In fact, every facility shall be afforded you, and I immediately place my whole house at your disposal, until you have satisfied yourself of the truth or falsehood of the rumours that have been spread abroad, relative to this fugitive

from justice. By-the-by, I have not yet been told the name of the person you are seeking for."

"That is the most disagreeable part of my mission," answered Colonel Latimer, "for the person is no other than Lord Arden, the brother, I believe, of Lady Aymot."

"My brother!" exclaimed Lady Eveline with alarm.

"Ay, my lady."

"Is he then suspected of being in this neighbourhood?"

"It amounts to something more than suspicion," answered the officer, "for it is well known that he has been lurking about the neighbourhood, and the last reports we heard stated that it was almost certain he had obtained admission into this house."

"From whom did you obtain this information?" demanded Sir Walter Aymot with surprise.

"From your steward—Jabez Sneed."

"Jabez Sneed may have been mistaken in his surmise."

"With respect to the person he may," answered the colonel; "but he is so positive that one of the fugitives is in your house, that I had no alternative but to come hither and satisfy myself whether any such person has thrown himself upon your hospitality."

"And do you," asked Lady Eveline, "upon the report of a treacherous servant, venture to take a step that cannot but cast suspicion upon the honour of my husband?"

"In the performance of my duty," answered Colonel Latimer, "I cannot show favour even to those who are nearest and dearest to me. That such a person may be here is quite possible, but even if we should find him it would afford no proof that Sir Walter Aymot was cognisant of the fact. However, I have no wish to create confusion in your family at this late hour of the evening, and I will, therefore, postpone my search until to-morrow, when it can be done without any one in the house being aware of the purpose that has brought me hither."

"Then you are not afraid that the person—if there be one here—may effect his escape?"

"Care has already been taken to prevent his escape," answered the officer, "for my people are watching round the house, and any attempt to leave the house would be followed by his instant death. My orders are strict, and I have no choice but to perform my duty, however painful it may be to do so."

"And all this," cried Lady Eveline reproachfully, "has been brought about by the malicious reports of an ungrateful servant!"

"The report has been confirmed by others," answered Colonel Latimer, "and under all the circumstances, I found myself compelled to adopt the course I have. At the same time believe me, I feel the deepest sorrow at being the cause of grief and uneasiness to the wife of one who has distinguished himself so highly in the service of his country."

"And what would be his fate," she asked "supposing such a person should be found ?"

"That would depend on circumstances."

"If he were to yield without resistance ?"

"He would be treated with every consideration, and probably his life would be spared on condition that he left this country under a promise never to return to it. If, however, it should prove to be Lord Arden, I would not answer for the consequences, because he is well known to be one of the most active of those who are endeavouring to restore monarchy in England."

"Alas !" sighed her ladyship, "is there any crime in advocating a cause that we consider to be a just one ?"

"I will not go so far as to say there is any crime in it," answered Colonel Latimer, "but such persons are dangerous to the peace and safety of their country, and it behoves those who are in power to prevent the mischief that may be anticipated. The Protector has found it necessary to support his authority with a firm hand, and those who endeavour to involve the country in another civil war can scarcely expect to be treated with leniency when they fail in their mischievous designs."

"But those who are still loyal to their king believe they are only performing a duty in endeavouring to restore him to the throne from which he has been forcibly driven."

"These would be dangerous words if uttered by a man," replied Colonel Latimer, "but they may be safely uttered by the wife of an officer who has so often proved his devotion to the cause which has driven the Stuarts into exile. Sir Walter Amyot knows the difficulty in which I am placed, and whatever may be the result of this visit of mine, he will at least exonerate me from all desire to annoy or perplex him. In short, there is reason to believe, that by some means or other a Cavalier has found refuge here, and I should have been forgetful of my duty had I omitted to make the necessary inquiries as to the truth or falsehood of the reports that have been spread abroad."

"But, as I said before," answered Lady Eveline, "the reports which caused your visit, were circulated by a domestic, who desires to revenge himself for having been accused of acts of dishonesty."

"Yet he may have spoken the truth," replied the officer, "and it was at any rate my duty to convince myself whether he has stated that which would lead to the discovery of a fugitive enemy. Be it understood, however, that I do not for a moment imagine that you are in any way connected in assisting the escape of any of the people who have been accused of fomenting disaffection in the country."

"But Jabez Sneed has said as much."

"I am aware of it," answered Colonel Latimer, "but you may suppose how little reliance I place in that part of his information from the fact of my not commencing a search through the house till the morning. Had I believed you guilty of such an act, it would have been my painful duty to place you under restraint until the affair would be properly inquired into."

"He has dared then to accuse me of having afforded a refuge to one of those who have been compelled to seek safety by hiding themselves wherever they can find a resting-place?"

"He has."

"Does he venture to say that he has any proof ?"

"He boldly asserts that a search through these premises will soon convince me that he has spoken nothing but the truth. Nay, he has gone so far as to name the particular room in which the fugitive is secreted."

"What room did he speak of?"

"One that is called the Bower Chamber."

"And yet you have not proposed going there ?" exclaimed Lady Eveline.

"To-morrow will be soon enough for my purpose," answered the officer, "for I have placed so many persons round the premises to watch who comes in or goes out that any attempt to escape would be certain to end in defeat. In the morning, however, I shall thoroughly search every portion of the premises; and should any suspicious person be found, I shall immediately convey them to London, in order that no delay may take place in the trial. In the meantime, Sir Walter and yourself will pardon me for taking up my quarters here for the brief period that it will be necessary for me to remain."

"I should have been glad had your visit been occasioned by a different object," answered Sir Walter Aymot, "but under any circumstances I cannot be otherwise than pleased to meet with a comrade in arms who has proved himself so zealous a defender of our republic. By-the-by," he added, during the pause that followed, "I forgot to mention that at an early hour this evening we arrested a man that was lurking about these grounds, and who I have reason to believe was looking for some one who is endeavouring to leave our coast for some part of the continent."

"Is the man known ?"

"Perfectly well."

"What business does the fellow ?"

"That of a smuggler; and if reports are to be believed, he is one of the boldest that infest our neighbourhood."

"Is he still in your custody ?"

"Yes, I have ordered him to be confined in a dungeon that is beneath my house."

"To-morrow I will see the man and question him upon the object that brought him here," exclaimed Colonel Latimer. "He may be able to give us some important information about the fugitives; for I suppose he will not be proof against the temptation of a bribe, if a sufficiently large one is offered to him."

"The man is far more stubborn than I expected to find him," answered Sir Walter Amyot, "for neither threats nor promises seem to have the least effect upon him."

"Then we must try what imprisonment will do, since it is necessary that we should discover the retreat of all the fugitives, in order that we may obtain future peace for the country. These smugglers, indeed, are generally found to be actively engaged in assisting the royalists to escape from the country; and it seems to me that we may obtain some important information from the man you have taken into custody. Let him, therefore, be well guarded, that he may have no chance of making his escape from the dungeon you have confined him in."

"I have already given orders to that effect," returned the knight, "and two of my men servants are so placed that it will be impossible for him to leave his prison till he does so with my permission, which will not be given until he has answered all questions to my entire satisfaction."

"Are there any other persons," asked Colonel Latimer, "whom you have reason to believe are likely to assist in effecting the escape of the person I suspect to be concealed here."

"I know of none," answered the knight, "unless, indeed it may be some of the comrades who have by this time learnt the fate of Mark Bentley, the man I have been speaking of. They are desperate enough to attempt anything, though I fancy they will meet with a repulse, now that we have so many persons who are determined to prevent the escape of any one who may have come hither for the purpose of secrecy."

"Should any attempt be made," exclaimed Colonel Latimer, "we will give them so warm a reception that few would be left to carry back the news to their companions. We will have no mercy upon them, for my orders are positive, and I am determined to strike terror into the hearts of all those who would assist in carrying the fugitives to a foreign land."

"And it seems," answered Lady Eveline bitterly, "that you would also terrify those who are merely *suspected* of having connived at the preservation of one of these unfortunate royalists whom all ought to pity."

"Pardon me, my lady," he replied, "for though I must necessarily appear harsh, I am most anxious to discharge my duty with as much care and tenderness as possible. Indeed,

my own honour is at stake; and where I to show any remissness of duty, I should most deservedly bring upon myself the anger of those who have entrusted me with the task of routing the royalists from this part of the country. Sir Walter Amyot, at least, will do me the justice to admit that I was bound to make this visit, however averse I may have felt to disturb the peace of his family."

"You had no other alternative to pursue," answered the knight, "and I have reason to be rather pleased than otherwise at your having come here, because I shall be able to prove to the satisfaction of everybody that I knew nothing of any one being concealed beneath my roof. Nay, more, on further steps being taken, it will be seen that I am anxious to afford all the assistance in my power towards apprehending any enemy of his country, even though he should be allied to me by the closest ties of family or friendship."

"This night then we will keep watch together," exclaimed Colonel Latimer, "for there shall be no escape suffered through any carelessness or negligence of my own. With your leave we will occupy the library, which, if I am not mistaken, overlooks the terrace and the adjoining plantation, so that an important portion of your premises will be immediately under our observation."

"And what," asked Lady Eveline, "if you should see anything to lead to the supposition that the person you suspect is here is about to leave the place?"

"In that case I should raise an alarm, and the pursuit would follow so immediately that there would be no probability of an escape."

"And you would do so though the person had never done anything to injure you?"

"Personal injury is the last thing I have to do with," answered Colonel Latimer, "for the duty I owe to my country and the government I serve, should be the only guide in a situation like the present. Even friendship must give way under such circumstances, and should be sacrificed rather than have afterwards to endure the reflection that I have been guilty of an unworthy act."

"Lady Amyot knows the duty of a soldier," exclaimed Sir Walter, "and whatever happens she must set all down to the score of a stern necessity. If she has been rash enough to afford protection where she ought rather to have given an offender up to justice, she must not blame those who resolve to act in a case of this difficulty with firmness and determination."

"Has Colonel Latimer any sufficient ground for believing that I have acted in the manner you have supposed?" she asked.

"He could not have avoided taking this step," exclaimed her husband, "for when information reached him that one of the fugitive was supposed to be here, he had no alternatives but to satisfy himself of the truth or falsehood of what he had been told."

"I have uttered no word of complaint," answered Lady Eveline, "but I still think might have received the story with some feeling of suspicion, seeing that it proceeded from one whose assertions were hardly worthy of credit."

"Believe me, Lady Aymot," replied the officer, "I place no reliance whatever on anything reported by your steward; but as the assertion has been made, I am bound not to let it pass by without making a full and searching inquiry. That all will end to my satisfaction I have no doubt; and it is my most earnest wish

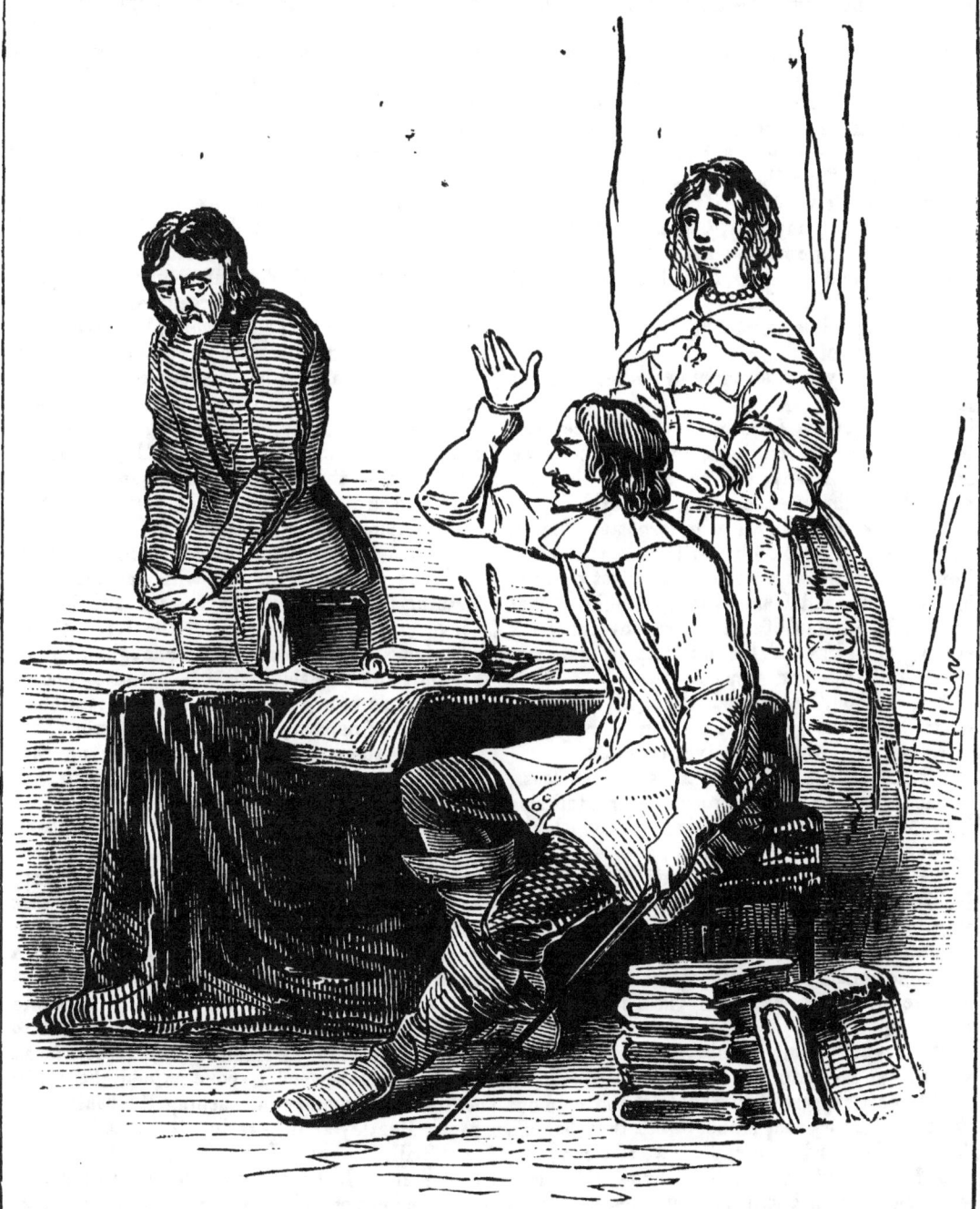

[SIR WALTER AYMOT EXAMINES THE ACCOUNTS OF JABEZ SNEED.]

that I may have to report at head-quarters that no royalists have been sheltered beneath your roof."

Having pronounced these words with more courtesy than he had hitherto observed, Colonel Latimer accompanied Sir Walter Amyot from the room, and Lady Eveline was left to ruminate in solitude upon the dangers with which her brother was threatened. To procure the safe removal of Lord Arden seemed to be impossible, for every avenue appeared to be closed against him, and to attempt an escape under such circumstances, would expose him to the certainty of being captured by his enemies. In the midst of these melancholy reflections the faithful Maud entered the room, and having first ascertained that no one besides her mistress was present, she ventured to announce in a whisper, that she was going to visit Mark Bentley, and devise means for his escape from the dungeon.

"It would be in vain to make the attempt," answered Lady Eveline, "for both my husband and Colonel Latimer are going to keep watch all night, and numbers have been placed round the house, with orders not to let any one pass in or out until questioned as to who they are, and what their business is!"

"I know it, my lady," exclaimed the girl, "but Tom Dingle has promised to lend me his assistance, and we shall find him very useful in an affair of this kind."

"Do you think he may be depended on?"

"I'm sure of it."

"Perhaps you are rather prejudiced in his favour?"

"I don't think I am, my lady," exclaimed Maud, "for the truth is, we quarrel often enough to lead any one to suppose that we were the bitterest enemies in the world."

"Lovers' quarrels are soon forgotten, Maud, and then they become better friends than ever. You seem, however, to place the fullest reliance in this man, and I am willing to believe that he would be faithful if there were any chance of serving the cause of his mistress in this moment of distress and suspense."

"A method," answered the girl, "has already been thought of, and Tom is ready to begin as soon ever he receives orders."

"What chance is there," asked her mistress, "that he will be able to procure your admission into the dungeon in which this Mark Bentley is confined?"

"Why, my lady," whispered Maud, again looking round to satisfy herself that no one was listening, "as good luck will have it, the two men that are placed as a guard over Mark, are uncommonly friendly with Tom, and I believe he could persuade them to do almost anything."

"Except letting their prisoner escape," sighed her ladyship.

"I don't suppose they would let the man out wilfully," answered Maud, "but they happen to be rather fond of a cup or two of strong ale, and Tom Dingle is going to invite them into his room, so that I may have an opportunity of entering the dungeon without being seen."

"How can you do that when the door is locked, and Sir Walter himself holds possession of the key?"

"Ay," answered the girl, holding up another key, "but I happen to have a duplicate of it, and if I can only see the coast clear, I'll soon find means to let Mark Bentley out of his prison."

"How can that be done," asked Lady Eveline, "when the house is surrounded with watchers, who will permit no one to pass without questioning them as to their business?"

"Why, the truth is, my lady," she replied, "I was once shown a secret passage that leads from near the dungeon, under the moat, to the wood on the south side of the hall. Every one seems have forgotten it but me, and I have a great notion that it will serve our purpose admirably."

"Is the passage open from end to end?" asked Lady Eveline.

"Sufficiently so for us to pass through without any very great difficulty," she replied.

"Then why cannot my brother escape by that way at once?" demanded her ladyship.

"Because nothing is in readiness for him," answered Maud, "and it would be almost certain destruction if he were to venture out of this place till there is a boat ashore ready to convey him to the vessel which is waiting for him. And that, my lady, I hardly need tell you, cannot take place till Mark Bentley is able to go and make the necessary arrangements."

"And are you sure he will remain faithful to his promise after so narrow an escape?"

"I think there can be very little doubt of it," she replied, "for he will not receive a farthing of the promised reward till he has conveyed Lord Arden beyond the reach of his enemies. So there is reason enough why he should remain faithful to his promise, and as matters are now going on he has no occasion to be afraid of being interrupted in his work."

"Are there no persons watching on that part of the coast where the vessel is lying?"

"At one time there were several," answered Maud, "but they have grown tired, I suppose, for they have all come closer to the hall, because they feel pretty certain that his lordship is concealed somewhere in the house. Jabez Sneed has taken care to impress them with that notion, and so far he has done us a good service, for whilst these people are keeping close watch and ward in the immediate neighbourhood of the place, I shall be able to lead his lordship, by means of the subterranean passage, to the wood I spoke of, and there will then be no difficulty in reaching the boat which Mark Bentley will have in readiness."

"Still," sighed Lady Eveline, "I cannot help fearing lest some mishap should occur."

"I hope you will get rid of that notion as soon as possible," exclaimed the girl, "for I feel quite satisfied that with a little care everything will go on as smoothly as possible. There's not a soul in the place, except Tom Dingle, that knows anything of this secret, and I have confidence enough in him to believe that he would rather suffer his tongue to be cut out than say a word that would make me angry with him for ever."

"Are you sure," asked Lady Eveline, "that the secret passage you speak of is not watched?"

"There was no one near it half an hour ago when I went to see how the land lay," answered the girl.

"Do you know where the steward is?"

"Prowling about the place and looking as savage as possible," answered Maud.

"And still," observed her mistress, "as determined as ever to revenge himself by causing the arrest of my brother?"

"By the appearance of him," answered Maud, "I should say that his temper has not been at all improved by the disappointment he has suffered. That, however, matters very little, for I shall be too cunning for him yet, and I feel quite certain that he will soon have more cause than ever to vow vengeance against me."

"Beware what you do, my poor girl," exclaimed her mistress, "for we have already seen enough of that man's revengeful feeling to know that he will stop at no act of villany when his own evil passions are to be gratified. I tremble at the bare thought of his even suspecting that you are concerned in shielding a cavalier from those who are in search of him."

"Why, he suspects that already," answered Maud, "and no doubt I should before now have felt the effect of his vengeance but that he knows I am rather a favourite of your ladyship's, and he cannot tell how far his interfering with me may give rise to the displeasure of Sir Walter."

"Perhaps he is only waiting for an opportunity."

"That is exactly what I have thought myself," answered the girl, "and I have taken good care that he shall not see anything in my conduct to lead him to guess what is actually passing in my thoughts. He is always peeping and prying about in the hope of making some notable discovery; but he has a cunning one to deal with, I can tell him, and will find out by and-by that he has been outwitted by a woman."

"And then," sighed Lady Eveline, "you will be made to suffer for your faithful conduct to your mistres."

"And what care I for anything may happen," exclaimed Maud, "so long as I know that I have spared you the pain of seeing your only brother taken away a prisoner from your presence?"

"But you may yourself be made to suffer for the faithful discharge of your duty to me."

"I can bear anything," answered Maud, "so that we can only frustrate the designs of Jabez Sneed, who has too long carried on his shameful doings without a check."

"But a check will soon be given to him," answered her ladyship, "when Sir Walter has convinced himself of his dishonesty by a careful examination of his accounts. Then, at least, we may hope to see the house freed from his presence, and he will sink into the contempt he so richly deserves."

"There would be some consolation in that thought," returned the girl, "if it were not that I fancy Sir Walter will always remain prejudiced in his favour. The old man boasts of having been a long time in the family, and he still has a strong hold upon the feelings of his master, though everybody else can see plainly enough that he ought to have been dismissed from the house long ago."

"My husband will soon be able to judge for himself," exclaimed Lady Eveline, "and when once he sees through the baseness of his servant he has confided in, his anger will know no bounds."

"Is is not strange," asked Maud, "that the accounts have not yet been examined?"

"At present," answered her mistress, "Sir Walter has had little time to spare for a task that will necessarily require a great deal of care and attention. The arrival of Colonel Latimer has taken us all by surprise, and till our house is cleared of the soldiers who accompanied him here, Sir Walter will be in no humour to attend to other matters."

"Are they likely to remain much longer, my lady?"

"I hope not," she replied; "but that will of course depend entirely upon circumstances. If my brother should fortunately escape, there will be no further necessity for the intrusion of these strangers here, and then, perhaps, we may we allowed to go on in peace and quiet as we did before the late outbreak. I am afraid, however, that my husband is angry with me for having been the cause of this unpleasant intrusion, and the thought of it makes me sad, even though I would fain appear cheerful."

"Ah, my lady," cried Maud, "this is a severe trial, indeed; but things may not be quite so bad as they appear to be, and I would have you take heart, since all the grieving in the world will not serve to make matters a bit the better."

"I have endeavoured to look forward to the best," answered Lady Eveline; "and have so far conquered my melancholy as to appear more cheerful than I really am. It was, indeed, necessary for me to do so, for Sir Walter observes me with a keen eye, and his suspicions would be easily roused, if he saw alarm expressed in my countenance at the arrival of these troopers in search of my fugitive brother."

"At least, my lady, I hope you are convinced that I will do all in my power to assist the escape of Lord Arden?"

"I am sure you will, my poor faithful Maud,"

she replied; "but when the danger is so imminent, I am afraid to hope anything even from your well-tried zeal in my service."

"Why should you give way to despair?"

"Because I know all eyes are upon us, and the least act of thoughtlessness would serve to convince those whom we wish to deceive, that the person they are in pursuit of is secreted somewhere within these premises."

"Why, they think as much as that already," answered the girl, "and yet we have contrived to keep him out of their sight."

"True, yet we may not be able to do so much longer."

"He must not be here much longer," said Maud; "and I think, with the assistance of the secret passage there is not much reason to fear that before daylight to-morrow his lordship will be on board the vessel which is to convey him to the opposite shores. If ever he reaches his place of his destination, it is to be hoped he will never again attempt to set foot upon his native land till the king returns by the unanimous call of the nation."

"Such a time I once looked for," sighed Lady Eveline, "but so little progress in the right direction has been made of late that I almost begin to despair."

"Well," answered the girl, "I don't pretend to understand such matters, but I have heard people say that the time will come when the king will be welcomed back by all Englishmen."

"How can that be expected," asked Lady Eveline, "when Cromwell is as firmly at the head of affairs as ever he was?"

"That may be all very true as far as *he* goes," answered the girl, "but I have heard say that his son Richard Cromwell is too quiet and easy a man to hold the same power that his father does, and whenever he succeeds to the Protectorate, people think the nation will be glad to make a change. You shake your head, my lady, and can see no hope of such an event taking place, and perhaps I was foolish to say what I have heard; but it was done to show you that there is still a chance of Lord Arden's return."

"If such should ever be the case," sighed her ladyship, "what would be the consequences to my husband, who took so active a part against the exiled king."

"As for that answered Maud, "his Majesty would have so much reason to congratulate himself upon his happy return, that he would hardly feel any revenge against those who followed the fortunes of Cromwell. Such, at least, is my opinion, and I hope your ladyship will pardon me for speaking my mind upon a subject that I had no right to mention."

"Your meaning was a good one," she replied, "and I should be ungrateful indeed to feel angered by that which was intended to raise me from the despondency into which I am too apt to fall. We will now, however, return to the subject of my brother's escape, for, till that has been accomplished, I can encourage no hope that a brighter prospect is before us."

"Your ladyship thinks, then," said Maud, "that I shall be able to extricate him from his danger?"

"So far as making every effort goes, I can place the most unbounded reliance in you," answered Lady Eveline. "That you will succeed however, is a matter of so much doubt and uncertainty, that I dare not hope for the success I am so anxious for."

"All will depend upon how far I am able to deceive the ever-watchful eye of old Jabez," exclaimed the girl, "since he is the only one that is likely to be lurking about the entrance of the passage."

"Is he aware of the existence of such a lace?"

"I should think he must be, from the long time he has been in the house," replied the girl; "but even if he is, I don't think there is much chance of his venturing into the passage."

"Why do you think so?"

"Because he is terribly superstitious, and the gloomy look of the place is quite enough to frighten a stouter heart than his."

"But if his suspicion should be roused," observed Lady Eveline, "his feelings of revenge towards me might urge him to do that which he would otherwise shrink from."

"Depend upon it, my lady, he will never venture to enter such a dark, horrible place as it is," replied her attendant.

"Yet it seems you have been there."

"So I have," she replied; "but it was only when I saw there was no other chance of Lord Arden's making his escape from this house; and to tell you the truth, I was glad enough to get out of it again, for there were plenty of rats scampering about, even if there were no worse company to be dreaded. However, be that as it may, I will act as the guide of his lordship, and glad enough shall I be to return with news of his having been able to get beyond the reach of his enemies."

"Alas!" sighed Lady Eveline, "how shall I ever be able to reward such generous devotion?"

"My best reward will be in the approval of my own heart," answered the girl; "for never can I forget the kindness I have ever received from my dear mistress. Oh! my lady, only let me see you once more cheerful in the certainty of your brother's safety, and I shall be as happy as the days are long;—that is to say, if we are well rid of Jabez Sneed, whose presence in the house is alone enough to give one the horrors."

"Leave the old man to the remorse that

must fill his heart when he has time and opportunity to reflect upon the evil of which he has been guilty," answered her ladyship. "Now he is exulting in the mischief that he thinks is about to fall upon me, but when he finds that all his base plots have been of no avail, he will repent that he has ever acted the part of a spy upon one whom he was bound to serve rather than to injure. Let this suffice you, Maud. And now, if you are indeed able to assist the escape of Lord Arden, let not another moment be wasted that may be profitably employed in his rescue."

"I go, my lady," answered the girl, "but it is in the hope that you will endeavour to console yourself with the reflection that I will suffer no opportunity to escape that may serve to relieve you from your terrible anxiety. If I succeed, I shall, indeed, be most happy; but should I fail in the attempt, it shall be no fault of my own that I do so."

Upon this, Maud left the room to go on the task she had volunteered to undertake. Lady Eveline, however, dared not venture to hope that her errand would prove successful;—she saw insurmountable obstacles in the way, and sat trembling, as she awaited the return of her faithful attendant.

CHAPTER XII.

THE STEWARD IS STILL BUSY AND INQUISITIVE.—MAUD PROVES MORE THAN A MATCH FOR HIM, AND HE IS AGAIN DISAPPOINTED.—HE MEETS SIR WALTER AMYOT, AND RENEWS HIS INSIDIOUS HINTS.—TOM DINGLE AND MAUD SET THEIR WITS TO WORK TO KEEP THE COAST CLEAR, AND A PLAN IS ARRANGED.

BAFFLED as he had hitherto been in the course he had been pursuing, Jabez Sneed was still determined not to let matters remain as they were. Every succeeding hour served but to increase his suspicions that a cavalier was concealed in the house; and feeling convinced that Lady Eveline had thus laid herself open to the censures of her husband, he saw no means so ready to accomplish his revenge, as to prove that she had afforded an asylum to one of the fugitives who had lately been routed in an attempt to overturn the then existing form of government. Could he but do that the bitterness of his hatred would be satisfied, and he saw no great difficulty in the way, now that a troop of parliamentarians had arrived for the purpose of apprehending all persons who had not yet succeeded in their attempt to leave the country.

Full of such thoughts, he made his way towards the Bower Chamber of Lady Eveline in the full expectation that something might arise to confirm that of which he was already almost certain. With slow and noiseless steps he crept along the corridor that led towards the apartment, now and then pausing to listen, and glancing round to observe whether any one was watching his progress. At length he came within sight of the room, and just as he did so, Maud came from it, closed the door quickly after her, locked it, and deposited the key in her pocket. All this was done in an instant, and the old man had not time to conceal himself before she hastened to the spot where he had paused, uncertain what to do.

"So, Mr. Jabez," she exclaimed, "you are well set to work, I'm sure, watching about the house, and creeping from place to place, as if you thought something very dreadful was going on. Pray, sir, what have you to say for yourself, or what excuse can you make for dodging my steps in the way you do?"

"Minx!" muttered the old man, "I have good reason to believe you are committing an act of treason against the state."

"Indeed! did you ever here of a woman plotting against the state?"

"Perhaps not," he replied, "but there are ways by which to assist those who are known to be enemies."

"And you think I am doing so?"

"I am sure of it."

"Explain yourself."

"It will be enough for you to do that when I have succeeded in what I am trying to do," he replied. "I have got my eye upon you, girl, and you must beware, or this wilful act of yours will bring you into more trouble than you perhaps anticipate."

"You are very kind, Jabez, to give me the hint," exclaimed the girl with a sneer; "but as I am not aware of having done any harm, I see nothing whatever to be afraid of."

"Then why don't you let me see whether anybody is concealed within the chamber you have just left?"

"Because the apartment belongs to my mistress," she replied tartly, "and I would not suffer even Sir Walter himself to go into it unless I had my orders to do so."

"Then you lay yourself open to suspicions."

"Very likely I may," answered Maud, "and what care I for the suspicions of such persons as you? I know my duty, Mr. Sneed, as well as you do yours, and am neither to be threatened nor coaxed by such as you, when my orders are that no one shall for the present enter the Bower Chamber."

"Which is a proof that some one is concealed there."

"Think just as you please about it," answered Maud, in a tone of indifference; "raise all sorts of stories to injure my mistress; but do not, at the same time, forget that you may by-and-by see bitter reason to repent the impertinence you have been guilty of. My lady is not yet quite so friendless as you imagine, and Sir Walter will not fail to punish those who have taken part in these unmanly attempts to bring her into trouble."

"Tut—tut," exclaimed the old man, "I am only performing my duty when I have reason to believe that the house has been made the refuge for one, if not more, of the fugitive malignants."

"Your suspicions are groundless."

"So you would have me believe," he replied, "but if there be any truth in your assertion, why do you not convince me of my error by throwing the room open for my inspection?"

"Because I don't choose to encourage impertinent curiosity," she replied, "and your conduct has not been such as to induce me to show you any favour."

"What complaint have you to make against my conduct?" asked the old man.

"They are so many that I have no inclination to enter into an explanation of them just now," she replied. "Another time you may perhaps hear more than will be exactly agreeable; and, depend upon it, whenever the opportunity does arrive, I shall not be very sparing. This much I will say, however—you have acted the part of a mean, paltry spy upon your mistress, who has never done anything to deserve such conduct from your hands."

"But consider my duty, Maud."

"If *you* had considered it," she replied, "you would not have stood in the disgraceful situation you do at present!"

"Would you have me remain silent when I have reason to believe there is at least one traitor to the country in the house?"

"Psha! 'tis a mere groundless suspicion."

"Prove it, girl," he exclaimed, "and I will at once own that I am in the wrong."

"How would you have me prove it?" asked Maud.

"By suffering me to enter the room you have just left," replied the steward. "Your frequent visits are not paid there so often for nothing; and when I suspect there's mischief in the wind, it's time I spoke out, lest my master should suffer through the indiscretion of his wife."

"What a pity it is, Jabez Sneed," exclaimed the girl, with marked emphasis, "that you have not always been as careful of the interests of your master."

"Hah!" cried the old man, "am I to be taunted by such as thee?"

"Ay, Master Sneed," she replied, "you must expect to hear the truth when you take so much pains to bring upon yourself the contempt of everybody. You want to pry into a secret that you have nothing whatever to do with, and I, for one, am determined that you shall continue to grope on in the dark."

"Prithee, maiden," exclaimed the old man after a pause, "how is it that I have brought upon myself your severe displeasure?"

"Humph!" she replied, "I should have thought there was no occasion for such a question."

"Why refuse me an answer?"

"Because none can be required, when you have only to ask your own conscience—that is to say, supposing you had such a commodity about you, Master Jabez Sneed."

"You are pleased to be caustic, girl," he exclaimed, "but luckily I am in no humour just at present to lose my temper on such frivolous grounds. It would be as well for you, however, to recollect that no good can possibly come from your being so severe, though you may materially serve yourself by answering the one or two questions I have to put to you."

"I dare say now," she replied, "you have not given up all notion of persuading me to turn against my poor mistress?"

"Understand me, Maud," returned the steward. "I have no wish to see you become a traitress to the Lady Eveline, who I still regard with all the reverence that is due to her; but you might confess to me what you know about the person who is concealed here, and I will undertake to say that no harm shall happen either to your lady or yourself."

"And pray, Mr. Sneed," she asked, "upon what authority do you presume to say that there are more persons in this house than ought to be here?"

"Psha! I am not bound to give up my authority," answered Jabez Sneed.

"Nor have you any right, sir, to imagine that I would make a confident of one who has a heart filled with nothing but mischief."

"Indeed, girl, you wrong me."

"So much the better for your own conscience, Mr. Jabez," she replied; "but it requires something more than your own bare word to convince me that you are not trying to do all you can to injure my mistress."

"Nay, I am only anxious to ascertain whether there are those in the house who ought not to be here."

"And what is it to you, even supposing your evil-minded suspicions were perfectly correct?" asked the girl.

"Why, in that case, Maud, I should be obliged to perform my duty, however painful it might be to myself."

"Painful? why the more mischief you could do, the more pleasure you would find it, I believe."

"There again you wrong me," exclaimed the steward; "for my heart knows no such feelings as you imagine."

"Then why have you taken so much pains to worm out an affair that exists only in your own imagination?"

"Because I know the danger that awaits all

those who venture to screen offenders from justice. Sir Walter himself would not give shelter to any of those who are the declared enemies of our republic; yet would he incur as much danger from the vengeance of the laws, even though he might not be aware of his wife having been rash enough to afford an asylum to any of the fugitives."

"Who besides yourself, Mr. Sneed, will ever dare say she has done such a thing?" she asked.

"There are many others who suspect it."

"Then all I know about it is, that they have not presumed to speak their mind as you have."

"Very likely," answered the old man, "and that proves that they are not quite so honest."

"Honest!" exclaimed Maud, sharply; "it will be time enough to boast about that when Sir Walter has examined your accounts and expressed himself satisfied with them."

"Ah!" muttered the steward, shrinking from the fixed look with which she regarded him; "you speak of that which you know nothing about. My accounts will bear the closest inspection, and so my master will acknowledge when he has an opportunity of going carefully through them."

"Which you may depend on it will not be long first."

"The sooner the better," he replied; "for no one can be more anxious than myself to put an end to the scandalous charges that have been brought against me. Is it to be borne that I who have spent the greater part of my life in this family, am to be at last accused of acting with duplicity and dishonour?"

"If you are able to clear yourself as easily as you say you can," exclaimed Maud; "I am sure no one will be better pleased to acknowledge your innocence than my mistress. She is not, however, apt to form her conclusions without sufficient grounds; and for my own part I am inclined to place every reliance in what she says rather than in your denial of it."

"That may be," he replied; "but for some reason or another, Lady Eveline is strangely prepossessed against me; and under false impressions, she has made an accusation that cannot be satisfactorily answered till her husband has devoted sufficient time and attention to the examination of my accounts. When that is done, there is little fear but he will do me the justice I expect."

"Perhaps if he does that," answered Maud, "he will not suffer you to remain much longer in his house."

"There, it strikes me," exclaimed Jabez Sneed, "you speak the wishes of your heart."

"Well, to tell you the truth, I do," she replied, "for when people are so mischievous, the sooner one gets rid of them the better; and all your actions have proved that you have determined to do all the mischief you can, unless care is taken to prevent it."

"'Tis false!" exclaimed the steward, "and even if there was any truth in what you say, there could be no wonder at my feeling aggrieved when I experience the consequences of the accusation that has been made against me."

"I know nothing about that, Mr. Sneed," answered the girl; "but this I do know—my mistress is not one who would bring a serious charge, unless she was quite able to substantiate it."

"So she may think, perhaps," he replied; "and I, on the other hand, shall be able to prove that she has afforded shelter and protection to at least one of the enemies of the republic."

"Pray, sir, how will you prove any such thing?"

"By conducting Colonel Latimer to the chamber that you have just now left," he replied.

"Villain! you do but deceive yourself," she exclaimed, "for, search the room when you may, you will find no one who ought not to be there."

"That we shall see."

"Ay, and great will be your disappointment when you discover that all your mischievous schemes have been thrown away."

"Girl, I am not sure yet that they will be thrown away."

"No," she replied, "but you will make the discovery by-and-by, and then it will be my turn to triumph in your disappointment. So take good advice, Mr. Jabez Sneed, and give up this villanous pursuit of yours whilst there is yet time to get yourself out of an awkward scrape."

"Not I," exclaimed the old man, doggedly; "I know the duty I owe to my master, and will not see him plunged into danger merely that a rebel to the state should be suffered to scape."

"Will nothing convince you of your mistake?"

"Nothing."

"Then you are an obstinate old fool for your pains, and will have no pity from any one, whatever may happen from it."

"Nay," exclaimed Jabez Sneed, "the obstinacy is rather on your side, for all this might have been easily avoided if you had suffered me to examine the Bower Chamber when I first spoke to you upon the subject."

"And why should I encourage impertinent curiosity?" she asked. "My mistress, for reasons of her own, ordered me not to let any person enter the room, which has been specially set apart for her service, and I know my duty too well to disobey her commands."

"It may be all very well to pass it over in that way," exclaimed the steward, "but your refusal was likely to give rise to all sorts of surmises, and I am not to blame for what has been done, when I had reason to believe some person was concealed there."

"What reason had you beyond your own suspicions?"

"Everybody in the house is talking about it."

"Indeed! then I think servants might find something better to do than to be prying into the affairs of their masters and mistresses. So you may take the hint if you please, for even if there were any secret, you would never be able to worm it out of me."

"Remember," he said, "any assistance you may afford will be amply rewarded."

"I daresay it would," answered Maud, "but neither you, nor your master himself will ever be able to make me unfaithful to my trust. So now, Jabez Sneed, I hope you see that it would be labour thrown away to press me any further upon the subject; and if you take my advice you will not trouble you head any more with an affair that don't concern you in the least."

Having uttered these words, Maud left the old man, whose rage and disappointment may be more easily imagined than described. In his own mind, however, he was more than ever convinced that his suspicions were correct, for the slight glance he had obtained of the stranger through the window was quite enough to urge him on in a pursuit that, if successful, would satisfy his deep feelings of revenge against Lady Eveline. Full of these thoughts, he made his way towards the garden, where he soon met with Sir Walter Amyot; who, full of perplexity and doubt, was wandering up and down one of the walks in anxious reflection upon the events which had occurred to disturb the usual serenity of his mind. So wrapped up was he, indeed, in his thoughts, that he was unconscious of the presence of Jabez Sneed till the voice of the old man broke upon his ear, humbly asking if he might be permitted to say a few words.

"Speak if you please," he replied, moodily; "but I can at once guess what you have to say to me."

"That is easily accounted for, Sir Walter," exclaimed the steward; "for you may suppose that I would not have disturbed you except to speak of the arrival of these troopers and the cause that had unfortunately led to it."

"Why," demanded the knight, sternly, "should you remind me of that which I would fain forget?"

"Pardon me, my dear master," answered the hypocrite, "but I am only anxious to spare you the affliction that must follow if it should be publicly known that Lady Eveline has assisted in screening a traitor from justice."

"And if any such an exposure should take place," demanded Sir Walter, "who shall I ave to thank for it but yourself?"

"Do you blame me for what I have done?"

"I do."

"Then it must be done without reflection," exclaimed Jabez Sneed; "for had a moment's thought been given to it, you must have seen that I had no other course to pursue. I knew the consequences that would fall upon yourself if it should be known that your house had been made a refuge for any of those who are fleeing from the offended laws of the country; and unworthy should I have been of your many acts of kindness had I remained quiet whilst you were exposed to danger."

"Nay, sirrah!" returned the knight, "you have been actuated more by a feeling of revenge than any service that you thought you were doing me. Nay, interrupt me not, for I know the blackness of your heart, and can see clearly that you are actuated in this affair by a fiendish desire to inflict a heavy injury upon Lady Amyot."

"Why should I endeavour to injure her, Sir Walter?"

"Because she has discovered your dishonesty, and made me acquainted with it."

"When the proper time comes, I can easily prove that I have been cruelly wronged," exclaimed the steward; "nay, even were it as you suppose, I can still justify myself for having made known my suspicions that the house contained those who ought not to be in it."

"Ay," replied the knight; "but villain as you are, you would have impressed upon my mind the lie that the person you suspect to be here is a rival to me in the affections of Lady Eveline."

"Was I wrong then," asked the hypocrite, "in endeavouring to preserve your honour from the taint of suspicion?"

"Who, besides yourself, dare suspect the honour of Lady Amyot?"

"I have not gone so far as to say she was guilty of any treachery towards you," exclaimed Jabez Sneed; "but you were yourself a witness that she was on familiar terms with this stranger."

"I was," answered the knight; "but on taxing her with it, she implored my patience for a brief period, and assured me that all should be explained to my satisfaction."

"Why did she delay the explanation?"

"I know not her reason, nor did I think it necessary to press her for one just then."

"So far you were considerate," answered Jabez Sneed; "and yet I should have supposed that the sooner she had satisfied your mind the better it would have been for all parties."

"She went so far as to tell me that she had been intrusted with an important secret that she dare not divulge just now."

"Methinks a wife should have no secret from her husband."

"In most cases that is true," answered Sir Walter, "but such is my confidence in *my* wife, that I can wait patiently till she finds herself able to afford the explanation. And, indeed, her conduct through life has been so loving and faithful, that I should ill deserve so exemplary a wife were I to suspect that she has now deceived me."

"'Tis most kind of you to place such unbounded confidence in her," exclaimed the steward ; "but it unfortunately happens that kindness is sometimes thrown away, though

n the present instance, we may hope that it has been properly exercised."

"Again you suffer your own evil feelings towards Lady Amyot to overcome you," said Sir Walter.

"Indeed, sir," he replied, " I have no evil feelings towards her, nor should I have ventured to say so much but that I thought I might give utterance to my fears without giving offence. And I believe the world will justify me for having done so when it is known that I had good reason for suspecting that a stranger was secreted in a chamber devoted to the use of her ladyship."

"Ay," exclaimed Sir Walter, "no doubt you will colour the affair highly in furtherance of your own ends; but though people may be deceived for a brief period, they will ere long be made to see that Lady Amyot's character has been traduced merely to satisfy the private malice of one who ought to have defended her from such vile assertions."

"We shall see about that when Colonel Latimer has made his promised search over the house."

"If Colonel Latimer has a spark of honour about him," exclaimed Sir Walter, "he will leave unsearched a room which belongs exclusively to her ladyship."

"But he must perform his duty."

"Which will be sufficiently done even though he excludes that one chamber from his search."

"So you may imagine," answered Jabez Sneed, "but as a soldier he knows that he is bound to obey his orders, however he may pain those whom he ranks amongst his friends. Besides, he himself suspects that one or more of the fugitive cavaliers are secret beneath this roof, and he dare not leave your house till he has subjected every part of it to a strict search. And surely Sir Walter Amyot will not be the man to throw any obstruction in the way when the enemy is to be routed?"

"I know my own duty, sir," replied the knight, sternly, "and shall perform it after my own fashion. There must, however, be some consideration shown towards Lady Amyot or I shall feel called upon to afford her the protection of a husband. And hark ye, Jabez Sneed, dare not to whisper any of your foul suspicions in the ear of Colonel Latimer, or I may hereafter punish you to the very fullest extent of the law."

"That is to say if you find there is any truth in the charge that Lady Amyot has made against me?"

"Ay," exclaimed Sir Walter, "you carry it off bravely, but where an assertion is so broadly made, I cannot do otherwise than give credence to it."

"Why, then, have you not before now examined the accounts which have been stated to be false?"

"Because I choose to bide my own time," answered the knight.

"Yet, in justice to myself, not a moment ought to have been lost when my character is at stake."

"Your character will not suffer much if your conduct has been as honest and straight-forward as you would have me believe," answered Sir Walter Amyot. "At present I have given no opinion either way, nor shall I do so till a thorough investigation has been made into the affair."

"And when that has been done," returned the old man, "you will see how unjustly I have been accused."

"I hope Lady Amyot may have fallen into some mistake," answered the knight; "but, to speak truly, I hardly see how that can be possible, when she has herself examined the accounts, and asserts that they contain many palpable false statements. The only thing, therefore, in your favour is, that she does not thoroughly understand such matters, and that you may be able to explain that which has led her into error."

"Which I believe will be very easily done when the time comes for entering into the matter," answered Jabez Sneed. "I do not, however, pretend to assert that it is impossible an error may have crept in, for Lady Amyot has refused to let me see the accounts since I delivered them into her hands, and I have, therefore, had no opportunity of correcting any mistake that I may have fallen into."

"Let not that trouble you," exclaimed Sir Walter, "for there shall be no unnecessary delay in the investigation, and you may depend I shall proceed in the matter without the slightest feeling of prejudice against you. So now leave me, and, as you value my future favour, dare not utter another word that may injure the fair name of your mistress."

There was something so resolute in the manner with which this was said, that Jabez Sneed immediately obeyed the command, and turning away, entered the house full of rage and disappointment at the result of his interview.

We must now follow Maud, who, after leaving the steward, proceeded in search of Tom Dingle, whose assistance she required to liberate the smuggler, upon whose aid the ultimate escape of Lord Arden so much depended. She found the object of her search alone, and having satisfied herself that no listeners were near, entered at once into the subject which had led to their meeting.

"If you expect either favour or kindness from me, Tom," she said, "you must now oblige me by doing all in your power to assist the escape of a certain person whose life will be endangered if he remains much longer in this house."

"What's all this mystery about a *certain person?*" demanded Tom Dingle, whose suspicions and jealousy had been excited by the frequent stolen visits of Maud to the Bower Chamber. "Tell me who he is, or I'll not stir a foot to lend you any help."

"You wont?"

"I'll not, so there's an end on't."

"Then you are an obstinate fellow for your pains," exclaimed the pouting girl, "and it would serve you right if I were to desire you never to speak to me again. However, I suppose I must humour you for this once, but it must be upon your solemn promise never to mention it again to anybody."

"Oh, I'll promise that," he replied.

"Well then," exclaimed Maud, "you must know that the person who is concealed in the Bower Chamber, is the brother of Lady Eveline, and as he happens to be a cavalier, he will be certain to be sent to the scaffold if he should unfortunately fall into the hands of those who have been sent here to search for him."

"Then you mean to tell me," returned Tom Dingle, "that it's no one I need be jealous of?"

"To be sure I do; so now I suppose you will have no objection in assisting me in effecting his escape?"

"Nearly all my objections are removed now," he replied; "but it is still necessary that I first of all ask if there is likely to be any danger to myself if I do what you have asked?"

"Not the slightest, I can assure you." answered Maud. "All you are required to do is to get into conversation with the two men who are watching at the dungeon door where the smuggler is confined, and to try whether they are not to be persuaded to leave their post for a little while just to take a cup or two of wine by way of passing off the wearisome task they have been employed upon."

"Never fear about their doing that," returned Tom, "for they are a couple of arrant topers, and will not refuse to drink with me if I only make them the offer."

"And can you manage to keep them in conversation for about an hour, do you think?"

"Two or three if you wish it," he replied, "for so long as there is plenty of drink, they'll not want to leave my company."

"And I may depend upon your keeping your promise?"

"Ay, that you may. But, I say, Maud, what tricks are you going to be up to next?"

"Why, I'm going to pay a visit to the smuggler in his prison."

"For what purpose?"

"To set him at liberty, to be sure."

"Humph!" ejaculated Tom Dingle; "he must have found great favour in your sight for you to feel so interested in his behalf."

"To tell you the truth, Tom," she replied "I care nothing about what may happen to the smuggler, but as it happens to be in his power to assist in the escape of Lord Arden, my lady's brother, I am anxious to set him at liberty as soon as possible."

"How can he help the gentleman you speak of?"

"I don't know that I am bound to answer all your questions," she replied, "but as you have promised to keep the secret, I don't mind telling you that he has engaged to take his

lordship in his vessel over to the opposite coast, and when that has been done, he may set all his enemies in this country at defiance.'

"All that may be very well," exclaimed Tom Dingle, "but what would happen to me where it to become known that I had a hand in setting Mark Bentley free?"

"Never think of that," answered the girl, "for Sir Walter, though he is obliged to appear anxious to secure those who have been compelled to flee their country, is by no means desirous that any of them should be taken through his exertions; and I may venture to say, that those who take the most active part in hunting out the fugitives will not be afterwards regarded with much favour."

"In that case," observed Tom Dingle, "what may our o'd steward have to expect after the pains he has taken to discover who it was that my lady concealed in her Bower Chamber? By-the-by, though, I believe Sir Walter Amyot was never very friendly towards Lord Arden, and perhaps he may be angry when he finds out that he has been suffered to make his escape."

"Never be afraid of that, Tom," answered the girl, "for though, as you say, he never liked his lordship, I believe he is the very last that would give him up to his enemies."

"How can that be when I have heard him say that he would not spare any of the cavaliers if chance should throw any of them in his way?"

"Ay," returned Maud; "but as it happens that Lord Arden is the brother of her ladyship, our master would rather sacrifice his own feelings than afflict her by surrendering into the hands of the government one who is so dear to her. Besides, I have been told that his lordship once saved the life of Sir Walter on the field of battle, and, surely, gratitude for that act of kindness would lead him to favour even an enemy in a moment of extremity like this."

"Gratitude is a very fine thing to talk about," observed the groom; "but it's very seldom thought of when most needed. However, as you say I am not likely to get into a scrape through doing a good turn for his lorpship, I'll see what can be done towards giving you an opportunity of entering the dungeon without the two sentinels being any the wiser for it."

"That's well said, Tom," she exclaimed; "and depend upon it, I'll not forget you for it by and by."

"Will you reward me for it?"

"To be sure I will."

"Then you must not go on continually postponing our marriage as you have done," he replied; "you must name the day as soon as I have performed the task you have imposed upon me; and then I shall think the service has been liberally repaid."

"We'll talk about that another time."

"Oh, but we must not confine ourselves to

talking," answered Tom Dingle; "for it strikes me there has been enough of that already, and that it's now time we should finish our arrangements."

"Surely, you would not have me leave my mistress, who has always been so kind to me?"

"Why, you can't want to stay with her all your life?" exclaimed her lover.

"I don't want to leave her at any rate," she replied; "especially just now, when she has so much need of some one to console her under her afflictions."

"There's no occasion for you to leave her," answered Tom; "for I don't mean to give up my situation here; and if her ladyship is as fond of you as you say she is, she will still keep you, rather than there should be a parting. So now, say how it is to be, for I'll not afford my assistance, unless you promise that there shall be no delay in our marriage after I have aided in effecting the escape of this Mark Bentley."

"Well," she replied, "perform your task to my satisfaction, and I will go so far as to promise that I will ask for no unnecessary delay. Indeed, my gratitude will be so great, that I don't know whether I shall ask for any delay at all."

"Then the bargain is made," exclaimed Tom Dingle, snatching a kiss from her rosy lips; "and now, since the bargain is signed, I'll go and see whether I can't persuade those two chaps to leave their post long enough for you to get the prisoner clear away."

Thereupon, he left her to go and put his plan into immediate execution, and was soon afterwards followed by Maud, who was resolved to watch them from a distance, in order that she might have the earliest intimation of a favourable opportunity.

———

CHAPTER XIII.

COMMENCEMENT OF TOM DINGLE'S STRATAGEM.—HIS PERSUASIVE POWERS PROVE TO BE IRRESISTIBLE, AND THE COAST IS LEFT CLEAR. — MAUD'S INTERVIEW WITH THE SMUGGLER, AND HIS ESCAPE FROM THE DUNGEON.

WHEN Love beckons on, who is there that can resist his power? Had this question being asked of Tom Dingle, he would have answered "No one;"—and he may be considered as some authority, for no sooner had he obtained a favourable reply from Maud, than he made the best of his way towards the place where the two sentinels were keeping guard over the prisoner. Unperceived by them, he paused for a few minutes, to consider the best way of accosting them, and, having arranged his plan of attack, he proceeded boldly with the task he had undertaken. Harry Simkins and Dick Crumple, the two men of whom we speak, soon perceived his approach, but not recognising him

at the moment, they shouted to him to stop, and raised their arquebuses to their shoulders, as a broad hint of what he might expect if he ventured any nearer. Thereupon, Tom Dingle burst into a violent fit of laughter, and having thus discovered who he was, professed a great deal of concern for the disagreeable task that had been imposed upon them, and proposed passing a little time with him, in order to cheer the loneliness of their situation.

"Humph!" exclaimed Simkins, "it's all very well to talk about cheering us up, Master Dingle, but if you had brought a bottle of brandy with you, we might have enjoyed ourselves, instead of shivering here like a couple of unfortunate devils as we are."

"Come to my room, just yonder," he replied, "and you shall both have as much drink as you like."

"Ah!" muttered the other, "it's all very fine to say so, when you know we mustn't leave our post."

"And why mustn't you leave it?"

"Because we are ordered to keep guard over the prisoner; and if he should happen to escape, we know what to expect."

"Poor fellow! he's only a smuggler," exclaimed Tom Dingle.

"Very true; but smugglers break the law; and this Mark Bentley has so long escaped justice, that Sir Walter is determined to hand him over to a magistrate to-morrow."

"Well, I suppose he knows best about it," answered the groom; "but for my own part, I don't see any great harm in a man dealing in goods that have not paid a tax. The brandy that we are going to drink presently is some that he gave me, and when you taste it, I think you'll say he knows what a good article is."

"Can't you bring it to us here?" asked Dick Crumple.

"No," he replied; "we must go and drink it in my room, I tell you."

"But we were told not to leave this place for a moment."

"What signifies their telling you so, when they had no right to give you such a disagreeable duty to perform? If they had asked me, I should have given 'em a plump refusal; for it's no joke to be pacing up and down this cold passage, when one ought to be comfortably in bed and asleep. So come along with me, my boys, and we'll make a jolly night of it, instead of being half perished, as you must be, if you remain here much longer."

"Suppose the man was to escape during our absence?"

"Impossible!"

"Sir Walter don't think it impossible," answered Simkins, "or he would not have set us here to keep watch."

"But common sense must convince you that there is no chance of his getting away," returned Tom Dingle; "is'nt he locked in the dungeon, and ain't Sir Walter got the key in his own possession in order that the prisoner shall not have a chance of escaping? So, as its all right, my lads, come with me to my room, and we'll have a jovial hour or two together, instead of being wretched and uncomfortable."

"Are you sure there's no trick intended?" asked Dick Crumple, whose suspicions began to be a little excited.

"Trick! what do you mean?"

"Why, I thought you might want to make us both drunk, and then there'd be a pretty fuss if it should come to the ears of Sir Walter."

"Do you suppose I'd be guilty of such a thing?" exclaimed Tom Dingle, with seeming vexation; "did you ever know me to be fond of playing tricks, or getting any of my fellow-servants into trouble? No, no, I have the kindest feelings towards you, my boys, and it was only out of pity for your uncomfortable condition to-night that I have proposed a way of making the hours pass more cheerfully."

"Well," answered Simkins, "if you mean it out of kindness I don't know, but we may as well do as you have said."

"Ah!" exclaimed his comrade, "and suppose Sir Walter should come and find us away from our post?"

"He is gone to bed."

"But Jabez Sneed is not, and we know what a habit he has of prowling about the house whenever he thinks there is a chance of any mischief being done."

"Jabez Sneed is not master here," answered the groom, "and between ourselves, the old man has quite enough just now to look after his own affairs, for people say he has been cheating Sir Walter for some time past, and if it should be found to be correct, we shall have the pleasure of seeing him kicked out of the house."

"Do you know where he is just now?" asked Crumple.

"In his own room I believe," answered Tom Dingle, "and a rare ill humour he seems to be in, too, for he had been talking to Sir Walter in the garden, and I suppose something passed between them that was not very pleasant to him."

"In that case," exclaimed Simkins, "he'll want to vent his spite upon some one, and no doubt he'll be this way presently to catch us if we should happen to neglect our duty."

"Let him come if he likes," answered Tom, "for we shall be sure to hear him the moment he enters the other end of the passage, so that there will be plenty of time for you to run out and take up your old posts again."

"Ay," returned the other, "but I cannot help thinking what a scrape we should get into if the prisoner happened to make his escape during our absence."

"Nonsense! how can he get out of the dungeon when he has been securely locked in? Besides, if there was a chance of his breaking through the door, it would be as well for you not to be near the place, for Mark Bentley is a terrible fellow when driven to extremities, and you might both of you be killed if any attempt were made to prevent his making his way out of the house."

This latter suggestion was not without the desired effect upon the two men, who, after having listened at the door to convince themselves that all was quiet, followed Tom Dingle to an adjacent room, where he placed before them the bottle of brandy he had promised. After having taken a glass or two each, their alarm for the safety of the prisoner began to subside, and thus an opportunity was afforded Maud to put into practice the plan she had formed. The quick ear of Tom Dingle caught the light sound of her footstep as she passed the room on her way to the dungeon, and fancying that his two visitors were rather suspicious that something was going wrong, he plied them with more liquor, and talked away to them in order to detain them till he was sure the scheme had been carried into effect.

"By-the-by, my friends," he said, "there has been a great fuss going on in the house about some one that is supposed to have been secreted in some part of the premises. For my own part I have not seen any person except those that have a right to be here, and I dare say you will both agree with me that there is no truth in the report which has been spread upon no better authority than that of the old steward, Jabez Sneed."

"But the old man may have spoken the truth for once," exclaimed Simkins, "and I for one am determined to keep a sharp look out, for I am not over-fond of these cavaliers, and the more especially as there is a large reward offered for the apprehension of them."

"Who do you suppose there is in this house," asked Tom, "who would conceal an enemy of the republic?"

"I don't mean to say anything against our lady," answered Simkins, "but we all know that she belongs to a royalist family, and there may, therefore, be some truth in what Jabez Sneed says."

"Jabez Sneed would say anything to revenge himself on Lady Amyot, now that she has detected his villany."

"Very likely," returned the other, "and yet there are many things that confirm what he has said. In the first place, what reason can her ladyship give for not allowing any one to enter the Bower Chamber?"

"Why, it's her own private apartment," replied Tom Dingle, "and I suppose she has a right to do as she likes about it."

"That's all very well," exclaimed Crumple;

"but if it was all right, she would throw the room open for every one to enter, if it was only to show that nobody is concealed there."

"And why should she do that unless Sir Walter desires her to do so?" asked Tom Dingle.

"Just for the sake of satisfaction, that's all."

"Satisfaction!" he exclaimed; "and who, I should like to know, has any right to suspect her?"

"I'm sure I don't want to believe that she would keep a secret from her husband that he ought to know," answered Simkins, "but there are some things that cannot be denied, and Jabez Sneed has sworn that upon looking through the window of the Bower Chamber he saw a man there, dressed in the gay garb of a cavalier."

"Do you believe him?"

"How can we help doing so," asked the man, "when Sir Walter himself saw the shadow of just such a person as has been described as he was passing along the terrace? That there is something in it I feel pretty certain, and it shall be no fault of mind if I don't find out the truth before long."

"Have you no fear, then, of offending our mistress?"

"I should be sorry to do that," answered the man, "but what can be done in a case like this, when there is a heavy punishment against all those who assist in concealing those who are looked upon as enemies of their country?"

"Come, come, old fellow," exclaimed Tom Dingle, "confess at once that you have got your eye on the reward that has been offered."

"Well, there's something in that, to be sure," he replied; "and who can blame me when, at the same time, I can do my duty and yet get well paid for it into the bargain?"

"So, then, you would not mind afflicting your mistress so long as there's money to be put into your pocket?"

"Why," he replied, "the truth of it is, somebody must get the reward, and I don't see why I should not have it as well as any one else. Besides, we have the authority of Sir Walter Amyot for apprehending any strangers that may be found lurking about the house, and it is our duty, you know, to obey his orders."

"Inclination, I rather think, is stronger than duty."

"Nay," answered Crumple, "I'm sure both of us would do anything in our power to serve her ladyship, and it would go to our hearts to wound her feelings if it could be helped."

"Hypocrites!" exclaimed Tom wrathfully. "how can you say such a thing when you are trying to do all you can to afflict her?"

"Oh!" returned the other, "then you confess there is some truth in the report that some one is concealed in the house?"

"How can I confess when I tell you I don't know anything at all about it?" demanded the groom. "Her ladyship don't condescend to make me her confident, and it's not likely that I should go prying into affairs that I have nothing to do with."

"But Maud is in her confidence though, and you may have heard all the particulars from her."

"If Maud has been trusted with a secret," he replied, "she is not quite so treacherous as to tell me or anybody else of it. And even if she had done so, I would have kept it to myself rather than Lady Amyot should be made unhappy through my means."

"Well," answered Simkins, "of course you will do as you please about it, but we are not bound to follow your example, nor shall we hesitate to secure the intruder if by any chance he should happen to come in our way."

"You will be spared the trouble," exclaimed the groom, "for now that Colonel Latimer has arrived here with his troops, he will take good care that the honour of making the discovery shall fall on himself. Not that he will find anybody, I believe, though he intends searching the house from top to bottom in the morning."

"Then you think the person, whoever he is, will be assisted to escape in the meantime?"

"I have told you that no such person as you suppose has been concealed in the house."

"Humph!" ejaculated Dick Crumple, "in that case a good many people must have been greatly deceived."

"No doubt they have been deceived," exclaimed Tom Dingle, "and it's not to be much wondered at either, for you have all been looking out for the reward, and were, therefore, willing to believe every idle story that has been flying about. As for no one being allowed to enter the Bower Chamber, there's nothing very remarkable in that, seeing that her ladyship has a right to show her determination when she sees such an anxious desire to be peeping and prying into the only room that she can properly call her own."

"For my own part," observed Simkins, "I should have thought she would have been glad to get rid of the suspicion at once, when it could have been done so easily."

"Ay," answered the other, "so you may think; she does quite right in saying that no one shall enter the room till she chooses to give permission. Sir Walter himself is quite willing that she should have her own way; and I don't believe that anything people may say will ever make him suspect that his wife would deceive him."

"Perhaps he will be convinced, though, to-morrow, when Colonel Latimer has searched the house."

"I tell you, neither Colonel Latimer nor

anybody else will ever find a stranger concealed here."

"How do you know that?"

"I don't pretend to know," answered Tom Dingle; "but from her ladyship's general conduct, I must give her the credit of believing that her actions are open and fair in all things. And it's pretty clear that her husband thinks so too, or he would have insisted upon going into the room before now."

"If he thinks so," answered Crumple, "it's no fault of old Jabez Sneed, for he has done his best to convince Sir Walter that something has been concealed from him that he ought to know."

"Ah!" exclaimed Tom, "but luckily he knows what a precious old scoundrel Jebez Sneed is, and most likely receives all his information at its just value. Indeed, it's hardly to be supposed that he would pay any attention to hints and insinuations of a man who has been detected in cheating him, and who has his own private revenge to carry out."

All this time Tom Dingle had been plying the liquor pretty freely to his two companions, and thus taking their attention from the object in which they had been engaged. In the meantime, making the best use of the opportunity which was thus given, Maud quietly proceeded in the task which she had at set herself, and having first ascertained that the two men were engaged in conversation with Tom Dingle, she hastened to the dungeon, the door of which she easily opened with the key with which she had provided herself. On entering, she again closed the ponderous portal, so that no suspicion might arise in the event of any person passing that way; and then rousing Mark Bentley, who was sleeping with his head upon the table, she informed him in a few hurried words that she had come to release him if he thought proper to make use of the opportunity she offered. For a moment or two he seemed to think that he was still dreaming; but at length, taking her hand, he exclaimed—

"What's the meaning of all this, my girl? You talk about me being at liberty to leave this place when I please, but for the life of me I can't understand why you have taken so much interest in my fate."

"Do not be deceived, Mark," she said "for what I do is by command of my mistress, who has desired me to arrange a plan for your escape from this house. I have obeyed her orders, and nothing now remains but for you to leave as soon as you like."

"Is there no trick in this?"

"Why should you suspect me," she asked, "when there can be no other wish than to set you at liberty?"

"Then of course I am expected to do some favour in return for it?"

"No other than the one you have already undertaken."

"What is that?" he asked.

"That you convey abroad, without delay, the fugitive cavalier who is concealed in our house."

"It shall be done."

"And when it is done," answered Maud, "you will receive from her ladyship five hundred crowns in payment of the service. Will that satisfy you for the task you have to perform?"

"It will."

"How soon will you be ready?"

"To-morrow at midnight."

"Where will you meet the person you are to convey away?"

"Among the rocks down on the sea shore.'

"You may be watched there."

"That's not very likely," he replied, "for there will be no moon up, and I shall so manage affairs that no one will have reason to suspect that anything particular is going on. My boat will lie snug enough close by; and when I have conveyed the gentleman on board the lugger, we shall lose no time in making for the opposite coast, where he'll be safe enough till this storm blows over."

"But in the meantime you must keep yourself concealed," observed Maud, "for should you be apprehended again, there will an end of the only hope of the fugitive's escape."

"You need not be afraid of my showing myself," answered Mark Bentley, "for I have no wish to get into this dungeon again, and especially as I should not have such another opportunity of making my escape. By-the-by, I must not make too sure of it as it is, for there are people watching all round the house, and it will be trouble enough, I dare say, to get off without being seen.

"There is neither trouble nor difficulty about it," exclaimed the girl, "for I will conduct you through a subterranean passage which leads from this place to the thicket on the opposite side of the moat. When there, you must arrange all your actions with great caution, and no doubt you will succeed in the design to the utmost of our wishes."

"Are you sure," he asked, "that Sir Walter has no notion of the plot that is in progress?"

"He cannot have any," she replied, "for it is known only to my mistress and myself, and neither of us are likely to speak of a matter upon which so much depends. Everything will therefore rest upon yourself, and there is no fear of the most complete success, if you perform your part with spirit and decision."

"You may depend upon it I shall not fail to do my best," answered Mark Bentley, "for if by any ill-luck I should fall again into the hands of my foes, it would be all up with me, for those that are found out endeavouring to assist in the escape of any of the fugitive cavaliers, are adjudged to perish on the scaffold, and that is a sacrifice that I am not at all inclined to make."

"I run the same risk," exclaimed the girl, "and yet I can look upon the consequences without fear. Besides, if there be some little danger the reward will be a large one, and it will surely be yours if you only act with determination and care."

"But how am I to come back and claim the money ?"

"That may be done without fear," she replied, "for no one will suspect how the gentleman got away from England, nor will anybody suppose that you have had any hand in it. You have, therefore, nothing to fear, but may return without the slightest chance of punishment for what you have done."

"You seem to forget," exclaimed the smuggler, "that Sir Walter Amyot will order my arrest as soon as he knows that I am in England."

"Leave that to her ladyship," replied Maud, "and she will intercede with her husband for your pardon."

"And after all," exclaimed Mark Bentley, "I have been shut up in this gloomy dungeon for no worse a crime than that of having been found upon the premises."

"And not giving a satisfactory account of yourself."

"Which, by the way," answered the smuggler, "was not very easy to do, seeing that I could not tell him I was waiting for one of the fugitives who wanted to get over to France or Holland. However, thanks to your assistance, I am likely to regain my liberty, and you may rest quite content that I will do my best to bring this affair to a satisfactory conclusion."

"But what in the meantime is to be done with the person who is about to escape ?"

"You must keep him snug where he is."

"That will be impossible, for the place is now filled with troopers, and to-morrow the house is to undergo a thorough search."

"You must exercise your wits then," exclaimed Mark Bentley, "for it will be impossible for me to get him away sooner than the time I have named."

"Might it not be done at once ?"

"Impossible," he replied, "I must have time to make arrangements with my crew, and they will not be able to get the vessel ready for sailing earlier than the time proposed."

"Are your sure," asked Maud, "that everything will be prepared by to-morrow at midnight ?"

"Oh yes," replied the smuggler, "I'm quite sure of that, so bring him down to the shore and you'll meet me there according to my promise; and if the wind holds fair, the gentleman will be in a place of safety in a few hours after we leave this coast."

"When that is done," exclaimed Maud, "you may honestly claim your reward; and if the matter be concluded to the satisfaction of my mistress, she will not fail to prove it by an additional present by way of marking her approval of your conduct."

"That's all right," answered the other, "but by the way though, my girl, you have not yet told me who the gentleman is."

"Nor does it matter that I know of," answered the girl, "for its quite sufficient that he requires your assistance, and that you will be well paid for any service you may do him."

"You may tell him, though, that he must disguise himself somehow or another," returned Mark Bentley; "for he will hardly escape the notice of the people here if he ventures out with the gay garb of a cavalier."

"Leave that to me," she replied, "and I'll take care that nothing shall be omitted that will help to get him safe out of the country."

"How came he to this house at all ?"

"That's almost more than I can tell you," answered Maud; "but here he is, and all we have got to do is to take care that he don't fall into the hands of those that are looking for him."

"And he must mind what he's about," exclaimed the smuggler, "for his enemies are both numerous and wary, and if they should lay hold of him he knows what he has to expect."

"Ay, and so does my lady, too," she replied, "and I verily believe it would be the death of her if any misfortune were to happen to him."

"Isn't Sir Walter jealous of her anxiety on his account ?"

"He has not said much about it," answered the girl, "but his steward has taken care to do his best to make him jealous, in order to gratify his own feeling of revenge. He will not, however, I believe, be able to succeed in that, because her ladyship has never, till now, done anything to occasion distrust, and she has promised to give very soon such an explanation as will set her character in a fair light."

She now listened, to ascertain as far as she was able, whether the two sentinels had resumed their post, and feeling convinced that the coast was clear, ventured to open the door and look round to see if anybody were near the place. In a few moments she beckoned for Mark Bentley to follow her, and then leading the way to another point, descended about a dozen steps, which brought them to the entrance of the subterranean passage of which she had spoken. Assisted by the light of a lamp, which she had carried, they made their way, slowly, along, in spite of the many obstructions which lay scattered in their path, and at length reached another flight of steps which gave egress to the place of which she had spoken. Here the smuggler proceeded in advance, in order to raise up a large stone flag with which the entrance was concealed, and having removed the obstacle, they stepped forth, and found themselves in a thicket, near the moat, which surrounded the mansion. Having thus far accomplished her purpose, Maud took leave of the smuggler, and returned by the same way she had come.

CHAPTER XIV.

THE FAITHFUL EMISSARY GIVES AN ACCOUNT OF WHAT SHE HAS DONE — ANOTHER VISIT TO THE FUGITIVE, AND FINAL ARRANGEMENTS FOR THE ESCAPE ARE MADE. —MAUD MEETS WITH HER MASTER, AND IS SUBJECTED TO A STRICT EXAMINATION AS TO HER CONDUCT.

UPON once more emerging from that part

MAUD AND THE SMUGGLER.

of the subterranean passage which opened within the precincts of her master's mansion, the faithful Maud proceeded at once to the chamber where she was almost certain to find her mistress. Fortunately Lady Amyot was alone, and putting aside the volume which she had been reading to divert her mind from thoughts of sorrow, she eagerly demanded from her attendant how she had succeeded in the somewhat hazardous task she had undertaken.

The smiling countenance of Maud, however, assured her that no misfortune had occurred, and her fears vanished almost before a reply was given.

"So far as Mark Bentley is concerned, my lady," answered the girl, "I have succeeded to the utmost of my hopes, and he has promised to set sail to-morrow night, with the fugitive, if we can only contrive to get him out of the house without being observed."

"Which seems to me almost impossible," returned her ladyship, with a deep sigh.

"We might have thought the same with respect to Mark Bentley," exclaimed the girl, "and yet, you see, when I make up my mind to do anything, it is almost sure to be accomplished."

"I have, indeed, reason to be grateful for the generous zeal you have shown in my service," replied Lady Amyot, "and I feel certain you will do all in your power to rescue my brother from the perilous situation he is in. There is, however, so strict a watch kept over the house, both by the troopers and the domestics of Sir Walter that I fear it will be impossible to leave the place of concealment without being discovered."

"And yet there is the same passage open to Lord Arden that served me so well to-night."

"But all eyes are now directed towards the Bower Chamber, and I see no way by which my brother can leave it without being certain of falling into the hands of those who are hunting him to destruction."

"There may be a little more difficulty in the way to be sure, my lady," answered Maud, "but if I put my wits to work, I believe we shall find that there are means left by which we may disappoint those who are so eager to capture his lordship."

"Have you thought of any plan yet?"

"None that pleases me exactly," she replied, "but I think, with the assistance of Tom Dingle, we shall not find so much difficulty in the way as you imagine."

"May be be depended on?"

"I'm sure he may or I would not have trusted him so far as I have. Besides, he knows he he had better mind what he is about, for if he were to deceive me in the slightest degree I would never allow him to speak to me as long as he lives, and that alone would be quite sufficient to make him mind what he is about."

"But Jabez Sneed is still as malignant as ever, and he will leave no means untried to draw from this young man all that he knows of the mystery of the Bower Chamber."

"Tom don't like the old man well enough to humour him by answering any of his questions," answered Maud; "and he'll get no good by making his inquiries in that quarter."

"Will he be able to resist the offer of a bribe?"

"When the happiness of his mistress is concerned I'm sure he will."

"But what would be the consequence if Sir Walter were to question him as to who is concealed here?"

"His master would not be able to get anything out of him any more than Jabez Sneed," answered the girl. "Tom Dingle is not to be tampered with, either by angry words or promises of money, and you may rely upon it the secret will remain safe enough in his possession, even though he should be threatened with instant dismissal."

"And this Mark Bentley, may we depend on him?"

"I believe so."

"That is to say if no reward is offered him on condition of his revealing the secret."

"I rather think no offer of that kind would tempt him," answered the girl, "for Mark Bentley is a bit of a royalist in his heart, and would rather favour the escape of one than deliver him up to his enemies. Besides, he has no great reason to like the present government, seeing that he is being continually annoyed for following the pursuit of a smuggler."

"Then you really believe no apprehension of treachery need be felt on his account?"

"I am sure of it."

"So far you have relieved my mind," exclaimed Lady Amyot, "but still I cannot but look forward with apprehension to the chance of his being retaken before he can have the opportunity of carrying his promise into effect. Should that misfortune occur, all my hopes would be at an end."

"Mark Bentley is too wary and cunning to fall into the hands of his enemies after having once escaped from them," exclaimed Maud. "Besides, my lady, the only charge against him, is that he was found on the premises of Sir Walter, and that he refused to give any explanation why he was there. Now, there's no very great crime in this that I can see, and I think he was shut up in the dungeon for no other reason than that it was thought he knew something of the secret they want to find out."

"Still," answered her ladyship, "I cannot help thinking that steps will be taken to recapture him as soon as it is discovered that he has contrived to make his escape."

"That, I think, is not at all improbable," returned the girl, "but I very much doubt that their attempt will prove successful. He knows plenty of hiding places where he will not be easily found, and when he gets abroad with Lord Arden, he can remain there till this storm has blown over. And to-morrow night, if fortune favours our endeavours, he will set sail, and all further fears be at an end."

"You seem to forget, Maud, how many people are watching round the place to prevent his escape."

"No, my lady," returned the girl, " I have not forgotten it, but I think I can be a match for them in spite of all they may do to carry their malicious designs into effect."

" Still I feel that my conduct is open to censure for having kept this secret from my husband."

" There was no help for it," answered Maud, " and there is, at least, the consolation of knowing that Sir Walter will be perfectly satisfied when he hears the explanation you have to give."

" Alas!" sighed her ladyship, " how can I expect him to be satisfied when he hears that I have given shelter to one to whom he would have refused it ?"

" But surely he can no longer be jealous when he hears that the person was your own brother."

" My brother and Sir Walter have never been friends."

" Perhaps not, my lady," she replied, " but I should think he would not do anything to injure one who is so dear to you. The secret, too, may soon be explained, so that he will not be kept in any great deal of suspense."

" Yet he will blame me for having afforded protection to a fugitive from the laws."

" He cannot do that long," answered Maud, "for you had no idea of his lordship coming here, and the thing was altogether so unexpected that there was no time for you to reflect whether the act of affording assistance to your brother was right or wrong. Nay, to be offened with you would be unreasonable, for who is there who would close their doors against one who is dear to them, and whose life was in danger."

" It is not that I believe Sir Walter will be seriously angry with me," answered Lady Amyot, " but he will, himself, be liable to fall into disgrace for allowing a cavalier to be concealed in his house, and should that be the case, how bitterly should I reproach myself for having been the occasion of it."

" How could he fall into disgrace when he has had nothing to do with the concealment ?" asked Maud. " For my own part I am willing to take all the blame upon myself, and will suffer any punishment they may think proper to inflict rather than you, my lady, should be made to feel the weight of their wrath."

" My good girl," cried Lady Amyot, " each day serves to prove more and more the fidelity with which you have attached yourself to me. If there is any blame, there fore, for what has been done, I will take the consequences upon myself rather than you should be made to suffer for the fault of your mistress."

" Fault !" exclaimed Maud, with surprise, " can even your worst enemies throw any blame upon you for affording a few hours concealment to your brother when his enemies were pursuing him to death ?"

" There is no saying what light they may place my conduct in when they hear the artful representations of Jabez Sneed."

" True, my lady," answered the girl, " we know pretty well that he will not fail to make matters appear as bad as possible; but there are others who know the motives of the old man, and will take care that all his baseness shall be fully exposed. In short Jabez Sneed had better mind what he is about or he will find himself in a very awkward situation."

" Beware of him, Maud, for he is an enemy to be feared."

" Not so much as your ladyship thinks," she replied; " for the good-for-nothing old fellow has crimes of his own to answer for, and he may be brought to account sooner than he expects. However, I shall not just now mention what I suspect him of doing, but before long, I expect to make a discovery that will bring upon him a very severe punishment."

" Are you alluding to the false accounts he has lately rendered ?"

" Not altogether, my lady," she replied; " for there are other matters he is concerned in, and he little suspects that I guess what is going on, with as much secresy and caution."

" Perhaps you are mistaken ?"

" That is impossible," she replied, " for I took the trouble to convince myself before I ventured to mention it, even to you. However, as I have now given your ladyship the news of Mark Bentley's escape from this house, I will next go to Lord Arden, and tell him he must be in readiness for leaving here to-morrow night, as soon as all the people have gone to their beds."

Without waiting to hear any reply to this, Maud left the room, and made her way towards the Bower Chamber, luckily without meeting any person in her way thither. On entering she was eagerly welcomed by Lord Arden, who had been anxiously waiting the arrival of intelligence as to when or how his escape was to be contrived. Upon learning, however, that no steps could be taken till the following night, he expressed no little disappointment, and declared that at all hazards, he would leave immediately.

" And why should you do so, my lord," she asked, " when evil will be sure to come of it ?"

" It is for my sister's sake," he replied; " for my presence here does but injure her, and I feel that I have already brought upon her more affliction than she deserves."

" Nothing, my lord," exclaimed Maud, " could afflict her so much as to know that you run an unnecessary risk, and that you would do in this case; for, since the arrival of Colonel Latimer and his troopers, every part of the place is so closely watched that there is no moving about the place but one is sure to meet some of them."

"It is supposed then, that I have sought refuge here?"

"I don't think they suspect you to be the person," answered Maud; "but the steward has taken care to let them know that one of the royalists is concealed in the house, and a watch has been set upon it, to-night, previous to a general search that is to be made to-morrow morning."

"Then, it is impossible for me to avoid falling into their hands?"

"I don't exactly think that must happen, my lord," exclaimed the girl; "for there is still a way left to save you from being taken."

"Then, their search will not be a very strict one."

"Depend upon it they will not suffer a room to escape their attention," she replied.

"How then can I avoid detection?" he asked. "This chamber will, of course, be carefully examined, and I cannot hope for concealment behind the arras, as on a former occasion."

"True, my lord," she replied, drawing back a portion of the tapestry, and moving a sliding panel in the wainscot; "but within you will find a small room that I think is not likely to be very easily discovered."

"Why was I not informed of this before?" he asked.

"Because I had forgotten it," answered Maud, "and might never have remembered it again but for a dream that I had last night. So far, then, fortune seems to have favoured us, and it appears to me a good omen that this affair will end better than we fancied."

"Is there any means of escaping from the room?"

"There is no other entrance to it but the one you see," answered Maud, "for it seems to have been contrived only for the purpose of concealment. The only light admitted is through a small hole, so that you will not find it very comfortable, even for the short time you may have to remain there."

"Are you sure no one else in the house, besides yourself, knows of this room?" asked Lord Arden.

"Her ladyship I know does," she replied, "because it was she who told me soon after I came to live in her service. That none of the servants know anything about it I am very certain, for they would have been sure to talk of it had they known anything of there being a secret room in the house."

"Then there is, indeed, some hope," ex-claimed Lord Arden, "and even now, in the midst of my despair, I see a chance of escape that, but a short time since, I thought was impossible."

"And especially," added the girl, "as Mark Bentley may be relied on in the part he has undertaken."

"You think there is no doubt of him then?"

"If you may judge by his promises there is not the slightest," she replied; "for he appeared to be satisfied with the reward that has been offered; and it will, besides, be rather convenient for him to leave the country for awhile till his recent escape has been forgotten. Not, I believe, that Sir Walter had any other motive for locking him up, than that he thought it would be the most likely means of making him confess who it is that has sought refuge within his house."

"It is strange," observed his lordship, "that Sir Walter has not insisted upon entering this chamber whenever he pleases, believing as he does that some one is concealed here."

"As far as my master is concerned I do not believe you have anything to fear," answered the girl. "He has too much regard for his wife to cause her either alarm or uneasiness, but this affair has given rise to so much talk, that for his own honour he is obliged to submit that is house shall be searched for the suspected person. Colonel Latimer seems glad that he has an opportunity of showing the power he is armed with, and——"

"Colonel Latimer happens to be my most deadly enemy," exclaimed the fugitive, "and should it be my evil destiny to fall into his hands, I have no mercy to expect."

"Your lordship will be spared the pain of being made a prisoner by him," returned Maud; "for this secret panel is not known to anybody but ourselves; and concealed as it is by the tapestry, there is no chance of it's being seen."

"But how am I to leave the house?" asked his lordship, "even supposing I am not discovered here."

"More easily than you expect," answered Maud; "for there is a secret underground passage that I have made use of to-night, and which leads to the very spot where Mark Bentley will be waiting to receive you."

"And is that place far from the coast?"

"Not more than a quarter of an hour's walk, and as the boat will be in readiness, you will be conveyed without loss of time to the lugger which is to take you to a land of safety."

"Is all this excellent arrangement your own?"

"Only part of it, my lord," she replied, "for Mark Bentley deserves the greatest share of praise if any be due, and you will perhaps own now that he may be depended on in the service he has undertaken to perform."

"Well," exclaimed his lordship, "circumstanced as I am, there is no alternative but to place myself in his hands. If he be faithful to his promise I will not fail to reward him liberally for it; but should he prove treacherous his life should be the first that is sacrificed in attempting to defend myself."

"You mean, my lord, I suppose, if he should lead you into the midst of the enemy?"

"I do."

"Depend upon it he will do nothing of the kind," exclaimed the girl; "for though a smuggler, and perhaps rather a desperate character, I believe he means to act fairly and honourably towards you, and that he would rather fight in your defence than do anything that might bring you into trouble."

"Why do you think so?"

"Because he takes part with the king's friends, as you do, my lord."

"If that be the case I can have nothing to fear from him," exclaimed the fugitive, "and I will place my life in his hands in the fullest confidence of finding him true to his charge. In the meantime do you be guarded in the presence of those who are endeavouring to worm out this secret, for an incautious word might be enough to bring my enemies upon me before I had time or opportunity to place myself out of their reach."

"They'll not be able to get anything out o, me so they need'nt expect it," exclaimed Maud "Indeed, none of them now attempt to question me upon the subject as they did at first, for they found it was of no use, and they are now trying what they can do with Tom Dingle, because they think he knows something."

"Is he aware of my being here?"

"Yes, my lord," she replied; "I was obliged to tell him because we shall require his assistance by and by, and I believe we shall find him of a great deal of use."

"Can I rely upon him?"

"I'm sure you may," she replied, "or I would not have trusted him with the secret."

"But you say others suspect that he knows something more of this affair than they do?"

"Ay, my lord, but its only suspected, and the poor fellow would rather suffer his tongue to be cut out than say anything that he knows would displease me. So I am quite sure he may be relied on, and your lordship may rest easy that so far there is nothing that need cause any alarm."

"Do you know at what time they intend to search the house?"

"I only know that it will be early in the morning," answered Maud, "for Colonel Latimer has given orders to his troopers to be in readiness to march away at mid-day. You will, therefore, be prepared for their coming by availing yourself of the sliding panel as soon as possible after I have brought your breakfast."

Soon after this, Maud bade his lordship good-night, and left him to the enjoyment of such

repose as he could obtain in the dangerous situation in which he was placed. Having fastened the door after her, she was making her way along the corridor, when footsteps were heard in advance, and shortly afterwards Sir Walter Amyot was seen approaching. He instantly perceived her, and quickening his pace, accosted her with more abruptness than usual.

"You have come from the Bower Chamber?" he exclaimed.

"I have,' replied the girl, quite undaunted by the anger that was expressed in his countenance.

"Who sent you there?"

"My mistress."

"With some message, I suppose, to the person she has been so imprudent as to conceal there?"

"Excuse me, Sir Walter," answered the girl, "but I am not bound to reply to questions that I don't like."

"Why," he demanded, "should there be any secrecy with me?"

"With any secrets of my own I can do as I like," she replied, "but it is another thing when I am asked about those that belong to others."

"At least," exclaimed Sir Walter, "I have a right to know who is concealed in my house."

"Ask her ladyship, then," returned Maud, "and she will do as she pleases about giving an answer."

"Your mistress has already refused to do so."

"But only for a short time," answered the girl, "and if you have but patience to wait till the day after to-morrow, she will, I dare say, clear up everything to your satisfaction."

"Why should there be any delay when I have a right to demand an immediate explanation?"

"I can only reply that I have no right to speak upon a subject that is forbidden."

"Have I not a right to know who has been brought to my house?"

"No one has been brought here, Sir Walter, I know," she replied; "so if anybody is here, it is certain he must have brought himself."

"He has been allowed to remain," exclaimed the knight, "and I must bear the consequences if he should be discovered to-morrow by Colonel Latimer. And all this mischief as been occasioned because your mistress was so far unmindful of her duty as to receive a fugitive cavalier into my house."

"Her ladyship," replied Maud, "knows her duty so well that I am certain she has not forgotten it in this instance. And even if she were ever so much to blame it would be no part of my duty to say anything that might cause her more affliction and trouble than she already suffers."

"Whatever she may suffer," exclaimed Sir Walter Amyot, "has been brought on by her own imprudence. I have myself been brought into a most difficult and trying situation through one act of thoughtlessness that never ought to have been committed."

"Only wait with patience a short time longer," answered the girl, "and I'm sure you will not be angry at what has been done."

"I do not believe your mistress capable of any serious fault," exclaimed Sir Walter Amyot, " but as I have never proved myself unworthy of her confidence, I think on this occasion she has not acted wisely in keeping me in ignorance of that which I ought to know."

"Had *she* thought you ought to know it, there would have been no secret [made of the affair," replied the girl. "She knows, however, that it was better for you to remain in ignorance for a little while; and so you will admit yourself, when informed of that which just now appears to be so full of mystery."

"But I suspect, nay, feel almost [certain that some person is concealed in the Bower Chamber."

"Well," she replied, "and even if it were so, you have too much confidence in her, I hope, to believe she would admit a stranger into the house from any improper motive?"

"I may flatter myself with such a notion," he replied, "but the world may think otherwise."

"The world's opinion is hardly worth thinking of, so that yours is favourable to her."

"You speak boldly and freely, girl," exclaimed the knight, "and would have excited my anger before now, but that I like your fidelity to your mistress."

"Then I hope, Sir Walter," she replied, "you will not again ask me to give up a secret that I have promised to keep."

"That will depend upon how much longer my patience is to be tried."

"Perhaps you can wait four-and-twenty hours?"

"Ay, on condition that no further delay is required."

"I believe I may venture to promise that by that time your curiosity will be gratified."

"May be sooner," exclaimed the knight, "for to-morrow the house will undergo a thorough search, and the Bower Chamber will be the first place examined."

"That will matter very little," answered Maud in a careless tone, "for Colonel Latimer will find no one there, though he search till he is weary of it."

"Do you mean to assert, then, that no person is there?"

"You will be able to judge for yourself after the room has undergone a search," she replied. "For my own part, I can only laugh at the idea of how great the disappointment will be when it is discovered that all this noise and fuss has been made about nothing."

"We shall see how that will turn out," exclaimed Sir Walter, "for, at present, I can see no reason why Lady Amyot should have excluded all persons from the room but yourself, unless some one were there. I would have spared her the pain of a public exposure, but she has obstinately refused to answer my questions, and must now take the consequences."

Having given utterance to these latter angry words, Sir Walter Amyot turned away and went in search of Lady Eveline, whom he still hoped might be prevailed on to confess the secret.

CHAPTER XV.

THE STEWARD TRIES TO INSINUATE HIS POISON INTO THE EAR OF COLONEL LATIMER. —THE SEARCH COMMENCES, AND ENDS IN THE DISAPPOINTMENT OF SOME AND TO THE SATISFACTION OF OTHERS.—THE FLIGHT OF THE SMUGGLER IS DISCOVERED.—THE PURSUIT AFTER HIM.

THE next morning, Jabez Sneed was up betimes, for he anticipated no little gratification from the result of the search, and his only fear was lest Colonel Latimer might suffer himself to be prevailed upon to omit the Bower Chamber from the search that was to be made for the fugitive royalist. This would be a disappointment that he could not endure the thought of, and knowing that the officer had gone to take a morning stroll upon the terrace, he proceeded thither in search of him. In a few minutes he found the object he was in search of, and putting on a more than usually pleasant countenance, he inquired if he might be allowed to ask a few questions.

"You can do so if you please," answered Colonel Latimer, "but they must be brief, for our search will take place presently, and immediately after it is over, I take my departure."

"It was upon the subject of the search that I wished to speak," returned the old man, cringingly.

"Have you any new light to throw upon the subject?"

"Nothing particularly new, sir," he replied; "but I have been thinking it very likely an attempt might be made to prevail upon you to pass over the Bower Chamber, and it may be as well to hint, that in my opinion that is the place where you will find the person you are in quest of."

"I have myself a suspicion of the same kind," answered the officer. "and, therefore, your suggestion is of no use. But how is it that you are so anxious for the discovery of the fugitive to take place, when the consequences would be so serious to the family you are engaged to serve?"

"It is no unworthy motive," answered Jabez Sneed, in a tone of hypocritical humility, "but duty requires the sacrifice, and I must perform it, let what may happen."

"Is there no private revenge in the affair?"

"None, I assure you."

"Have you any information to give, by which I may discover the person I am in search of?"

"I can only say that a person dressed in the gay clothing of a cavalier has been here."

"Have you seen him, that you speak with so much confidence?"

"I have," answered the steward; "for feeling certain that my own suspicions were well-founded, I climbed, by means of a shrub that grew against the wall, up to the window of the Bower Chamber, and there saw such a person as I have described, in conversation with the favourite attendant of Lady Amyot."

"Did they know that you were acting the part of a spy upon them?" asked the colonel.

"The girl saw me immediately," answered Jabez Sneed, "and uttering a scream of terror on discovering that they had been watched, I was obliged to descend with all haste."

"Then I suppose you had not time to recognise the features of the man?"

"I had not."

"Should you know him again?"

"It is scarcely possible that I should," replied the steward, "for his back was towards me, and the glance was so brief a one, that I could only remark the fact of his being habited as the royalists mostly are."

"The fact is then, your information amounts to little or nothing."

"But it may lead to something important, for I am certain he still remains in the house."

"How are you certain of it?"

"Because I have been on the watch ever since, and am able to declare positively that no such person has gone away."

"Do you think it impossible he can have escaped in disguise?"

"I am sure he has not, for I have taken particular notice of all persons who were not known to me, and no one has left the house whose figure corresponds with that of the man I saw in the Bower Chamber."

"Of course you mentioned your discovery to your master?"

"I did," replied Jabez Sneed.

"And what said he?"

"It seemed rather to startle him," answered the old man, "but he made no particular observation, on account, as I suppose, of the awkward situation in which her ladyship is placed."

"I don't see why Lady Amyot should be blamed," returned the colonel, "for it appears to me that this person, whoever he is, has been brought into the house by the servant unknown to either her master or mistress."

"Ay sir," exclaimed Jabez Sneed, "but if that were the case, how do you account for her ladyship having ordered that no person shall for the present enter that particular apartment?"

"Who can account for the caprice of a woman?"

'No one has more right to say that than myself," returned the steward, "for her ladyship has taken it into her head to make some unfounded charges against me, and—"

"Ah!" exclaimed Colonel Latimer, "I see how it is then; you are actuated by feelings of revenge, and have taken this means to pay off old scores."

"Indeed, sir, you wrong me," answered the hypocrite, "for I only perform what I conceive to be my duty in trying to procure the arrest of a man who is considered as an enemy of our republic. That such a person is still in this house, I am ready to swear, and you will, therefore, do well to let the Bower Chamber be the first place you search."

"There is no occasion for your suggestion, for it was my intention to do so," returned the officer. "The duty that has been thus forced upon me is a particularly unpleasant one, because there has long been a feeling of hostility between myself and Sir Walter Amyot, and my proceedings in this case may be looked upon with some little prejudice."

"But of course you will not afford any opportunity for the fugitive to escape?"

"There is little fear of that, if he has not already left."

"Which I know to be impossible."

"Humph!" exclaimed Colonel Latimer, "you think your watch has been so well kept that there was no chance of his leaving?"

"I am as sure that he is still here, as I am of my own existence."

"Well," answered the officer, "if your information be correct, there is nothing to prevent his falling into my hands, for no part of the place shall go unsearched till he is found."

"And what will be his punishment?"

"The same that has befallen all the rest who have been taken," answered the other. "He will be tried by a court-martial, and ordered to be shot, as an example to all other traitors who are inclined to disturb the peace of the country. So, if he should be any one that is dear to your mistress, old man, you will be revenged to your heart's content."

"You think, then, that I am acting as I have done only to serve my own purposes?"

"That," answered Colonel Latimer, "is an affair that I shall leave between yourself and your own conscience. My business here is to capture one who is dangerous to the peace of the country, and not to pass my judgment upon the actions of a person that I have nothing to do with. Proceed, therefore, with your task of mischief, but do not again presume to suggest what I ought or ought not to do."

" If I have offended you, sir, I——"

"There is no occasion for an apology, old man," interrupted the colonel, " for all I desire is that you will not repeat what I complain of as being an act of impertinence to one who knows, and is prepared to do his duty."

"Nay, I only thought her ladyship might endeavour to persuade you to omit searching the chamber in which I feel certain the person I speak of is concealed."

" Nothing would induce me to commit so flagrant an act of disobedience to my orders," answered the Colonel, " and it will presently be seen that I will not leave the house until I have either secured my prisoner or been convinced that he is no longer here."

" Again I repeat—he has not left the place."

" And again I repeat," exclaimed the officer, " that he may have done so in spite of all your boasted watchfulness."

" Then he must have found wings to fly away with."

"Psha !" ejaculated Colonel Latimer, " this is no matter to speak lightly of ; and without any of your interposition, I should have performed my task to my own satisfaction and, I hope, to that of those who have employed me."

" May I be allowed to go into the chamber when your people do ?"

" If you promise not to interfere with me in any way, I have no objection to your doing so."

" I will do nothing more than point out any places where it is likely the fugitive may be concealed."

" In that case you may follow me when I go, which will be as soon as I have seen Sir Walter Amyot."

Having thus far succeeded in obtaining permission to do what mischief he could, the old man turned away, and took his departure, well pleased that his purpose had not been entirely frustrated. Colonel Latimer watched his retiring form with a look of angry impatience, and then resuming his walk, proceeded towards Sir Walter Amyot, who he perceived at the further end of the terrace. The plans they were to act upon were then arranged and adopted, and a sufficient number of men having been placed round the house to prevent the possibility of an escape, they set forth towards the Bower Chamber, accompanied by four of the troopers, who were considered quite sufficient to make the intended search.

On reaching the door of the suspected apartment, they were joined by Jabez Sneed, who, in spite of the reproachful look directed towards him by his master, followed them with a heart exulting in the mischief which he anticipated with so much inward satisfaction. To his mortification and surprise, however, though every place was examined with the most scrupulous care, nothing could be seen of the person who was suspected to be there, for even the steward was ignorant of the sliding panel ; and, as may be imagined, Lord Arden had taken refuge in the secret apartment immediately upon a hint being conveyed to him by Maud, that the persons in pursuit were about to make their appearance. Every hole and corner was examined ; the tapestry, which was supposed might conceal him, was drawn back, and every portion of the wainscot sounded, but without effect. It was clear then to all that no one was in that portion of the house ; and the party then proceeded to the other rooms, all of which were subjected to a similar minute examination, with precisely similar results. Thus frustrated in their expectations, orders were given to the soldiers to look through the out-buildings, and other places where there was a possibility the fugitive might have sought concealment ; and, in the meantime, Colonel Latimer and Sir Walter Amyot, followed by the steward, proceeded to the dining hall, there to await the result of the search that was then going on.

" This has been a painful hour to me, Colonel Latimer," exclaimed the knight, throwing himself into a chair ; " but I have, at least, the satisfaction of knowing that you must, by this time, be fully convinced that the suspicion against us was unfounded."

" I am glad to say you have passed through the ordeal with honour," answered the squire ; " but methinks the countenance of your steward betrays that he is not equally well satisfied with the result of our labours."

" That he is not here now appears to be certain," replied Jabez Sneed ; " but that such a person has been concealed in the house is as sure as that I now venture to make the assertion."

" So you would have us believe, old man," exclaimed the Colonel ; " but even if there is any truth in your statement, it is nothing to the purpose, since my business here may now be said to be at an end ; indeed, under any circumstances your master stands clear of all suspicion."

" Can you say the same of my mistress ?" he muttered.

" Dare to breathe another word defamatory of her, and, old as you are, I'll strike you to the earth !" exclaimed Sir Walter, passionately.

" I have no wish to injure her ; but it must be owned that ——"

" Too long already has she suffered under your vile aspersions," interrupted the knight ; " and I will no more endure that she shall be the mark for your malignancy and falsehood. The purpose for which you have designed this wrong is known, and, therefore, your evil reports will be no more listened to."

"Indeed, Sir Walter," exclaimed Jabez Sneed, "you wrong me in suspecting that I have been moved by revenge. I had every reason to believe some one was secreted in your house; and would it have been the part of an honest servant to see his master endangered by an act that he was not cognizant of?"

COLONEL LATIMER INTERROGATES LADY EVELINE.

"You talk of honesty, Jabez," retorted the knight, "as if nothing had ever occurred to throw a doubt upon yours."

"My character has been blackened and villified," he exclaimed; "but I have the satisfaction of knowing that it will be honoura-bly cleared whenever you think proper to examine my accounts."

"Which will be almost immediately, now that this great anxiety has been removed from my mind."

"You are satisfied, then," said the steward

" that no one has found refuge in your house ?"

" Most assuredly I am."

" Then her ladyship excluded you from one particular chamber, without having any reason for it?"

"What her reason may have been, I feel no wish to inquire into," answered Sir Walter. "The room you speak of has always been devoted toer own especial use; and she was perfectly justified in refusing admission, when she knew it was only demanded to gratify an unpardonable curiosity."

" But if there was no one there, how is that her ladyship's favourite attendant has gone three or four times every day with provisions to the Bower Chamber?"

" I never asked the question."

"I have though," answered Jabez Sneed; and she has prevaricated so often in her story, that there was reasonable grounds for believing that her errand was one which she wished to keep secret."

" *You* had no right to question her upon the subject."

" I should not have done so," said the old man, " but that I feared that something was going on which would get you into trouble. In truth, Sir Walter, I have not lived so long in this family without feeling that it is my bounden duty to guard the honour of my benefactor by every means in my power."

" Then the course you have pursued is a most extraordinary one," retorted the knight, " for you it was whoe verywhere spread rumours that have occasioned this search to be made. But why should I reason thus with a hypocrite whose malice and evil motives I have sifted to the very bottom? You have proved yourself unworthy of all further confidence, and I believe an examination of your accounts will satisfy me of the truth that Lady Amyot was right in the suspinions she formed of your conduct."

Before Jabez Sneed could make any reply to this the troopers who had been sent to search the remaining part of the premises, returned with an intimation that they had not succeded in making a discovery of the person they were in pursuit of. They, however, brought the intelligence that Mark Bentley had made his escape from the dungeon, and from the previous examination of the place there was sufficient ground for the assertion that there was no probability of his being anywhere in the premises. This served greatly to incense Sir Walter Amyot, who declared that some one in his employ must have assisted the prisoner in his escape.

" That is perfectly clear," observed Colonel Latimer, " and the next thing is to discover who the guilty party is."

" I think I can make a tolerably good guess in the right direction," exclaimed Jabez Sneed.

" Indeed !" exclaimed the knight; " who is it you suspect ?"

" Maud, my lady's favourite attendant."

" And because she is no favourite of yours," returned Sir Walter, " you would basely throw the blame upon her !"

" Nay, there you wrong me again, for I have no antipathy against the girl,"

"Then why do you come at once to the conclusion that she assisted the escape of the prisoner ?"

" Because she is over-cunning in all things," answered the steward, " and I believe it was through her means that both the cavalier and the smuggler have got away."

" Do you think there is any truth in this man's assertion, Sir Walter ?" asked the colonel.

" Indeed I do not," he replied, " for we have lately seen so much of his bitterness of spirit that I begin to think him capable of any act of baseness in furtherance of his own views. That he has a mortal dislike to her, I know, and hence arises a charge that he is well aware is without foundation."

" Really, Sir Walter," exclaimed the steward, with well-feigned humility, " you seem to have formed a strong prejudice against me, though why or wherefore, I am unable to say."

" It is," answered Sir Walter Amyot, " because I have discovered that you are influenced by evil passions; and from various things that have occurred of late, I see that you are unscrupulous whenever your own private feelings are to be gratified. The girl's chief defect, in your eyes, is the strong attachment she has always manifested towar dsher mistress, and it has been chiefly through her means that your evil deeds have been brought to light."

" I have no ill-feeling against her," answered Jabez, " though it could scarcely be wondered at if I had, seeing that it is through her that I have lost my master's confidence."

" Nay, in that respect she is entirely without blame, for the first intimation of your suspected dishonesty was given to me by your mistress."

" That may be," answered the crest-fallen steward, " but her ladyship would never have thought evil of me if it had not been for the base suggestions of her attendant. I shall, however, yet triumph over my enemies, for not one word of this accusation can be proved against me, whilst, at the same time, there is no doubt I shall be able to show that she has had a hand in assisting the smuggler, Mark Bentley, to escape from your custody."

" Show me any motive she can have had for

doing so, and I may begin to believe the asser-tion."

"At present I am not prepared to do so," answered Jabez Sneed, "but in a little time I have no doubt I shall be able to substantiate the charge I have made."

"Really, Sir Walter," exclaimed Colonel Latimer, "I can see no probability that the escape has been contrived or assisted in any way by a female. That there is treachery somewhere amongst your servants, there can be no doubt; but just now we have no means of judging from whom the mischief has come."

"And why," demanded the steward, "should not an artful woman be capable of this act?"

"Because there was danger in it," an-swered Colonel Latimer, "and it is the nature of females to shrink from peril."

"But suppose she was desired to do so?"

"If you allude to her mistress," exclaimed Sir Walter, "I can answer for her that she would feel no compassion for a smuggler who has made himself notorious by his many acts of lawlessness. Nay, she would rather assist in the detection of such a man than suffer him to return to his old habits."

"I suppose, Sir Walter," returned the steward, "it will not be considered meddling on my part, if I endeavour to prove that my suggestion is a correct one?"

"You will act as you think proper," he replied; "but before you commence with your task, I warn you that it will terminate in your own disappointment and chagrin."

"That we shall by and by see."

"If you take my advice, you will leave the matter to take its own course," answered the knight, "for a failure will but serve more and more to convince me of the malice of your heart."

"Perhaps," returned Jabez Sneed, "I may be able to show that my conduct has been looked at in a wrong light, and that I have judged, in this case at least, with more dis-crimination than I have hitherto had the credit for. The girl whose part you take, is artful and designing enough to have under-taken such a task as the one I have accused her of."

"How can you prove it?"

"By means of the man who has escaped."

"Is it likely that he would betray the per-son, whoever it was, that did him the service?"

"There is no doubt of it," answered the steward, "for when he finds himself once more in custody, he will make no scruple to expla all we want to know."

"Then," exclaimed Colonel Latimer, "he must be a scoundrel for his pains, and he ought receive the heaviest punishment that can be awarded in such cases as his."

"That has nothing whatever to do with it," answered Jabez Sneed. "It only remains to search after the man who has taken so uncere-monious a leave of us, and when once he finds himself deprived of liberty, with no chance of a second escape, we shall see whether he will not confess how and by whom the first was contrived."

"Why of course it could not have been con-trived or executed by any other person than himself."

"It is impossible," answered the steward, "for the dungeon is strong enough to prevent any person getting out of it, and I myself saw that the door was well secured, because I knew the desperate character of the man we had in charge. I am, therefore, convinced that he must have been assisted, and, in my opinion, no one was so likely to do so as Maud."

"She ought to be very much obliged to you for the opinion you have expressed," returned Colonel Latimer, with a sneer.

"Ay," muttered the old steward, "because my suspicions happen to be directed towards a woman, they must needs be thought to be wrong. A short time, however, will serve to prove that I have not judged too hastily, and that other persons are as likely to form a wrong opinion as myself."

"But it seems you entertain a prejudice against the girl," observed the colonel.

"So people choose to say, but I deny it," he replied. "If there is prejudice in the case, it is on her side, for she has an antipathy towards me, and takes every opportunity that offers to do me all the injury in her power. And she is welcome to do so, for the time may come when she will have bitter reason to regret the evil she has tried to heap upon me. And now sir, perhaps you will excuse me for saying that we waste time in talking that would be better employed in searching after the man who has been suffered to slip through our fingers."

Impertinent as this suggestion was, Colonel Latimer did not condescend to make any reply to it, but calling his men to him, he desired them to proceed without delay in pursuit of Mark Bentley, and to return with him with all possible dispatch, as it was his inten-tion to take his departure from that neighbour-hood as soon as possible. Jabez Sneed gladly volunteered to accompany them, in order to identify the smuggler in the event of his falling in their way, and immediately afterwards they all left the mansion on the errand with which they had been charged. Sir Walter Amyot and Colonel Latimer remained some little time longer in conversation upon the matter which had occupied so much of their attention, and then proceeded to the apartment of Lady Eveline, in order to acquaint her with all that had taken place during the time they had been absent from her. The escape of the smuggler however, was not even alluded to, as it was considered to be unnecessary just then to inform her of the charge which had been made against Maud by the steward.

CHAPTER XVI.

A CONSULTATION BETWEEN MARK BENTLEY AND A COMRADE UPON MATTERS OF IMPORTANCE.—NEWS OF THE ENEMY'S APPROACH, AND PREPARATIONS TO AVOID THE DANGER.—JABEZ SNEED FINDS HIMSELF IN AN UNPLEASANT PREDICAMENT.

During the time that the search was going on at the Hall, Mark Bentley and his comrade, Ned Longley, betook themselves to the thicket, of which we have spoken, to make their arrangements for getting the lugger in sailing order by the time that had been appointed for meeting with the fugitive cavalier. The place in which their consultation was held afforded them complete concealment from any persons who might be in search of them, and possessed, besides, the advantage of not permitting any listeners to approach without their presence being known. This apparent security, however, did not prevent them occasionally casting around them an inquisitive glance, in order to satisfy themselves that they were not the objects of dangerous curiosity.

"I don't know what you may think of it," at length observed Longley after they had been somewhat alarmed by a sound, the cause of which they had not been able to discover, "but somehow I fancy you are not quite so safe as you imagine, for depend upon it they will not suffer this affair of your escape to pass over without making an attempt to carry you back to the quarters you complain of as being uncomfortable."

"They can try it, by all means, if they like to be so fool-hardy," answered Mark Bentley, "but if they come near me with any such intention, there'll be warm work of it, for I'll never surrender myself up whilst I've the means left to slay any of my pursuers."

"Nonsense man!" retorted his companion, "matters are bad enough as it is, but they'll be a great deal worse if there should be any bloodshed."

"Would you have me surrender myself up quietly, then?"

"No, but you might get clear away from this place instead of waiting till they come after you."

"How am I to leave," demanded Mark Bentley, "when I have undertaken to convey a gentleman cavalier over to the continent?"

"Leave the gentleman cavalier to his fate, and look to your safety before all other things."

"It's all very well to say that," answered Mark, "but I have been promised a large sum of money if I complete my bargain, and it wont do to go away and give up that chance. Besides, I shall have to remain abroad till this affair has blown over, and how am I to live there unless I have something to keep me in a foreign land and among strangers?"

"Well," returned Ned Langley, "you know your own business best, I suppose; but one thing is very certain, and that is, that you must not expect to get your liberty in a hurry if you should happen to fall into their hands again."

"Which I don't think is very likely," he replied, "because I know of plenty of hiding places, where I shall be safe enough till the time comes when we are to set sail, and, once more on board our little craft, there'll not be much chance of our being overtaken by the swiftest sailing vessel they may send after us."

"Ay, ay," exclaimed the other, "you think because you have just now been able to escape so easily that the same thing will happen on the next occasion. But there's not the least chance of it, for if you get locked up in a dungeon again, you'll not have the good luck to meet with another girl like the one that helped you to get clear away from the hall."

"Ah!" returned Mark Bentley; "she was a trump, indeed, when I stood most in need of a friend, and perhaps some day or other she may have to thank her stars that she did a good turn to a fellow that is not altogether ungrateful for past favours."

"Have you any notion what it was that induced her to set you at liberty?"

"Not any particular regard for myself, I believe," he replied, "but because there was a royalist fugitive in the house, and there was no chance of his getting clear away from England except through my means. However, it matters very little, for here I am, and that through means of a girl that I should have thought would have been among the last in the world to lend a helping hand to Mark Bentley the smuggler."

"She forgot, I suppose, what a devil of a scrape it would get her into if it should be found out that she had anything to do with it."

"I don't know how that may have been," replied Mark, "but it seems certain that she is very faithful to her mistress, and as the cavalier seems to be a favourite of her ladyship's there was a determination to get him away at all hazards, and fortunately for me, it appears, the girl fancied that I was the most likely chap to lend him assistance that would be serviceable."

"And you have been promised a handsome reward if you succeed in getting him abroad?"

"Ay; and, what's better still, there seems

to be no doubt that I shall fairly earn it. All we have to do will be to be upon the alert till midnight, and the moment the gentleman makes his appearance, there must be no time lost in getting him into the boat and then rowing him off as quickly as possible to the vessel, which you must take care to have in readiness for immediate sailing. A few hours will then take us over to the opposite coast, and once there, we may snap our fingers at those we leave behind."

"Humph!" exclaimed Langley, "to hear you talk one would think the affair is certain to end well."

"And so it is," he replied, "if those I depend on will only act as if they wished to succeed. So far, as you see, no attempt has been made to find me, and I have a notion that they'll not think it worth while to cause a pursuit to be made, because they know well enough that I have done nothing to deserve being—like a felon—locked up in a dungeon."

"As for that," exclaimed Ned Langley, "it would be easy to make a charge against you for having been found lurking on the premises of Sir Walter Amyot without any sufficient excuse for being near the place. And it's ten chances to one but before this time they have made up their minds that you were there for the purpose of assisting the escape of the fugitive cavalier that report says was concealed there."

"And what can they make of such a charge, even if they should bring it?" asked Bentley.

"It's all very easy to say that," replied the other, "but such people as you have got to deal with can make mountains of molehills when it suits their purpose; and if there is a determination to crush you, they will not fail to carry their purpose into effect. Then you have an enemy in old Jabez Sneed, and all the world knows that he sticks at nothing when once he has made up his mind to ruin anybody."

"The old villain had better mind what he's about," exclaimed Mark, "for I owe him a grudge, and shall not fail to pay it off the first time I have an opportunity."

"Which will not be very soon, if you are going to keep out of the country for a time."

"Soon or late, he shall suffer for the many evil turns he has done me," returned the other. "The scoundrel has two or three times brought the officers on my track when pursuit was made after me, and once I had very nearly fallen into the hands of my enemies through the contrivance of that hoary-headed scoundrel."

"I rather think you needn't give yourself any trouble about him," observed Ned Langley.

"How do you mean?"

"Why, if report speaks true, he has been robbing his master to a great extent, and would have gone on no one knows how much longer, if it had not been for Lady Amyot, who discovered that his accounts were incorrect."

"I wish they would only give him his deserts, and hang him for it," exclaimed Mark Bentley, bitterly; "he is a complete curse to the neighbourhood, for all the tenants of Sir Walter Amyot look upon him with dread, and many's the poor family he has turned out of house and home, when his master, if he had known their circumstances, would have given 'em time to get over their difficulties as best they might. But this Jabez Sneed has not a spark of pity in his heart, and would rather crush a poor man at once than give him a chance of recovering himself."

"Well," laughed Ned Langley, "it's a good thing for him that he's not likely to come in your way, for if he did, I rather think there would be warm work between you."

They were now startled by the sound of some person making his way through the underwood, and in an instant both the men grasped a pistol in his hand, so as to be in readiness in the event of any sudden attack being made. Their alarm was, however, quickly quieted by the appearance of Stephen Bourne, another of their comrades, whose appearance denoted that he was the bearer of important news.

"If you want your presence here to be unknown," he exclaimed, on approaching them, "you must not speak so loud, for I was wondering where to meet with you till I heard your voices in conversation together."

"What did you want to meet with us for?" asked Mark Bentley.

"To tell you of something I have just seen and heard."

"Are they in pursuit of me?"

"Ay."

"In what direction?"

"When I saw them," answered Stephen, "they were on the sea shore, just under an excavation in the rock where I had thrown myself down to sleep. The noise they made awoke me, and peeping down, I saw four or five troopers and some of the servants of Sir Walter Amyot."

"Did they discover you?" asked Mark Bentley, anxiously.

"No," he replied, "I took good care to prevent that by drawing a little further back into the cave, where I could hear all that passed, without the risk of being seen."

"What did you learn from their conversation?"

"That they were looking for you."

"Could you hear whether they had any clue to the place where I was likely to be found?"

"They were all abroad upon than subject," answered Stephen Bourne, "but I heard quite enough to convince me that they mean to catch you if you are anywhere in the neighbourhood. You must understand, however, that when I say *they*, I mean the servants belonging to the

Hall, for the troopers are under orders to march from this neighbourhood in the course of a couple of hours."

" Who are the servants?" asked Mark.

" There was only one that I knew among them, and that was old Jabez Sneed."

" Ha!" exclaimed the smuggler, " I thought he would not be far off when there's mischief in the way. Well, I was wishing to fall in with him, and perhaps the chance is not far distant when I shall have an opportunity of giving him his deserts."

" Don't be a fool, Mark, and get yourself into trouble, when there's no need for it," returned Stephen Bourne. " The old fellow is near enough to his grave as it is, and it's hardly worth your while running the risk of swinging on the gallows merely to revenge some injury he may have done you."

" Leave me alone for taking care to keep myself out of the danger of that," he replied. " I know best what sort of punishment to give him; and if chance should throw him in my way, in the humour I am in at present, I shall have the satisfaction of knowing hereafter, that I did not leave England till I had fulfilled the oath I made about that man."

" Surely you won't kill him?"

" That will be as it happens," answered Mark; " but at any rate, if he lives, it shall be to remember to the last moment of his existence the injuries he has tried to do me. If he dies, there will be little harm done, for the world can well enough spare one who was never so happy as when he was doing mischief."

" But," observed Ned Langley, " it's not worth your while, I'm sure, to run the risk of the gallows for such an old villain as he is. Let him live the few days that may remain for him."

" You think, I suppose, that as he draws nearer to the grave, he will repent his evil deeds?"

" I believe it's not at all unlikely, and that would be far worse for him than immediate death."

" If we meet together," answered Mark Bentley, " he must take any chances that follow; for in addition to other injuries that I have received from him, he has taken it into his head to guide the troopers to the places where I am most likely to be found. But this last act of his may cost him dear, for I will not suffer myself to be taken till he, at least, has fallen by my hand."

" You had better by half hide yourself till the pursuers have tired themselves with a vain search," observed Stephen Bourne.

" In what place can I remain in greater safety than where I am?" he asked.

" Well then, stay here," exclaimed Langley " and if you like it, Stephen and I will watch

from different points at the borders of this thicket, and give you notice of approaching danger."

" How can you give me notice?"

" By a signal; a loud whistle, for instance."

" Do so if you like," answered Mark, " only keep a sharp look-out, for I don't want my enemies to come upon me unawares, lest I should fall into their hands too easily."

" And do you take care not to shed any blood," exclaimed Stephen Bourne, " for this neighbourhood is almost too hot for us as it is, and if any life should be lost, ours will be sure can be sacrificed afterwards in revenge."

" Are you afraid of a bit of blood shed when we are driven to it for our own defence?" demanded Mark Bentley.

" I am no coward, as I believe you most own yourself," replied the other, " but I see no use in risking our lives merely because you don't like this Jabez Sneed."

" He is too contemptible for me to seek for the purpose of revenge," answered Bentley, " but if he acts as a guide to others to show them where I may be found, he can expect neither quarter nor favour from me. Whilst he remains quiet, I shall not seek to harm him, but when he proves himself to be venomous, it will be high time to rid myself of a dangerous enemy."

" Can't you think of any other way of revenging yourself besides taking his life?"

" I have not said that I mean to kill him, Ned," replied the other, " but that will depend upon the humour I am in at the moment when we happen to meet. He may provoke me beyond all bearing; and if so, his blood be upon his own head."

" Remember, he is old and harmless now."

" Old he may be," answered Mark Bentley, " but harmless he will never be as long as he lives. His only object seems to be to do all the mischief he can, and if one won't punish him for the evil he has done, another ought to do it, that's all I know about it."

" Not at the risk of being hanged for it, though."

" Hanged! I could submit even to that for the consolation of knowing that I had relieved the world of a villain."

" Then you are more patriotic than I can pretend to be," exclaimed Ned Langley, " for I have no notion of risking my neck for the sake of getting rid of an old feellow that nobody cares about."

" He has made many a one suffer, though," returned Mark Bentley, " and it's only fair that his own turn should come at last. However, you may rest content that I have no idea of putting him to death unless I should be driven to it by sheer necessity. So now, go and keep watch as you have promised, and upon hearing the signal you have proposed, I shall stand ready to act just as circumstances may oblige me."

The two men then left as he had directed and as soon as they were gone he examined his pistols to see that they were ready for immediate use. Having fresh primed his pistols, and arranged his dagger so that he might grasp it in an instant, should there be any occasion for it, he paced up and down, glancing occasionally towards the mansion of Sir Walter Aymot, which he could just see through the trees which intervened.

"Well," he muttered to himself, "they have advised me wisely, no doubt, for 'tis hardly worth my while to hazard my own life merely to revenge myself upon one who is beneath contempt. Yet if he ventures hither in pursuit of me, I must act in my own defence; and should he lead others who are determined on my capture, I may then be forced to revenge myself upon him in a way that I would fain avoid. But for him, I dare venture to say no pursuit would have been thought of, and yet to gratify the maliciousness of his heart, I must needs be dragged back to the loathsome dungeon from whence I was rescued by the kindness of a woman! What satisfaction he can derive from it I know not, unless, indeed, he delights in human suffering, and can gloat over the agonies of a miserable victim, condemned to pass the remainder of his years in hopeless captivity. And that such would be my fate there can be little doubt, for—"

At that moment a shrill whistle was heard, and immediately afterwards the report of a pistol announced that danger was close at hand. Again Mark Bentley clutched his weapons with a convulsive grasp, and placing his back against a tree, to be prepared in case of being attacked by overpowering numbers, he stood prepased to sell his liberty as dearly as possible. There wss, however, no necessity for this precaution for on his looking round and perceiving Jabez Sneed and three men approaching, the latter took to their heels, leaving the steward to bear the brunt of the affair as best he could. Upon finding himself thus deserted, Jabez Sneed would have followed their example had not the smuggler sprang forward and interposed himself so as to prevent his flight.

"Old man," exclaimed Mark Bentley sternly, "you have thought proper to follow me here in the hope of capturing me, and it is now my will and pleasure that you remain where you are till I have heard what excuse you have to make for having thus led my enemies against me."

"'Tis a mistake to suppose that I have done anything of the kind," answered the steward, every limb in his body trembling with fear. "I was merely walking this way with three or four of my master's people, and had no thought of meeting with you on this spot."

"Liar!" exclaimed Mark Bentley, passionately; "you are capable of any act of villany, but are too great a coward to avow it when your vile schemes has been discovered!"

"Indeed, you are wrong, Mark Bentley," repeated the steward: "I had no thought of attempting to capture you. And you must feel assured that I speak the truth; for what interest could it be to me to injure one who has never done me any harm in his life?"

"But I may, before I have done with you, though," returned the other, grasping his arm forcibly. "You say you came not out in search of me—how is it, then, that you were seen scarcely half an hour since on the sea-beach, with four or five of the troopers under the command of Colonel Latimer?"

"I—I—was with them by chance," stammered the old man.

"Where they not out in search of me?"

"No."

"What was their object, then?"

"To look for the fugitive who has contrived to escape from my master's house."

"'Tis false!" exclaimed Mark Bentley, "for he who informed me of what was going on overheard some of the conversation that took place, and I need not remind you that I was the principal subject of it."

"Your name may have been mentioned," answered the old man, still further alarmed at the discovery that had been made; "but it was merely by chance, and not at all in connexion with the object that brought us out from the hall."

"Do you mean to tell me, then, that you did not offer your services to act as guide to the men who were sent out to capture me?" asked Mark Bentley.

"I have told you that we had no notion of searching for you," exclaimed the steward, obstinately persisting in his lie, in dread of the consequences of an admission of the fact.

"Had you not heard of my escape?"

"Yes—I admit that."

"And did you say nothing to Sir Walter about it?"

"Why should I?" he asked. "Sir Walter is master in his own house, and will not be dictated to by any one."

"This shifting and shirking will not serve your purpose," exclaimed Mark Bentley, "so come to the business at once, and answer truly all questions I put to you."

"I have answered you truly."

"These falsehoods," returned the smuggler, drawing forth a pistol, which he deliberately cocked, "will only serve to drive me to do that which I would have avoided. I will have the truth from you, old man, or it may be that you will never leave this place alive."

"Mercy—mercy!" cried the old man, falling on his knees. "Spare my life, and I will answer all the questions you may be pleased to put to me."

"Ay, upon compulsion, you may; but will you answer them in plain, honest truth?"

"I will."

"Confess, then, that you and your companions who just now took to their heels were sent to capture me."

"Well," groaned Jabez Sneed, "if the truth must be told, we were out in search of you."

"Yet, just now," exclaimed Mark Bentley, "you lyingly denied the fact that you now admit."

"Ay," answered the old man; "but that was because I was in dread of your anger."

"And you have cause to be so now," returned the smuggler, "for you and I have a long score to settle together, and we shall not part till I have had my full amount of satisfaction."

"Ah!" groaned the old man, "then I am to be treacherously murdered in cold blood!"

"Coward! are you afraid of me?"

"I am," he replied, "for the flashing of your eye tells me that there is danger to be apprehended."

"Don't your own conscience tell you so as well?"

"I have never done anything to injure you," exclaimed the old man.

"What!" cried Mark Bentley, clutching his arm still more forcibly; "are you not out at this very time to act as a guide to the man that have been sent in search of me? Never injured me! Why, you would have sent me to the gallows if it had been in your power."

"Indeed, Mark, you judge me too harshly."

"I know you to be an infernal old scoundrel," exclaimed the smuggler; "and 'twas a good chance that threw you in my way, just when I was wishing for such an interview."

"But you will not lay violent hands on me?"

"Don't make too sure of that," exclaimed Mark Bentley; "for when men have received an injury, they seldom let pass an opportunity of revenging it when it offers. You know your deserts, Jabez Sneed, and must not expect to get off without receiving them."

"What good will it do you to injure me?"

"It will satisfy me," replied the smuggler, "and I shall fulfil a vow that I made long since."

"Have you no pity for an old man?"

"Ay," he replied, "as much as you have ever shown to others. Your whole life has been devoted to mischief, and the time has at length come, when you must expiate your evil deeds."

"Hah! you mean to kill me, then!" exclaimed Jabez Sneed, attempting to throw himself on his knees, which was, however, prevented by his more powerful antagonist.

"Nay, you shall not kneel to me," returned the smuggler; "for neither prayers nor entreaties shall save you from the punishment you have brought upon yourself. As for killing you, that will depend upon whether you are able to swim or not; for I am about to hurl you into the moat, and there leave you to sink or swim, according to what fate may happen to decide."

Thereupon, he lifted Jabez Sneed in his arms, with as much ease as if he had been a child, and bore him with the swiftness of thought to the edge of the moat. The cry raised by the horror-stricken old man was loud and long; but Mark Bentley was dead to all feelings of mercy, and having released himself from the convulsive grasp with which his victim had seized him, he dashed him, with one violent effort, into the midst of the water.

CHAPTER XVII.

THE UNEXPECTED ESCAPE OF JABEZ SNEED AND THE PROMISE HE MAKES TO HIS PRESERVER.—TOM DINGLE NARRATES THE AFFAIR, AND RECEIVES A COMMISSION FROM MAUD.—THE KNIGHT'S INQUIRIES RESPECTING THE PERPETRATOR OF THE VIOLENCE PROVE TO BE UNAVAILING.

FORTUNATELY for himself, the outcry raised by the steward was heard by Tom Dingle, who, running with all his speed towards the place from whence the sounds came, beheld with astonishment the old man vainly struggling to extricate himself from the perilous situation in which he found himself. At such a moment as that, the good-natured groom forgot the dislike he felt towards Jabez Sneed, and throwing off his outer garment, plunged into the water to preserve the old man from a fate that would otherwise have been inevitable. Another instant would have been too late, for, exhausted by the efforts he had made to support himself, Jabez was upon the point of sinking to the bottom, when his arm was grasped by his preserver, and in a minute or two afterwards he was dragged in a state of insensibility to the land. Luckily, another of the domestics had been brought to the spot, and with his assistance Jabez Sneed was conveyed into the house, and from thence to bed, where, under the skilful treatment of his friendly preserver, he was soon so far restored to consciousness as to be able to explain the means by which he had been placed in so perilous a situation. Tom Dingle, however, could not at first be made to believe that the violence had been committed by the smuggler, who he thought would naturally, for his own safety, have fled far from a place where he was in danger of being retaken.

"There must be some mistake in this account of yours, I'm certain," he exclaimed, "for Mark Bentley has something else to think of just now, when he has got quite enough to do to keep himself clear of those he has been fortunate enough to escape."

"I tell you it was he, and no other person, that threw me into the water," answered the old man. "I was in conversation with him nearly a quarter of an hour before the violence was committed, and, therefore, can have made no mistake."

JABEZ SNEED WATCHES MAUD ENTER THE BOWER CHAMBER.

"Do you mean to tell Sir Walter the same tale?"

"Of course I do."

"Then I tell you, old gentleman, you must do nothing of the kind."

"Why not?"

"Because," replied Tom Dingle, "it is my desire that you don't mention his name in this affair."

"Your desire?"

"Yes!" he exclaimed; "haven't I a right to expect as much from the man that I have saved from death? Recollect, Master Sneed, if it had not been for me, you would at this very time have been lying at the bottom of the moat."

"I'm obliged to you for the service you have done me," answered the old man, "but Sir Walter will ask me how the affair happened, and I shall be obliged to tell the truth."

"The truth must not be spoken in this instance, at any rate," exclaimed Tom Dingle, "and as I have happened to render you a very important service, you must repay it by doing me another, and that is—not to mention Mark Bentley as being the man that threw you into the moat."

"And why," asked the old man, "do you wish to save such a scoundrel as he is from punishment?"

"I'm not going to enter into an explanation about it," answered the other, "nor have you any right to ask for one."

"But Sir Walter will insist upon my telling him who, it was that made an attempt upon my like."

"He'll ask you the question I daresay," explained Tom Dingle, "but you must make the best excuse you can for the present, and when I know that Mark Bentley is beyond the reach of danger, you may tell Sir Walter anything you like."

"But how am I to know that another attempt will not be made against my life?"

"You have to keep within doors for a day or two, and you will then hear of his having left his country, most likely never to return to it again."

"And when that is the case, I may tell Sir Walter all about it?"

"Oh, yes, you may tell him then whatever you please. So give me your promise, or the next time you find yourself in danger, you may get out of it the best way you can."

"Well," replied Jabez Sneed, after a pause, "for a day or two I'll keep the secret as the only return I can make for the service you have just now done me. I, however, make this promise with reluctance, for the man is a very great villain, and ought not to be allowed to escape the punishment he deserves."

"So you may think," exclaimed Tom Dingle, "but I have a motive for what I have asked that I cannot explain just now. Not that he and I have ever been any great friends, but I expect he will have it in his power to do a certain person a very important service, and for that reason I would not have Sir Walter lay hands upon him again."

"The scoundrel laid his hands pretty roughly upon me though," answered the steward, "and he has no right to expect any mercy, seeing that he wouldn't show me any when I prayed of him to spare my life."

"You have had a quarrel with him, I suppose?"

"Not I," replied Jabez Sneed; "but he took it into his head that I was acting as a guide to the men that were searching for him, and in revenge he threw me into the moat."

"But not to drown you, I dare say."

"What else could the villain have intended to do?"

"I'll be bound to say he only wanted to frighten you a little."

"There you and I differ," he replied, "for I'm sure he intended nothing less than to kill me."

"Had he any weapons?"

"Yes, I saw a brace of pistols and a dagger."

"Then if he had meant to kill you, couldn't he have put you out of the way at once by either shooting or stabbing?"

"I don't know anything about that," answered Jabez Sneed, "but it's most likely he thought drowning was the most secret way of getting rid of me. I might have laid a week or two in the water without anybody being aware of what had become of me, and in the meantime the murderer would have got away out of England."

"Which I am in hopes he will be able to do as it is," answered Tom Dingle, "for he is engaged to assist some of the fugitive royalists to escape abroad, and if anything happens to him, there'll be an end to the chance they have been looking forward to."

"Are you in favour of the royalists, then?"

"I'm neither for nor against 'em," answered Tom, "but I think there's been quite enough blood shed to satisfy even the most malignant among their enemies. Some few have contrived to hide themselves, and all I hope is that they'll not be found by those that would exult at seeing them sent to the gallows."

"Well," observed the steward, "and as disturbers of the public peace, they deserve whatever may befall them."

"Does everybody meet with the punishment he deserves, eh, Master Sneed?" asked the groom, ironically.

"Humph!" he replied, "I don't know how that may be; but there's no rule without an exception, and I can't see how it can apply in the present instance. By the by, talking of the cavaliers, reminds me of asking whether you happen to know anything of one of them being concealed in this house?"

"I have heard some foolish people say something of the kind," answered Tom; "but for my own part I never believed it, and still less do I do so now that the place has been searched and no one found either in the house or the outbuilding."

"That's because we have cunning people to deal with," replied the steward, "and the fugitive was got away as soon as it was known that Colonel Latimer and his troopers had come here to look for him."

"Who are the cunning people you speak of?"

"At present I shall mention no names," he replied, "but I know more than they suspect I do, so they had better look to themselves, for it will not be long before I turn the tables on them.

"I hope you don't suspect me?" exclaimed Tom.

"No, I believe you are tolerably clear," answered Jabez Sneed, "and even if you were not, I should leave your name out of the question, because I feel grateful for the service you have done me. In short, they are women that have entered into this plot, and I'll—"

"Women!" interrupted Tom Dingle; "what has put such a notion as that into your head?"

"Oh, I've plenty of reasons for what I've said," he replied, "and you'll know what they are all in good time."

"And why should you, Master Sneed, trouble your head with matters that don't concern you?"

"Because its my duty to prevent the mischief that threatens Sir Walter," replied the hypocrite. "He is not aware of what has been going on in the house, yet for all that he would get into trouble if it should be hereafter discovered that an enemy of the republic has been concealed in his house."

"Nonsense!" exclaimed the groom; "haven't we just seen that there was no truth in the rumour?"

"Nobody was found, I grant you," answered the old man; "but that don't convince me against the evidence of my own eyesight. I saw the man plainly enough when I looked through the window of the Bower Chamber, and I am ready to swear to it whenever I may be called upon to do so."

"Very pretty!" exclaimed Tom Dingle; "so you would actually swear to a thing that would get your master into trouble?"

"My master should have believed me, then," replied the old man, "when I told him there was somebody here that ought not to be. He, however, thought proper to throw a doubt upon my words, and I was even reprimanded in no very gentle terms for venturing to speak my honest conviction. So, whatever may happen, he will have no just cause to throw any blame upon me."

"Well, of course you'll do as you like about it," exclaimed the groom; "but, at any rate, you must not forget your promise to me, or it will be a poor return after risking my own life for the sake of getting you out of the water. Remember my words, Master Sneed, or you and I shall not be friends much longer."

Upon this, Tom Dingle left the steward to his own ruminations; and having changed his clothes for dry ones, sought out Maud, to whom he related the adventures which had just happened, and which had nearly terminated fatally. The girl listened to him with considerable uneasiness; and upon his concluding, expressed her fears that the acts of violence committed by Mark Bentley would prevent him from giving the assistance which he had promised towards the escape of the concealed visitor.

"Don't be alarmed about that, Maud," replied her lover, "for I have the word of Jabez Sneed that he will not mention the name of the person that threw him into the water till I give him leave."

"Do you think he will keep his promise?"

"One can hardly answer for him, to be sure," he replied; "but let us hope that for once he will not break his word,"

"That's all very well," exclaimed the girl, "but I can see clearly enough that Sir Walter will insist upon having the whole truth."

"Which he will not easily get out of Jabez Sneed," answered Tom Dingle, "for the old man can be as obstinate as anybody; and in this instance, I think we may rely upon his word."

"At all events, it seems we must trust to him," returned Maud. "And now the next thing we have to do is to learn from Mark Bentley whether he will be ready by the time he promised."

"How are we to know where to look for him?"

"Very easily," she replied; "you have only to pass through the thicket on the other side of the moat, and make your way towards the sea-shore, where you will be sure to meet with him. But you must be very careful in all your actions, for some of the people here may take it in their heads to watch where you are going to, and then the whole affair would be ruined."

"Never fear me," exclaimed Tom Dingle, "for they'll be cunning people, indeed, if they succeed in learning anything through a want of caution on my part. If I see anybody following out of curiosity, I'll alter my course, and lead them such a dance that they shall be heartily tired of it before I've done with 'em."

"And if they should ask where you are going to?" said Maud.

"I shall tell 'em to mind their own business and not interfere with other people's."

"Which will excite their suspicion still more."

"Never fear about their being any the wiser for asking questions from me," he replied. "The only one that I hardly know how to deal with is Jabez Sneed, and I don't think it's very likely that he will get out of bed for this day or two."

"Unless he thinks there's any mischief to be done," replied Maud, "and then he would be out of bed if he scarcely knew how to stand upright. The very spirit of mischief seems to be in him, and never is he so happy as when planning how he shall make other people miserable and uncomfortable."

"Your opinion of him, like mine," said Tom Dingle, "is not a very flattering one. However, the old fellow don't seem to care much about what people think of him, for he still goes on in the same way, till at last, I suppose all his villanies will be found out."

"Why everybody knows what he is, except Sir Walter," replied the girl, "and he appears still to be undecided whether to believe him innocent or guilty."

"At all events," observed her lover, "there's a consolation in knowing that he'll very soon appear in his proper light, for now that this search is over, Sir Walter will make a strict examination of his steward's accounts, and if any acts of dishonesty should come out, Jabez Sneed may expect to be punished according to his deserts."

"Not according to his deserts, I'm afraid," returned Maud, "for his master happens to be too lenient towards those who do wrong, and I suppose the heaviest punishment he would think of inflicting would be to rid himself of his unjust steward."

"Which would be a mere trifle to Master Jabez Sneed," exclaimed the groom, "for no doubt he has feathered his nest well since he has been in service here, and in that case he would pass the remainder of his days in ease and comfort."

"But his conscience will be troubled, I should think."

"He has no conscience to trouble him," returned Tom Dingle, "or he would never have acted in the way he has. So now you know what my opinion of him is, and the only thing that surprises me is how I ever came to risk my own life by jumping into the water to save him."

"Why you couldn't see a man drowning, Tom, without putting out a hand to help him."

"True," he replied; "and if it had been a dog instead of him, I believe I should have done the same thing. So, Jabez Sneed has not much to thank me for after all, seeing that it was from no respect to him that I saved his life. And, what's more, I mean to keep a sharper eye upon him than I have done, for he just now told me that he has his eye upon certain females in this house, who he suspects to have assisted a fugitive royalist in his escape; and as that is his notion, you may depend upon it we shall before long witness some more of his villany."

"No doubt he'll try to do his worst against me," answered Maud, "but we have the consolation of knowing that he has pretty well run out his course, and as Sir Walter will no longer be his friend, he will find all his evil practices turn upon himself. So, in spite of his suspicions, I shall still lend my assistance towards securing the escape of the person who is concealed here, and in order that all may go well, you must see Mark Bentley and ascertain from him whether the appointment he made still holds good."

Acting upon this suggestion, Tom Dingle left her, and was endeavouring to make his exit from the house without being observed, when Sir Walter Amyot suddenly appeared before him.

"How now," exclaimed the knight, "whither are you going in such a hurry?"

"I was merely going to the stables, Sir Walter, to look after the horses," answered the groom.

"Stay a moment, then, and answer some questions that I have to put," said the knight "Hearing of what has occurred to Jabez Sneed, I have just been to see him, but the old man seems anxious to avoid an explanation of how the affair took place, and I can only learn that he was thrown into the moat by some person who suddenly rushed upon him."

"He didn't tell you, then, who the man was?" exclaimed Tom Dingle eagerly.

"No," answered his master, "he pretends that he did not see his assailant; but I have my own reasons for believing that he keeps back the truth from me. You, however, it seems, rescued him from his perilous situation, and it is, therefore, of course in your power to supply the information he refuses to give."

"I'll answer any questions you put to me, Sir Walter."

"In the first place, then, did you see the man who perpetrated the villanous act?"

"Indeed I did not."

"Were you not near the spot at the time?"

"I was near enough to hear the cries of Jabez Sneed for assistance," answered the groom, "but not to see him till after the man who threw him into the moat had escaped. On arriving at the place, I saw your steward struggling in the water, and, of course, without waiting to see who had done the act, I plunged in, and with some difficulty succeeded in saving him."

"'Twas bravely done," exclaimed Sir Walter, "and I shall not fail to reward your conduct as it deserves. You must, however, make inquiries in every direction to ascertain who was the perpetrator of the villanous act, for I am determined to punish him with the utmost severity that the law will allow."

"I'll do my best towards it, you may depend," answered Tom; "but I'm afraid it will be of no use, for it seems there were no witnesses of the deed, and of course, the man, will not be the first to criminate himself."

"But circumstances sometimes arise that serve to direct us in the right course," exclaimed the knight, "and I think if your inquiries are properly conducted, there is very little doubt that we shall succeed in our object. Nay, in order to induce persons to give the necessary evidence, you may offer in my name fifty crowns to any person who will prove to my satisfaction the guilt of the delinquent."

"I'll follow your instructions faithfully, Sir Walter," answered the groom. "I'm afraid the offer of so large a sum may tempt some one to accuse an innocent man."

"Such a thing is indeed possible," answered the knight, "but I will trust to my own penetration to discover whether the evidence is worthy of being received; and if an act of villany such as you have alluded to should be practised, the scoundrel, instead of receiving the reward, shall be punished according to his deserts."

"And you are quite sure, sir," asked Tom Dingle, "that Master Sneed is not able to speak as to the man that threw him into the water?"

"I have questioned him closely upon the subject," answered Sir Walter, "but, though I fancied I detected some hesitation in his manner, he repeatedly assured me that he could give me no further information upon the subject."

"I should think there can be no reason to doubt him," observed the groom, "for it can't be supposed that he would favour the man that tried to take away his life; and it's most likely the fellow that did it pounced so suddenly upon Jabez Sneed, that he was unable to get a glance of his countenance."

"That is very likely," answered the knight, "and I also think it probable that my steward has not yet sufficiently recovered the use of his faculties to recollect all the circumstances attending this extraordinary affair. By tomorrow he will be more calm and composed, and I will then question him minutely, in order that this diabolical offence may be rigidly inquired into."

"I'm glad to hear you say that, sir," exclaimed Tom Dingle, scarcely knowing what answer to make, "for that which has happened to Jabez Sneed to day may come to somebody else's turn to-morrow if the villain is not taken up and punished."

"And punished he *shall* be, if any exertions on my own will bring him within the clutches of the law."

"I suppose, sir," inquired Tom Dingle, "the steward can't even guess who the man was?"

"The old man is too much bewildered just now to answer any questions very clearly," returned Sir Walter; "but a few hours' rest and quiet will, I dare say, serve to restore him, and his memory may then serve him better than it does now. Such, at least, are my anticipations, and I hope they will not be disappointed, for I confess nothing will afford me more satisfaction than to bring the delinquent, whoever he may be, to justice."

"You may rely upon it, sir, I'll do my best to discover who it is," answered the groom "and I dare say in the course of a few days I shall be able to give the information you want. But the worst of it is, the man may leave the neighbourhood, or perhaps the country altogether, when he finds how determined you are to make him answer for his evil. deeds."

"For which reason you must at first be very cautious in your inquiries," replied Sir Walter Amyot; "asking only of those upon whose secrecy you can rely, and promising them my favour and protection in the event of our efforts proving successful. Indeed, you cannot be too careful in your management of this affair since everything will depend upon your skill and address."

"Don't you think, sir," asked the groom, "that Jabez Sneed himself would be the best person to undertake this affair?"

"He may not be able to leave his bed for two or three days," replied Sir Walter, "and in the meantime the villain who sought his life might find means to escape beyond my reach. You will, therefore, obey my orders; and should anything transpire, let me know of it immediately, in order that no chance may be given for the escape of the ruffian."

"I'll do my best to give you satisfaction, sir," exclaimed the other; "but, for the life of me, I don't know how to begin my task."

"In the first place," returned Sir Walter, "you should contrive to get into conversation with some of the smugglers, for I have a great notion that they are able to give the information we require."

"But the question is whether they will give it," asked Jabez Sneed

"Offer them money," answered the knight, "and they will no longer screen the offender from justice."

"And what if they should refuse?"

"Then tell them, that upon the first opportunity that offers, I will make them suffer for it."

"Very good, sir," replied Tom Dingle, "I'll not fail to follow your instructions to the letter, though I am still of opinion that neither threats nor promises will be of any service."

"Why do you think so?'

"Because I've always found that these fellows are very chary of opening their minds to people that don't belong to their band. They are suspicious of everybody, and will hold no communication with us, lest they should get themselves into trouble."

"I dare say you are right there," answered the knight, "but the experiment must be tried, nevertheless, for I am determined not to let slip any opportunity of punishing the scoundrel that has committed the great outrage. Not that my steward deserves much commiseration, perhaps; but if this affair be suffered to pass over quietly, we knew not what may follow next."

"Then, you think, sir, I had better go in search of some of these smugglers?" asked Tom Dingle."

"Ay, and that, too, without loss of time. You have no reason to fear any violence from them, for they know I have it in my power to bring destruction upon them at any time if they break the law."

"I'm not afraid of meeting them, sir," answered the groom, "but I thought it would be giving them a notion of what's going on, and that they will be sure to assist the man, whoever he may be, to get beyond your reach."

"Never mind your own opinions upon the subject," exclaimed Sir Walter, "but observe my directions, and leave all the rest to chance. My first wish is to ascertain who the guilty party is; and when that is done, it shall not be long before I retaliate upon him the violence he has dared to commit against one of my servants."

Having uttered this in a tone of decision, Sir Walter Amyot turned away to seek for Lady Eveline. The groom pondered for some few minutes upon the task that had been imposed upon him; but seeing that he must needs submit, he made his way at once towards the place where he was most likely to meet the men he was in search of.

CHAPTER XVIII.

COLONEL LATIMER MEETS WITH THE SMUGGLERS, AND QUESTIONS THEM.—THE NECESSARY ARRANGEMENTS FOR SAILING ARE COMPLETED.—TOM DINGLE ARRIVES ON HIS MISSION, AND AFFORDS SOME INFORMATION THAT WAS REQUIRED.—A LITTLE FURTHER PERPLEXITY.

At the time when the preceding conversation was going on, Colonel Latimer had strolled down to the sea beach, not with any definite object in view, but rather that he might reflect without interruption on the steps he ought to take, now that his search for the fugitive had proved unsuccessful. Whilst thus occupied, his attention was attracted towards a boat filled with sailor-looking men, who were rowing towards the shore; and thinking it possible he might obtain some information from them, he made towards the spot to which they seemed to be urging their way. On landing, the men dragged the boat high and dry upon the beach, and whilst they were thus occupied, Mark Bentley approached the stranger, and by way of sounding him upon the object of his being there, inquired if he was looking for any one.

"Why do you ask that question?" returned the colonel, surprised at the bluntness with which it was put.

"Merely because I thought I might be able to assist you," was the reply. "They say some of the royalists are hiding in these parts, and as you seem to be an officer, I thought it very likely you might be upon the look-out for them."

"Well," returned Colonel Latimer, "and supposing that to be the case, may I reckon upon your assistance?"

"That would depend upon circumstances."

"Humph! you would help me on condition of being paid liberally for your services?"

"Perhaps I might."

"In the first place, then," exclaimed Colonel Latimer, "do you give me your word that you are not already engaged in assisting the fugitives to escape from justice?"

"If I was, I should hardly be fool enough to let you into the secret," answered Mark Bentley. "We'll, therefore, say no more upon that subject, but come at once to any other questions that you may feel inclined to put to me."

"Well, then, to come to the point, do you know whether any of the enemies of the republic are lurking about here?"

"I know nothing more than from hearsay," answered the smuggler, "and it would be useless to deny that people talk a good deal about one of them having been concealed at the hall."

"Which report I have every reason to believe is correct," returned the colonel, "though he has, by some extraordinary means or other, continued to elude my search."

"Indeed! there must be some clever people, then, working for him," exclaimed Mark Bentley with a sneer. "You soldiers, I thought, were never to be defeated, and yet you are about to return to those who sent you on this errand with an admission that you have taken all this trouble for nothing."

"It must be confessed I have hitherto failed in my object," answered the colonel. "The fugitive has, for a short time, succeeded in placing himself beyond my reach, but even now I do not despair of placing him under arrest."

"What if he happens to have escaped over to France or Holland?"

"That is what I am sometimes afraid of," answered Colonel Latimer; "and the thought just now strikes me, that you may have been concerned in assisting his escape."

"I!" exclaimed the smuggler. "Why should you suspect me of doing anything of the kind?"

"Because, if I am not very much mistaken you belong to the band of smugglers that I have heard so much talk of, and your vessel offers the ready means for assisting the escape of any one who may be able to pay for your services."

"Well, then, to put you right upon that point," answered Mark Bentley, "I declare that I have not been concerned in anything of the kind."

"Do you know, then, whether the person I am in search of has left this part of the country?"

"I've not heard anything of the kind."

"Do you know where he is likely to be found?"

"No," replied Mark Bentley; "and even if I did, I don't know that I should give the secret up to you."

"Beware what you say," exclaimed the colonel, "for I have the power to arrest all persons who are suspected of aiding the enemy, and it may appear necessary for the ends of justice that I convey you before those who will not be satisfied without a more satisfactory explanation than you are willing to give me."

"And what would my friends yonder be about if you attempted to put your threat into execution?"

"They might resist probably," answered Colonel Latimer, "but of what avail would that be against the troopers that are under my command? However, I am not disposed to bandy unnecessary words with you, so let us have no more differences upon the subject, but rather come to the point at once by telling me upon what terms I may reckon upon your assistance."

"Well then," exclaimed Mark Bentley, "the long and the short of it is, that I don't mean to have anything to do with it."

"Then you will render yourself liable to punishment."

"What for?"

"For refusing to aid in capturing a man who has lately been in arms against your country."

"Pooh!" ejaculated the other, "first prove me guilty of having done so, and then talk about punishing me. I know no more about where the man is than you do yourself, and yet you threaten me as if I had been guilty of some great offence."

"Come, come," exclaimed the colonel, "why should you refuse to give me the information I require, when you will be well paid if it should lead to the apprehension of the fugitive?"

"I have no information to give."

"Do you mean to say you have not seen him?"

"Not that I know of," he replied. "I see a great many strangers every day of my life, but I don't stop 'em to ask who or what they are."

"Again I ask whether you have heard whether he has been lurking in this neighbourhood?"

"I know nothing more than you do yourself," answered Mark. "People say he has been at the hall, but it turns out to be a false report, or you have managed your search after him very clumsily."

"I have done all that lay in my power to find him," exclaimed Colonel Latimer; "but he has been aided by people in the house or I am very much mistaken."

"Who do you suspect?"

"The female attendant of Lady Amyot."

"And pray, sir, who may have put that notion into your head?"

"The steward."

"What, old Jabez Snead?"

"That, I believe, is his name," answered the colonel. "However, be that as it may, the man speaks very positively upon the point, and I am inclined to believe he is not mistaken."

"Have you questioned the girl?"

"Not at present," he replied, "but I may feel it my duty to do so by and by, and my only reason for not having done so already, is that Lady Amyot seems to have been concerned with her in concealing the royalist, and I feel averse to bring upon her the punishment that would follow such a discovery."

"Do you think it likely," asked Mark Bentley, "that her ladyship would run such a risk?"

"Extremely so," answered the colonel, "for she belongs to a family that has always supported the cause of monarchy, and nothing, therefore, can be more likely than that she should afford assistance to any of the fugitives, should chance throw them in her way."

"And very right of her, too, in my opinion," exclaimed Mark, "for none of us know but we may some time or other require the same sort of assistance, and a person must have a hard heart, indeed, to refuse shelter to a poor fellow that has been hunted through the country like a mad dog."

"But our feelings must not be suffered to interfere with our duty," answered the officer, "and Lady Amyot, notwithstanding her high position, would feel the heaviest weight of the law, should it be proved that she has endeavoured to defeat it."

"And you would be base enough to bring all this upon her?" exclaimed Mark Bentley.

"Your expressions might be more courteous," answered the other, "especially as I have so far refrained from taking those steps which would bring out the whole truth."

"But it seems to me," returned Mark,

"that you suspect her only upon the lying reports of Jabez Sneed."

"I know not that he has spoken an untruth."

"Ay, sir," answered the other, "but I happen to know that he is capable of any base act; and as for his word, I wouldn't take it if he were to swear till he was black in the face."

"You are prejudiced against him perhaps?"

"For that matter, sir, I believe most people are of my way of thinking; and one thing is certain, a great deal of mischief would have been prevented, if Sir Walter had dismissed him from his service a year or two ago."

"But as Sir Walter did not do so," answered the officer, "I think we may fairly presume that he is perfectly well satisfied with the conduct of his steward. However, be that as it may, the old man's word is as good to me as that of any other person."

"You believe him, then, when he says that Lady Amyot has given shelter to a royalist?"

"I do."

"Then if there were no other reason for it you shall have no assistance from me," exclaimed Mark Bentley. "So now, sir, you may go your ways, and as far as I am concerned, I heartily hope you will not succeed in finding the poor fellow you are looking for."

Upon saying this, he turned upon his heel, and Captain Latimer finding that it would be in vain to urge the matter any further, left the place, somewhat angry at the defiance with which his proposition had been met. Mark Bentley, on the other hand, went to rejoin his comrades, to whom he related the subject of the conversation in which he had been engaged.

"So you see, Ned Langley," he added, "there's a determination not to give up this pursuit just yet, and I begin to see it's not exactly so easy as we at one time expected."

"Do you think it's likely the colonel suspects what the lugger's lying off yonder for?" asked the person he had addressed.

"He didn't say anything about it," answered Mark, "but there's no saying what notions may get into his head, and we must, therefore, be the more cautious in our actions. Everything is quite ready for a start if we have but an opportunity; and when once our little craft is under sail, we may set all pursuit after us at defiance."

"Ay!" exclaimed Ned Langley, "and even if we should come to close quarters, we have plenty of arms on board, and we know how to use 'em, to, when there's occasion for it."

"But there won't be any occasion," returned the other, "for we shall so manage the business, that no one will know of our departure till we are far enough off to set them at defiance."

"And after taking all this trouble and risk upon ourselves," interposed Stephen Bourne, "do you think we shall get paid anything that's worth our while accepting?"

"Who can doubt it," demanded Mark, "when the money is to be paid directly afterwards by Lady Amyot?"

"That may be all very true," answered the other, "but if Sir Walter happens to learn the fact, he would take good care that not a farthing should reach us."

"Well, then, the gentleman himself must pay us, that's all I know about it," answered Bentley. "So don't begin to raise a parcel of objections, for if we mean to succeed in the job we have undertaken, there must be a determination to go through with it in spite of all the difficulties that may be thrown in our way."

"For my own part I don't see any difficulty at all," observed Ned Langley, "for all our arrangements are perfect enough, and, of course, the gentleman won't think of venturing here unless he is quite sure that the way is clear before him. Even if matters should come to the worst, and the soldiers should come down upon us, we have plenty of arms in our possession, and I for one would fight to the very last rather than fall into the hands of the enemy."

"Ay, we all of us need do that," exclaimed Mark, "for we know what to expect if they should lay hold of us. But never mind, don't let's look at the worst side of the question, but make up our minds that all will go right, and that the money will be ours as soon as we have fairly earned it."

At this juncture, their conversation was interrupted by the appearance of Tom Dingle, who, in obedience to his master's orders, was on his way to make inquiries which he knew would be perfectly useless. Upon seeing him, all but Mark Bentley retired, and as the groom came up to him, he narrated the object of his visit, explaining at the same time his own unwillingness to come upon so useless an errand. The smuggler laughed heartily, and bidding Tom to be under no apprehension of any serious consequences, he inquired of him if he knew anything of the fugitive, and whether he would be ready to go on board at the appointed time.

"Ah!" exclaimed the groom, "you have asked me a question that I'm quite unable to answer, for the truth is, they keep one as much in the dark as possible, and I know no more what has become of the gentleman than you do."

"Don't you know whether he is at the hall or not?"

"Yes, I know he is still there," replied Tom, "but they must have found out some other cunning hiding-place in the house, for, though the Bower Chamber and every other room in the place were searched, nothing could be seen of the person they were looking after."

"Another clever contrivance of Maud's, I'll be bound to say," observed the smuggler.

"Oh, yes, there's no doubt she's at the bottom of it all," answered Tom, "for her ladyship leaves everything to her management, and the fugitive owes his safety entirely to her."

"For which, no doubt, she will be liberally rewarded."

"I don't know how that may be," answered the groom, "but Maud has too much spirit to do a good act, merely for what she may receive for it. All she cares about, is to please her mistress, and she knows nothing is so

likely to do that, as to lend a helping hand towards the escape of this unknown person."

"Do you think he's an old lover of Lady Amyot's?"

"If he were," answered Tom, "he should

receive no encouragement to visit her, now that she is married to another."

"He would not be encouraged to do so, perhaps," exclaimed Mark Bentley, "but it would be a very good reason why she should afford him shelter and concealment, supposing he was to be in need of them. It only struck me that it might be so, and, therefore, you needn't feel so mightily offended at my having mentioned it."

"I don't know what Maud would have said to it, if you had said as much to her," replied the groom. "She thinks there's not such another woman in the whole world as her mistress, and would, I verily believe, go through fire and water to serve her."

"Hasn't the girl told you who the gentleman is?"

"No," replied Tom Dingle, "she keeps everything snug and quiet to herself, and would never have let me into the little I know of the secret, if it hadn't have been that she saw I was getting jealous of her frequent visits to the chamber where the fugitive was concealed."

"Do you happen to know whether Lady Amyot ever goes to see him?" asked Bentley.

"She has been once or twice I believe," he replied, "but being afraid of arousing the suspicions of Sir Walter too much, she sends Maud to him instead of going herself."

"And nobody in the house is able to guess who he is?"

"Not a soul," answered the groom. "Even Jabez Sneed is unable to make that out; and if anybody could have done it, he would long before now."

"The old rascal," exclaimed Mark Bentley "would only have met with his deserts if he had died in the ditch."

"Ah!" returned Tom, "so a good many would have thought, and it surprises me that Sir Walter should be in such a furious passion against the man that threw him there."

"You, it seems, took enough pity on the old scoundrel to jump in after him."

"So I did," answered Tom; "and I should have done exactly the same if it had been a dog instead of a human being. However, I have pleased my master by doing as I did, and he has now trusted me with the task of finding out who it was that made the attempt upon the old man's life."

"But what made you come here to make your inquiries?"

"I came by his orders."

"Does he suspect that I had any hand in it, then?"

"If he had thought that," answered Tom, "it's pretty certain that he would have given orders for your arrest. He only thought I might hear something among your people, and I was sent here to offer a reward to any one that would throw a little light upon the subject."

"Then you may take word back to him," exclaimed Mark, "that it will be useless for him to repeat the offer, because no one of us would say a word upon the subject even if we could. And you may also tell him that Jabez Sneed is not worth the trouble and expense he is putting himself to."

"I'd rather be excused telling him that."

"Are you afraid of his anger, then?"

"I'm not afraid of it," replied Tom, "but I don't see the use of making him more angry than he is already. Besides, I don't want him to know that I have seen you."

"Why not?"

"Because he would persuade Colonel Latimer to send a party of his men to take you."

"I have just seen the person you speak of, and have been in conversation with him some time."

"Did he know you?"

"I should suppose not," answered Mark, "or if he did, he took good care that I should not be aware of his discovery."

"If you take my advice," observed Tom Dingle, "you'll get yourself out of sight as soon as possible, or, instead of setting sail in your vessel, you'll stand a very awkward chance of finding your way back to the dungeon you have so lately had the good fortune to escape from."

"They'll have some little trouble to take me, though," exclaimed the other, "for I'm well provided with weapons, and will never surrender myself up alive."

"What's the use of talking like that," returned Tom, "when you may keep yourself so easily out of harm's way? You have only to conceal yourself all night, and if you tell me where you are to be found, I'll come by-and-by to let you know whether or not the gentleman will be able to leave the hall to-night."

"Oh, there's no occasion for that," replied the smuggler, "for he knows well enough where I am to be found at the proper time, and I shall wait there as long as I see any chance of his coming. You can tell Maud so, if you please, and the gentleman will, of course, hear of it through her."

This Tom Dingle promised to do, and having so far performed the errand with which he had been commissioned, he took leave of Mark and turned his steps homewards in order that he might give an account of what he had done. Having entered the house, he was about to make his way to the apartment usually occupied by his master, when he was encountered by Maud, who had been looking for him a long while in order to relate some little circumstance which threatened to overturn all their plans for the present.

"Would you believe it, Tom," she exclaimed, "that good-for-nothing old fellow, Jabez Sneed, has been at his mischief-making again, and if we don't mind what we are about, the person that has been concealed here will be taken, after all."

"How can Jabez have been at mischief

when he is too ill to leave his bed?" asked her lover.

"It don't matter about his being ill and a-bed," she replied, "for when he's determined to do a thing, there's nothing that will prevent him. Master has been up in his room since the return of Colonel Latimer, and the consequence is that those noisy troopers have orders to remain here some days longer."

"How do you know that was in consequence of anything that Jabez Sneed has said?"

"Because the men have been told that there is no doubt of the fugitive being still in the house, and they have received strict orders to keep a careful watch upon every part of the premises, so that there shall be no chance of any one leaving, if these suspicions are correct. So the consequence of all this is that we shall not be able to get the poor gentleman out of the house to-night."

"Then Mark Bentley's trouble will all be thrown away?"

"You must go, Tom, and give him information of the unfortunate change that has taken place in our plans."

"That I'll do," he replied; "but you had better tell me what is to do next, for he'll be sure to ask."

"I don't know what to advise or how to act," answered Maud, "but perhaps you can ask him to come as near to the house after night-fall, and then, perhaps, I may have another message to send him. Perhaps, too, he'll order all his people to be in readiness, for something lucky may turn up when it's least expected, and I am determined to get our unfortunate visitor out of the house, if there be any possibility of it. At all events, we must not leave a chance untried, or all the trouble we have been at will have been thrown away."

"Are you sure there is no way of his leaving the house without being discovered?" asked Tom

"I can see none at present," replied the girl; "but we must be in readiness to take advantage of any opportunity that offers."

"And you think all this mischief has been done by Jabez Sneed?"

"I'm sure of it."

"Then I'm almost sorry that I picked him out of the moat when he was drowning," exclaimed Tom Dingle. "The old rascal don't deserve any pity; and if I were to see him in danger again, hang me if I think I should put out a hand to save him."

"Well, we'll not talk about that now," she replied, "for we have matters of more consequence to think of just at present. There's my poor lady almost heart-broken at this fresh misfortune happening, just when she began to think all the danger was over; and if anything should happen to the gentleman, I believe it would be almost the death of her."

"By the by, Maud," exclaimed her lover,

"I should like to know how it is she feels so much interest for him."

"I dare say you would, sir," she replied, "but you must have a little more patience, for even Sir Walter cannot be trusted with his wife's secret, and it's not very likely you are going to know it before he does. Let it suffice that her honour will suffer no injury from what has taken place, and, when all is known, those who now censure her, will be among the first to acknowledge she has only performed a duty."

"That may be," answered Tom Dingle, "but I'm afraid she'll get into trouble for having concealed a royalist."

"There's no fear of anything of the kind."

"So much the better, if it be so," returned her lover, "for no one would be more sorry than myself to see her suffer for doing what, after all, is only an act of kindness towards a person who is fleeing for his life. For my own part I have never had any doubt of her good intentions, but I was afraid lest Sir Walter should not be equally well satisfied."

"You may take my word for it, that he is too fond of his wife to be angry when he has heard her explanation."

"In that case, Maud, she needn't care what any body else may think of her. Then there is, besides, the satisfaction we shall enjoy at the discomfiture of Jabez Sneed when he finds that all his plans have been defeated."

"So there will, Tom," she replied, "and we shall afterwards have the still greater satisfaction of seeing him turned out of the house, like a good-for-nothing old mischief-maker as he is. He deserves all that will happen to him, however bad it may, and I don't think there's a soul in the world that will pity him. But we must now be stirring, Tom, for there's a great deal to be done, and if we don't mind what we are about, it is ourselves that will see the overturning of all our plans. So as soon as you have seen Sir Walter, lose no time in finding out Mark Bentley, and tell him all you have heard from me."

This Tom Dingle willingly promised to do and snatching a kiss, he hastened to the apartment of Sir Walter Amyot.

CHAPTER XIX.

THE FUGITIVE RETURNS ONCE MORE TO THE BOWER CHAMBER AND HEARS TIDINGS FROM MAUD.—SHE MEETS WITH COLONEL LATIMER, AND UNDERGOES A SHARP EXAMINATION.—THE MESSENGER RETURNS WITH NEWS THAT IS ANYTHING BUT CONSOLATORY.

LORD ARDEN, from his place of concealment behind the sliding panel, overheard all the conversation that occurred in the Bower Chamber amongst those who were seeking for him.

Notwithstanding the assurance given by Maud that there was no chance of the secret recess being discovered, he stood ready prepared for the worst; and when at length he heard them sounding the wainscot with the pommels of their swords, he every moment expected to see an irruption of the enemy into his little place of retreat. In this state of suspense he remained for about half an hour, when, to his great relief, he heard Colonel Latimer give orders to his men to leave that room, and prosecute their search in other parts of the house. Soon afterwards all became as still as the grave, yet he ventured not to remove the panel, lest any person should have remained behind to watch for him. Thus he remained for the space of two hours or more, when, as all remained perfectly silent, he ventured gently to remove the panel and to look round the room in search of any person who might be there. By degrees he enlarged the space so as to increase the field of vision, and being at last satisfied that no one was present, he stepped into the chamber, leaving the recess open in case anything should occur to render his return to the hiding-place imperative. His next care was to secure the door against intruders, and then advancing towards the window, he stationed himself at such a distance as to leave but little chance of being seen by any one from without, and from thence could plainly see his foes as they hurried from place to place in eager pursuit after their expected prey. There he remained almost motionless for three or four hours longer, till a gentle tap at the door roused him from his reverie, and having opened it, he gave admittance to Maud, who entered on tiptoe, and having again fastened the entrance, inquired in a whisper if anything had occurred to alarm him since the departure of his pursuers.

"No one has returned here," he replied, " but I have been in almost continual expectation of Jabez Sneed, whose furious hostility to me has led to so much difficulty and danger."

"And so I dare say you would, my lord," she replied, "but the old man has nearly lost his life, and is now confined to his bed, where he is likely to remain for at least three or four days."

"Has he met with an accident?"

"I don't know the truth of it exactly yet " answered the girl, "but they say he was thrown into the moat by somebody, and he would certainly have been drowned but for Tom Dingle, who jumped in and saved him just at the moment when he was sinking to the bottom. So, for a little while, he will not be able to do any mischief, which, I dare say, will grieve him as much as anything could."

"And when is Colonel Latimer expected to leave?"

"That nobody knows at present," she replied. "Orders were at one time given to his troopers to be in readiness for marching by mid-day; but since then, something or another has happened, and they are going to remain no one knows how long."

"Do they still suspect I am here?" asked his lordship.

"I believe so," answered Maud; "but there is so much secrecy observed, that it's impossible to learn why or wherefore the sudden change has taken place. The men, however, have been ordered to keep a careful watch all round the house, and I'm afraid there will be no way left for your lordship to get away without being seen by some of the scouts."

"Is there not the subterranean passage by which you contrived the escape of Mark Bentley?"

"That is the very way I intended to lead you, my lord," she replied, "but, as ill-luck will have it, guards are stationed near the entrance, and we are, therefore, deprived of the only means that were left us."

"Cannot the men be seized and secured till after I have made my escape?" asked Lord Arden.

"It would be impossible to prevent them raising an outcry," she replied, "and that would bring certain destruction upon you."

"Then, I suppose I must remain where I am till a more favourable opportunity presents itself?"

"At present I can see no other way," answered Maud; "but I would have you be prepared for escaping at a moment's notice, for I shall watch every chance that may occur, and Mark Bentley has received a message from me to conceal himself in the thicket on the opposite side of the moat, in order that he may be in readiness if I am able to think of any scheme for getting you out of this house. Perhaps, however, it would be better to remain where you are a little longer, for here you are at least tolerably safe; and when once the troopers have left, there will not be much more difficulty in the way."

"Your zeal deserves the warmest thanks," exclaimed his lordship, " and, depend upon it, I will not forget the determination of purpose with which you have laboured in my behalf."

"I am more than repaid as it is," she replied, "by the success which has hitherto rewarded my efforts. It is enough for me that I have relieved some of the anxiety and fear of my poor mistress, who, I verily believe, would have died of grief had any unfortunate occurrence thrown you in the way of your enemies."

" Does Sir Walter still suspect that she has given shelter to a rival?" asked Lord Arden.

" He says nothing about it just now," answered Maud, "but I dare say he is only waiting till it has been clearly shown whether the reports he has heard are true."

"Is he still upon kindly terms with Lady Eveline?"

"So far I can see no difference," answered the girl, "except that he is more silent and thoughtful than usual. He has expressed great anger, too, against Jabez Sneed for the reports he has raised, and the old man has received strict orders never to repeat them whilst there is a doubt remaining."

"Which orders will not be obeyed, I suppose," observed Lord Arden, "for he seems determined never to give up his infamous designs till he has ruined the character of my sister."

"Ah! my lord," exclaimed the faithful girl, "he will not find that as easy a task as he may 'magine, for Lady Eveline Amyot is beloved iby every one, whilst her dastardly accuser is well known for the old villain he is. Besides, his accounts are soon to be examined; and if—as I suspect will be the case—they are found to be incorrect, he will be sent away in disgrace, and must ever afterwards hide himself from the world that despises him."

"But he may not give up the mischievous designs in which he seems to delight so much."

"And who is there that will ever believe him after all his evil practices have been exposed?" asked Maud. "No no, he may say and act as he will, but he is about to be deprived of the little credit that may have been once given him, and he must be content to pass the rest of his days in contempt and neglect. However, for a few days we have, I believe, nothing to fear from him, and in the meantime it shall be my care to watch for the first favourable opportunity that may offer for your lordship to escape from this house to the place where you are to meet the people who have undertaken to convey you to France."

"The men may become tired of waiting."

"Never, whilst they have a large reward in view," answered Maud, "for her ladyship has promised them a sum of money sufficient to secure their fidelity, and they have promised to run all risks on purpose to earn it."

"Is their vessel ready for sailing?"

"Mark Bentley," she replied, "has promised to set sail the very moment you set foot on board; and if his word may be relied on, there's no chance of his being overtaken, even if another vessel should be sent in pursuit."

"You have made all your arrangements admirably," exclaimed Lord Arden, "and I feel every confidence in their success, if we can but find an opportunity for leaving this house without being seen. But you have not yet told me of my sister—Cannot I have another interview with her before I leave?"

"Her ladyship is as anxious upon that subject as you are," answered Maud, "but after much consideration, she has resolved to sacrifice her own feelings rather than you should run any risk of being discovered."

"What fear is there of that?"

"Her actions are closely watched," replied the girl, "and were she seen coming to the Bower Chamber, it would be imagined that you were still here. Under these circumstances, anxious as she is to see your lordship before your departure, she is willing to sacrifice her own feelings rather than risk further danger."

"Tell her, then, from me," exclaimed Lord Arden, "that we may see each other again sooner than she expects, for the king designs a speedy descent upon the English coast to claim the crown of which he has been unjustly deprived; and with the foreign assistance that has been promised to him, there is little or no doubt that the attempt will be a successful one."

"Ah!" cried Maud, "so it has been thought before; but when the time came, those who called themselves his friends declined to give the assistance they promised."

"That must be admitted," answered Lord Arden, "but his party has since gained experience, and numbers of people in this country will gladly hail his return, rather than submit any longer to the military government of the Protector. Such, at least, is my confident expectation, and it is, therefore, with the less regret that I am now about to take a temporary leave of my native land."

"Ah, my lord," exclaimed the girl, "has not the bitter experience of the last three or four weeks served to damp your zeal for a cause that most people think is hopeless?"

"Why should they think it hopeless," asked his lordship, "when there are so many who are willing to risk their lives in order to restore monarchy to this unhappy country? These who were once fierce republicans have long since seen that their anticipations are never to be realised; and the king is constantly receiving letters from England assuring him that he will meet with a loyal reception, whenever he may be pleased to come and claim his own."

"That may be," answered Maud, "but there are many thousands in England like my master who will never submit to the restoration of monarchy till they are compelled to do so, which can only be after much deadly strife and bloodshed."

"Nevertheless, maiden," exclaimed his lordship, "you will, I hope, live to see my words come to pass. This, however, is not a subject to dwell upon just at present, and we will, therefore, return to that of what we were but now speaking. You will, of course, remain in communication with Mark Bentley, upon whose exertions so much must depend: and when the way is clear before me, I will place myself under your guidance to reach the place where my deliverer is to be found."

Maud gave him her renewed assurance that nothing should be neglected on her part to render his escape easy and certain; and having first listened to ascertain whether any one was in the passage, she ventured to open the door. Fortunately, no person was near, and having once more turned the key upon the fugitive, she was going in quest of Tom Dingle, when she was intercepted by Colonel Latimer, who, taking her by the arm, said—

"Whence come you, girl ?—I have been seeking you in all parts of the house, and was just now on my way to the Bower Chamber, where I made sure to meet with you."

"Indeed!" she exclaimed with affected surprise, "and pray, sir, why did you suppose I was there ?"

"Because your visits to that place are so frequent, that people say you must have some motive for it."

"People had much better minds their own business than incerfere with other," she replied tartly. "I certainly go very often to the Bower Chamber, but it is nothing to any one why I do so."

"Yes it is," exclaimed Colonel Latimer, "for it has been said that a fugitive royalist found protection there, and the matter is still the subject of general conversation."

"Again I say, sir, it would be much better if folks didn't interfere with their neighbours' affairs quite so much."

"Where there is secrecy observed," he replied, "we may be excused for entertaining our suspicions."

"Secrecy!" exclaimed Maud; "I have done nothing more than prevent people from entering a room that has always been considered to belong entirely to my mistress. Besides, what doubt can there be upon the subject, after you and your men have so thoroughly searched it without effect?"

"The truth is, my girl," he replied, "I have many reasons to believe the person we are in search of is still secreted within this house, and I should be guilty of an unpardonable omission of duty if I were to leave till thoroughly convinced of the truth or falsehood of the notion I have formed."

"Are you going to search the house again then?" asked Maud, concealing her alarm as well as she could.

"That will depend upon circumstances," he replied; "but, at all events, I and my men will remain here to keep watch, so that no one shall have a chance of leaving without being seen."

"Well," answered Maud, in a tone of affected indifference, "your doing that won't matter much to anybody except yourselves, for all this trouble will be thrown away, and we, who can see the folly, will afterwards laugh at you for your pains."

"I have a notion it wil b quite ether-wise, and that you will prove to have been concerned in an unlawful act."

"What do you mean by that, Colonel Latimer?" she asked petulantly.

"Neither more nor less," he replied, "than that you have concealed a traitor to his country, and are, therefore, liable to receive a very severe punishment."

"You think to frighten me, sir, but that will not be done very easily, since I am not conscious of having acted wrong."

"That may be your notion, my girl," exclaimed the colonel, "but time may prove that you have formed a wrong one, for if my suspicions should prove to be well founded, you you will be placed under arrest till your conduct has been inquired into."

"Oh," retorted Maud, "I am not to be frightened, I can assure you."

"So it seems at present," answered Colonel Latimer, "but a short time may effect a great change in your courage."

"You suspect me, then, of concealing a royalist?"

"I do."

"Upon what grounds, sir?"

"Your frequent visits to the Bower Chamber is one reason, and another is founded on the reports of Jabez Sneed, who is ready to declare upon his oath that he has seen a person habited in the garb of a cavalier in conversation with you there."

"If you take his word, sir, you will find yourself deceived," she replied sharply.

"Then tell me why you so often go to that particular room, and always with so much caution."

"Chiefly to amuse myself, by exciting the suspicion of those who are over-curious."

"That cannot be your only motive for going there."

"I am not bound to reply to all your questions," she said, "but in order to satisfy you, I will further say that I am frequently sent there by my mistress when she wants anything that has been left in her own room; and at other times, as is my duty, I go to dust and arrange the furniture against her ladyship chooses to return there."

"But Jabez Sneed tells me he has seen you taking a basket of provisions into the chamber."

"He may have seen me with a basket," she replied, "but I defy him to prove there was anything in it."

"Come, come, my girl," exclaimed Colonel Latimer, "be honest and confess the truth to me at once. Admit that you have done as I suspect, and instead of punishment, I will take care that you receive a suitable reward."

"I have told you all that you are likely to hear from my lips," she replied, resolately.

"Then the consequences be upon your own head if a discovery should take place."

"Even if I were guilty of an unworthy act," answered Maud, "I have too much spirit to be intimidated by the threats of any one except my mistress. I, however, am not conscious of having done wrong, and neither you, nor those who are above me, shall induce me to yield to threats."

"Remember," exclaimed Colonel Latimer, "we may yet discover this fugitive, and if we do so, you and your mistress will at once be charged with having concealed him."

"Think what you please sir, of me," returned Maud, "but my mistress may surely be free from your evil suspicions."

"Nay, even her husband believes she has been guilty of deceiving him in this respect."

"Sir Walter would never have done so," answered Maud, "if it had not been for the suggestions of a parcel of evil minded persons. He loves his wife for her fidelity and attachment to him, and as a proof of it, he would not cause a search to be made in her room till after he was compelled to do so for fear of the consequences of a refusal."

"That may be," exclaimed Colonel Latimer. "And now, as a last effort for your own good, I ask if you will confess who is concealed in the Bower Chamber."

"I have nothing to confess, sir," she replied; "and even if I had, it should not be to you who have brought so much confusion and alarm into this family. This, Colonel Latimer, is my only answer, and it will, therefore, be useless for you to put any further questions to me."

She spoke this in a tone of so much firmness and determination, that the colonel made no further effort to detain her, and she was permitted to leave him without another word of threat or expostulation. Finding herself thus free to go whithersoever she pleased, Maud was making her way through a little side entrance which led to the gardens, when she was encountered by Tom Dingle, who had just returned from the errand upon which she had sent him.

"Well, sir," she exclaimed, as he approached, "what news do you bring me from Mark Bentley?"

"Nothing that's very good," he replied, "for the troopers have so completely surrounded the house, that I was not suffered to pass on my way till I had answered the questions of about half a dozen of them."

"What did they ask you, Tom?"

"All sorts of things," he replied, "and some of them went so far as to say that I was the person they are searching for."

"Why they surely couldn't take you for a cavalier?" exclaimed Maud, hardly able to refrain from laughing.

"Yes, but they did, though," replied Tom Dingle. "They thought I was disguised, and it was not till one of my fellow servants came up and called me by name that they would let me go my ways."

"And did you see Mark Bentley?"

"Yes."

"Does he see any chance of getting the gentleman off to-night?"

"Not the least," he replied, "for the soldiers seemed determined not to let any one pass without first questioning him, and he thinks the gentleman had better remain snug where he is till after Colonel Latimer and the troopers have left."

"Which," answered the girl, "I am sorry to say, is not very likely to take place so soon as we expected. They have determined to remain where they are, Tom, and goodness only knows what will become of me if they should find the fugitive here after all."

"Why," answered Tom, "as long as he remains in England he is in constant fear of being sent back to the dungeon you helped him to escape from. He knows his own danger, and may not feel inclined to run the risk of staying here any longer, now that he finds it is uncertain when the gentleman will be able to leave."

"Then you should have told him," exclaimed the girl, "that we are in momentary expectation of getting him off."

"I said as much as that to him," he replied, "but there's very few of us that would lose our liberty when there's a chance of keeping it, and no one would blame Mark Bentley for looking to his own safety."

"Now that's what I call speaking sensibly," exclaimed Maud, "and depend upon it I shall not forget you for it. So don't feel hurt at anything I have said, but take the earliest opportunity you can find to seek out Mark Bentley once more, and persuade him not to leave England without the unfortunate gentleman, who will be lost but for his assistance."

"Make yourself easy about that," answered the groom; "for rather than give you any cause for vexation, and as a proof that I mean what I say, I'll go at once to see Mark, and persuade him to have a little more patience before he thinks of leaving us in the lurch."

In pursuance of this resolution, Tom Dingle retraced the path he had just come, much to the gratification of Maud, whose only hope remained in the assistance he might be willing to afford.

CHAPTER XXVI.

JABEZ SNEED MAKES ANOTHER DISCOVERY AND COMMUNICATES IT TO HIS MASTER —SIR WALTER'S JEALOUSY, AND THE DETERMINATION HE COMES TO.—INTERVIEW BETWEEN THE HUSBAND AND WIFE. —THE PASSPORT.—AN ALARM, AND THE DISCOVERY.—CONCLUSION.

DURING the last interview that had taken place between Lady Eveline and her brother, Jabez Sneed, who, unobserved, had watched her to the Bower Chamber, stealthily took his way to the terrace, and climbing up a tree that stood opposite the window, observed from his place of concealment all that was necessary to confirm the suspicions he had formed. Exulting at the discovery he had made, the old man stirred not till Lady Eveline had left the room, and then cautiously descending to the ground, he went in search of his master, who he found looking over his accounts in a room adjoining that with respect to which so much mystery had been observed. Unable to control his impatience, he lost not a moment in revealing all that he had seen, and if anything could have increased the malicious gratification of the old man, it was the marked change which his information had effected in the countenance and demeanour of the knight, who, after a brief pause, demanded whether he might not have been deceived by his anxiety to discover the secret.

"It is impossible there can have been any mistake," answered the steward, "for I had my eye on them both nearly half an hour, and from the manner of their parting they seemed to be on the most intimate terms with each other, for her ladyship at parting threw herself into the arms of the stranger, and seemed no way displeased at a kiss with which he saluted her lips."

"Then her affection for me was dissembled," groaned Sir Walter, "and I have been the dupe of her upon whom I placed all my confidence and love. But this discovery shall cost her dear, for though my own heart should break, I will henceforth cast her off as unworthy of the confidence she has betrayed."

"Nay," exclaimed the hypocrite, "if I may venture to offer my advice, I should recommend you to see her ladyship once more before you part, in order that she may have an opportunity of answering the charge I have made.'

"It shall be so," answered Sir Walter, "for though the task be a most painful one, I will see her once, and only once more. Go to her, and say that I am waiting here to see her."

Secretly exulting in the mischief he had been doing, Jabez Sneed's first care was to send off a messenger to Colonel Latimer, requesting him to come immediately to the hall with his troopers, to capture the fugitive royalist, whom he had at length succeeded in discovering to be concealed there. This done, he next went in search of Lady Eveline, to whom he communicated the errand with which he had been charged. The message was immediately obeyed, but the alarm of her ladyship may be more easily imagined than described, when she saw the fearful alteration in the countenance of Sir Walter since last they had met. She anxiously demanded if he were ill, or if any misfortune had occurred to him; his utterance, however, seemed to have failed him, and it was not till he had in some slight degree recovered himself, that he informed her of what he had just heard from Jabez Sneed, who had not hesitated to accuse her of having acted unfaithfully to her marriage vows. Filled with grief and indignation, the afflicted wife demanded whether he could place any reliance in the accusation of a man whose hatred towards her had been already proved.

This earnest appeal was, however, made in vain, for now everything served to contribute more and more to the fact of his having been dishonoured by the woman he had confided in, and he was about to make an angry reply, when a servant entered the room to announce that Colonel Latimer and his troopers had just arrived to make another search over the house or the royalist officer who was suspected to be concealed there. Sir Walter Amyot heard this intelligence with a look of sullen indifference, and after a moments' silence, desired that the officer should be immediately ushered into his presence. In a brief period afterwards, Colonel Latimer made his appearance, and having communicated the intelligence he had just received, apologized for having again obtruded himself by an assurance that nothing but his own sense of duty would have induced him again to disturb the domestic quiet of the house. Sir Walter felt the degradation to which he was forced to submit, but assuming an appearance of composure that was foreign to his heart, he said, with chilling indifference:

"He who has been busy enough to have sent for you here, might have known that I, at least, ought not to be suspected of harbouring any person who is suspected of being a dangerous enemy of my country. I have, however, till the last few days, been absent from home on duty, and my wife yonder can best answer for herself, whether such a person as you speak of, has been suffered to find a refuge beneath my roof."

Bowed down with grief and terror, Lady Eveline cast an imploring look towards her husband to spare her these reproaches, but he heeded her not, and Colonel Latimer advanced towards the room in which Lord Arden was still concealed. At any other moment her heart would have failed her, but the imminent danger that threatened her brother, seemed to inspire her with more than a woman's courage, and throwing herself before the door, she, in frantic accents, declared that no one should pass her whilst she had strength to resist the intrusion. Startled by her attitude of firmness, the colonel paused for a moment, but again remembering the duty he was called upon to perform, he was about to force his way into the chamber, when the better feelings of Sir Walter Amyot returned, and in a stern voice of authority, he, in virtue of his own superior

military rank, commanded the colonel to leave his house without prosecuting his search any further.

Perhaps not altogether unwilling to yield to this injunction, and wishing to avoid giving offence to one whom it was his duty to obey, the officer immediately left the room, but it was only to give directions to his men so to place themselves round the house that it should be impossible for any one to leave it without being seen. Being thus once more left alone with his grief-stricken wife, Sir Walter informed her, that, as no doubt remained in his own mind of her guilt, he would from that moment discard her for ever from his house.

Lady Eveline heard all these reproaches in a state of fearful agony; she would have given all she possessed in the world to convince him of her perfect innocence of the foul charge that had been brought against her, but this it was utterly impossible to do without betraying her brother's secret, and thus risking a life for which she would have sacrificed her own. Sir Walter believing her to be fully convicted of having proved false to him, immediately afterwards quitted the room; and as he did so, the terrible words again rung upon her ears that she was to see him no more!

Thus left alone in her misery, Lady Eveline sank nearly fainting upon a chair, in which state of wretchedness and grief she was soon afterwards found by the faithful Maud, by whose care and attention she was at length restored to a consciousness of the terrible scene which had just passed. Tears fortunately came to her relief, and having by degrees summoned fortitude enough for the task, she related, as briefly as possible, the conversation which had taken place between herself and her husband. Maud could scarcely restrain her indignation at hearing the calumnies with which her mistress had been assailed, but she exerted herself to console the grief of Lady Eveline, who, by her advice, was induced to seek one more interview with her husband in order to make one last effort to banish from his mind the injurious suspicions which he so groundlessly had entertained against her.

This interview was granted without much hesitation, but unhappily she found Sir Walter in no humour to listen to her request, that he would suspend his judgment for a short time longer. Jabez Sneed had, in fact, been again pouring into his ears the vilest slanders against his wife, which confirmed all his worst suspicions, that she had been unfaithful to him. With a harshness which, till very recently, she had never experienced from him, he commanded her to leave his house within an hour, and to seek an asylum with her brother, Lord Arden, who, he believed, had succeeded in making his escape to France. As a guard, however, was stationed round the neighbourhood to prevent any one leaving the country, he wrote a few lines which were to serve as a pass for the bearer, and would enable her to reach in safety the ship which was then ready to sail for the opposite coast. Having done this, he threw himself upon a chair, and seemed to wait with impatience for her to leave the room.

Maud, however, who had been present during the whole of this interview, had suddenly conceived a design which could scarcely fail being of the greatest importance. Her quick eye instantly observed that the passport which had been given did not mention the name or sex of the person who was to use it, being merely intended to prevent the detention or delay of the bearer. She saw then that it would be a ready means for the escape of Lord Arden, who was now only waiting her return to leave his hiding place for the purpose of attempting to reach the vessel which was to convey him to a place of safety. The thought which had so opportunely struck her she whispered to Lady Eveline, who, rejoicing in such an opportunity to insure the successful flight of her brother, delivered it into the hands of her faithful attendant with a brief injunction to lose no time in getting him from the house.

Upon the departure of Maud, the sorrowing wife remained silent for some few moments, in the hope that Sir Walter would relent, and speak to her in those accents of kindness which had once been the chief source of her happiness. Finding, however, that he still maintained a sullen silence, she ventured, as a last effort, to entreat him to discard from his mind the injurious reports which had been invented only to plunge her into ruin.

She waited anxiously for his reply; but no attention was paid to her appeal, for just at that moment he was standing at the window, where his attention was occupied by something that was going on outside the house. She stood watching him with intense anxiety, as if a foreboding of evil had found its way to her heart; and at length, to her horror, she heard him exclaim, in a tone of exultation, that the troopers were in pursuit of a fugitive royalist officer, who was making with all speed towards the sea-shore! In an instant the terrible thought flashed upon her mind that it was her brother of whom they were in pursuit; and then, losing all further control, she threw herself upon her knees before him, supplicating, in the most earnest accents, that he would interpose his authority to save an unfortunate fugitive from the fate that would befal him should he unfortunately be captured by his relentless pursuers. But her words were either unheard or unheeded, for no reply was deigned, and the next moment the loud report of fire-arms conveyed to her the harrowing intelligence that the life of her brother had in all probability been sacrificed in his attempt ro escape. Still no heed did Sir Walter pay to the despairing sobs of his wife, and he was about to leave the room to learn what had occurred, when loud shouts of triumph were heard in the entrance-hall, and in a few minutes more Lord Arden, who had fortunately escaped uninjured, was brought into the room by the men who had succeeded in capturing him. The surprise of Sir Walter Amyot, on recognising the brother of his wife, was great, but the meeting between the cavalier and the roundhead was cold and distant. In a short time, however, this began to wear off, and then an explanation took place, which afforded satisfactory evidence to the knight that all his suspicions against his wife were false and unfounded. A reconciliation immediately took place between Sir Walter and Lord Arden, and the former, addressing himself to Colonel Latimer, who had just entered the room, said—

"You have come, I suppose, to claim your prisoner, colonel; but I, who have been invested with an authority superior to your own, do not intend to part with him till I have communicated with our government upon the subject. In a word, Lord Arden has only to pledge his word that he will not again draw his sword against this country, and I feel assured that my interest will procure for him a full pardon for the past."

"And I for one," exclaimed the colonel, extending his hand towards the young nobleman, "will be the first to offer him my congratulations upon the fortunate escape he has had. I can guess, too, the reason for Lady Amyot's having concealed him when no other asylum offered, and can answer for it, that she will incur no displeasure for affording shelter to a royalist under such circumstances as these."

"But what punishment," demanded the knight, as he pressed Lady Eveline to his bosom, "can be sufficient to meet the deserts of the cold blooded villain who sowed dissention between myself and the wife whom I was fool enough to suspect of infidelity?"

"If you speak of Jabez Sneed," answered the colonel, "it may afford you some consolation to learn that he has been arrested by my orders, and will be conveyed to London, where certain allegations will be made against him."

"Of what offence has he been guilty?" asked the knight.

"He is strongly suspected of having been concerned in assisting the escape of many of the royalists."

"How is it, then, that he has shown so much anxiety to cause the capture of the one who sought shelter in my house?"

"I believe, Sir Walter," answered the colonel, "a solution to that answer may be found in the fact that he sought to revenge himself against Lady Eveline, for having discovered the dishonesty he has been practising whilst in your confidence. That, however, will form no part of the inquiry, for if the other charge can be proved against him, of which there can be very little doubt, he will deservedly meet his end upon a gibbet, as a warning to others who betray their country under the specious mask of being more patriotic than their neighbours. The old man, too, seems to know what his fate may be, for he already gives himself up for lost, and piteously bewails the destiny that is in store for him. And, now, having performed all the duty that was required of me here, I will take my leave, with an earnest wish that the happiness which has been so unexpectedly restored, may never again be dimmed through the evil meddling of such a hypocrite as Jabez Sneed."

"Can you not spare time to pass a few days with us to witness our restored happiness?" asked Sir Walter.

"Another time I may do so," answered Colonel Latimer, "but at present I have a duty to perform, and that is to return to head quarters, and render an account of what I have done. So farewell, and may Heaven's blessing rest upon all here."

The officer shook hands with them, quitted the room, and within a few minutes afterwards rode away with his troopers towards London. As for Sir Walter Amyot, he had become an altered man from the moment when the discovery had taken place. He had ascertained that the fugitive whom he had suspected of being the lover of his wife was no other than her own brother, from whom he had been estranged many years, and who had obtained shelter from Lady Eveline only for a few days, till he could find an opportunity of making his escape to France. The secret which had nearly been of such fatal consequence to the happiness of two persons had been discovered to be a perfectly harmless one; and Sir Walter, as we have seen, was no sooner made aware of the error under which he had been lying, than he made all the reparation in his power by acknowledging the wrong he had done. In a few days afterwards the knight received a letter from government, stating that the prayer of his petition had been considered, and that, on certain conditions, Lord Arden might either pass over to France, or remain an inmate in the house which had received him, when he was a fugitive, from his pursuers. It is, perhaps, hardly necessary to say that his lordship gladly embraced the latter proposition, and that he maintained a perfect neutrality in all political affairs till the restoration of Charles the Second, which happened about six years afterwards.

PUBLISHED BY E. LLOYD, SALISBURY-SQUARE, FLEET-STREET.